WALK IN TWO WORLDS

BY

S. B. MILLER

D0112192

Copyright © 2012 S.B. Miller
All rights reserved.
ISBN: 148028081X
ISBN 13: 9781480280816
LCCN: 2012921488
CreateSpace Independent Publishing Platform
North Charleston, South Carolina

CAP-TIVE

1. One, such as a prisoner of war, who is forcibly, confined, subjugated, or enslaved

2. One held in the grip of a strong emotion or passion

   —*The American Heritage Dictionary*

"White children who were adopted were treated well and became members of the tribe. Indians don't discriminate when they adopt someone. Hell, I saw runaway slaves welcomed into some of the different tribes as full warriors! Whites don't do the same. Indian children that were taken by whites were treated poorly by most; not any better then slaves. It ain't no wonder most Indian children went to brush the first chance they got, while most white children never had a mind to leave their Indian families."

— *Stephen Ruddell*

SHAWNEE WORDS AND TERMS

No'tha – **My father**

Ni-je-ni-nuh – **My brother**

Jai-nai-nah – **Blood brother**

Ni-kwith-ehi – **My son**

Ni-t-kweem-a – **My sister**

Dah-nai-tha - **My daughter**

Ni-da-ne-thuh – **My husband**

Ni-wa – **My wife**

Keewa - **Your wife**

Ne-kah-noh – **My friend**

Weshemoneto – **Great Spirit**

Matchemenetoo – **Bad Spirit**

Psaiwiwuhkernekah Ptweowa –
Great White Wolf

Shemagana - **Soldier**

Shemanese – **White man**

Nilu famu – **Sacred Tobacco**

Mat-tah - **No**

La-yah-mah - **This**

Wi'si - **Dog**

Msipesi - **Panther**

Bezon - **Hello**

Oui-shi-cat-to-oui – **Be Strong**

Neahw – **Thank you**

Psai-wi-ne-noth-tu - **Great Warrior**

Baaga'dowe - **Lacrosse**

PROLOGUE

KANSAS TERRITORY
OCTOBER, 1834

THE FORT GATE EXPLODED inward from the impact of the cannonball showering the defenders with a barrage of deadly splinters and dense smoke. The settlers screamed and milled about in confusion as the red and black painted warriors rushed through the ruined gates, whooping victoriously. Chaos spread through the compound as the unarmed inhabitants fled before the attacking Indians.

An auburn-haired woman clutched an infant close to her chest and frantically searched the compound for her oldest son. She screamed his name again and again as the attackers fell on the settlers around her. The woman looked up as a large warrior materialized from the smoke in front of her like an apparition released from the gates of Hell. His face was painted black and twisted into a menacing grimace, but to the woman's amazement she saw that his exposed skin was white, and his shoulder length hair was the same shade of red as hers. She looked up at him, her eyes wide with shock and desperate with pleading.

"Have you seen my son?" she cried "Please help me find him!"

The white warrior snarled and grabbed the woman by her long hair, roughly jerking her head back.

"Sorry, Ma," he growled, raising his tomahawk to strike. "I'm a Shawnee now, and you are my enemy!"

The woman's eyes froze wide open in terror. Her desperate scream echoed across the valley as the tomahawk swept down.

The hunter gasped and struggled out of his bedroll, his heart beating rapidly. He shook his head and took a deep breath to calm himself. Slowly, he became aware of his surroundings. The fire in his hunting camp had burned low. He added a few sticks, and the flames soon illuminated the dark night. The hunter reached into his saddlebag and pulled out a quart bottle of whiskey. He grabbed a tin coffee cup from beside the fire and used his teeth to uncork the bottle. The hunter poured a generous portion of the liquor into the cup and drained the contents in two gulps.

He sighed and set the bottle down within arm's reach, not certain that one drink would be enough. He closed his eyes and ran his hand across his sweaty brow.

"You damned fool!" he scolded himself quietly, lying back down on his bed roll. "It's only a dream!"

His own words provided little comfort. On this evening his heart ached as much as it did the day his mother died, over fifty years earlier.

The doe sniffed the air and slowly moved down the game trail toward the Neosho River. Autumn had been dry west of the Mississippi, and the deer was thirsty. The sun was just starting to rise in the eastern sky, and a light, early morning fog lay over the narrow river valley. A slight breeze was at the doe's back, denying her the ability to smell the danger ahead of her. Thirst lessened her cautious nature as she moved steadily along the trail toward the sandy river.

Thickets and briars covered the river bottom. Cottonwood trees lined the riverbank, adding additional cover for the hunter who waited patiently. The man had been there for several hours awaiting the coming of day, and he now covered the deer traveling the same trail with his flintlock rifle. He had worked his way into a thicket that gave him a clear view of the deer now moving toward him. He let out his breath to steady the rifle. He squeezed the trigger as the doe crossed in front of him. The pan flashed, and the report of the rifle echoed across the quiet valley. The deer staggered and took two more steps before collapsing.

The hunter reloaded his rifle before moving out of the thicket. The lead ball had smashed through the deer's lungs, killing her quickly. The man drew a skinning knife from his belt and expertly gutted the doe. He cut the still warm heart from the animal's chest and held it toward the sky, offering a small prayer. He then took a small bite of the bloody flesh and chewed it slowly. Satisfied, the man wrapped the rest of the heart in a handkerchief and placed it in his side pouch. The hunter scratched his chin, feeling the stubble that had grown since he started this hunt, five days ago. He looked at the large doe at his feet. This deer made fifteen. He allowed himself a nod of satisfaction. Not bad for an old man.

He set his rifle against a cottonwood tree and stretched his stiff back. He was still a large and strong man, even at the age of sixty-six. He bent and tied the hide hoppusing tugs around the deer carcass before hoisting the load across his shoulders and standing easily. He adjusted the weight and tested the balance. Satisfied, he gathered up his rifle and made his way down the trail toward his camp, over a mile away.

White Feather Village came into view as the hunter crested a low ridge. The Shawnee had founded the village near where the Neosho flowed into the Missouri after the 1825 treaty of St. Louis had forced the tribe to give up their lands around Cape Girardeau and move farther west. The old man reined his horse to a halt and scanned the village. Dirt trails spread like a spider web among the haphazardly constructed buildings. Most of the village consisted of single story wooden shacks or sod houses, but a few ill-constructed wigwams and long houses stood among the various structures as well. Pigs, chickens, and dogs ran free in the streets. It looked nothing like the orderly Shawnee villages of Ohio that he had known as a youth. That was a different time, he reminded himself. The Shawnee of his youth were a fierce and proud people. Those left were defeated and struggling to survive. The hunter forced the disappointment from his face and rode down to the village, his pack horse loaded with deer meat in tow.

Susan White Feather worked stoically, sweeping the dirt out of her cabin door. She stopped and looked up from the doorway as the village dogs barked at the new arrival. White Feather put her broom down and strained her eyes to make out the figure. She was no longer a young woman and could not see as well as she used to. She smiled when she recognized the old hunter walking his horse toward her. She smoothed down her wool skirt, trying to cover the poor moccasins that covered her feet. She stepped from the porch and moved out to meet him. The hunter grinned as White Feather made her way toward him. He had not seen the Shawnee woman in four years. Times had been hard and she had passed into middle age. Her body had become plump, and gray was beginning to show in her hair. Wrinkles had worn their way into the corners of her eyes and mouth. The hunter could remember when White Feather had been born. She was the youngest daughter of the Shawnee chief, Black Hoof. She had been among the last Shawnee to be removed from Ohio. The old man himself had gone to Ohio and helped White Feather and her family make the trip to Missouri. It had been the least he could do for the daughter of his adopted father.

"Greetings, *ni-je-ni-nuh*," she said, using the Shawnee word for brother. "I see that you have had a successful hunt."

"I've had many considerable hunts, *ni-tkweem-a*," he responded, using the term for sister. "I fear that my success has done little to help the people. What I have with me is for you and those of this village" he added, gesturing to the deer carcasses hanging from the pack horse.

"We're grateful," she replied, signaling to several of the men who had gathered. The villagers rushed forward eagerly and began unpacking the meat. "The government supplies are slow in coming and usually less then what we need," she added, a frown replacing her smile.

"I'd expect no less," the old man snorted. "It's always been that way with the American government in dealing with the people. Each promise has only been good until the Shawnee have given up more land, and now there's nothin' left to take!"

The hunter stepped down from his horse and hugged the woman. "I didn't expect to find you here. I looked for you in the other villages."

"There was no room for those of us who came from Ohio. *Tenskwatawa* opened his village to us," she explained. "We're in his debt."

The old man scowled. "He's the one who is in debt! In debt to you and the entire Shawnee people."

White feather shook her head. "You shouldn't be so hard on him, *Sinnatha*" she said, emphasizing his Shawnee name. "He made mistakes, but he cares for the people."

Sinnatha snorted. "*Loud Noise* has never cared for anyone but himself!"

White Feather returned the old man's scowl. She had the same dark eyes and heavy brow of her father. She looked much like the old chief when he became angry. "Black Hoof made his peace with the Prophet before he died. You should do the same. There are too few of us left to hold to old grudges!" she chided.

"Never was he a Prophet!" Sinnatha growled, his eyes flashing.

"He gave our people hope" White feather whispered.

"Hope? What does he give his people today?" he pressed.

White Feather hung her head. Before she could answer, there was a commotion at the edge of the crowd as Tenskwatawa pushed his way forward to see the visitor. The former Shawnee Prophet was a large, ugly man. He still dressed in the deerskin robes of a shaman and kept his long, graying hair wrapped in a red, silk turban. He wore an eye patch over his missing right eye, as he had for much of his life. He was dark skinned and unlike most Indians, had a thin mustache above his upper lip. Now over sixty, alcoholism had ruined his health. The fat man wheezed and coughed as he made his way toward White Feather. Sinnatha's horse kept him obscured from the village leader's view.

"Who's that with you, *ne-kah-noh?*" the Prophet rasped between coughs. "I've come to give my blessing to one who has been so charitable to our people."

Sinnatha stepped around his horse and faced the one man he most blamed for all that went wrong. "I would give all creation to our people freely, which is more then I can say you have ever done" he stated, "and I would rather stuff a rattlesnake down my leggings then receive any blessing from you."

Tenskwatawa stood in stunned silence at the old man's insults. His jaw dropped as he looked into the man's hard, blue eyes and recognized who he was. "Ruddell? I thought you were dead!"

"I reckon not," the old man chuckled.

"Why have you come? You are not welcome in my village," the Prophet hissed through clenched teeth.

"Seems we've had this fix before," Ruddell replied. "I didn't give a shit what you thought then, and I reckon I don't give a shit now."

"Seize him!" Tenskwatawa ordered, gesturing to a couple of young men standing at the edge of the group.

Ruddell leveled his long rifle at the Prophet and cocked the flintlock hammer. "I allow that it pained me that I never kilt' you in my younger days, Loud Noise," he stated, his eyes narrowing. "If your men budge, I'll fix your flint."

"Enough!" White Feather cried, stepping between the two men. "*Ni-je-ni-nuh,* it's best that you leave. We are thankful for the meat that you have brought us, but nobody wants to see any more blood spilled among our people."

"Very well, *ni-t-kweem-a,*" Ruddell said, uncocking the hammer of his rifle. "I'll leave out of respect for you and our father." He swung up on to his horse, never taking his eyes from the one-eyed leader.

Ignoring the angry man, he reached down and took White Feather's hand. "Be well, *ni-t-kweem-a.* Write to me when this coot has passed on and I'll do all creation I can to help the people of your village. Until then, farewell."

Sinnatha kicked his horse into a gallop and rode from the village. White Feather raised her hand after him, "Goodbye, *ni-je-ni-nuh,*" she whispered. "May we meet again in a happier time."

She turned and took up her broom; there was still dirt to be swept from her floor.

CHAPTER I

QUINCY, ILLINOIS
SUMMER, 1845

DR. LYMAN DRAPER gripped his writing box firmly and winced as the wagon he was riding in bounced across another rut in the narrow road they were traveling outside the town.

John Ruddell smiled over at his passenger. "Hang on, Doctor. The ride home can be a bit rough on the bumfiddle!"

The writer smiled nervously and clutched the writing box tighter to his chest. He was beginning to question the wisdom of traveling to the bustling Mississippi town to interview one old frontiersman.

The sun had set and stars were starting to appear in the sky when they reached the Ruddell homestead. The road, if that was what the dirt path they had bounced on for the last mile could be called, ended at the Ruddell's doorstep. Lyman was surprised when their final destination was a fine, two story brick home that sat on a bluff overlooking the Mississippi. The house was surrounded by pasture and hayfields. A large wooden barn was built into the side of a bank adjacent to the house.

"You have a likely home, Mr. Ruddell" Lyman complemented, stepping down from the wagon and rubbing his bruised backside. "I'm surprised so see a brick home built this far away from town."

"Thank you, Dr. Ruddell, and please call me John. My father had this home built when we settled here over twenty years ago.

The bricks were toted up by barge from St. Louis and he built a wench to raise them up the bluff. It was a considerable feat!" John stated proudly.

Their conversation was interrupted by a high pitch whoop as a boy of about ten rushed from the front door and jumped into John's arms. The boy wore a hawk feather in his hair and carried a wooden tomahawk. He wrapped his arms around his father's strong neck.

"Pa! I kilt two rabbits with my bow today!" the boy cried, his chin held high. "Ma is cooking them in a stew for dinner."

"Two rabbits? Why you may end up as powerful a hunter as your grandpa!" John replied, causing the boy to blush. John put the lad down and turned toward their guest. "Dr. Draper, this is my son, Stephen."

Lyman ruffled the boy's hair. "Named after the great frontiersman, I'll allow!"

The little boy looked up at him, his jaw set. "My grandpa was a Shawnee warrior!" he boasted. "And I will be too some day!"

John patted the boy on the head. "Go tell your mother that our guest is here."

The boy let out another whoop and rushed into the house, yelling for his mother.

Lyman chuckled, "I hope he doesn't take after his grandfather!"

John shook his head. "All to pieces; my father has filled his head with many a tale!"

Draper dusted himself off and reached for his bag. "I must admit that your letter interested me. I found details about your father as a minister, but little on his early life."

Ruddell nodded. "There wouldn't be; he's never spoke of it to anyone outside our family."

John gathered up the rest of Draper's luggage and set it on the porch. "If you'll pardon me, Dr. Draper, I must see to the stock. Please go in and refresh yourself and I'll be along directly."

John climbed back onto the wagon and drove the horses toward the barn as Lyman made his way up the steps and onto the porch.

Lyman washed his hands and face in a white basin that sat by the kitchen door of the home. He wiped his face with a towel handed to him by John Ruddell's wife, Sarah. "Thank you, Mrs. Ruddell," he sighed. "I feel much better."

"Please Dr. Draper, call me Sarah. We have a guest room all set up for you," she replied with a smile as he handed the towel back to her. "You're welcome to stay with us as long as you need to."

Lyman scanned the house once again. The floors were made of polished oak and covered with knit rugs in all the rooms. All the windows, which were open to the humid, summer night air, were framed by drapes. Well built furniture adorned every room.

"You have a likely home, Sarah," he complemented.

Sarah smiled, beaming with pride. "Thank you. I helped my late mother-in-law, Susan, decorate it when John and I first married. We had few visitors back then, but we took pride in our diggings!"

"I'm very grateful for your hospitality, Sarah," Lyman said, sniffing the wonderful aroma of cooked food coming from the kitchen, "but I only figure to be here a few days. I'll leave just as soon as I've put together my notes from your father-in-law. Where is Mr. Ruddell? I wish to meet him."

Sarah smoothed out her apron and cleared her throat. "Well, I think maybe John should talk to you..." she began.

Sarah was interrupted by a commotion from outside. John Ruddell entered the house, little Stephen hanging from his shoulders.

The big man laughed. "He ambushed me at the porch, nearly gave me a cocked hat." John's smile faded as he saw his wife's expression. He put his son down and moved to her side.

"Land sakes! Has something befallen Mr. Ruddell?" Draper asked, his eyes widening. "I feared with his age...."

John's merry laughter cut the smaller man off. "My father's as fit as a hoss! He's gone to brush. I reckon he's huntin' on the far side of the river."

Lyman's jaw dropped. "Hunting? At the age of seventy-seven! When will he return?"

Sarah looked down. "Well, we really don't have a notion..."

"It's alright, Dr. Draper." John cut in, patting his wife's hand. "Pa goes hunting quite regular and he is always has considerable luck," he explained, a hint of pride in his voice. "We never have a mind to when he'll be home. Sometimes it's a day, sometimes it's a coon's age."

"Didn't he know that I was coming?" Draper asked, still trying to digest the information.

"Oh, he knew!" John replied, his cheeks reddening. "I told him you were due today, but he went to brush anyway. Pa has always been known to do what he found likely, and there's no stoppin' him!"

"I see," Draper replied with a sigh. "Well, Sarah, it seems I'm your guest until Mr. Ruddell comes home." Lyman sniffed the air again. "If that roasted rabbit is as good as it smells; I'll have to thank Mr. Ruddell for his absence from the dinner table."

John's booming laughter echoed through the night air.

Morning along the banks of the Mississippi was usually a very tranquil time. Fog and mist swirled about the bluffs as animals made their way to the banks of the mighty river to drink before the suns' rays burned off the natural cover. This morning was different as a loud noise from the Ruddell home reverberated across the bluff and the river below, driving the wary animals back into the dense cover along the river bank.

Dr. Lyman Draper lay upon the guest room bed snoring loudly. The man had remained in a deep slumber as the night sky turned to early morning daylight. The intense snoring sounded much like a backsaw being drawn across a log, over and over. The door to the guest room opened without a sound. A man with a rifle in his hand made his way across the room silently. Dr. Draper snorted and choked as a rifle muzzle entered his mouth in mid snore. Lyman's eyes flew open to find an old man in buckskins with a shock of white hair and a thin beard holding a rifle in his face. The old man grinned.

"Boy, you snore louder then a Cherokee squaw I use to know! I found more interestin' things to stick in her chops to get her to shut pan!"

Lyman scrambled away from the wild man. He let out a screech as he tumbled off the bed and crashed to the floor.

John Ruddell rushed into the room. "Pa! What're you doing?"

"I told you I would get him to shut his bone box!" the old man cackled.

"Dr. Draper, please pardon my father..." John began.

Draper staggered to his feet, his cheeks flushed. " Pardon him? I'm quite finished with your designs, Mr. Ruddell! I've better things to do then be harassed by some old coot!"

Lyman began to gather up his clothes and stuff personal items into his travel bag. He had left his hat hanging from the back of a chair and reached for it. Draper gasped as the hat disappeared from his hand. He looked up to see that it was pinned to the bedroom wall by a large knife. Lyman looked back, his eyes wide. The old man stood in the doorway, his arm extended and a scowl upon his face.

"You can lay off your conniption fit. My son has opened his diggins to you. I might have a mind to fix your flint if you don't shut pan!"

The old man turned and sniffed the air before smacking his lips. "It smells like Sarah has breakfast about ready. Well, don't just stand there! Get your clothes on so we can eat!"

Still sniffing and talking to himself, the old man turned and wandered from the room.

Lyman watched him go and then stared at the knife sticking from his hat. "That was your father?" he whispered.

John nodded. "Don't that beat the Dutch?" he sighed

Sarah Ruddell entered the dining room with platters of food as her father-in-law set his rifle down in the corner. The summer morning was already heating up so she had decided to do her cooking in the summer kitchen. She had heard the commotion from the guest room. She glared at the old man as he moved to his place at the table. He smiled at her and poured himself a cup of coffee from the pot she had placed in the center of the table.

"Pa, you shouldn't treat our guest that way!" she scolded. "He came a far piece to see you!"

Stephen sipped his coffee and gestured toward the guest room. "I reckon I didn't hurt him any, and it was time for him to get up."

"That's not the point!" she continued, "You know better than to treat a guest that way. It was ornery!"

"Guest?" the old man grumbled. "I reckon guests don't get coin to come visit. I'd allow that he's a fool who needs to get up and earn his bread!"

Sarah sighed and shook her head.

Stephen chuckled and looked the table over. "What are the fixins for breakfast?"

"Hotcakes, bacon, and eggs, same as every Sunday. Will you be joining us at church today?" she replied, moving on to another subject.

The old man ignored the question and nodded toward the kitchen table where a large turkey lay. "How do you like what I brought you for supper? One shot took his head clean off," he stated proudly. "Considerable for an old man, eh?"

"It will make a right smart Sunday supper," Sarah replied without looking at the bird. "I just wish you would join us at church; everyone misses you!"

The young woman had moved to sit beside the old man. He reached out and patted her hand gently. "I'm pleased that you feel that way, Sis. Fact is, I don't have any hankering to go where I'm not wanted. I'm a body of the past they're sour on."

"You are not..."

The conversation ended as John Ruddell and little Stephen entered the room, followed by the now dressed Dr. Draper. The little boy ran to his grandfather's arms. "Grandpa! Did you bring me anything?"

Stephen chuckled. "I reckon so!" He reached into a large pouch at his side and pulled out a small, steel tomahawk that he handed to the delighted boy. He ruffled the child's hair. "I'll learn you how to toss it after breakfast. It's a sight different than the wooden one you've been using!

"Everyone sit down!" he commanded. "Let's enjoy this feast that Mrs. Ruddell has put together for us!"

Everyone obeyed the old man's command and took their seats at the table. Dr. Draper moved to the only remaining open seat, next to Stephen. He eyed the old man. As everyone around the table linked hands to pray, Stephen took Draper's hand and gave him a wink.

"Don't fret, I won't bite. Unless you get your hands close to my plate!"

Lyman opened his mouth to reply, but the old man bowed his head and began to pray. "Lord, we thank you for this wonderful meal and the health that you have bestowed upon us. We thank you for this wonderful day and our 'guest' whom you have sent to us. We pray that he does not irritate and cause me to inflict upon him bodily harm. In your name we pray, Amen!"

"Amen!" everyone repeated as Dr. Draper looked at Stephen incredulously.

The old man sat in a rocking chair on the front porch packing tobacco into a clay pipe. John and Sarah Ruddell, dressed in their Sunday clothes, finished packing their wagon for the trip to church. Dr. Draper stood near the wagon as John helped his wife up to the wagon seat.

"Are you certain you don't want to come?" John offered Lyman again.

"Yes, or at least I think so," Lyman replied, glancing toward the old man in the rocking chair. "I came here to talk to him. I suppose if I spend some time he might take a liking to me."

John shook his head and smiled. "Good luck."

The sound of metal splitting wood brought a sigh from Sarah Ruddell. "Stephen, time to go" she shouted. "Leave off with that tomahawk and get in this wagon!"

The little boy ran from behind the house where his grandfather had sat up a throwing block for him to practice. He leaped into the back of the wagon with a whoop and waved toward the old man. "Bye, Grandpa!"

The old man chuckled and waved back as the wagon moved down the road. Dr. Draper tentatively made his way to stand at the edge of the porch steps. After several quiet moments Stephen sighed and pointed to a chair beside him and held up a small pouch.

"You want a gage?"

"Why, yes!" Draper replied his eyes widening as he quickly climbed the porch steps. "Thank you, Mr. Ruddell."

Lyman eagerly packed his pipe and light it. He took one long puff and began to cough. He looked down at the glowing tobacco, his nose crinkled. "Damn! What's this?"

"It's an Osage Indian concoction," Stephen replied, blowing out a puff of smoke from his own clay pipe. "I suspect its a little more considerable then you're used to."

"It tastes like shit!" Draper complained

The old man shrugged. "Could be. I never asked. It takes a coon's age to get used to."

Dr. Draper looked at the pipe and frowned. He emptied out the homemade concoction and refilled his pipe with his own tobacco. He looked up in time to see a canoe piloted by a pair of Indians float by on the river below. He stood up and ran to the edge of the porch. "Are those wild Indians?"

Stephen waved at the Indians as they paddled down the wide river. Recognizing him, the pair smiled and waved back as they disappeared around the river bend. "Wild? If you allow them that. They're Iowa, on their way to St. Louis to trade for whiskey and gunpowder. Ain't you never seen an Indian before?"

"Well, not in his natural habitat," Lyman exclaimed.

The old man scratched his head and frowned. "His what?"

"Habitat! I mean, the way he is supposed to live," the younger man explained.

"Well, you still ain't seen an Indian in his 'habitat.' You are seein' him in the one the whites have made for him," the old man growled. "Say, you're a doctor, right?" he continued his eyes suddenly lighting up. "My knee has been acting up; do you have anything for it?"

Lyman chuckled. "Oh, I'm not a medical doctor, Mr. Ruddell. I'm a professor of history."

"What?"

"I study the past."

Stephen puffed on his pipe for a few moments, contemplating the younger man. "Well, I reckon that's better than some of the coots I've known. Most of them were nothin' but barbers and horse doctors!"

Lyman shook his head and looked after the departing canoe. "You truly live on the frontier, Mr. Ruddell."

Stephen nearly choked on his pipe as he laughed at the younger man's comments. "Frontier? Hell, this ain't no frontier! Now, when I started my church Twenty-five years ago, it was a frontier. There ain't no frontier left!"

"How can you say that?" Lyman began to argue. "Why it was not that long ago that the Black Hawk war..."

Stephen cut him off with a loud snort. "Black Hawk was a tired ol' cully who was tryin' to hold on to what he had left. He knew he didn't have a chance when he fought that war. He just hankered to go out like a warrior before they budged his people to the other side of the Mississippi and the 'new' lands for the Indians, that is until the greedy landgrabbers want it to."

"You don't think the government will honor the treaties it has made with the Indians?"

Stephen laughed and slapped his thigh. "The United States has never honored a treaty it signed with an Indian nation! I'm cock-sure, I was there for a boodle of them."

"Well, times have changed," Lyman argued.

"Have they? I hear all creation blusterin' about annexing Texas and California. This country won't stop until it has all the land from here to the Pacific Ocean. If times are changing for the Indians, then they're gettin' the little end of the horn."

Lyman released the brass latch on his mahogany writing box and flipped down the tri fold top to form a writing slope. He took out a sheet of paper and a sharpened pencil and laid them on the velvet writing surface. Hopeful of keeping the old man talking, he took the conversation in a different direction. "So, you're a minister?"

"Was for more than half my life. I was always on the frontier, until my retiracy here."

"If you don't mind me asking, why don't you go to church with your son?"

Stephen remained silent for several moments, rocking in his chair. Finally, he put down his pipe and looked at the younger man, his blue eyes distant. "I started that church in 1820. Back then this was a pretty rambunctious place, just the kind I take a cotton to. A frontier preacher needs to be full of fire and brimstone to save the wicked. After I brought my wife and children in, other families came in as well. Then all creation started to become civilized. Civilized places tend to get sour on a frontier preacher. So, after my wife died, I gave it up. The congregation acted grum, but they were relieved. They were able to bring in a young, high-falutin minister to shepherd over them. It's alright; I had other designs to tote in the name of the Lord."

"Such as?"

Stephen smiled. "My grandson reckons that I hunt all the time. I really spend most of my time helpin' provide for some of the lost souls on the other side of the river."

"You mean the Indians?" Lyman asked, looking up from his note taking.

"Well of course I do!" the old man growled. "Sickness and rum have done up many a proud tribes. They need all the help they can get."

Lyman continued to scribble down notes as Stephen smoked his pipe. Finally, he looked up and smiled. "Can we talk about your early years? I heard you spent considerable time with the Shawnee Indians."

"No," Stephen replied, his eyes hardening.

"But, your son told me ..." Draper began.

The old man rose from his seat and glared at Lyman. "My son and I differ all to pieces about recollectin' yarns!" Ruddell stormed to the edge of the porch and leaned against the railing, staring toward the river.

Lyman sighed and sat quietly for a few moments. He finally rose and moved to stand beside the old man. "I understand how you feel, Mr. Ruddell, but have a mind to hear me," He said quietly. "The heart and soul of this land is in the folks who have lived and perished here. Shouldn't they be the ones who tell the history that is passed down to our grandchildren's children? If you don't tell your story, who will? Will you let someone in Washington or Philadelphia write lies about the times you've lived in? You are the last of your kind, Sir. After you're gone, who will pass the yarns on? Please, let me tell the country about the life you've lived."

The old man stood silent for several moments. Finally, he turned toward Draper, his cheeks wet with tears. He reached for his jug and took a long pull, his throat working as he swallowed. He wiped his mouth with the back of his wrist and sat back in the rocking chair. "I'll recollect a tale for you. Once I'm finished, we'll fix the flint on tellin' the rest of the country about it."

Lyman nodded in agreement and waited in silent anticipation for the old man to begin.

Stephen looked out across the Mississippi. His eyes seemed focused on some distant point as he remembered back to another time. "I reckon this circumbendibus should begin the day my life changed. I wasn't any different then any other brat reared on the frontier during the war. All creation changed the summer of 80'. I still recollect the day I met Tecumseh. It's been sixty-five years, but how could a body forget the day they saw their kin's blood spilt on that dark Kentucky soil?"

CHAPTER 2

RUDDELL'S STATION, KENTUCKY
SUMMER, 1780

ELIZABETH BOWMAN RUDDELL wasn't happy. She had been making blackberry pies all morning and was ready to bake them, but wood had not been brought in and the fire in the hearth had not been banked. She looked at the smoldering embers and frowned. She wiped the dough from her hands on her apron and stepped outside the door of the log cabin her husband had built a year earlier. Her daughters Mary and Ann were busy weeding and tending to the family garden. Her son Abraham was at the well, seeing to his duty of refilling the water barrel that sat by the cabin door. The baby Daniel began fussing from inside the cabin. She looked toward the wood pile and the half finished stack of split wood. Her anger began to swell as she looked toward ten year old Abraham.

"Where's your brother?" she demanded.

Abraham swallowed hard. He could see the anger in his mother's eyes and hear the impatience in her voice. His elder brother had threatened him with a beating if he told anyone where he had went, but the boy feared the wrath of their mother much more.

"He said he was goin' huntin', Ma," he blurted, pointing toward the woodpile. "See, he took his rifle."

Elizabeth glanced toward the woodpile to confirm what he said was true. She turned her steely gaze back on the child. "What else?"

Abraham kicked the dirt beside the well and hesitated. "I don't recall him saying anything else," he replied, his eyes down.

Elizabeth knew the boy was holding something back. She turned toward the girls, "Well?"

"He said he was goin' to the fort when he got back," eight-year-old Mary replied without hesitation.

"He told Abe he would blast' em if he told," little Ann put in with a giggle.

Elizabeth turned toward Abraham once again. "Is that true, Abe?" she demanded.

Abe sighed. "Yes'um."

Elizabeth smoothed out her apron and ran her hands through her long, auburn hair. She pulled a strip of leather from her dress pocket and tied her long locks back, preparing for the task ahead. The three children looked on, their eyes wide. Elizabeth looked around the wood pile and spotted a slender piece of split hickory. She wrapped her hand in a handkerchief and picked up the piece of wood. It was about two feet in length and sturdy. She slapped the wood against her own palm and nodded in satisfaction.

"See to the baby," she commanded Mary.

Mary nodded and ran toward the cabin. Elizabeth turned in the direction of the fort and glanced at Abe as she walked past. "I'll settle with you when I get back," she stated quietly, her blue eyes smoldering.

Abe's shoulders sagged and he sighed once again as his mother moved on toward the fort. No doubt she would give him a whipping for lying and his brother would still blast him for telling on him. "Damnation!" he exclaimed, kicking the ground.

"I'm tellin'!" Ann squealed, running toward the house.

Abe shook his head and kicked the dirt in frustration once again. Finally, he picked up his water bucket and trudged toward the house and the half full water barrel. He could not avoid the punishment he was due to receive for lying to his mother, but he could lessen it. Abe knew his mother would be pleased if she came home to find a full water barrel. That might soften the blows she had planned for him.

"Well, at least Ma will give Stephen a bellyful before she gets to me!" he said to himself, a slight smile on his face. "By the time she's done, she might not have a hankerin' to beat me much."

Ruddell's Station was a growing community. Many homesteads had sprung up near the fort Isaac Ruddell had built on the south fork of the Licking River in 1779. Ruddell had moved with his in-laws, the Bowmans, to the Kentucky frontier from Virginia in 1774. For a time the family had settled in Boonesborough and Isaac had served as a Captain in the Kentucky militia. His quick mind and steady demeanor had caught the eye of George Rogers Clark, who had trusted Ruddell in commanding the post Clark established on Corn Island during the Illinois campaign that ended British control over the Ohio Valley. On his return to Kentucky, Isaac had taken a liking to the area that would become known as Bourbon County and had established a homestead and a fort to protect his family. A year later, the rich farm land of the Licking was being cleared by numerous Pennsylvania German and Virginian families who had left the war torn east and moved down the Ohio to find a better life.

Hans Mueller was from one of those new families. His father was a blacksmith who had set up shop at the settlement. When not working the bellows in his father's shop, Hans amused himself by overpowering the other boys from the settlement in rough and tumble wrestling and boxing matches. At fifteen, Hans was bigger and stronger then many men. Most of the boys his age and younger avoided him, especially after they had seen him thrash several older boys the last few months. Hans was not content with the reputation he had established and had begun looking for fights. He had finally found one in the form of a lad named Will Danner.

Will's family was Scotch-Irish and had newly arrived from North Carolina. Will had been sent into town with a mare that needed shoeing. While he waited, the boy had pulled out his hunting knife and had begun whittling on a stick outside the shop. Hans had taken notice.

"That's a fine blade. Where'd ya get it?" he asked, a slight smile playing across his face.

"My pa gave it to me," Will replied without looking up.

"Your pa? That's a considerable knife for any coot of an Irishman to have toted," Hans sneered. "I reckon you stole it."

Will looked up, struggling to control his anger. His father had warned him about the blacksmith's son and his reputation for picking on new boys in the community. Will had promised his mother that he would do his best to avoid a fight. "I don't want any trouble," he stated quietly.

Hans snickered. "Well, I reckon there won't be any if you give me that blade."

Will sized the other boy up. Hans was two years older and at least fifty pounds heavier then he was. Will had never been afraid to fight and it hurt his pride to continue to back down, but he had promised his ma. He ran his hand through his curly, red hair.

"This knife is plum dear to me," he explained, trying one final time to avoid a fight. "It was my grandpa's."

Hans slapped his leg and laughed. "Land sakes, Irishman! You allow that your pa knew who his sire was?"

Will's nostrils flared. The smaller boy rose to his feet, his fists clenched at his side. "You fat headed bastard!" he yelled, stepping forward. "If it's a fight ya want, it's a fight ya'll get!"

Hans smiled, revealing a mouthful of yellow teeth. He held up his hand as the smaller boy advanced on him. "Not here, Irishman. I don't want to get whipped for a fight in my pa's shop." Hans pointed toward the fort. "We handle all bouts over by the west wall."

Hans chuckled again as Will turned on his heel and stormed toward the fort. He nodded with satisfaction when he took note of the group of boys who had begun to gather in anticipation of the fight. "Don't fret, boys. This won't take no coon's age!" he boasted, strolling toward the wall. "We all got chores to do, so I'll make it quick!"

The fight began as the smaller boy rushed at Hans, his anger driving him on. The larger boy sidestepped and clapped Will on the back of the head, knocking him into the dirt.

"Easy, Irishman," the blacksmith's son mocked. "It's still right early for even one of your people to be fallin' down."

Will screamed and rushed forward once again. Hans moved to sidestep, but Will pulled up from his rush and threw a right hook that connected with the larger boy's jaw. Hans grunted in surprise and lashed out at Will, staggering him with a punch to the shoulder.

"Is that it?" he taunted, spitting in the dirt.

Will rushed again, fists flailing. Hans slapped aside the smaller boy's blows and backhanded him across the face. Will tumbled against the wall and struggled to rise. A vicious kick from Hans knocked the wind from his lungs and Will slumped to the ground. Hans shook his head and smiled. He reached down and pulled the boy's prized knife from its sheath.

"Thank ya, Irishman. Sure wish it had been a right smart fight. All fire, I reckon that your givin' me this blade."

"Put it down," a voice from behind Hans commanded.

Stephen Ruddell stood outside the ring of boys. His long rifle lay in the crook of his arm and a pair of wild turkeys were draped over his shoulder. The boy was large for twelve, almost as large as Hans. His thick auburn hair had been sheared off just above his shoulders, and he was dressed in buckskin leggings and a blue linen shirt. He already carried himself with the confidence of a hunter and a frontiersman.

"What'd you say?" Hans asked, rising up to his full height to stare down at Ruddell.

"You heard me," Stephen replied, meeting the larger boy's challenge.

"It were a fair fit," Hans protested, looking down at the knife.

"I allow it wasn't," Stephen replied. He handed the turkeys to another boy before setting his rifle against the wall and stripping off his shirt.

"Give it back or I'll give you a belly full," he stated.

Hans hesitated. Stephen was the one boy in the country that he had avoided fighting. His father was the respected leader of the settlement, and Hans had heard many stories about his son's prowess as a hunter and a fighter. Stephen's confidence had made him uneasy and he did not want to fight the boy, but he could not back down. Ruddell had called him out.

"If I blast you, your pa will get huffed and my folks will end up with the little end of the horn," Hans protested, chewing on his lower lip.

Stephen chuckled. "My pa won't have no conniption fit over what happens between you and me. You blubber more then a gal after church! Now are you goin' to give that knife back or are you goin' to shut pan and fight?"

"All fire!" Hans growled, his anger rising as some of the boys around the circle snickered at the mild insult. He rammed the blade into one of the wall posts and held his fist up. "Come and get it!"

Stephen crouched and moved forward slowly.

Isaac Ruddell stood on the porch of the fort supply cabin, scratching his bearded chin. His brother-in-law, John Bowman, sat beside him. Bowman bit off a chaw of tobacco and looked up at Ruddell.

"It's true, Ike," he said, spitting tobacco juice across the porch. "The Shawnee are fixin' to come across the Ohio in force again!"

"I was cock-sure they learnt their lesson after George took Vincennes and you burned their towns last year," Isaac replied. "Their support from England is less considerable than it was just last year! Clark gave them a lickin' along the Mississippi."

John spat again. "Well, that high-falutin buckskin ain't never taken Detroit!" he sneered. "The British still have a right smart power base there. They've been blabbin' to the tribes and encouraged them to come against us in Kentucky again. The war ain't goin' well for them in the east so they need them red heathens to stir up more trouble in the west and hold more of the militia here while the British regroup in Virginia. If that damn Virginia dude had taken Detroit like he promised, we wouldn't be in this fix," he added, frowning deeply.

Isaac remained silent. He knew that John was being unfair to Clark. His ragtag army had been in no shape for a march on Detroit after their victory over Henry Hamilton at Vincennes the previous year.

Isaac looked around at the Fort. "Well, we can put the word out for everyone to hole up here. I reckon we'll be safe enough."

"You be careful, Ike," John replied, his brow wrinkled. "Simon Kenton has his scouts out workin' the friendly tribes. There's talk that there may be some British regulars come down from Detroit to help the Shawnee on a summer campaign. If it's true, they might bring a cannon with them."

Isaac glanced at his brother- in- law and rubbed his chin again. Their fort was strong, but it wouldn't hold up to cannon fire. "We'll send out more scouts and put the militia on full alert," he replied with a sigh. "If they do try and bring a cannon across the Ohio, we'll know in advance and will be ready for them."

John nodded in agreement. "You do that, Ike."

Rising from his chair, Bowman walked to the edge of the porch. "What's goin' on by the west wall?"

Isaac covered his eyes against the afternoon sun. "Looks like the blacksmith's son has picked a fight with one of the Danners."

"Patrick's boy?" John replied, squinting to make out the struggling figures. "His pa's a bluff fighter; does the boy have the same grit?"

Isaac nodded. "He's game enough, but he's overmatched."

Isaac looked on in disdain as Hans Mueller knocked the boy into the dirt and taunted him. Neither man moved from the porch to stop the fight. They both knew that frontier life was hard and required all children to develop a degree of strength and toughness in order to survive. Fights were common place among boys and were only stopped if they became too violent. Isaac noticed several other men watching the confrontation at a distance as well.

"That German brat seems pleased," John observed. "I take it there ain't been a body give him a cocked hat?"

"No," Isaac replied with a frown. "He's a bouncer, and ornery. He blusters the lads he knows he can lick. I suspicion he don't have the grit to stand against a considerable fighter."

Bowman smiled as he noticed his nephew move to the edge of the circle. "Well, I reckon we're about to fix the flint. Ain't that Stephen takin' the other boys' part?"

Isaac did not reply. He watched silently as his eldest son stripped off his shirt and moved in on the larger boy.

Hans took measure of Stephen as he moved toward him. Ruddell was advancing cautiously, prepared for whatever the older boy might do. Hans was not used to fighting a calm opponent. Anger caused a fighter to make mistakes and Mueller was used to angry boys rushing at him. He decided to try and taunt his opponent.

"Must make you proud, your pa bein' the captn' of Corn Island," Hans sneered. "The other officers went on to fit at Vincennes; your pa got left behind to guard the trace!"

"At least mine went along!" Stephen fired back calmly.

Hans grunted and swung at Ruddell as he moved within reach. Stephen dodged the blow and smacked Mueller across the face. The older boy growled and rushed forward. Stephen ducked out of Mueller's grasp and delivered a blow to his stomach as he rushed past. Hans staggered and stumbled to the ground, gasping for breath.

"What's wrong, Hans?" Stephen asked as he advanced toward him. "Don't you have the grit for a real fight?"

The German boy scooped up a handful of dirt and threw it in Stephen's face, blinding him. Seizing the advantage, Hans bull-rushed the smaller boy and drove him into the log wall. Stephen staggered from the force of the impact and stumbled to his knee. As he struggled to rise, Hans wrapped him in a powerful bear hug.

"Who's the gal now!" he howled triumphantly as he tightened his grip.

Stephen did not panic as the larger boy tried to crush the air from his lungs. He had been in many rough and tumble fights during his time in Kentucky. He calmly worked his arms to his sides to loosen Han's grip and he set his feet firmly against the ground. Stephen then used a trick his uncle John had taught him if he was ever caught in a more powerful man's grip. He exhaled and pushed off with his toes against the hard ground, slipping up in the larger boys' grip. This move cleared enough space for Stephen to arch his back and snap forward, driving his forehead into Han's face.

Mueller howled in agony and released his hold on Stephen. He staggered backward as blood gushed from his nose. Hans was bewildered by the sight of his own blood and wanted to quit, but he knew his reputation among the other boys was at stake. He growled in anger and rushed at Ruddell once again. Stephen did not side- step the rush this time. He set his feet and swiveled his hips as Hans attempted to crash into him. Stephen caught the larger boy's arm and used his own momentum to hip-toss him. Mueller sailed through the air and landed hard on his back, knocking the wind from his lungs. He groaned and tried to rise, but collapsed in a heap.

Stephen turned to Will Danner. "I reckon you can take that blade back, Will."

Danner took Stephen's hand. "Thank ya, Stephen. I'd been plum cow-hearted to go home without my grandpa's knife."

Hans had managed to rise from the ground and noticed all the boys around Ruddell, clapping him on the back. Many of them cast looks of disdain or snickers in his direction. He glanced at the knife that remained buried in the wooden post and he reached up to touch his broken nose. Mueller could feel the fire of hatred burning in his heart and he began to reach for the knife, his eyes focused on Stephen's unprotected back.

"I wouldn't," a calm voice from behind drawled. "He already blasted ya; you pull that blade and I reckon that boy'll kill ya!"

Hans whirled to find a frontiersman in buckskins standing beside him, his long rifle held comfortably in the crook of his arm. The man was of medium build with a large nose and piercing blue eyes. His clean shaven face looked youthful, even though he was in his mid- forties. Hans gulped as he recognized Daniel Boone standing before him.

Boone winked at Hans and moved past him to clap Stephen on the shoulder.

"I reckon you ain't got no less rambunctious since ya left my settlement, boy." He chuckled. "You still have a mind to pick fights with older boys."

"I still win," Stephen replied, returning the frontiersman's smile. "What are you doin' here, Daniel?"

Boone glanced past Stephen, the smile fading from his face. "To converse with your pa, but it looks like you have a more con- siderable fix to deal with."

"What?" he asked

Before Boone could comment, Stephen gasped in pain as his mother landed a stinging blow across his back with the piece of hickory she had picked up from the wood pile.

"Get back to the diggings and finish your chores!" she hissed, landing a second blow on the boy's exposed flesh.

The other boys scattered as Elizabeth Ruddell took out her fury on her eldest son. Stephen rushed to gather up his shirt, rifle and turkeys as his mother rained blows down on his unprotected back. He raced past his father and uncle as they came to stand beside Boone.

"Are you goin' to take his part?" John Bowman asked as he watched his sister keep stride with the boy. He winced as he heard another audible smack of wood on flesh. Isaac shook his head.

"I'm reckon the boy knew his ma would be huffed if he went to brush huntin'."

"Besides," he added, a slight smile on his face. "I suspicion she'd give me a blasting for taking up for the boy, and I don't want no part of that. He's on his own."

Boone chuckled. "I always allowed that you wasn't a coot, Ike. You plum just proved me right. Hell has no fury like an angry mother."

The three men moved off as Will Danner walked past Hans and retrieved his knife from the post. The smaller boy stopped beside Mueller and held out his hand.

Mueller looked at him in astonishment. "Why are ya offering me your hand? Your man beat me!"

Will nodded. "No worse then you blasted me. I suspicion getting' knocked on your bumfiddle might take some of the bluster out of ya. I reckon if you can shut pan and not be such a black guard, we could be friends."

Hans shook his head and chuckled. He reached out and took Danner's hand. "I reckon your right!" He reached up and felt his broken nose. "Sure seems like Ruddell left me something to remember him by!"

Will shrugged. "You should thank him; I think he made ya more likely!"

He sprang away as Hans swung at him and gave chase across the compound.

Stephen was lying on his stomach in the cabin loft when his father came home. His siblings all lay sleeping around him, but the boy's stinging back hurt too much for sleep to come. His mother had not lain off with the hickory switch the whole way home. Worst of all, she had sent him to the loft without any supper. He could bare the sting of her switch, but the boy had truly felt he was in agony when the smell of roasting turkey and freshly baked blackberry pie had drifted through the cabin. His mother had sent his sisters to smear a salve of bear grease and honey on his wounds, but neither of them had been allowed to sneak him any food. Stephen felt his empty stomach rumble once again and shook his head; his mother certainly knew the best way to get her point across! The boy sighed and scooted painfully closer to the edge of the loft to listen to any news his father might share with his mother.

Isaac Ruddell placed his long rifle on a set of pegs above the mantle and turned to his wife. Elizabeth sat in her rocking chair darning a pair of Abraham's socks.

"You're late," she stated pointedly.

"Aye, and you well know the reason why," he replied. "Daniel and John had all creation of news to share."

"And a jug of whiskey, no doubt." She added dryly.

"Let's not fight, Beth," Isaac replied, a crooked smile on his face. "Might there yet be some supper for me? I'm gut foundered."

Elizabeth pointed one of the needles toward a Dutch oven that sat near the fire. "I kept some warm for you."

Isaac smacked his lips as he reached for the fire poker and gently lifted the Dutch oven and set it on the cabin table as his wife brought him a plate. Elizabeth sat down across from him and silently watched her husband eat for several minutes. Finally, her patience wore thin.

"Well?" she stated.

"Both John and Daniel suspicion the Shawnee have designs another raid against the settlements before the harvest," he replied in between bites of turkey. "We need to send out more scouts and strengthen the fort in case we have to wait out a siege."

Elizabeth nodded in agreement. She had lived on the frontier for most of her life and she had seen many Indian attacks and her share of sieges. It was simply part of life in Kentucky.

"The turkey sure is good," Isaac said with a grin, deciding to change the subject. "Where'd you get it?"

Elizabeth's face flushed. "You know where it's from, that no account son of yours!"

Isaac chuckled. "I had a mind you'd go hard on him."

"This ain't no laughin' matter" Elizabeth cried. "The boy sets aside his chores to disappear into the woods to hunt and fight. Don't tell me you cotton to his behavior!"

"Cotton to my son putting food on the table? I reckon not," he replied, smacking his lips as he bit into another piece of moist turkey. "Or acknowledge the corn that he's a considerable hunter, plum better then most of the men in the settlement," he added pointedly.

Elizabeth shook her head. "That may be, but I caught him in a fight with the blacksmith's son!"

Isaac nodded. "Aye, he was. Mueller is a fat headed cully! He was blusterin' Patrick Danner's son, tried to take his knife from him. Stephen stood up for him."

"I can't abide him fighting." Elizabeth replied, her face softening. "He enjoys it too much. The boy is wild. I don't want him to become like Boone, Kenton, or some of them others who leave their families behind to wander over all creation!"

"We live on the frontier, Beth." Isaac reminded her quietly. "This is a hard land and it makes for hard people. Stephen's a good boy. Sure he's rambunctious and head strong, but he gets that honest enough. Do I allow pride that he can hunt and hold his own against boys older and bigger then him? All to pieces. I know you fret that he'll be like Boone, but I'm cock-sure we won't have to lie awake at night worryin' about him fendin' for himself when he has a notion to go off on his own."

Elizabeth ran her hands through her auburn hair and sighed. She hated it when her husband was right. "Well, he still earned a blasting for not finishing his chores," she grumbled.

"Rightfully so," Isaac agreed with a nod, "and in front of a boodle of his friends after he whooped Mueller. You Bowmans always have shown considerable skill in getting your point across. I'm sure you shamed the lad as much you actually hurt him."

Elizabeth smiled and moved to her husband's side. "That was the point, husband. I reckon the boy will think twice before he runs off on me again! His stingin' back, hurt pride, and empty belly should remind."

"Oh, you're an ornery one, Elizabeth Ruddell." Isaac cried, pulling his wife onto his lap. "To cook the turkey your son shot and not allow him a single bite, you're right smart at torture."

Elizabeth smiled and wrapped her arms around her husband's neck. "You'd do well to recollect that the next time you decide to cross me."

Isaac chuckled and moved to kiss his wife, but a knock at the door interrupted them. Elizabeth leapt to her feet and moved to the fireplace and took down the rifle resting above the mantle. Isaac reached under his chair and drew forth a flintlock pistol that he kept hidden there. He rose from the seat and cocked the hammer back and pointed it at the door.

"Who calls?" he stated calmly.

"Don't shoot, Captain Ruddell." a voice responded. "It's Tom Salyers. My Dorothy has gone into labor! Can Mrs. Ruddell come and help?"

Isaac closed his eyes and sighed as he uncocked the pistol. "Come on in, Tom."

The door opened and a young, slender farmer entered the cabin. Tom twisted at his hat nervously. "I'm sorry to call so late, but its Dorothy's first child and the labor seems to be considerable."

"All fire, Tom," Elizabeth scolded as she gathered up everything she would need to help the young woman give birth. "Birthing is considerable on all women, no matter if it is their first or their tenth, but havin' a fat headed man around is plum worse. Go tell Ann Compton to meet me at your house and then you come back here and wait with Isaac."

"But..." Tom began to protest.

"Forget it, lad," Isaac said. "Do as she says. Elizabeth has helped birth a right smart number of babies and knows all creation about what to do. It'll be easier on you to do what she says."

"Besides," he added with a wink, "we've got some celebratin' to do."

Tom managed a nervous smile as he turned from the cabin door and moved out into the darkness to do as the midwife had instructed him.

Elizabeth eyed her husband as she moved to the doorway. "Don't celebrate with the boy too much. He'll need to be able to hold his babe in the mornin' without his wife streaked about him droppin' the little one!"

Isaac waved her out the door. "Did I ever drop one of ours?"

"It might've done some good if ya had dropped the oldest one!" she fired back. "It might have knocked sense into him and then I'd have considerable less trouble with him!" Elizabeth turned on her heal and stepped out into the night without waiting for his response.

Isaac walked to a set of shelves opposite the hearth and took down a large clay jug. He gave the jug a shake and nodded. He estimated that it was more then half full, more than enough for this night's celebration. The frontiersman walked back to the table and sat down. He uncorked the jug and took a long pull of Kentucky whiskey. He smacked his lips and smiled as he felt the liquor warm in his stomach. This batch was over two years old and had aged well in maple barrels. Whiskey was made all over the Western frontier, but Isaac had never tasted any better then that made in Northern Kentucky. He watched the doorway for several more moments, making sure that his wife did not return for some forgotten item. Finally, he cleared his throat.

"Alright, you can come down."

The ladder creaked as Stephen climbed down from the loft and moved to his father's side. Isaac turned the boy and inspected the whelps and cuts on his uncovered back. He nodded and pointed to the chair beside him. "Do you have a mind for why your ma blasted you so?"

The boy nodded. "I didn't finish my chores and went to brush huntin."

Isaac shook his head. "No, son. That ain't why she whooped ya."

The boy frowned and shrugged, not understanding.

Isaac placed his hand on his son's shoulder. "What if there had been an Injun raid? Your ma would've had a conniption fit if she and the other youngins had to go to the stockade without you."

"I can take care of myself!" Stephen replied, sticking out his chest.

Isaac sighed. "I reckon you can, son, but what about your mother and the little ones?"

Stephen frowned once again.

Isaac remained patient. "You're almost a man, son. I wasn't lying when I said you're a better hunter then most of the other men in the settlement: it's a fact. You have the grit to be a fine frontiersman, but you need to think of your family. There's still a war goin' on and I'll be gone with the militia. What would happen to your ma and the rest of the family if a war party come upon them while I'm away and you took a hankerin' to go to brush huntin'? Who would look after'em?"

Stephen swallowed hard.

"I'm plum dependin' on you, Stephen," Isaac said gently, seeing the boy redden in shame. "Can I count on you to be more of a man?"

Stephen spit in his palm and held out his hand. "I won't let you down, pa."

Isaac smiled. He spit in his own hand and shook with the boy. "How's your back?"

"It stings to Sam Hill!" the boy admitted, wincing as he raised one of his arms.

Isaac chuckled. "I don't reckon the Mueller boy gave you a click as hard as your Ma did!"

"Aye," Stephen agreed. "At least I saw him comin'."

Isaac laughed again and uncorked the jug. "Here, it's better medicine for your wounds then any of your ma's salves."

Stephen took the jug eagerly and swallowed a mouthful of the fiery liquid. He sputtered and coughed as he handed the jug back to his father.

Isaac smiled. "It takes some getting' used to. You best eat some of that turkey you shot and have a piece of your Ma's pie. It's ain't a right smart notion to drink whiskey when your gut foundered."

"Ma said I couldn't," Stephen protested, already starting to feel lightheaded from the strong drink.

Isaac winked at the boy. "I won't say nothin' to her if you don't."

Stephen eagerly stuffed his empty stomach with the tender meat and sweet pie. Isaac sat back in his chair and packed his clay pipe with tobacco. He watched the boy eat as he blew smoke from his pipe.

The boy finally sat back and sighed with satisfaction. "Thanks, Pa."

Isaac uncorked the jug and took another swig. "I was proud of what you did today, son. It was a considerable thing, standing up for the Danner boy. Hans could have clawed you off, but you wouldn't budge. It takes grit to stand up for others, but a body has to be considerable to stand up in the face of danger. For that, you deserve a good meal. Now, get yourself back to bed before your ma comes home and takes her switch to the both of us!"

Stephen stood and moved toward the ladder. He hesitated for a moment and then turned back and flung his arms around his father's neck in a tight hug. "Thanks, Pa."

Isaac smiled. "Go on, son. Your ma will have chores for you to do in the mornin.' You need your sleep."

Stephen gave his father a final smile and climbed the ladder to the loft. As he lay down, he heard Tom Salyers enter the cabin once again.

"Come, lad," his father said, handing Tom the clay jug. "Have a horn: tonight you join me in the ranks of proud fathers."

Stephen drifted off to sleep, a smile on his face.

CHAPTER 3

NOTHERN KENTUCKY
SUMMER, 1780

CAPTAIN HENRY BYRD adjusted his red British officer's coat and nodded in satisfaction. After several months of hard work, Byrd's company had finally made their way from Detroit to the Kentucky side of the Ohio River. Byrd looked on as the cannon that had been hauled all the way from Canada was carefully unloaded on the Kentucky shore. The brass muzzle of the mighty weapon shone brightly in the morning sun. The cannon had left quite an impression on the different tribes Captain Byrd had visited on the long trip south. His men had put on demonstrations of the weapon's power in various villages along the way. Ottawa, Miami, Potawatomi, Delaware, and Shawnee warriors had eagerly joined the British officer and his company as they moved across the Ohio to attack the northern Kentucky settlements. Byrd had assured the tribes that none of the forts could withstand the power of the cannon and that every warrior would return home with his tomahawk wet with Long Knife blood. Byrd watched as almost eight hundred warriors silently made their way across the wide river. The Shawnee warrior, Chiksika, came alongside him as he stood on the river bank. The warrior was of medium build with well defined muscles and a scalp lock of dark, braided hair that hung past his shoulders. Chiksika wore buckskin leggings and a silver gorget hung over his bare chest. The British officer was amazed by the amount of silver the Shawnee warriors all seemed to wear. In addition to the gorget, Chiksika had both ears split and bound in silver twine as well as a pair of silver armbands clasped around each of his biceps. Many of the other Shawnee warriors wore even greater amounts of silver than their war leader. Byrd had heard rumors that the Shawnee had a secret silver mine in the Ohio country from which they were able to produce their extensive decorations. He deemed there to be sufficient evidence to investigate those rumors once this damned rebellion was put down. He noticed that Chiksika was now watching him intently, his expression stoic.

Byrd was a large, powerful man with a round face and a notorious short temper. His soldiers often faced his wrath and the man's physical presence intimidated most of the people around him. He was also a good judge of character and realized that the Shawnee warrior was not intimidated in any way. The British officer knew the reputation of the Shawnee as fighters, and he needed their support in order for this campaign to be successful: he treated the Shawnee with respect.

"Well Chief, how far are we from the nearest settlement?" he questioned.

Chiksika pointed to the mouth of a small river a few hundred yards down stream. "The *Shemanese* have settlements on the Licking River, north of the place they call Boonesborough. Our scouts can be there by tonight, but it will take at least two more days to bring the cannon to the place they call Ruddell's Station."

Byrd frowned. "What about their scouts? Two days is plenty of time to call their militia together. I don't want to walk into an ambush and end this campaign before it even begins."

Chiksika smiled. "My warriors will take care of their scouts. These men that we face are not Boone or Kenton: they are careless." He placed his hand on the fresh scalp at his side for emphasis. "The men they had watching the river are dead. We will catch or kill any we find. We will be at the gates of their forts before they know we are here," he added confidently.

"Good," Byrd replied. "Then send out your warriors to lead the way, my friend."

A slender Indian boy who could not have been more then twelve or thirteen years old had silently moved up beside Chiksika. Byrd didn't think much of it; as it was common to see boys of the same age within the British army as drummers and pages. Byrd was truly surprised when the warrior turned to the boy and instructed him to move ahead of the raiding party with the other scouts. The boy nodded and ran ahead without a word. Byrd watched as he disappeared swiftly into the woods.

"I say, Chiksika," he began, his eyebrows raised. "You are appointing scouting duties to a mere lad? I would feel more comfortable if you sent a proven warrior with him. These Kentucky frontiersmen are known for their skill in the wilderness. I must say that I am not comfortable intrusting our safety to some youngster."

Chiksika's scowled. "*Tecumseh* is a better tracker and hunter then all but a few of the warriors who have joined you on this raid, Father. He is my brother and destined to be a great leader. I trust him above all others," he added pointedly.

Byrd sighed. He had learned enough about native beliefs and superstitions during his time on the frontier to know better then to question the warrior's judgment. Byrd hated the fact that he had to rely on savages to complete this campaign, but he knew that he didn't have a choice. Regular British forces were spread thinly across the continent as the colonial war continued to rage. The Americans were being aided by both the French and Spanish and the war was losing support in England. The British needed some decisive victories, and Captain Byrd intended to deliver one on this campaign, whatever the cost.

"Lead on, *ne-kah-noh*," Byrd said, adjusting his coat once again. "If you and your scouts can get us within sight of the Long Knife forts, we'll let the cannon show them the price of stealing Indian lands."

Chiksika flashed the English officer a smile and disappeared after the other scouts into the forest.

Stephen lay motionless on a wooded ridge overlooking a bubbling spring. The boy was patiently watching a deer trail that ran beside the clear stream. He lay over fifty yards away from the trail, but had a clear view of the point from which the deer would emerge from the trees to drink from the stream. He had been silently watching the trail since the early morning mist had covered the area and the ground had been damp with dew. The sun had risen higher in the eastern sky and midmorning was approaching.

Still, the boy did not move. He knew that his patience would be rewarded in time. A movement caught his attention. He could not help but smile when he saw a large buck making its way cautiously down the trail. The deer stopped short of the stream and sniffed the air tentatively. Stephen knew that he was down wind of the buck and had not been detected. He eased his rifle up and carefully took aim, slowly cocking the hammer back. A slight noise caused the deer to straiten, sniffing the air once again. Stephen cursed silently as the buck leapt the stream and disappeared into a thicket. The boy slapped the ground in frustration and began to rise. He intended to give whoever was coming down the trail a piece of his mind for ruining his hunt.

The boy's jaw dropped in disbelief as a pair of Indians materialized from the forest. He kept his senses and dropped silently back to the ground. Stephen had seen Indians before in the different Kentucky settlements, but none that looked like these. The boy watched intently as the warriors moved forward, carefully examining the trail. He took notice of the warrior's scalp locks and painted faces. Both were heavily armed. Stephen hoped the pair might be hunting, until he saw the scalp of some dead frontiersman hanging from one of the brave's side. A chill went up the boy's spine; he knew these Indians were part of a war party. Another movement on the trail caught his attention. He watched as a green clad frontiersman moved up to join the pair. The trio communicated through silent hand signals for several moments before the ranger nodded and moved back up the trail. Stephen had seen enough.

He knew the ranger was a Canadian and the warriors were Shawnee. Stephen had listened to the conversations his father had with his uncles and other prominent frontier leaders enough to know that the presence of Canadians with hostile Indians meant there was a significant enemy force moving against Kentucky. He had to get back to the settlement and warn everyone before it was too late! Stephen quietly worked his way down the wooded ridge to the forest floor and ran toward the station.

Isaac Ruddell was hoeing corn in one of his fields when his eldest son burst from the forest and ran toward him. The militia captain dropped his hoe and picked up his rifle from its resting place beside the split rail fence. The boy's frightened expression had already set the frontiersman on alert.

"What's wrong?" he demanded, scanning the tree line.

"Indians, Pa!" the boy gasped, struggling to catch his breath. "Warriors with scalps, headed this way!"

Isaac cursed and cocked his rifle. "How far?"

"More then a mile, Pa," Stephen stated. "I saw them, but they didn't see me!"

Isaac nodded, never taking his eyes off the tree line. "Run on home and tell your ma and everyone else you see along the way. Help get your brothers and sisters to the stockade."

Isaac watched his son run toward the settlement before making his way toward the stockade. The frontiersman knew that the lad had observed a scouting party of a much larger force. The scalps more than likely belonged to some of the men Isaac had sent to patrol the Ohio River. Hopefully, Stephen's warning would give the settlement enough time to prepare. Isaac needed to get to the western ridge opposite the stockade and set the signal fire. The green sassafras used to build the fire would emit a heavy cloud of smoke that would be seen across the valley. All the settlers who saw it would know to get to the stockade and prepare to defend themselves. Isaac's face hardened. The war had come once again to Kentucky and was at the doorstep of his own settlement. He knew his people would be ready.

"Ma!" Abe Ruddell cried from the cabin door. "Here comes Stephen, and he sure is in a hurry!"

Elizabeth Ruddell peered out the cabin window as her eldest son staggered into the settlement. She stepped out of the cabin as the boy collapsed on the doorstep.

"What's wrong?" she demanded.

"I saw Indians in the woods!" the boy gasped. "Pa told me to help you get all creation to the stockade."

Stephen was surprised how calm his mother remained after hearing the news. She stood in the doorway for a moment, her expression emotionless.

"Go and tell the other folks," she replied, motioning to Stephen. "Abe, gather up all your pa's powder horns and spare bullets, we'll be needin' them at the fort." She turned to her eldest daughter as the boys sprang into action. "Mary, I need you to take the baby and Ann and walk toward the fort. I need to gather a few things and then I'll be along directly."

Mary bit her lip and nodded. She moved to follow her mother's directions as Elizabeth lifted a heavy gurney sack from a hook inside the cabin door and quietly went to work. Elizabeth had lived through many Indian raids during her lifetime and knew this was no time to panic. They could be in the stockade for a few days and she knew what her family would need during that time.

She filled the bag with all the smoked venison she had in the cabin, a bag of corn meal, and the last of her winter store of potatoes. Elizabeth added a heavy cast iron skillet for cooking and gathered up all the bandages she had stored. If the stockade was attacked, she knew there would be wounded. Satisfied that she had everything she needed, Elizabeth hoisted the heavy sack and stepped out of the cabin to join her children on the way to the stockade. She took note of the heavy white smoke rising from the signal ridge. Elizabeth knew her husband was trying to call as many of the area settlers as he could into the safety of the fort.

The stockade was filling quickly by the time Stephen joined his family inside the walls. The fort was not large, but it was sturdily built. There were few interior buildings, so most of the settlers would be confined to the open area of the parade ground. Several frontiersmen were erecting lean-tos for shelter against the hot summer sun. Most of the settlers went about their business inside the stockade calmly, being veterans of previous frontier Indian raids. A few of the newly immigrated German families from Pennsylvania sat huddled against the eastern wall, frightened and bewildered by all the activity and the thought of an Indian attack. Several frontiersmen already manned the stockade wall, silently watching the distant tree line with their rifles ready. Stephen gathered up his rifle and went to find his father.

Isaac Ruddell was at the main cabin, surrounded by militia officers. He had ordered a detailed inventory of stores, powder, and lead. Most raids were short lived, but a large force might lay siege to the stockade for several days. The fort had a deep well, so there was little concern about water. Over two hundred settlers would be packed within the forts protective walls before sundown. Isaac knew he could put close to a hundred men on the stockade walls, and all were experienced hunters and fighters. This would be more then enough to withstand a siege by any significant enemy force. As long as there was enough food and ammunition, the settlers within the walls would be safe. Isaac looked up from the reports that lay in front of him and smiled as his eldest son entered the cabin, his rifle resting in the crock of his arm. The boy already carried himself with the manner and confidence of an experienced frontiersman.

"Where do you want me, Pa?" he stated evenly.

"Go help your ma," Isaac replied. "Get the lean-to set up and have a fire goin'. She'll need your help watchin' over your brothers and sisters."

Stephen frowned. "I can fight, Pa! Why can't I be on the wall?"

Isaac took the boy aside. "Sure you can fight, son, but we have a boodle of men to guard the wall if we're attacked. I have to command the defense from here. I need someone I trust to look after our family. It's a considerable task that I'm trusting you with, boy."

Stephen nodded, "Yes, Pa." The boy was disappointed with his assignment, but he would not let his father down.

Stephen found his mother and siblings setting up camp near the western wall.

"What do you need me to do, Ma?" the boy asked, unable to hide his frown.

"What's wrong?" Abe taunted as he walked by with a bucket of water. "Pa won't let you stand on the wall with the rest of the men?"

Stephen clapped his brother on the back of the head, causing the younger boy to stumble and spill the bucket of water. Elizabeth looked up from her work and gave her eldest son a stern look.

"Enough of that!" she scolded. "You boys get the lean-to set up for me. I need to converse with your pa!" she commanded, brushing off her hands and walking toward the cabin.

Isaac frowned as his wife stepped onto the cabin porch. He had seen that look on her face many times over the years and knew that she had something on her mind that he would have to deal with immediately. "Pardon me, boys," he said, moving around the table that now served as his desk. He offered his wife his arm and they moved out onto the porch where they could converse privately.

"What do you have a mind on, Beth?" he asked.

Elizabeth placed her hands on her hips and looked her husband in the eye. "Your son can tote a man's share of work, Isaac. He's too proud to be left with his ma!"

Isaac sighed. "He's still young, Beth. I had a mind you'd want to keep him safe at your side if there's a fight."

"Well of course I do, you fool!" she scolded, tears filling her eyes. "What mother wouldn't? That's not the point." She wiped the tears away before fixing her husband once again with her stern gaze. "Stephen's a better frontiersman then most of the men here. He needs to help defend the fort. There's nothin' that I need him to do that Abe can't take on. It hurt the boy's pride to be sent back to the women and children. You must find some duty that's fitting for him. I pray that you don't put him on the wall. Yet for his sake you must find him a considerable detail."

Isaac shook his head and chuckled. "It's you that our boy gets his stubborn streak from."

He bent and gave his wife a kiss on the cheek. "Alright, I'll make him a courier. He can carry orders and messages to each of the wall commanders. It's an important job, but he should be safer then if he was placed on one of the walls. Go tell him to get himself back here."

Elizabeth smiled and planted a kiss on her husband's lips before turning and hurrying back toward their children, leaving the militia commander shaking his head.

Stephen nearly jumped with joy when his mother told him he was to be a courier for the militia. He gathered up his rifle and made to leave for the command post when his mother grabbed his arm.

"Be careful and do exactly what your pa tells you to do!" she lectured, her eyes moist. "Don't be reckless or try to be a hero; this ain't a game. Actin' fat headed can get you kilt."

"I'll be careful, Ma." he assured her with a smile.

Elizabeth wrapped the boy in a tight embrace. "See that you are. Now go. Your pa is expectin' you."

Stephen picked up his rifle and jogged toward the cabin as his mother wiped tears from her eyes.

Captain Byrd looked through his eyeglass at the stockade and settlement known as Ruddell's Station. He could make out frontiersmen on the walls of the fort, their deadly Pennsylvania long rifles glittering in the morning sun. The stockade had been designed similar to most other frontier forts. The forest had been cleared within two hundred yards of the walls, ample distance for sharpshooters to cover with their deadly rifles. The gate of the fort was cleared of all obstacles in the direction of the settlement, allowing the inhabitants to retreat within the relative safety of the walls. Byrd smiled; it would be this clearing that would be the fort's downfall. Byrd turned his gaze upon the heavy brass cannon. He would easily be able to set the weapon up outside the range of rifle fire and smash the stockade walls. Byrd nodded in approval. The effort to drag the cannon across the frontier had been worth it.

A commotion from the stockade wall brought Isaac Ruddell out of the command post.

"Captn' Ruddell." one of the sentries called down, his voice strained. "You'd better get up here and see this!"

Isaac quickly mounted one of the wall ladders and climbed to the rampart. He shielded his eyes to the bright summer sun and watched as a squad of British regulars rolled a cannon into place in front of the stockade gate. Outwardly the militia commander remained calm, but his heart skipped a beat and his stomach tightened at the sight.

Isaac glanced at the frontiersman beside him. "How far you reckon, Jacob?"

"Three hundred yards, captn'," the dark bearded frontiersman replied, spitting tobacco juice over the side of the wall. "Too far to pick off any of those cannoneers."

"How powerful of a cannon do you reckon it is?" Jacob asked, watching the British regulars train the muzzle of the cannon on the stockade and block the wheels against the recoil of the first anticipated shot.

"Powerful enough," Isaac stated, frowning at the sight. "Our walls won't hold long against cannon balls."

Jacob spat again. "Maybe we can rush 'em," he said, grasping for a solution to the dangerous situation. "I'd allow that we could drive them back long enough to spike the cannon."

Isaac shook his head. "They would suspicion such a move. Sendin' men outside the walls would be foolish."

Jacob tugged at his dark whiskers. "What do you have a mind to do, Captn'? We can't sit back and wait for them to blow the gate down."

"No we can't," Isaac agreed, moving toward the rampart ladder. "I'll have to go out and converse with the British officer."

"What for? Ain't it cock-sure what their designs are?" Jacob growled.

"It's one thing for men to die in a fight, but what about them?" Isaac replied quietly, waving his hand over the people below. "How many women and children will die in a fit that we can't win? My family's down there, Jake. I'll do all creation to protect them and everyone else in this fort. Those are British regulars down there, white men that can be reasoned with. If we don't go talk to them they'll blow the gates down and send the Injuns in. Is that what we want? The way I see it, talkin' is our only choice."

Jacob swore and shook his head. "I don't reckon we can trust them bloody backs anymore then the red bastards they brought with'em."

The sound of thunder echoed across the valley as the cannon fired its first shot.

"Get down!" Isaac screamed, dropping to the ramparts.

Stephen blinked in amazement as the stockade gates erupted in a shower of splinters and smoke. One moment the gates were there and the next there was a jagged, gaping hole where they had once stood. The boy's ears rang from the explosion. It took several moments for him to hear the frantic screams of the people around him. The next thing the boy knew, his father was at his side.

Isaac shook the dazed boy. "Are you alright?"

Stephen nodded in response, still too shocked to speak. Isaac hugged his son in relief. "Go find your ma and the youngins."

The boy nodded and ran off. Isaac ran forward toward the breach with several other men, expecting an attack. As the smoke cleared, the militia commander could make out the soldiers reloading the distant cannon. Isaac wiped his brow with his sleeve and appraised the situation as Jacob moved to his side. Nobody had been killed by the first cannon fire, but several people had been wounded and the gates were damaged beyond repair. The men within the fort could defend the gap against an attack, but not if the cannon continued to knock other holes in the walls.

Isaac looked around at all the men, women, and children who were depending on him to keep them safe. He knew that he had no choice.

"Find anything that can be toted in front of the gate. Keep your rifles ready and cover me until I get back," he instructed the men around him calmly as he tied a white handkerchief to his rifle barrel. "Be ready in case the Injuns rush the fort before I've had a chance to talk with their officer."

Isaac took a step toward the hole, but Jacob reached out and put a hand on his shoulder. "Wait, Captain. I'm comin' with you. You need to have at least one body you know you can trust out there."

Isaac managed a slight nod. "Thanks, Jake." Together, the frontiersmen stepped through the ruined gate.

Captain Byrd suppressed a smile as he watched the woodsmen slowly make their way toward his position beside the cannon. He turned to the Shawnee warrior, Chiksika. "Have your warriors ready to enter the fort, my friend."

The warrior nodded and moved away as the white men from the fort were brought before the British officer.

"I'd like to talk with the commandin' officer," The taller frontiersman stated, his blue eyes settling on Byrd.

Byrd clicked his heals and gave a slight bow. "Captain Henry Byrd, at your service."

The frontiersman nodded and leaned forward on his long rifle. "I'm Isaac Ruddell, Captain of the Kentucky militia and commander of this station. Do you mind tellin' me why you are attackin' our settlement unprovoked?"

Byrd's eyes widened and he could not suppress a laugh. "Why, we're at war, Mr. Ruddell! The American colonies that you are a part of have been engaged in open rebellion against his majesty's government for nearly four years. Surely, you wouldn't have me believe that you've not heard of the war, even in this most remote part of His Majesty's lands."

Byrd's laughter ceased as the burley, dark bearded, frontiersman beside Ruddell spat tobacco juice at his feet.

"We've heard of the war, Bloody Back. Do you see any colonial soldiers here? What the Captn' hankers to know is why you are attackin' non combatants. We're a peaceful settlement that's just tryin' to make a livin'. Why do you have a mind to make war on women and children?" Jacob demanded.

"Peaceful?" Byrd sneered. "It's well known that the Kentucky militia was among those who marched against the Royal outposts along the Mississippi with the Rebel commander Clark and attacked Governor Hamilton at Vincennes. Colonel Hamilton now sits in a rebel prison thanks to your 'peaceful' militia."

"That's right where 'Hairbuyer' Hamilton belongs." Jacob retorted. "The militia went against him cause he was payin' Injuns to bring in the scalps of white men, women, and children. I suspicion you have similar designs."

"You are in no position to lecture me, Sir." Byrd growled, his face turning a deeper shade of red. "You colonials who have settled in the lands west of the mountains have done so in violation of His Majesty's proclamation of 1763. You have engaged in open warfare against his majesty's loyal native subjects since that time, including their women and children. This rebellion will be put down and his majesty will no longer tolerate the insolence of his American colonists!"

Jacob was about to reply, but Isaac cut him off. "We know that the colonies and the crown are at war, Captain," he said quietly. "I allow that I took part in the fight that you just spoke of. We suspicion that you're part of a military campaign, and not a raid bent on murder. What are your demands?"

Byrd took a long breath and exhaled to calm himself. It was obvious that the backwoods militia captain had been schooled in the basics of military protocol. Byrd gave the man a slight nod of respect.

"My force has you outnumbered, outgunned, and overmatched, Captain Ruddell," he replied, sweeping his hand toward the cannon for emphasis. "You'll surrender your command to me and become prisoners of war. "

Ruddell remained silent for a moment. "What of our women and children?"

"They'll join us as well" Bryd replied with slight smile. "We wouldn't wish to leave noncombatant's unprotected on the frontier. Heaven knows what might happen to them."

"Our guns?" Isaac whispered, struggling to maintain his calm.

Byrd clasped his hands behind his back. "You're beginning to test my patience, Captain. Do I truly need to recite all the details of an unconditional surrender to you? What do you possibly believe you have to bargain with? If you don't surrender we will pound your stockade to bits with the cannon and send our force in to storm the walls."

"Do you reckon I would turn my people over to your savages unarmed?" Isaac replied through clenched teeth. "Everyone inside those walls knows how to use one of these!" He continued, shaking his rifle at the British officer. "How many of your force will fall to our guns before you wipe us out? Can your campaign afford the cost?"

"Very well, Captain Ruddell," Byrd replied, eyeing the rifle in the militia captain's hand. "This is what I'll offer. If you surrender your arms and force to me, I give my word that every man, woman, and child you protect will have safe passage to Detroit. In addition, you will arrange for the surrender of any other stations we come to under the same conditions."

Isaac was about to reply, but Captain Byrd raised his hand to stop him. "This is my only offer, Captain. Consider it well. If you refuse, I'll unleash my 'savages' upon your fort. You asked me if I could afford the cost of an assault against your rifles. The real question is if you and the men you command can afford such a cost. If you refuse my demands, you and every other man under your command will watch their families die before your very eyes. Which one of us has the most at stake?"

Isaac clenched his fists to his side and stared hard at the British officer. He did not doubt the man's words. He glanced back at the fort and thought of his wife and children; he knew that he had no choice.

"I'll need some time to tell my people and prepare to leave," he replied, his voice cracking.

"Of course. It is almost two o'clock and I intend to make camp for the evening. Your people may remain in the fort for the night and prepare to leave in the morning. Do we have terms?" Byrd replied with a smile, holding out his hand.

Isaac looked hard at the outstretched hand, knowing what the British officer expected. He exhaled slowly and hesitantly handed his rifle over. A Canadian Ranger roughly pulled Jacob's rifle away from him. Byrd admired the finally crafted weapon.

"Have your men stack their arms, rifles, pistols, tomahawks, and blades beside the gate, Captain," Byrd stated, glancing up from his examination. "Make sure nothing is left out or forgotten. The consequence for any prisoner found to be hiding a weapon will be severe. Do you understand my meaning?"

Isaac nodded, turned on his heal and made his way back toward the fort, Jacob in tow. The two men said nothing for several moments. Finally, Isaac looked at the bearded frontiersman, tears in his eyes.

"There's no other way, Jake," he whispered. "If we try and stand against them, they'll kill everyone. This is our only chance."

Jacob frowned. "I know, Ike. Everyone will abide your decision. We've got to do what's best for the settlement. Still, it ain't chirk to bow down to that bloody back and his heathen allies."

Isaac could only nod in agreement as the two men entered the ruined fort.

CHAPTER 4

RUDDELL'S STATION
SUMMER, 1780

STEPHEN'S EYES WERE WET WITH TEARS as he helped his mother gather what possessions they could before they were to become prisoners of the British. The boy had looked on in disbelief as his father returned from his meeting with the British officer and informed the people in the fort that he had surrendered to the enemy and that the frontiersmen had to turn over all their weapons before everyone was marched to Detroit as prisoners of war. Nobody had protested, but several men had grumbled and many had refused to look at his father as they stacked their weapons beside the fort gate. Stephen could not hide his own frown as he stacked his rifle against the wall and dropped his knife on the adjacent pile. Isaac had squeezed the boy's shoulder as he moved to stand beside him.

"Go help your ma gather what you can before we march out." he whispered, reading the disappointment on his son's face. "We may be split up and I'm countin' on you to help take care of a boodle of folks when we head north."

Stephen had nodded his head, too upset to speak. The boy had run off as his father watched with a heavy heart.

The boy's anger built as he gathered up the iron kettle and cooking utensils while his mother rolled blankets into bed rolls. Finally, he couldn't take it any longer. "I don't want to go to

Detroit!" he grumbled, slamming the lid on the kettle. "Pa should never have surrendered! We could've fought them off. Now we have to leave all creation behind!"

Elizabeth Ruddell had risen from the ground and was standing with her back to her eldest son. The boy was caught totally by surprise when his mother whirled and smacked him across the face. Years of hard living on the frontier had made Elizabeth strong and she hit the boy hard enough to knock him to the ground. Stephen blinked up at her in surprise as she stepped to his side and jerked him to his feet by his hair. She roughly grabbed his face and forced him to look at the gate.

"Look at what we're facin'!" she hissed. "One shot from that cannon took down our gate. What do you reckon would have happened if they continued to blast away? There's no way we could have held these walls. The British would have blown everything to hell and then sent those damn Injuns in to massacre all wrath!"

Stephen gulped. He had never heard his mother curse before. The woman jerked his head around to look at her angry face.

"This ain't a fort full of buckskins fightin' a battle between two armies," she hissed through clenched teeth. "There aint no rules or glory. Every man, woman, and child could have been kilt'. This ain't civilized warfare, son. Out here we're beyond civilization. Your pa knows that. You don't think he wanted to fight? He was thinkin' about you and the rest of his family. It plum humiliated him to have to surrender to the Bloody Backs. He did it because he cares about every single body in this fort and he knew it was the only way to save everyone. If you weren't so selfish, you would be able to see that. You should be thanking your pa for what he did!" Tears filled Elizabeth's eyes and she let the boy go, reaching for a handkerchief.

Stephen rubbed the side of his bruised cheek. "Sorry, ma," he whispered.

"I'm not the one you should apologize to, son." she replied, wiping the tears from her eyes. "We've some hard times ahead of us," she whispered in his ear. "Your pa and I will need you to be strong to help our family make it through. Promise me you'll do everything we expect of you."

"Yes, ma." the boy replied, wiping his own eyes. "I won't let you and pa down."

Chiksika glared angrily at Captain Byrd. "My warriors came with you because you said we would kill many Long Knives," he spat. "Your cannon has blown their fort open, yet we do not attack. Few warriors have new scalps hanging from their belts; this is not what you had promised."

Captain Byrd put his arms behind his back and sighed. " His Majesty wishes for peace between he and his subjects in America. As you know, he can be harsh to those who disobey his commands, but generous to those who obey him. The people in the fort have surrendered, so I must do as he commands and take them as prisoners back to Canada"

Chiksika shook his head in disgust. "This is not war!" he declared. "These *Shemanese* have stolen our lands and murdered our people. They have broken every treaty and burned peaceful villages time and time again. They deserve to die!"

"That may be, but I have my orders," Byrd replied, his voice hardening.

"My warriors have no orders," Chiksika replied coldly. "If you do not have the stomach for war, then maybe I will take my warriors and return to our villages until the British sends us a leader who will fight!"

The British captain knew he was in a delicate situation. He had promised his native allies glorious victories and many scalps in this campaign. He believed that Chiksika might take his warriors and return across the Ohio, effectively ending the Kentucky campaign. Damn this frontier warfare! If the crown would send more regulars to the frontier, there would be no need to deal with these savages. Byrd shook his head, knowing that British forces were already spread thinly across the continent fighting the Colonials, French, and Spanish. He needed Chiksika and his warriors; he had to find a way to placate them.

Byrd had placed the militia Captain's rifle against the cannon wheel. He looked at the weapon and smiled. He had intended to keep the finely crafted weapon as a spoil of war, but now found a more important use for it.

"These Long Knives all have fine rifles and good blades, as you well know," Byrd stated, picking up the rifle and once more examining it.

"Those weapons are all being stacked inside the gate as we speak." Byrd continued, tossing the rifle to Chiksika. "They're all yours to hand out among your warriors as you see fit. Consider them your people's reward for your role in this great victory."

Chiksika admired the weapon and bit his lip. The gun was beautifully crafted. The curly maple stock was crescent shaped with a brass butt plate and a silver inlaid patchbox. The .50 caliber barrel was a full forty six inches long and well maintained. Chiksika knew that the rifle was far more accurate then any British musket. Armed with guns such as these, he could lead his own people in open warfare against the Kentucky settlements. He would not need the support of the British with their cannon, red coats, and weak stomachs. Byrd had just awarded him the greatest spoils that his people had ever received. Chiksika would be recognized as a war leader on the same level as his father, Hard Striker. Still, he was a shrewd man and did not let his satisfaction show.

"There are many horses in the fort and the Long Knife fields. What will be done with them?" Chiksika stated smoothly.

Byrd smiled. "Why, they'll also be given to your people, as well as any items you find in the cabins that your warriors might find useful."

Chiksika nodded. "We will be taking many prisoners back to Ohio. What will be done with those who hide weapons or try to escape?"

Byrd's smile disappeared. "Your warriors have my leave to kill and scalp anyone who tries such folly."

Chiksika smiled. "I will choose warriors to enter the fort and send others to search the cabins and catch the horses in the fields. We will kill any animals that are left and burn the cabins when we are done."

Byrd nodded his agreement and the Indian leader eagerly moved away to set his warriors into action. The British officer rubbed his eyes. Once again, he was reminded of the brutal and savage requirements it took to fight a war in this distant place. He hoped his success on this campaign would warrant his reassignment to a more civilized location. For that, Captain Henry Byrd realized he would do just about anything.

The atmosphere was tense as Canadian rangers and Shawnee warriors made their way through the ruined gates to stare silently at the weaponless settlers. With their rifles and blades stacked,

Captain Ruddell had released most of the militia to help their families prepare for the long journey ahead. Now Ruddell and his core of officers stood at the front of the long train of prisoners. Isaac longed to be with his family, but knew that his place was at the front of the column. The Indians glared at the Kentuckians, fingering their knives and tomahawks. Many of the militia shifted uncomfortably and glanced toward the weapons that remained stacked beside the gate. Captain Byrd came forward.

"Are your people ready to go?" he questioned Ruddell, looking down the column.

"As ready as we're goin' be," Isaac replied, his voice tense as he eyed the large number of warriors entering the fort.

Byrd nodded. "I would remind you that the trip is long, Captain Ruddell. I hope your people have only packed what is necessary. We cannot tolerate anyone slowing down our advance."

"We Kentuckians pack light, Captain," he replied, fixing the British officer with an intense stare. "We won't slow you down anymore then you're used to. Not unless you were ever attached to Johnny Burgoyne at Saratoga or Willie Howe and his ladies when he was trying to run down General Washington a couple of years back. If you were with them, then I reckon you'll be slowin' us down."

Several of the surrounding militia smiled and snickered.

Byrd's eyes widened and his lips tightened at the comment. "That will be enough insults, Captain Ruddell," he stated indignantly. "You are a prisoner of war who is being treated well; I expect you and your people to respond in a respectful manner."

Isaac nodded. "My apologizes, Captain Byrd. Could I respectfully ask why so many of your savages have crowded inside the walls? They're makin' my people feel a bit peaked."

"It's no affair of yours," Byrd replied pointedly. "With your surrender of this fort, you and your people are prisoners of war. You may move your people out, Captain."

Isaac swallowed an angry retort and began moving forward, starting the whole column south. Byrd nodded to Chiksika, who signaled the eager warriors. Several Indians let out excited whoops as they rushed to the stack of fine, Kentucky rifles and sharp, steel blades. The militia looked on in shock and surprise, and then anger when they realized what was happening.

"Damnation! That fool of a Bloody Back is given' them savages our guns," Jacob hissed, moving beside Isaac. "Our weapons will be used in every raid and murder those heathen bastards take part in across Kentucky for the next ten years. We got to do something!"

Isaac grabbed Jacob by the shoulder as he took a step toward the excited warriors.

"Easy, Jake." he whispered. "There's nothin we can do now beside get everyone kilt. Settle yourself down."

Jacob swallowed hard and stepped back in line.

Will Danner was nervous. He instinctively reached for his grandfather's knife that he had secretly hidden in the seam of his breeches. Feeling the handle, he breathed deeply to try and calm himself. Everyone in the fort had been ordered to turn in all weapons, but Will could not bear to part with the knife. It was the only valuable possession that he had and the thought of it in the hands of an Indian warrior turned his stomach. He had taken his chances and concealed the blade carefully. Now as he watched the painted warriors push and fight over the surrendered weapons, he was glad he had hidden the family heirloom away Hans Mueller grumbled in anger beside Will as they moved toward the gate.

"Look" he huffed, pointing toward one of the Canadian rangers silently watching the moving line. "Can you allow that white men are helpin' these savages? Ya must be proud of yourself," the larger boy said, speaking loud enough to get the attention of the ranger.

"Let it go, Hans!" Will hissed, his heart racing. It was too late, the ranger made his way over to the boys.

"What'd you say?" the Canadian demanded.

"I said you must be proud," Hans shot back, meeting the ranger's hard stare. "Helpin' savages to take what belongs to other white folk. You should be ashamed of yourself."

The young ranger's face reddened with anger. "I'm a loyal subject of the crown," he replied indignantly. "These Indians are our allies in defending the rights and lands of his majesty's subjects against rebels such as you who take everything without consent! You're not even English, yet here your German arse is in English lands; you have no right to be here!"

Will frantically tugged at Hans' arm, trying to end the altercation before other rangers or Indians took notice of the situation. "Come on, Hans. We have to go!"

The German youth pulled his arm away. "Right?" he cried. "We've earned the right to live as we please. We pay for it with sweat and blood. If you Canadians had any balls, you'd all be helpin' us win this war rather then lickin' the boots of your British masters!"

The Canadian had heard enough. He responded to the insult by driving his rifle butt into Hans' chest, knocking him back into Will. The smaller boy stumbled as Hans crashed to the ground heavily. Will staggered and felt his hidden knife slip as he tried desperately to regain his balance. The boy looked down in horror as the blade tumbled from his breeches and landed at his feet.

"You Irish dog," the ranger growled, seeing the knife and moving in on Will. "All weapons were to be turned over. I'll teach you to disobey."

Before Will could explain, the Canadian hit him in the face with his rifle stock, knocking the boy to the ground. Will tasted blood in his mouth and curled up in a defensive ball as the furious ranger savagely kicked him in the ribs. The green clad soldier raised his rifle to strike again, a sneer on his face.

The blow never fell.

Will looked up as the ranger grunted. His expression had gone from rage to that of confusion and pain. The Canadian dropped his rifle and sagged to the ground, Will's knife buried in his back. Hans stood behind the fallen ranger, his hand covered in the man's blood.

"There's a lesson for you, you bastard." Hans said, spitting on the dead man.

Will collapsed into unconsciousness as the stockade erupted in chaos.

Stephen had looked up as the ranger clubbed Will Danner. Instinctively, he tried to move forward and reach his friend's side. He struggled through the crowd as Hans rose from the ground and drove Will's knife into the man's back. Stephen looked toward the group of Indians still bickering over the surrendered weapons and watched as several of them drew their weapons and ran toward the unarmed colonists. Stephen watched as a large, black and red painted warrior descended on Hans Mueller. The boy turned as the warrior arrived. Before he could move, the Indian split Hans' skull with a vicious tomahawk blow. The settlers panicked. Screams rent the air as the crowd rushed in different directions, trying to escape the onslaught of the attacking warriors. Stephen was knocked against the stockade wall and tumbled to the ground. The boy instinctively rolled against the wall to avoid being trampled. He rose quickly and looked for his family. He caught sight of Abe and the girls, cowering against the wall behind a couple of British regulars. Stephen frantically scanned the scene; where was his mother?

The boy caught sight of his mother standing in the midst of the chaos, holding baby Daniel. She clutched the baby to her and looked around the chaos, calling her eldest son's name.

"I'm here, Ma!" he cried, but the screams of the crowd drowned out his reply. Undaunted, Stephen began pushing his was through the chaos to get to his mother's side. A movement out of the corner of his eye caught the boy's attention. He looked on in horror as the same black and red warrior who killed Hans descended upon his mother.

Elizabeth clutched her baby closer as the grinning warrior appeared in front of her. The Indian grabbed the crying infant's arm and tried to pull him away from the struggling woman. Elizabeth screamed and clutched the baby closer, refusing to give up her child. Desperate, she kicked dirt in the warrior's face and turned to run.

The Indian growled in anger and grabbed the fleeing woman by the sleeve of her dress. Elizabeth struggled as the warrior wiped his eyes with his forearm and raised his tomahawk.

"No!" Stephen screamed as the Indian drove the blade into the top of his mother's head.

Blood burst from the woman's mouth as she sagged to the ground, still stubbornly clinging to the infant. The warrior reached down and pulled the child from the dying woman's arms. He let out a triumphant whoop and swung the baby by the leg and smashed its head again the stockade wall. Blood and brain coated the Indian as he dropped the dead child and turned from the gruesome scene.

A primal scream erupted from Stephen's mouth as he rushed at the warrior he had just watch murder his mother and brother.

The warrior smiled once again and raised his tomahawk to meet the enraged child. The boy skidded to a stop beside the fallen Canadian ranger and scooped up the dead man's rife. The Indian's smile disappeared as the young frontiersman raised the weapon and took aim, no more then twenty yards away. The warrior stepped forward and raised his tomahawk to throw, hoping to distract the boy's aim. The muzzle flashed and the shot reported across the compound as Stephen pulled the trigger. The lead ball tore through the warrior's throat and blasted him from his feet. Stephen dropped the rifle and ran forward, tears streaming down his face. The Indian had dropped his tomahawk as he struggled to his knees, clutching at the gaping wound in his throat as blood bubbling between his fingers.

Stephen picked up the fallen tomahawk.

"This is for my ma, you red bastard!" he cried, slamming the tomahawk down upon the warrior's exposed head with all of his might. As the Indian collapsed, the boy wrenched the tomahawk free and rained several more savage blows down on the motionless warrior.

Through his rage, Stephen felt a set of strong arms wrap around him. The boy struggled frantically and managed to twist out of the man's grip, minus the tomahawk. Stephen rolled away and scooped up his discarded rifle before he came to his feet, crouching in a defensive position.

The warrior that now stood before Stephen was not as large as the previous Indian he had killed, but looked no less deadly. His eyes were painted black and an eagle feather hung from his scalp lock. The Indian said something to him in a language he could not understand. When the boy did not respond, the warrior raised his tomahawk and advanced a step.

Stephen felt another set or arms wrap him in a tight embrace. As he struggled to free himself, his assailant stepped on his foot and drove Stephen to the ground. The attacker landed lightly on top of the boy, still holding him in a tight grip. Stephen realized whoever had hold of him was not as heavy as a man and twisted enough to see that he was being held by an Indian boy close to his own age. He looked up as the warrior advanced toward him, his tomahawk set to strike. Stephen continued to struggle, determined to die fighting. The Indian boy said something to the warrior that stopped his advance. He then bent close and spoke in Stephen's ear.

"Stop!" he whispered in surprisingly good English. "You are my prisoner; no one will hurt you unless I say so. Hold still if you want to live!"

The Indian's words, spoken in his own language, shocked and calmed the white boy. Stephen ceased his struggles and nodded as his rage dissolved into tears.

A single gunshot echoed through the stockade as Captain Byrd rode back through the gates, his flintlock pistol still in his hand. The officer had discharged the weapon into the air, drawing the attention of everyone involved in the melee.

"See here!" he cried sternly, looking around as his British regulars moved in to restore order. Byrd spotted Chiksika and nudged his horse toward the Indian leader as he examined the scene. The British officer took note of Tecumseh, holding a distraught colonial boy to the ground at his feet. Byrd's anger rose as he counted almost twenty dead colonists, many of them women and children, strewn about the stockade grounds.

"What's the meaning of this, Chiksika?" he demanded hotly. "No colonists were to be killed!"

Chiksika remained silent and walked over to the dead Canadian ranger and pulled the knife from the corpse's back. He threw the blade at the Byrd's feet as the officer dismounted his horse and then pointed at the body of Hans Mueller. "The young *Shemanese* had the knife hidden and used it on one of your soldiers. Did you not say to kill any prisoner who tried to hide weapons?"

"Aye!" Byrd agreed, his anger no less sedated. "But that doesn't account for all the other dead!"

Chiksika shrugged. "We went for the boy and the other Long Knives fought ."

"That one killed one of my warriors," he said pointing at Stephen. "We should kill them all; the trouble of moving them is too great!" he added pointedly.

"That we will not do," Byrd replied, his face darkening. "Any more killing and I will take my cannon and return to Detroit."

Chiksika shook his head and stalked away from the British officer. Byrd watched the warrior go before turning back to the gruesome scene. Cries of anguish rent the air as colonists ran forward to identify fallen loved ones. Byrd's chest tightened as he took note of the militia captain on his knees, clutching the body of a woman to his chest.

"My condolences, Captain Ruddell," he stated apologetically.

Isaac looked up, his eyes filled with tears. "Your condolences?" he whispered. "Will your condolences bring back my wife or son? Your savages broke the terms of surrender and killed unarmed prisoners, you bastard!" he cried.

Ruddell gently laid his wife's head on the ground and rose to his feet, his fists clenched to his side. It was then that he saw his eldest son being held to the ground by an Indian boy. The militia captain took several steps toward the boy as British regulars moved to block his path.

"Get out of my way!" he growled, attempting to push past the soldiers. "Let go of my boy!"

The click of a pistol hammer brought the distraught man's attention back to Captain Byrd. The officer had his pistol leveled at Isaac's head.

"Stand fast, Captain Ruddell," he ordered. "Your son was involved in this melee and he will be held until we can determine the extent of his crimes."

Isaac was about to reply when a large warrior pushed his way forward to stand in front of Byrd. The lower half of the Indian's face was painted black and he was angrily gesturing toward the boy with his tomahawk. Byrd could not understand the Shawnee tongue, but he could see that the Indian wanted to kill the boy. Chiksika stepped to the warrior's side.

"What's he saying?" Byrd asked.

"He wants the boy. The man he killed was his brother. Red Hawk wishes to kill him and take his scalp to avenge his dead brother," Chiksika explained in English.

Stephen had risen to his feet, even though the Indian boy still had a strong grip on his arm. Hearing what the warrior said, he became enraged and shook free of the boy's grasp, moving a step toward the Indian who wanted to kill him. Two rangers grabbed him by his arms and stopped him in his tracks.

"He kilt my ma!" the boy screamed, struggling to free himself.

"Enough!" Captain Byrd commanded, pointing his pistol at the angry boy. "Calm yourself, or I will kill you."

The Indian boy stepped forward and spoke to Chiksika in Shawnee. "Red Hawk cannot have him, brother," Tecumseh stated. "I have claimed him as my prisoner."

"Be quiet, *ni-je-ni-nuh*" the warrior replied, "The boy must answer for Black Bear's death!"

Tecumseh shook his head. "The boy speaks the truth, I saw everything. Black Bear did kill his mother. The fight between them was fair. It was wrong for Black Bear to kill them and the Great Spirit stood with the boy in the fight. Black Bear deserved to die and Red Hawk cannot claim his scalp when the fight was fair."

Chiksika looked thoughtfully at his younger brother, unable to dispute the boy's argument. The war chief had seen the white boy attack the warrior fearlessly. He admired his courage and respected the opinion of his younger brother.

Chiksika nodded. "He is yours until we return to Chillicothe. Keep the boy close to you; Red Hawk may still try to kill him."

Tecumseh watched as Chiksika moved before the angry warrior. Red Hawk shook his head in disgust and stalked from the fort when hearing the war chief's decision. He cast a murderous glance at Stephen as he exited the gate.

Tecumseh turned to the white boy. "I will stay close to you when we leave," he stated quietly. "As long as you are my prisoner, you are safe, do you understand?"

Stephen glanced at the Indian and nodded slightly before his gaze went back to his fallen mother. Tears welled in the boy's eyes and he began to struggle against the rangers grip.

"Let me go!" he sobbed.

Tecumseh nodded, and the rangers released the distraught young man who ran to his father's side. The other children had moved through the crowd and now stood in shocked silence beside their dead mother.

Captain Byrd uncocked his pistol and nudged his horse forward along the grieving family.

"There is no time to bury your dead, Captain Ruddell," he said, a hint of sympathy in his voice. "I am sorry, but we are at war. Our column moves out in one hour. You may do what you can for your dead, but they will be left for someone else to bury. Do you understand?"

The militia captain glanced up at the British officer, his face flushed.

"Thank you for your generosity, Captain," he replied hoarsely. "I pray I can do the same for you some day."

Byrd ignored the insult and kicked his horse into a gallop and rode from the ransacked fort.

Stephen stood beside the ruined for gates, tears wet upon his cheeks. He had helped his father wrap his mother and baby brother in a quilt before laying them inside the forts interior cabin. Some of the other women from the settlement had taken the younger children to care for during the march.

Stephen fell to his knees and sobbed. Isaac reached down and placed a supportive hand on the boy's shoulder.

"It's my fault, Pa!" Stephen cried. "I didn't stay beside her like you told me. It's my fault Ma's dead!"

Isaac dropped down beside his son and pulled the boy close. "Hush! It ain't your fault your ma died. It's that no account Bloody Back officer who's to blame! If you'd been beside your ma, I'd be mournin' you!"

Isaac pulled the boy's chin up and looked into his eyes.

"What's done is done," he stated evenly. "Your ma would expect you to be strong and watch over your brother and sisters. We've bluff days ahead of us, boy. I suspicion Captain Byrd will keep me away from you and the other youngins until we get to Detroit. He's streaked I'll be a black guard and he'll want to keep me close. I'll need you to watch over the others with your ma gone. Do you understand?"

Stephen nodded and hugged his father tight. "Yes, Pa."

A British regular moved up behind the grieving father and son. "It's time to go, Sir," he stated.

Isaac nodded and rose from the ground, pulling his son to his feet beside him. "We'll come back and give your ma and brother a proper burial when this is all over," he promised.

Stephen nodded silently and followed his father as they made their way toward the waiting column. The boy glanced back at the cabin.

"Bye, ma." he whispered before moving to his place in line as the column moved forward.

CHAPTER 5

SOUTHERN OHIO
SUMMER, 1780

THE COLUMN HAD MOVED down the Licking River to Martin's Station. The prisoners watched as Byrd's 8th regiment rolled the cannon into place and prepared to fire on the fort. The boy shook his head as the British officer sent his father forward to speak with the defenders. Within an hour, Martin's Station had surrendered and the number of Kentuckian prisoners had swelled to almost four hundred individuals. Byrd and the Shawnee leaders had argued over what to do next. The Shawnee wanted to kill most of the prisoners and move on to Boonesbourgh and Harrodsburg while they could still use the force of the cannon. Byrd refused, arguing that the prisoners were to be returned to Detroit. The Shawnee stated that they could not guard any more prisoners and that such a large number would allow Boone or Clark to raise an army and catch the slower moving force.

In the end, Captain Byrd refused to move against anymore forts until the prisoners had been taken to Detroit. The frustrated warriors had loaded the Kentuckians down with booty and forced everyone to march north toward the Ohio. Those settlers who were too old, sick, or weak to make the long trek were tomahawked and left along the trail, much to the chagrin of Captain Byrd. The warriors pressed the survivors forward, eager to cross the Ohio before they could be caught in the open by a frontier army bent on revenge. Byrd seemed to take on much of the Indians zeal at crossing the river. The British officer became cross and nervous as the column slowly moved up the Licking River. Byrd ordered that the men receive no more then a cup of flour each day. Women and children were allowed no more then a half cup of flour for their ration. The day before they reached the Ohio, Byrd eagerly pushed the worn out settlers into the night and did not allow them any rations. William Mahon, a member of a large family that had been taken at Martin's Station, called out to Byrd the next morning as the column was forced into motion.

"Captain Byrd, I suppose we may expect back rations today?" Mahon had dared ask as he marched by Byrd's horse.

"No such indulgence will be given to prisoners," Byrd replied pointedly, tipping his hat at the young frontiersman. "Pray that we reach the Ohio this day, for your next meal will not occur until we cross the river."

The column did make the Ohio by early afternoon, and Captain Byrd made the decision to cross to the north side of the river before nightfall. Crossing the wide river was a harrowing ordeal for the captives. The settlers were ferried across by warriors in birch bark canoes as summer thunderstorms rolled out of the western sky. The crossing had taken hours and Captain Byrd had become irritable as time slowly passed. He had exploded at Isaac Ruddell.

"Your people had better move faster, Ruddell," The British officer snarled. "If Clark or Boone are sighted on our trail, I'll be forced to have any prisoners left on this side of the river killed by the Shawnee. Encourage your people to hurry along."

"How do you allow I do that, Captain Byrd?" Isaac shot back. "Are you going to make more boats appear to tote everyone? These folks are doin' the best they can."

Byrd had stomped away, nervously eyeing the back trail for signs of pursuit.

Clark never came.

Stephen and Will Danner stood on the Ohio side of the river as the last canoes paddled across from the opposite shore.

"There's no way we could be rescued now," Will stated, staring at the Kentucky shore. "I hoped Mr. Boone or General Clark would have found us."

"Be thankful they didn't," Stephen replied, glancing at one of the warriors alertly guarding the prisoners. "These savages would have kilt all of us and went to brush. As it is, a grist of us might survive."

Will swallowed hard at his friend's honest statement and looked toward the opening of a stream that flowed into the Ohio no more then a hundred yards from where they stood. "What river do you reckon that is?" he whispered.

"The Great Miami," Stephen replied without looking, his stare fixed on Captain Byrd and the last of the canoes as they slid onto the Ohio shore. "They'll use it to march us all into Shawnee country."

Will shook his head and noticed the warriors were forcing the other settlers to move down the shore toward the mouth of the Great Miami.

"Come on, Stephen, we have to go," he said, slowly shuffling forward.

Stephen did not move. His gaze was fixed on the British commander as he made his way up the bank. He glanced down at a large piece of driftwood that lay near his feet. The boy calculated if he could scoop up the club and make it to the hated officer before anyone could stop him. He edged a step closer to the club, but stopped when he felt a hand rest lightly on his shoulder. He turned to find the Indian boy who had subdued him at the fort watching him intently.

"We are leaving," the boy replied in English. "Chillicothe is still several days away and we will move away from the river before night falls."

Stephen hesitated as he returned the boy's intent stare. The Indian boy stepped forward and whispered in his ear.

"You will do your people no good attacking the British man. You will be killed and he will be hard on the rest of your people."

Stephen's shoulders sagged at the realization that what the boy said was right. He turned and began following the other prisoners up the banks of the Great Miami. Soon, darkness began to fall and the settlers were herded onto a high, flat plain that overlooked the winding river. Stephen and many of the other men and boys were allowed to gather wood and build fires for the prisoners to dry out and keep warm through the night. Stephen noticed that both the Indian warrior who wanted to kill him and the boy who had spoken to him always remained nearby, watching him closely. He was warming himself by one of the fires when the young Indian appeared at his side.

"I am Tecumseh," the boy stated quietly.

"I'm Stephen," he replied, surprised to hear himself talking casually with one of his capturers.

Tecumseh nodded. "We will reach Chillicothe in two days. Many of your men will run the gauntlet."

Stephen knew about the gauntlet. He had heard stories of how Daniel Boone and Simon Kenton, both famous frontiersmen, had been forced to endure this form of torture when they had been captured by the Shawnee some years earlier. Every person in a village lined up in two parallel lines, sometimes stretching close to a mile in length. Unfortunate prisoners were forced to run between the lines as the village occupants beat them with clubs and sticks. If a prisoner fell, which they often did, he was beaten savagely before being drug back to the start of the line and forced to run again. Death was not common during this ordeal, but not unheard of. Simon Kenton had been taken throughout the Shawnee nation and forced to run the gauntlet over a dozen times during his time in captivity! Stephen could still remember the young frontiersman's words.

"Their squaws and youngins is ornery," Kenton had told a group of men at Boonesbourgh as Stephen stood listening behind a barrel. "They can't go out and fight like the warriors, so they take all their hate out on the prisoners that are brought back. They hit ya with all creation– rocks, thorn tree switches; some'll even sneak in a tomahawk. If ya fall down, it's the squaws that blast ya near to death. The warriors usually stand back and laugh."

Stephen shivered at the memory and felt pity for the men who would be forced to endure the same fate.

"You will run the gauntlet with the men as well." Tecumseh added.

Stephen felt his stomach tighten in fear. "What?"

Tecumseh did not blink. "You killed a Shawnee warrior. You have earned the respect of our warriors as a man. You will run the gauntlet with the other men to test your courage."

Stephen swallowed hard and tried not to show his fear. "My thanks for letting me know your designs."

Tecumseh nodded and turned to leave.

"Wait"

Tecumseh turned back toward the white boy.

"Thanks you for saving me at the fort," Stephen said, his face reddening. "I'd had been done in."

Tecumseh nodded and disappeared into the darkness, leaving Stephen to ponder the challenges that lay before him.

Chillicothe sat in a wooded valley along the banks of the Great Miami. Stephen had never seen an Indian village, but he was impressed with how clean and orderly the Shawnee capital seemed to be. He calculated there were over a hundred wigwams laid out in rows beside dirt trails that all converged on the center of the village and the great council house of the Shawnee nation. The prisoners were paraded before hundreds of cheering Shawnee men, women, and children as they were marched toward the council house. Captain Byrd was greeted by a middle-aged Shawnee chief with craggy features and a dark, heavy brow that gave the chief a perennial angry and brooding expression. The chief did not seem pleased with Byrd and the two men argued and gestured toward the prisoners. Stephen noticed that the warrior who led the Indians during the raid stood near the chief, frowning with his arms crossed in front of his chest. Tecumseh appeared at Stephen's side.

"Black Hoof is not happy," he said, indicating the Shawnee chief. "Few *Shemanese* were killed during the raid, and now Captain Byrd does not want to have any of the prisoners run the gauntlet."

Stephen almost sighed in relief.

His relief quickly turned to dread as he watched the British officer throw up his hands and stalk toward Isaac Ruddell and the line of prisoners.

"Have ten of your men step forward, Captain Ruddell," Byrd said, glancing back toward the Shawnee leader.

"Why?" Isaac replied, his eyes narrowing.

Byrd sighed. "Because our hosts require at least that many run the gauntlet before we move on to Detroit. I will leave it to you to pick ten that are capable of enduring the challenge."

Ruddell's face reddened and his eyes widened. "I won't do it! You promised us protection as prisoners of war. Be a man and stand up to these savages!" the militia captain exploded.

Byrd's mouth twisted and he stepped in close to the frontier leader.

"I have done my best, Ruddell. As it is, not a single prisoner will be fed or allowed to rest until their demands are met," he hissed through clenched teeth. "Be thankful only ten will run. If it was up to these 'savages' every man, woman, and child would face the gauntlet. If I hear more insults from you, then I will give them what they want."

Isaac bit his tongue and glared at the British officer.

"If you don't pick, then I will," Byrd stated coldly. "I don't have a mind to the mettle of your men. I suspect some of my choices could be poor."

Isaac shook his head.

"Alright Captain, but allow that I intend to make a full protest of your actions to your commander in Detroit."

Byrd snorted. "As you will. Now have your men step forward; our hosts are becoming impatient."

Stephen watched as his father called nine young frontiersmen forward. They were all known as good hunters and fighters. None of the men were married or had family to care for. Isaac stepped forward with the other men.

"Stand down, Captain Ruddell," Byrd ordered. "I will not risk your injury in this contest. You are too important in getting all these people to Detroit safely."

Isaac refused to budge, glaring at the British officer. Jacob stepped forward and placed a hand on the militia captain's shoulder.

"He's right, Ike," the frontiersman whispered. "We won't make it to Detroit without you; I'll take your place."

Jacob stepped up to stand before Byrd.

"I reckon I'm the tenth man, Bloody Back." he drawled. "Let's get this shindig started."

The prisoners watched as the Indians lined up in two lines that stretched over one hundred yards. The frontiersmen were stripped of their clothes and stood naked at the head of the line. The Indians all held sticks, switches, thorn branches, and even green briar switches in their eager hands. Stephen swallowed as he watched Jacob step to the front of the line. The frontiersman's easy smile did not match the worry that showed in his dark eyes. He managed a nervous laugh.

"Watch me lads, I'll show you how this is done!" the brave man drawled.

He looked at the Shawnee chief, Black Hoof. "I'm ready."

Black Hoof nodded toward the frontiersman, pleased by the man's courage. The Shawnee leader raised his hand and the crowd became silent. He chopped his hand down quickly, signaling to begin. Jacob exploded forward, screaming at the top of his lungs. Several of the Shawnee missed the charging frontiersman completely as he raced between the lines. Unfortunately, the line was long and the Shawnee closer to the middle of the line were able to time their strikes better and soon the frontiersman was taking several hits. Stephen grimaced as he heard the meaty smack of wood against the man's bare skin. Jacob staggered from the abuse and almost fell. He managed to right himself and stumbled toward the finish line. A slender warrior near the end of the line stepped out and tried to trip the frontiersman. Jacob showed great agility in side stepping and knocking the warrior out of his way.

Jacob staggered past the end of the line and touched a pole set before the Council lodge. The assembled Indians cheered at the frontiersman's brave run and laughed at the warrior who tried to trip him as the man arose sheepishly from the ground. Jacob stumbled back toward the prisoners.

Stephen could not take his eyes off the man. Blood flowed from more then a dozen cuts and abrasions that cris-crossed the man's body. His back and shoulders were already turning black and blue from the abuse he had taken. Jacob wiped blood from his eyes and spit out one of his teeth.

"Don't slow down, boys," he advised through clenched teeth. "If ya fall, ya have to run again. Best you get it over with the first time."

Jacob winced as a warrior clapped him on the back and gave him his clothes back. "Thanks," he grumbled.

The settlers watched as the next man stepped to the front of the line. It was Will Mahon, the young man who had protested to Captain Byrd over the lack of rations given to the prisoners a few days earlier. Will rubbed his hands together nervously.

"I'm ready," he said.

Black Hoof dropped his hand and Will sprinted down the line. The Indians along the gauntlet were more prepared then they had been for the first frontiersman. Will was unfortunately not as fleet as Jacob and received many more blows. Still, Will was a powerful man and was able to drive his way through the vicious strikes. Near the end of the line, a large warrior stepped into his path. Will did not attempt to side step the warrior as the agile Jacob had. The young frontiersman lowered his head like a bull and charged straight at the large men, bellowing in anger. The surprised warrior was knocked from his feet, and Will staggered forward to collapse at the base of the pole as the prisoners and Indians cheered his successful run.

Stephen swallowed hard as a couple of warriors helped the frontiersman to his feet and half carried the semiconscious man back to the group of prisoners. Will sported twice as many wounds as Jacob had received and both his eyes were swelling shut. The warriors dumped him unceremoniously at the feet of the other prisoners.

The next man in line was not as lucky as Jacob and Will had been. He was a smaller man chosen from among the prisoners from Martin's station. He hesitated when Black Hoof signaled the start of the gauntlet. A warrior shoved the timid man forward and vicious blows quickly rained down on the man from the eager Indians. The man cried out in pain and staggered forward. He stumbled half way down the line and fell to the ground. Several Indian women and boys gathered around the prone man and enthusiastically beat him. Finally, a pair of warriors pushed the crowd back and dragged the man back to the beginning of the line. The frontiersman slumped to his knees, sobbing.

"Get up, man!" Jacob cried, stepping forward. "They'll give ya a belly full if you don't budge!"

The settler seemed to hear Jacob's plea and managed to stagger to his feet. Black Hoof signaled again and the prisoner stumbled forward. He made only a few paces before he was knocked from his feet again. Once again, the surrounding Indians beat the man savagely. This time, warriors were unable to revive the man from Martin's station. One of the warriors looked at the chief and shrugged. The little man had died from the beating. His body was dragged from the gauntlet and tossed to the side as the horrified settlers watched.

Jacob turned to the remaining men set to run.

"This ain't no Sunday stroll," he cried, "You'll end up cold as a wagon if they think your cow hearted."

None of the remaining men died in the gauntlet. They each bravely stepped to the line and ran for their lives. A couple were knocked from their feet and had to run a second time, but they all eventually touched the post. Every man was covered in blood and bruises by the time he finished and few could walk unassisted, but they all made it. Black Hoof seemed pleased with the prisoner's show of courage and seemed about to end the torturous activity when Chiksika stepped to his side and whispered in his ear. Stephen's heart sank as the Shawnee chief's eyes came to rest on him. Black Hoof nodded and a pair of warriors grabbed the boy and shoved him before the eager line of Indians.

"What's this about?" Isaac Ruddell demanded, straining against a pair of rangers as he watched his eldest son being undressed before the gauntlet.

"Byrd! Stop this. Our men have already met their demands. Don't make my boy run, I beg you," the frontiersman pleaded.

The British officer turned to face him, pity in his eyes. "My apologies, Captain Ruddell, but there is nothing I can do. Your son distinguished himself when he killed that warrior. The Shawnee had decided to test his courage before we ever left your station."

"I'll be alright, Pa," Stephen said, trying to sound brave. "I'm cock sure what to do."

Stephen caught sight of Tecumseh standing back from the line and the Indian boy nodded at him. Stephen took a deep breath to calm himself and set his feet against the ground and bent low, his hands gripping the loose dirt on the path in front of him. He saw the Shawnee chief raise his hand out of the corner of his eye. The boy had watched the Indian signal the beginning of each of the previous gauntlet runs and knew he did the same thing each time; exhale his breath right before he brought his hand down. Stephen watched, his body coiled to spring forward. Black Hoof exhaled and began to bring his hand down, but the boy was already gone.

The redheaded boy exploded down the right side of the surprised line of Indians. He ran so close to the outer edge of the gauntlet that the participants could not swing their clubs and sticks at the boy in full force. Stephen had taken only a couple of glancing blows as he passed the halfway point. A warrior stepped into his path, looking to slow the progress of the fleet young man. Stephen had anticipated the move and swerved toward the left hand side of the gauntlet without slowing. Several squaws and younger warriors made ready to strike as the boy moved across. Stephen used his next trick and flung a handful of dirt in the face of the eager Indians. Several cried out and sputtered as they were momentarily blinded. Stephen sped past the surprised assailants and neared the end of the gauntlet. The boy's eyes widened as Red Hawk stepped out in front of the finishing post. The warrior was swinging a tomahawk and grinning wickedly. Stephen glanced left and right, there was no way around the man. The boy gritted his teeth and charged forward. Red Hawk raised his tomahawk as he neared, eager to strike. Stephen flung his second handful of dirt in the warrior's face and dove to the ground. Red Hawk snarled and swung blindly, missing the boy as he rolled between his legs.

Stephen lashed out with his foot and kicked the warrior in the groin as he completed his roll. Red Hawk dropped the tomahawk and fell to his knees as the lad scrambled forward to smack the finish pole. The crowd stared at the white boy in stunned silence. No one had ever run the gauntlet in such a way! Stephen stood at the pole defiantly, barely a mark on him. The assembled Indians erupted in cheers and whoops of approval. Several Indian boys ran forward and eagerly pounded him on the back in congratulations. Stephen smiled when he realized that he had earned the respect of the tribe.

His smile disappeared as the enraged Red Hawk pushed through the crowd and approached Stephen, his tomahawk raised to strike, his teeth bared. Suddenly, Tecumseh was standing in front of the boy, his arms crossed defiantly. Red Hawk hesitated, but growled something at the Indian boy in Shawnee and gestured for him to move. Tecumseh shook his head. The Shawnee warrior snarled and attempted to push Tecumseh out of the way. The boy stumbled but held his ground. Red Hawk raised his hand to strike.

Suddenly, Red Hawk was knocked from his feet. The warrior groaned and lay still when he realized that Chiksika had knocked him down and now held a razor sharp knife to his throat.

"You dare strike my brother, *ne-kah-noh?* Your brother's death has caused you to go mad! You would kill a helpless boy who has proven his worth in the gauntlet? I should kill you for the disrespect you have shown here today."

"Enough, Chiksika." Black Hoof ordered, pushing his way through the crowd. "Let him up."

Chiksika hesitated, but finally removed the knife from Red Hawk's throat and stepped back beside the Shawnee chief. Red Hawk eyed Chiksika cautiously and bent to pick up his tomahawk.

"Stop," Black Hoof ordered, his face dark. "Your actions have been shameful. You will leave your tomahawk as a gift for my new son to make amends."

"What!" Red Hawk gasped, his eyes widening.

Black Hoof stepped forward. "This boy has proven he has the heart of a warrior, which is more then I can say for you. I have decided to adopt him as a son. Your tomahawk will make a fitting gift as he is welcomed into our tribe."

"You shame me!" Red Hawk cried

"You shame yourself." Black Hoof scolded. "You are no longer welcome in this village. You will go to one of the villages on the upper Auglaize. I will not stay Chiksika's hand if you bother my son again! Do you understand?"

Red Hawk nodded silently and moved to leave. Chiksika stepped forward and took the warrior's arm.

"I will be watching you," he hissed. "If you harm my brother or the white boy again, your scalp will hang from my belt!"

Red Hawk swallowed hard as he looked into Chiksika's eyes and realized the war leader was not making an empty threat. He pulled free of the man's grip and hurried to leave the village as quickly as possible.

Tecumseh stepped forward and picked up the tomahawk. He dusted the weapon off and brought it back to Stephen. He held the tomahawk out to the stunned boy. Tecumseh smiled at Stephen for the first time as the white boy hesitantly accepted the weapon.

"Welcome to the Shawnee nation, son of Black Hoof," Tecumseh said in English.

Stephen stared at the Indian tomahawk that he now held in his hand, still trying to digest what had just happened.

CHAPTER 6

CHILLICOTHE VILLAGE
SUMMER, 1780

STEPHEN STOOD BEFORE HIS FATHER, trying to fight back tears. "What should I do, Pa?"

Isaac stared at his eldest son, his stoic features masking the sympathy and concern he held for the child.

"Hush, boy!" the frontiersman replied sharply. "It's a far piece to Detroit and it's hard to tell what might happen to the rest of us. Captain Byrd's promises are no account. These savages might kill us all at the next village! You and your brother are at least safe."

Isaac put his hand on his son's brow. "I'm proud of the grit you've shown, Stephen. The Shawnee cotton to it as well. That's why they're adopting you. You'll be treated as one of their own, and I reckon you'll be safe until I can get us out of this fix. Look after your brother; I'll come for you when I can."

Stephen wiped a tear from his cheek. "I'll do my best, Pa."

The frontiersman pulled the boy into a fierce hug. "I know you will, son."

Stephen watched as two rangers escorted his father back to the line of prisoners slowly making their way north on the trail toward Detroit. Stephen wiped the tears from his eyes and tried to make sense of what was happening. His successful gauntlet run had been exhilarating. Stephen had accepted the tomahawk Tecumseh had presented him and he had shaken the weapon in the air triumphantly. His joy had turned to shock and bewilderment when he learned that he would not be traveling north to Detroit with his father and the rest of his family.

"What do you mean I've been adopted?" Stephen protested. "I'm ain't no orphan! I want to go with my pa!"

Tecumseh shook his head patiently. "That cannot be. Black Hoof has claimed you as his son. It is a great honor to be adopted by a chief."

"Black Hoof can go to hell!" Stephen spat. "I won't leave my family."

Tecumseh's eyes narrowed. "You are brave, but don't be foolish. If you refuse, you'll be killed for the disrespect you would be showing to Black Hoof and the Shawnee."

Stephen had swallowed hard and watched as the Shawnee boy stalked away.

The prisoners had been kept at Chillicothe for another day, before they were forced along the trail toward Detroit. Stephen had been separated from his father and was forced to stay in the wigwam of the sharp-eyed chief. Tecumseh had come to Stephen in the morning and let the boy know that a family from another village had decided to adopt his younger brother as well. Stephen had fought to hold back his tears of anger and frustration. His family was being torn apart!

"Please, ask the chief to let me to see my pa before they go." Stephen pleaded.

"Why?" Tecumseh asked suspiciously.

"So I can at least tell him goodbye."

Tecumseh looked at the distraught young man for several moments. Finally, he moved to where Black Hoof sat outside the wigwam, smoking a pipe and watching the boys intently. Tecumseh spoke to the chief quietly in Shawnee. Black Hoof scratched his chin and looked at the boy. Finally, the chief gave a slight nod.

Tecumseh moved to the white boy's side. "Black Hoof agrees, but I must go with you."

Now Stephen watched as his father disappeared from sight. Overcome by grief, he did not hear Tecumseh approach.

"I understand your sorrow," the Indian boy whispered. "It has been a year since I had to watch my own mother leave."

"What?" Stephen replied

"Many of our people grew weary of the endless fighting with the Long Knives and the loss of loved ones. Half of the tribe decided to give up the fight and move to lands outside of those claimed by the *Shemanese*. Most moved across the Great River. My mother went with them. She was never the same after my father was killed," Tecumseh explained, sadness filling his voice.

"How did he die?"

Tecumseh sighed. "Fighting the Long Knives. He was the war leader of our people and died in battle. Chiksika was with him, but I was only six and too young to go to war."

"Who cares for you with your parents gone? Your brother?"

Tecumseh smiled. "I spend much time with Chiksika. He has taught me how to hunt and be a warrior, but he is also gone much of the time. My younger brothers and I were adopted by Black Fish, chief of all the Shawnee."

Stephen had heard of Black Fish. Daniel Boone had spoken well of the chief. Black Fish had adopted Boone several years earlier and saved him from being burned at the stake. Boone had lived with the Shawnee for several months before escaping to Kentucky after he had learned of a planned raid on his settlement at Boonesbourgh. It was rumored that Black Fish had taken the frontiersman's desertion hard, and now swore to kill the white man if he ever fell into his hands again.

Stephen sat down on a stump as the last of the Kentucky prisoners disappeared up the trail. "I don't have a notion on what to do," he whispered, his voice cracking. "I ain't an Indian. I don't want to be adopted by Black Hoof; I want to go with my own people."

Tecumseh squatted down in front of the boy. "Of course you do," he agreed. "You do not know our ways yet and do not feel that you belong. I am sure that the life of an Indian boy is much like your own. We hunt and fish, play games, gamble, and learn to be warriors. Is this not what you have done?"

Stephen nodded. "Partly. What chores do you have to do?"

Tecumseh was puzzled. "What are chores?"

"You know, things such as work in the fields, gather firewood, care for the animals."

Tecumseh chuckled. "What you speak of are the duties done by the women of our village. A warrior would not shame himself by doing such things."

Stephen's jaw fell open in amazement. "Are you tellin' me you don't have to do anything besides hunt and play?"

"Yes."

Stephen scratched his head. "What happens if you get in trouble? Does your ma take a switch to you?"

Tecumseh again looked confused. "What do you mean?"

Stephen shook his head in amazement. "Hasn't anyone ever hit you with a stick or a belt for not doing what you are told?"

Tecumseh scowled. "A Shawnee would never treat their child in such a way. They might scold them or even throw water on a pair of boys who are hurting each other in a fight, but they would never hit their child for something as simple as doing what they wanted to do."

Stephen scratched his head once again. "I reckon the life of an Indian boy is sounding better all the time."

Tecumseh laughed once again. "Come, *Sinnatha*. Black Hoof has said that you may come to my sister's wigwam to eat. She makes good succotash and if we don't hurry, her husband Stands Firm will not leave any for us."

"What'd you call me?"

Tecumseh rose to his feet and offered Stephen his hand, deftly pulling the larger boy up. "*Sinnatha*. It is the name that you will be called from now on."

Stephen stopped in his tracks, "I already got a name."

"That is your white name. We have given you and Indian name. Everyone's name has special meaning and is a part of who they are and their place in our tribe."

"What does your name mean?"

"Panther Crossing the Sky." Tecumseh replied solemnly. "The eye of the *Msipesi*, what you know as a panther, was seen in the sky the night I was born. Our medicine man, Change of Feathers, declared it an omen that I would be a *Psai-wi ne-noth-tu*, great warrior of our people."

"What does my name mean?" Stephen asked, his eyes widening.

Tecumseh smiled. "Black Hoof admired the way you ran the gauntlet and I told him how hard you were to catch back at the fort. He has given great thought to your name. It means Big Fish."

Stephen's jaw dropped. "Big Fish? I'm to be known as Big Fish?"

Tecumseh laughed again. "Do not be upset! It is the big fish that is always the hardest to catch."

Sinnatha, the white boy who had been known as Stephen Ruddell, adjusted to life as an Indian quickly. The somber Black Hoof treated the boy well and took great pride in Sinnatha's transition. Black Hoof's wife, White Swan, showered attention on the boy. Her own daughters were grown and married and the couple had no sons. White Swan quickly fashioned the boy a set of moccasins and leggings to wear to replace his torn breeches and linen shirt. Sinnatha and Tecumseh were constant companions. Sinnatha quickly learned the basics of the Shawnee language. He took great pleasure in the time he spent with Tecumseh and the respected elderly chief, Black Fish.

Black Fish was a small, slender man who was well beyond middle age. Gray streaked his long, dark hair and deep wrinkles creased his face at the eyes and lips. The old chief had an easy smile and pleasant laugh. He was a stark contrast from the serious Black Hoof. Yet he had a strong voice and quick mind and was respected by everyone as the principal peace chief of the Shawnee nation. Tecumseh had explained that there were several *septs* of the Shawnee tribe. Tecumseh's father, Hard Striker, had been war chief of the *Kispoko*, or warrior sept of the tribe. Black Fish was of the *Chalagawtha* sept.

"He's your adopted father; does that mean you could be chief?" Sinnatha had asked.

Tecumseh shook his head. "Only a *Chalagawtha* may be principal chief of our people. I am *Kispoko*. I hope to one day be war chief, as my father was before me."

"Why can't you be both?"

Tecumseh shook his head again. "That is not how *Weshemoneto* has set forth how the Shawnee should live."

Sinnatha scratched his head. "Who's Weshemoneto?"

"The Great Spirit."

"Oh, you mean God!" Stephen replied.

Tecumseh shrugged and smiled.

Sinnatha wondered how Tecumseh had learned English so well. Tecumseh chuckled when the white boy asked him. "Do you think you are the first white man to come to live among the

Shawnee? I remember *Sheltowee*, the Big Turtle. You know him as Boone. He lived with Black Fish for a time and I learned much from him. Many other whites have been adopted into the tribe, and there have been many English traders who have visited our people. Most Shawnee can speak at least some English, but most choose not to."

One individual that Sinnatha often saw in the village was the dark-haired American traitor, Simon Girty. Simon, along with his brothers James and George, were infamous and hated across the frontier. They were excellent trackers, hunters, and fighters. They had maintained their loyalty to the British crown and had joined the Shawnee and other tribes on countless raids throughout the Revolution. Simon was a lean man who wore his hair to his shoulders and dressed in buckskins. His heavy, dark eyebrows added to his perpetual scowl, intimidating the boy. Still, Sinnatha worked up the courage to approach the man one day as he sat quietly smoking outside of Black Hoof's wigwam.

The frontiersman raised an eyebrow as the redhead boy approached. "Have you come to speak to me, Big Fish?" he rasped.

Sinnatha was taken back that the man knew him. Girty chuckled. "Don't be so surprised. Black Hoof is a good friend of mine. He speaks of you often, but you've always avoided me. So, I'm curious to why you suddenly appear before me. I reckon you must have something you want to speak about."

"My uncle told me you was a traitor. I'd allow that I'm curious to know why you turned your back on your own people," the boy replied evenly.

Girty's eyes narrowed. "I have a mind you're talkin' about your white family," he replied, switching to English. "What buckskin would happen to be your uncle?"

"John Bowman," Sinnatha replied, sticking his chin out proudly.

"I know him," Simon replied with a chuckle. "He's the coot that led the squaw campaign a couple of years back. It's because of black guards like him that I finally sided with the British. I was plum sour on the clankers the *Shemanese* had me tellin' the tribes in order to steal more of their land."

"That's a lie!" the boy replied hotly. "My pa never stole anything, he tried to live in peace with the Indians and they attacked our station. Now my ma and brother are dead."

Girty eyed the distraught boy carefully. "I have a mind to why you're so huffed. I reckon your Isaac Ruddell's boy. I plum forgot how old you was. It all makes sense now."

The frontiersman leaned forward. "Your pa is a good man. We met a few times before the war and I always knew him to keep his word. It grieved me to hear about your ma. I wish I had been here when Byrd brought your people in. I might have been able to arrange his release before he was sent on to Detroit."

Sinnatha snorted. "You expect me to believe that?"

Girty's hand shot out and he grabbed the boy by the throat, his strong hand easily cutting off his breath. "I've listened to enough of your insults, brat," he hissed through clenched teeth. "I've allowed your gum because of the considerable ordeal you've been through, but my patience has run out. Another word and I'll bust your chops!"

The dark haired man released his grip and the boy dropped gasping to the ground. "I'd allow you should forget about your old life. The Shawnee will treat you well and raise you to be a good man, which is more then I can say about a grist of the buckskins I've known. Learn all creation you can from them and you'll end up a better man for it."

Girty emptied his pipe and rose from the ground. "I found it more likely when you avoided me. I'd allow that you should do so again. I suspicion I won't be as understandin' the next time you insult me."

Sinnatha rubbed his throat and watched as the man stalked away.

Another individual that Sinnatha avoided was Tecumseh's younger brother, *Lalawethika*. Tecumseh had told Sinnatha that the boy's name meant "Loud Noise." Sinnatha could not imagine a more appropriate name for the nine-year-old. Loud Noise had been one of the Indian boys who eagerly rained blows down on the white boy when he ran the gauntlet. Loud Noise was everything that Tecumseh was not. He was fat and ugly, with a large head and even larger mouth. The boy boasted of his skill as a hunter and a medicine man in training. He followed Change of Feathers around, constantly pestering the medicine man until he was shooed away. The boy was a gluten and lacked any social graces. He would loudly pass wind while greedily eating in any family wigwam. Loud Noise would giggle at the looks of disdain and embarrassment that were cast his direction. Sinnatha often observed Loud Noise abusing and taking things from younger Indian children, but never saw anyone stop him. The boy had no friends, save one. Tecumseh patiently supported his younger brother and allowed him to follow him everywhere.

Sinnatha asked Black Hoof why everyone tolerated Loud Noise's antics.

The war chief snorted and his eyes flashed at the mention of the boy's name. "You know that your friend Tecumseh was born under a great sign sent by Weshemoneto?"

Sinnatha nodded.

"Loud Noise was born under a sign from Weshemoneto as well. He was one of three children born to Hard Striker and Turtle Mother that night. Three is not a good sign and no mother in the Shawnee nation had ever birthed so many. The other two babies were fine and healthy. Loud Noise screamed like a panther, night and day. I tried to convince Change of Feathers that the baby had an evil spirit and should not be allowed to live. The medicine man said that Loud Noise's destiny was mixed with that of Tecumseh. Now, he is tolerated, even when all he does is bad, because of his connection to his brother."

Black Hoof spat on the ground. "I still see the evil in the boy and fear that any destiny he may be apart of will only lead to sorrow for our people."

Loud Noise had treated Sinnatha with disdain at first, and then with open hostility as he observed the close friendship forming between Tecumseh and the white boy. Sinnatha did his best to ignore the younger boy, but the tense situation escalated during a game of *baaga'adowe*.

Sinnatha had seen the game played before in open fields during large gatherings on the frontier. He had heard a French voyager refer to the game as "Lacrosse." The Shawnee men played the game with enthusiasm. Tecumseh had explained to him that baaga'adowe was seen as a way to train warriors for battle and boys were encouraged to play from an early age. A game between mature warriors could take place on a field over a mile long and last several days. The Indian boys played on a field of around two hundred yards in length. The rules were simple. Each player carried a forked stick that had strips of leather woven around the end of the club to form a small net. The players would use this net to throw and catch a small leather ball. A player scored by advancing down the length of the field and throwing the ball in between two stakes at the end of the field. The other team worked to intercept the ball and stop the other team from scoring. There were few rules and games could become very physical. While serious injuries were rare, many players left the field with sore heads, missing teeth, and occasional broken bones.

Sinnatha found out very quickly that he loved the game and was a natural. His strength and size allowed him to out-muscle most of the boys in the tribe in the scramble for the ball, and his quick reflexes made him a great defender. Tecumseh would always try and pick the white boy for his team. Together, they were unstoppable. Tecumseh's speed and balance matched Sinnatha's raw power as they easily worked the ball down the length of the field for countless goals. Soon, all the other boys protested and would no longer allow the two friends to be on the same team. Both boys responded by battling each other relentlessly, doing everything in their power to lead their team to a victory.

It was in such a game that the trouble had begun. Tecumseh led a team of thirty boys that included Loud Noise against Sinnatha and a team of equal size. The game had shifted back and forth closely for several hours. Both Tecumseh and Sinnatha had scored several goals for their teams. Loud Noise had grown tired of the constant running back and forth and remained back in defense of his team's goal. Cold Water, a Shawnee boy of about fourteen, intercepted a throw by Tecumseh's team and flung a long pass toward Sinnatha as he streaked toward the opposite goal. He caught the ball in stride and side stepped a defender to give himself an open look at the goal. Loud Noise moved in from his left, too far away to intercept Sinnatha. The white boy set his feet and reared back to make a goal. His head exploded in pain as Loud Noise smacked his club into the side of Sinnatha's face. The boy collapsed to the ground and lost the ball. Loud Noise let out a whoop and scooped up the loose ball and moved toward the other goal. Sinnatha shook his head to clear his vision. He could feel blood trickling down his neck from a gash above his ear. He staggered to his feet and gave chase. Loud Noise made a clumsy throw that was once again intercepted by Cold Water. Tecumseh moved to block the older boy's path, and Cold Water once again whipped a long, high pass to Sinnatha. The white boy leapt as high as he could for the ball and was undercut by Loud Noise. Sinnatha winced and bit his tongue as he landed hard on his shoulder.

"You cannot seem to stay off the ground *Shemanese*," Loud Noise jeered. "Maybe you should just stay there."

Stephen felt his anger flaring as he rose to his feet. He knew how to handle the situation. He shook dust from his shoulder length red hair and followed the flow of the game closely, always keeping his eye on Loud Noise. It was not long before the deer skin ball was thrown his way and he once again found Tecumseh's younger brother between him and the goal. Sinnatha feinted as he had before and made to set up for another shot at the goal. Loud Noise charged forward, eager to strike another blow. Sinnatha ducked low at the last moment and charged under the surprised boy's swing. Sinnatha caught the younger boy's momentum on his shoulder and heaved upward. Loud Noise was heavy for his age, but Sinnatha was powerful and easily flipped the boy's bulk into the air. Loud Noise landed hard and did not move. The path to the goal was open and Sinnatha scored easily.

The white boy's teammates cheered and congratulated Sinnatha after the goal. They were so busy pounding their star player on the back that nobody took notice of Loud Noise rising from the ground and pulling a small knife from a sheath woven within his moccasin. The Indian boy advanced on Sinnatha from behind, his face twisted into a snarl. Sinnatha had not lost sight of the treacherous youth and whirled to face him, his club held before him defensively.

"I wouldn't," he stated calmly. "You should leave before you do something you will regret."

Loud Noise hesitated, but Sinnatha could read clearly the hatred upon the boy's fat face. He set his feet beneath him, preparing for an attack.

"STOP!"

Loud Noise halted in his tracks at the command and turned as Tecumseh stalked toward him. All the players on the field fell silent and watched the unfolding confrontation.

Tecumseh knocked the blade from his younger brother's hand. "You bring shame upon our family. You would attack a fellow tribesman who has beaten you fairly in a game?"

"He's white." Loud Noise hissed

"He's Shawnee." Tecumseh retorted. "You will respect him as such."

Tears began to flow down Loud Noise's fat cheeks. "You take his side against your own brother? It is you who should be ashamed," he sobbed. "You care for him more then me, just as you did Kumsaka."

Tecumseh's face softened at the mention of the name. "That is not so."

Loud Noise turned and ran sobbing from the field.

Tecumseh turned back toward Sinnatha. "I am sorry for my brother's behavior," he apologized. "He cannot help the way he is."

Tecumseh turned and ran after the younger boy without waiting for a response from his friend.

Later, Sinnatha and Cold Water had bathed in a clear stream to remove the sweat, blood, and grime from their bodies after the game had ended. The gash above the white boy's ear had sealed and he gingerly ran his wet fingers through his red hair, washing out dried blood. Sinnatha had been amazed how often the Shawnee bathed, at least once or twice a day. He had taken up the practice as well. He reckoned that he had bathed more in the past three months then he had in the previous two years combined.

"Who is Kumsaka?" he had asked.

Cold Water frowned. He cupped clear water in both his hands and splashed it in his long, dark hair. "He was one of Tecumseh's brothers," he replied hesitantly. "There were six children born to Hard Striker and Turtle Mother. Chicksika is the eldest, followed by their sister, Tecumpese. Tecumseh was then born under the great sign of *Weshemoneto*. Last came the triplets, *Lalawethika*, *Sauwaseekau*, and *Kumsaka*

"What happened to him?" Sinnatha persisted.

Cold Water looked around to see if anyone was near by. Satisfied that they were alone, he turned back to Sinnatha. "We do not speak of Kumsaka out of respect for Tecumseh and his family. It has been almost two years since he died and it still pains

Tecumseh. Still, you and Tecumseh have become friends, and you should know why he tolerates Loud Noise's behavior the way he does."

The older boy turned and pointed to a high bluff that over-looked the river valley. "Do you see where this stream cuts through the bluff before it joins the Great Miami?"

Sinnatha nodded, leaning closer to hear Cold Water's tale.

"We call that place the 'Warrior's Leap,' and boys who think they are ready to become full warriors test their courage by leaping across the chasm."

Sinnatha looked up. He gauged that the distance across the opening was over ten feet. The drop to the rocky stream bed below had to be at least fifty feet. The boy felt his throat tighten. "I see why it would be a test of courage."

Cold Water nodded. "The distance across is not great for a mature man or even a young warrior. An elder must give his consent before a boy is allowed to attempt a jump. This allows our elders to determine when a boy is ready and have warriors stationed on the other side to help catch anyone who attempts a jump."

"Has anyone ever failed?"

Cold Water nodded, his frown deepening. "I have only known one."

"Kumsaka?"

Cold Water nodded again and sighed. "Kumsaka idolized Tecumseh. Two years ago, Tecumseh climbed the bluff and made the jump, without permission. He was only ten and his feat was greatly celebrated throughout the village. Loud Noise had become jealous of the attention that Tecumseh had received. He had come upon Kumsaka pretending to be Tecumseh by jumping across a stream at the edge of the village. What took place next still tears at Tecumseh's heart as if it had happened yesterday."

Loud Noise snorted in disgust as he moved up beside his brother as he leapt across the little stream. "You don't look much like a 'Cat that flies in the air.' You look more like a frog jumping in a puddle,' he taunted, referring to the meaning of the other boy's name. "If you truly were courageous, you would stop pre-tending to be Tecumseh and you would leap the bluff as well!"

Kumsaka had grown angry at the insult. "I will make the jump when I am old enough."

"Do it now!" Loud Noise had persisted eagerly. "I will cast a spell to help you."

The boy looked at his brother suspiciously. "What are you talking about?" he asked.

"I have been watching Change of Feathers and I have learned some of his secrets," Loud Noise replied, his eyes glistening. "I will go with you and cast one of his spells. You will make the leap and we will both be honored. You for your bravery as a warrior and me for my skill as a medicine man!"

"I don't know," Kumsaka had replied hesitantly.

"Bah! I knew you weren't has brave a Tecumseh," Loud Noise spat, turning away.

"Wait," Kumsaka had growled. "Are you sure your magic will be strong enough to help me get across?"

Loud Noise had smiled widely. "Of course, brother."

Both boys climbed the bluff and Loud Noise had kneeled beside the cliff. The boy picked up a handful of loose dirt and began to chant in a low voice. Kumsaka looked on as his brother raised his hands to the sky and then walked toward him. Loud Noise continued to chant as he sprinkled the dirt on Kumsaka's head and shoulders.

"There," Loud Noise stated confidently. "I have placed the Great Spirit's blessing on you. You will be able to make the jump."

Kumsaka nodded and exhaled as he looked at the wide chasm. He dearly wanted to be like Tecumseh and was willing to risk death to make his older brother proud of him. The boy let out a whoop and charged toward the edge of the bluff, leaping forward with all his might.

The boy's cry changed to a scream of terror as he fell short of the opposite side and tumbled to the rocky stream bed below.

Loud Noise moved toward the edge of the bluff and looked into the gorge. He winced and began to wring his hands when he saw his brother's lifeless body, broken and twisted on the rocks below. He scrambled back from the edge of the cliff and ran from the bluff, looking for a place to hide.

Sinnatha stared at Cold Water, his mouth agape.

"When the boys did not return at night, the family went looking for them. It was Tecumseh who found Kumsaka's body. Loud Noise was found hiding beside the river. Chiksika had to threaten to beat the boy before he finally told his family the truth of what happened. Tecumseh has held himself responsible for the accident ever since."

"It wasn't his fault." Sinnatha argued. "Loud Noise tricked Kumsaka, so he is responsible for the death."

"I agree," Cold Water replied, "but Tecumseh does not see it that way. Kumsaka made the jump because he wanted to be like Tecumseh. Loud Noise goaded Kumsaka into the attempt because he was jealous of Tecumseh. Tecumseh accepts responsibility for the accident because he is expected to lead and set and example. If he had not jumped the gorge without permission, Kumsaka might still be alive today."

Sinnatha shook his head in frustration at the reasoning. Still, he now understood Tecumseh's relationship with his younger brother much better after Cold Water's story. He also realized just how far Loud Noise was willing to go in order to gain attention and power. He would keep his eyes and mind alert when he was around Tecumseh's treacherous sibling.

One day Tecumseh led Sinnatha into his wigwam and pulled a heavy leather satchel from under the sleeping platform. Tecumseh carefully removed a pair of leather bound books from the satchel and passed them to Sinnatha. The white boy opened them and flipped through the pages. The books were well worn, but in good condition.

"Where did you get these?"

"Chiksika brought them back from a raid," Tecumseh explained. "He thought I might like them, but I cannot understand them. I have kept them in case I could find someone who could teach me the words; you are that person, Sinnatha."

Sinnatha scratched his head. He could read and write, because his mother had forced him to learn the basics, but the boy had never been a great student. He had preferred to spend his time hunting and fishing. "I'm not cock-sure that I'd be a very good teacher."

Tecumseh smiled. "A poor teacher is better then no teacher. I am sure you will do your best, *jai-nai-nah,*" he said. "You can start by first telling what these books are about."

Stephen felt his chest tighten in pride. He had learned enough Shawnee to know that Tecumseh had just called him his "blood brother".

"Well, this is a history book of the world, and this is a Bible." he replied, indicating the thicker of the two books.

"Bible?"

"It tells about God." Sinnatha explained.

"God? This is the name you used for Weshemoneto! Are you saying the whites have written down the Great Spirit's words?" Tecumseh said, looking at the books in awe.

"Well... I reckon so. The preachers are always sayin' that God's words are in the Bible when they give a sermon. My ma used the Bible to help teach me to read, and there's some stories that I took a cotton to," Sinnatha replied, handing the Bible back to Tecumseh.

"Could I learn more about the *Shemanese* from these books?"

"Yes!"

Tecumseh passed the book back to Sinnatha. "You will teach me the white man's signs so I may read these books. I wish to learn everything I can."

Sinnatha nodded. "I'll do my best. Why do you want to learn so much about the *Shemanese*, Tecumseh? Their way of life is one that you've made powerful clear that you do not agree with."

"You should always know all that you can about your greatest enemy," Tecumseh replied solemnly.

Sinnatha had been with the Shawnee for three months when revenge for Captain Byrd's Kentucky campaign was exacted upon the tribe in the form of a force of one thousand Kentucky frontiersmen led by George Rogers Clark. Clark was greatly respected and feared by the Shawnee for his winter campaign that had captured all the forts in the lower Illinois country in the winter of 1778-1779. He was a courageous and cunning leader who was to be feared at the head of any force. Not only was the frontier general leading a force of battle-hardened and tough fighters, but he was bringing a cannon against the Shawnee as well.

As if Clark was not enough, other great frontiersmen marched with the army. *Sheltowee,* otherwise known as Daniel Boone and *Psaiwiwuhkernekah Ptweowa,* The Great White Wolf, who the whites called Simon Kenton, scouted the trail for the advancing army. Black Fish had shaken his head when he heard the news. It was the time of the hunter's moon and most of the warriors were out on long hunts. Winter was fast approaching and much meat was needed to feed the tribe through the months ahead. The Shawnee head chief had summoned Black Hoof to his wigwam. The tribal leaders sat beside the fire, contemplating the best course of action their people should take.

"We are too few to hold the village," Black Hoof stated bluntly, his features dark with anger.

Black Fish blew smoke from his pipe and nodded his head in agreement. "We could gather no more than a hundred warriors to stand against Clark. Our only hope is to leave enough warriors to burn the town and slow Clark's army while the rest of our people make their way up the Mad River to Piqua town. There are log houses and a fort there that might be defended. This might also give us enough time to raise a strong enough force of warriors to turn Clark back."

"Who will stay and fight? Chiksika, Blue Jacket and our best warriors are hunting along the upper Wabash."

"You are chief of the *Kispoko,* and therefore our war chief. You will pick the warriors who will stay and fight, but Chillicothe is my village. I will lead the warriors and decide when to burn the town."

Black Fish could see the relief in the war chief's eyes. He did not let his disappointment show. Black Hoof had always been a brave warrior and had fought the *Shemanese* his entire adult life. He had been a solid war party leader and capable sub chief under Hard Striker. The war chief's death six years earlier had thrust the full responsibility of leadership on the stoic warrior's shoulders. He was very cautious and self conscious of the shadow the popular and respected Hard Striker cast over his role as chief. In addition, Hard Striker's sons, Chiksika and Tecumseh, seemed to be destined to be great warriors and leaders. This made the less popular Black Hoof worry about his future role as chief. He was suspicious that many among the tribe were watching and waiting for him to make a mistake that could cause him to be replaced. As a result, the cautious leader took few risks.

"We will not be able to keep Clark's army here for long," Black Fish said, blowing smoke from his pipe into the fire. "We should be able to buy you enough time to set warriors along the trail to Piqua town. There are many good places to ambush the Long Knives and slow them down. This task I leave to you, Black Hoof. More warriors will join you each passing day. Position them wisely and make them pay for invading our country."

Black Hoof nodded and his craggy face set in determination.

Tecumseh lay hidden in a wigwam at the edge of Chillicothe. He watched Black Fish move among his warriors as the *Shemanese* army entered the far end of the burning town. The smoke hung thickly about the village, adding cover for the warriors as Clark's army advanced forward. A sound from the wigwam entrance caused Tecumseh to turn quickly, his rifle held ready.

Sinnatha stood in the entrance, his hands on his hips. "What are you doing?" he whispered harshly. "Black Hoof said we couldn't be here."

"I'm staying," Tecumseh replied evenly. "Black Fish may need help."

Sinnatha cursed and looked out of the wigwam. He could glimpse buckskin clad frontiersmen moving cautiously through the village among the heavy clouds of smoke. He knew that Black Fish and his warriors were hidden throughout the wigwams, ready to ambush the advancing army.

The white boy's heart skipped a beat. He could slip away into the smoke and easily join up with Clark's army without being seen. He would be able to make it home.

Home.

The place he had known as home was now nothing more then some burned out cabins and a ruined fort. He hoped that somebody had given his mother and brother a proper burial. He had heard more then a few stories of burial parties cleaning up after wolves, foxes, and buzzards had scavenged a battlefield. The thought of doing the same for his dead family sent chills down his spine.

What else did he have to go back to? His father and sisters were in Canada, if they were still alive. Any other relation he had were scattered across the war-torn frontier. There was also his brother to consider. What might the Shawnee do to Abe if his brother were to escape? Sinnatha made his decision.

"Alright! I'll stay with you, but don't do anything foolish." he hissed. "Those are Kentucky sharpshooters out there. They can knock a squirrel off a tree branch from a hundred yards while riding a hoss! They'll put a bullet between yer eyes easy enough. We can watch Black Fish and help him only if he needs us, agreed?"

Tecumseh nodded wordlessly.

Both boys ducked low to the ground as gunfire erupted outside the wigwam.

Several frontiersmen staggered and collapsed after the surprise volley. The Shawnee warriors whooped and quickly reloaded their rifles. Sinnatha hugged the ground closely as the frontiersmen returned fire and bullets whistled through the air above them. Cries of pain from the wounded echoed through the heavy smoke. Above all the noise, Black Fish could be heard encouraging his warriors.

"*Oui-shi-cat-to-oui!* Be Strong!" he bellowed.

Sinnatha and Tecumseh watched as the battle raged. Warriors darted among the wigwams under the cover of smoke, furiously returning fire as the white army pushed through the village. The fighting became more intense as the frontiersmen reached the center of the village and the blazing council house. Several warriors lay dead among the wigwams and the wounded had been helped from the field. The army's advanced stalled in the face of the Shawnee defense. Black Fish seemed to be everywhere, his deep voice resounding through the smoke as he cheered his warriors on.

Suddenly, Black Fish's voice went silent.

"Something's wrong," Tecumseh hissed through gritted teeth. "We need to help Black Fish."

Sinnatha nodded and moved forward cautiously. "Stay low, *ne-kah-noh*," the boy warned. "Or someone will be looking for us."

Tecumseh did not respond, but listened to his friend's warning and moved forward cautiously into the smoke.

Black Fish lay on the hard packed ground beside the council house, his teeth clenched against the horrible pain he felt. A musket ball had torn through his left hip, shattering the bone and leaving a gaping wound. The old chief had been wounded many times in his life, but nothing had been as bad as this. Black Fish could tell he was not dying, at least not yet. It was only a matter of time before one of Clark's soldiers came upon him and finished him off. The old man opened his eyes at the sound of footsteps to see Tecumseh and Sinnatha carefully making their way through the smoke. He managed a smile at the sight of the boys.

"You should not be here, *ni-kwith-ehi*," he gasped, sweat drenching his face.

Tecumseh took his adopted father's hand. "I know, but I knew you would need my help." The boy's chest tightened as he looked at Black Fish's wound. "Do not fear; we'll get you out of here!"

Sinnatha had disappeared into a nearby wigwam and had emerged with a white, linen shirt. The boy moved to Black Fish and quickly wrapped the wound with the garment and tied it off to staunch the flow of blood. The warrior gasped in pain as the boy drew the makeshift bandage tight.

"Sorry, chief," Sinnatha apologized, "but you'll bleed to death if we don't plug the wound."

"I fear my death is only a matter of time," Black Fish gasped. "Go! Save yourselves. The Long Knives will be coming soon."

"I am not leaving without you," Tecumseh responded. "Be strong, Father. We will carry you to safety."

Black Fish was not a large man and Tecumseh and Sinnatha together were able to carefully lift him from the ground. The wounded man gritted his teeth against the pain, but did not cry out. The boys carried the chief between them to the edge of the village where several warriors were waiting. A litter was quickly made and the wounded chief was laid upon it. Black Fish took the boys' hands as the litter was lifted to carry him away.

"You are brave, my son," he gasped, squeezing Tecumseh's hand. "Our people will need your courage in the time to come. The Long Knives will win their war with the British and they will be hard on our people for supporting the Red Coats. There will be many days of blood for the Shawnee in the years ahead. I will not be there to lead our people forward; that task will fall to you."

Tears welled up in Tecumseh eyes as he squeezed his adopted father's hand tightly.

Black Fish turned his head toward Sinnatha. "You're heart remains torn between red and white, Big Fish," the chief whispered, looking into Sinnatha's blue eyes. "Yet you remained loyal to Tecumseh when you could have run back to the *Shemanese.*"

"You are both of the blood of the panther," Black Fish stated, clasping their blood soaked hands together. "You will need each other in the years ahead, this I have seen. Watch over each other as brothers in the dark days ahead."

The old chief grew quiet as a pair of warriors lifted the litter and carried the wounded leader away from the battle. Tecumseh turned to the redheaded boy. "*Neahw,* Thank you, *jai-nai-nah.*"

Sinnatha shrugged. "I wouldn't leave you to face death alone, and I'll always be there when you need me. Come, we should leave before Clark and his boys find us."

Tecumseh disappeared into the smoke. Sinnatha, the boy who had been known as Stephen Ruddell, glanced back at the advancing army of frontiersmen and hesitated before disappearing into the undergrowth as well.

CHAPTER 7

QUINCY, ILLINOIS
SUMMER, 1845

"AMAZING!" DR. DRAPER EXCLAIMED. "You had a chance to escape and you stayed? Extraordinary."

The old man eyed the writer and shook his head. He carved off a plug of tobacco and slipped it inside his bottom lip. "There weren't nothin' "extraordinary" about it," he drawled, spitting tobacco juice off the side of the porch. "It was a matter of survival."

Draper frowned. "I don't understand?"

Stephen spat again. "I'm sure you don't. You ain't never seen the elephant, have ya?"

"What?"

"Been around a battle, ya fool," the old man growled.

Draper didn't respond.

"I thought so. Listen, boy. It sure ain't no likely affair or some grand adventure that all these coots who are clamorin' to go to war with Mexico think that it is. I fought in many a battle in my day, and there ain't never been a time that I wasn't streaked. I weren't no coward, but I was never fat-headed enough to get myself kilt. I had been with the Shawnee three months when Clark attacked. I would've been plum happy to hook up with his army and get back home."

"Sure, I cotton to Tecumseh well enough, but he was the only one I was sour on leavin' at the time, with maybe the exception of

White Swan. She was Black Hoof's wife and she treated me as her own son," the old man admitted. "I didn't try to escape because I would've gotten myself kilt."

"It seems to me that it would have been easy for you to hide in the woods and then presented yourself to Clark after the Indians had all left," Draper argued.

The old man laughed. "You reckon the Indians left? There never was a time where there weren't a boodle of warriors watchin' every move Clark and his boys made. If I tried to hide in the trees, some pissed off warrior would have slit my throat and taken my hair before I had gotten close to Clark."

"Well, you still had a chance to hide in the village and then slip away during the battle," Draper continued to argue. "It would appear that your love for Tecumseh caused you to hesitate."

Stephen shook his head. "Ain't you been listenin'? There was smoke everywhere and all creation of shootin' goin' on. Them frontiersmen would have shot me dead if I had run out to them."

"Surely not! They would have recognized you as one of their own. You had red hair and blue eyes, and you would have spoken to them in English."

The old man leaned forward. "You ever heard tell of Joseph Rogers?"

Draper shook his head, not recognizing the name.

"Well, Joseph was the cousin of General George Rogers Clark. He was captured by the Shawnee in 76' and lived with them almost four years. I met him once. He lived in one of the Piqua towns. He was redheaded, just like all the Clarks. Well, Joe dearly wanted to get back with his family in Virginia. Clark marched his army on the villages of the Mad River after he destroyed Chillicothe. Black Hoof and his warriors put up a fight, but Clark was able to destroy that town as well. Joe saw his chance, and he hid outside the village and ran toward Clark when the battle was over. Do you want to know what happened?"

"What?"

Ruddell spat again. "Them frontiersmen didn't see a redheaded white man running at them through the smoke. They saw a body dressed in buckskins with long hair charging at their general. Hell, he was even shouting 'George!' in English. They shot him down like they would have done Indian brave they saw in the battle. Oh, Clark ran down when he recognized him. They say the general was blubberin' and holdin' Joe's body, but that didn't make him any less dead. Clark and his boys packed up and headed back to Kentucky after that."

Stephen moved to the edge of the porch, looking toward the broad river. "So Doc, I allow that was a sad story about Joe Rogers, but he made a fat-headed mistake. He reckoned other white men would have recognized him and spared his life, but he was wrong. Simple fact is there have been plenty of other whites who fought with the Indians on the frontier. Alexander McKee, The Girty brothers, even that bastard William Wells before he switched sides. If somebody comes at you in battle, you don't hesitate. You kill them. So, if I had run out to Clark and his boys at Chillicothe, with my long hair and wearin' my buckskins, shoutin' 'I'm a white man!' what do you suspect would have happened?"

Draper looked at the ground. "We would not be speaking today."

The old man spit out his tobacco and nodded. "I didn't make any mistakes. I was able to survive."

Draper scribbled down several things on a sheet of paper as the old man moved back to his rocking chair and took another swallow from his whiskey jug.

Finally, Draper looked up. "What happened to you after Clark's campaign?"

Stephen sat back in his chair and scratched at his beard. "Life went on. Clark's army destroyed most of the crops around Chillicothe and Piqua town. The tribe settled in for a harsh winter along the Great Miami. I was probably gut-foundered more that winter then I was anytime in my life. I hunted with Tecumseh a right smart amount. I was a good hunter, still am as a matter of fact. Yet I ain't never seen anyone who could hunt like Tecumseh. Once, we ran into a herd of buffalo. I kilt one with my rifle. Tecumseh kilt sixteen with his bow. Sixteen arrows, sixteen kills. Tecumseh was good with a gun, but he usually hunted with a bow; he allowed it was more natural."

The old man frowned. "Those last years of the revolution were hard on the frontier. The Shawnee wiped out many a flatboat full of people that come down the Ohio during that time. Militia killed almost a hundred Christian Indians at Gnadenhutten. The

Shawnee ambushed a boodle of Kentucky Militia at Blue Licks and kilt seventy five, includin' one of Daniel Boone's sons. Another army came up the Little Miami and burned Chillicothe, again. Then Simon Girty came and told everyone how Washington had won the battle of Yorktown and beat the British. It wasn't long before the war was over and the United States was claimin' all the land in the Ohio Valley, even though they had yet to defeat the tribes in any major battle. Yes sir, the revolution had ended, but the fighting along the Ohio was just gettin' started."

"Did Tecumseh take part in the fighting?"

Stephen nodded. "You bet he did. Black Fish didn't die right away. That wound festered for weeks before he finally passed on. Tecumseh had seen two fathers die at the hands of the *Shemanese*. He became a full fledged warrior after Clark's campaign and was at just about every major fight over the next thirty years, and he didn't lose very many. He was as smart as a steel trap in battle, yet treated prisoners well. He wouldn't stand for a body to be tortured. Oh, he kilt more then his share of innocent people, but he never tortured any."

"Were you made a warrior during this time?" Draper asked, scribbling furiously.

Stephen scratched his nose. "Well, not for a coon's age. Black Hoof knew that my heart was troubled and he wouldn't send me out with the war parties. As head chief of the Shawnee, Black Hoof was very busy. He kept me huntin' to help feed his family. I was actually grateful; I was always cow-hearted I might look through my gun sights and see one of my uncles standin' there. I suspicion Tecumseh knew how I felt and he never said anything."

"Did you ever see your brother Abraham?"

The old man frowned. "Not much. He was adopted into a family in a village far up the Great Miami. Abe was never as chirk as me and more of a loner. I got to see him every once in a while when the tribe had large gatherins', but that was only a few times. Abe was never plum happy to see me. I reckon he blamed me for the fix we were in. He allowed the tribe adopted him because of how I run the gauntlet and how well the Shawnee admired my grit. I reckon it makes sense to think that. He was my younger brother and the same blood ran through our veins. That ain't the reason he was adopted. Sickness and war had done up the Shawnee for years. They was just like every other tribe on the frontier; they wanted to survive. They were always eager to adopt young captives to replace family who had died. That's what happened to Abe."

"Yes, it amazes me how many white children the different tribes took over the years. White culture certainly did not take many Indian children," Draper observed.

"That ain't a good thing," Stephen growled. "You know what frontier families was told about their children bein' takin' by Indians?"

Draper shook his head

"Don't worry about them. The Indians would treat them well. It was always a mistake to chase after a raidin' party. If they got too close, the Indians would kill the captives and go to brush. Few rescue parties succeeded in bringing anyone home alive. The best way to get a body home was to work with a trader who moved among the tribes to buy them back. That's what my pa tried to do." The old man leaned forward in his chair. "White children who were adopted were treated well and became members of the tribe. Indians don't discriminate when they adopt someone. Hell, I saw runaway slaves welcomed into some of the different tribes as full warriors. Whites don't do the same thing. Indian children that were taken by whites were treated poorly by most, not any better then slaves. It ain't no wonder most Indian children went to brush the first chance they got, while most white children never had a mind to leave their Indian families."

"Are you suggesting that white children were happier among the Indians than with their own families?" Draper replied indignantly.

Ruddell chuckled. "Well, all the ones I knew seemed to be. Don't misunderstand, Doc. I missed both my ma and pa, but I never had a hankering to be a farmer. Life huntin', gamblin', and playin' games fit me just fine. Everyone shared among the Shawnee. I could eat at anyone's wigwam. Nobody ever kept more then they needed, and they gave to those who would have been without. Whites could have learned a thing or two from the Indian nations they've pushed out of their way."

Draper could see the anger building in the old man's face and decided to change the subject. "You mentioned that Tecumseh had some books. Did you teach him to read?"

The old man laughed and slapped his thigh. "Well, I reckon I can take some credit as his first teacher. You got to remember, I never went to school on the frontier. I learned the basics of readin' and writin' from my ma. I passed what I could on to Tecumseh. He was quick to pick it up. It wasn't long before he could read as well as me. I taught him about Caesar and the Roman Empire and William the Conqueror and the Normans takin' over England. I think his favorite stories come out of the Bible. He loved hearin' about Moses leadin' his people to the Promised Land and how David kilt' Goliath. Tecumseh asked so many questions that my head hurt. That boy could have been a regular scholar at Harvard."

Draper eagerly scribbled notes down. "Did Loud Noise learn to read as well?"

Ruddell's eyes flashed. "That no account sack of shit? He was too busy pretendin' to be a medicine man and making fun of Tecumseh learning to read to attempt it himself. Oh course, that was also before he lost his eye and became even more no account."

"Ah, yes!" Draper exclaimed. "All the stories say he lost his eye in a hunting accident. Were you there? What really happened?"

The old man snorted. "Oh, I was there. It sure as Hell wasn't any hunting accident that caused Loud Noise to lose his eye."

"I don't understand."

Ruddell leaned forward again. "Doc, do you want to know what really happened? I never told anyone else the truth, not even Tecumseh. Loud Noise lost his eye trying to kill a body. It so happen that it was me. I took his eye, and taught him a lesson. I'll tell you about it."

Sinnatha worked his way slowly along the edge of the meadow. The fifteen-year-old had grown taller and thicker over the three years he had lived among the Shawnee. He was now bigger then many of the warriors that were raiding along the Ohio River. The war between the British and the American colonists had ended. Now settlers were pouring down the Ohio and into Kentucky. Knowing that their former hunting grounds were lost, the Shawnee were determined to keep any settlers from establishing farms and towns on the north side of the great river. Few warriors were left to hunt for the village, so more of the task fell upon the redheaded teenager.

Sinnatha did not mind. He was proud of his skill as a hunter and the important role he played in caring for the tribe. He looked down at the bow in his hands. Powder had become scarce and had to be saved for the raiding warriors. Tecumseh had taught the white boy how to make a bow and the arrows to go with it. He had practiced all summer to become proficient enough to hunt. He was not yet confident enough to stalk a deer as Tecumseh or some of the other hunters would have done. Instead, he had chosen a set of smaller arrows and was now stalking rabbits as they fed on the last of the fall grass, fattening up for the coming winter.

The boy already had four large rabbits hanging from a thong at his waist. He stopped as he caught sight of another rabbit in the tall grass. He had just fit an arrow to his bow when a movement among the trees caught his attention. He was surprised when the warrior Red Hawk stepped from the forest, a rifle in his hands.

Sinnatha recognized the weapon. It was the very same gun he had stacked against the stockade gate the day he was taken captive. The boy had not seen Red Hawk in three years, not since the day he had run the gauntlet. Laughter from the woods drew Sinnatha's gaze away from the Shawnee warrior. Loud Noise stepped into view, a wide smile upon his face.

"Red Hawk and I have waited too long for this day, *Shemanese!*" the thirteen-year-old cackled. "I have watched you poison my brother's mind with your book stories and false friendship for too long, I know your heart. You will be the death of Tecumseh!"

"As you were the death of Kumsaka?" the redheaded youth retorted.

Loud Noise's face twisted in rage. He turned to Red Hawk. "Kill him!" he snarled. "For both of our brothers!"

Red Hawk raised his rifle and smiled.

The warrior grunted in surprise and dropped the gun. He clutched at the arrow shaft that had buried in his throat. Red Hawk fell to his knees and pitched forward into the grass, dead. The arrows that Sinnatha carried were meant for small game, but could be deadly to larger prey if shot with enough force. Loud Noise looked on in astonishment as the angry young man stalked toward him and his dead companion, his bow still griped in his hand.

"I'd say Tecumseh has taught me to use a bow well enough," Sinnatha stated calmly. "I reckon I'll take back the rifle that rightfully belongs to me."

Loud Noise scrambled toward Red Hawk at the mention of the weapon.

"Don't!" Sinnatha warned. "I have no designs to shed anymore Shawnee blood on this day."

Loud Noise hesitated and then went for the gun. Sinnatha was on the younger boy before he could bring the rifle to bear. Both boys held tight to the barrel and struggled for control. Loud Noise was large for a boy of thirteen and Sinnatha was surprised by his brute strength. They stumbled to the ground and rolled back and forth, scattering arrows from the quiver Sinnatha carried across the ground. Loud Noise refused to lessen his grip on the rifle and jammed the stock into the white boy's throat.

"Now you die!" he cried triumphantly, bearing his weight down against the stock, trying to crush Sinnatha throat.

Sinnatha pulled down on the barrel and kicked up with his feet. The unexpected move flipped Loud Noise over the top of Sinnatha's head, sending him crashing to the ground. Sinnatha scrambled to his feet, in control of the gun. Loud Noise rose from the ground as well, his knife in his hand.

"It's over!" Sinnatha stated, pointing the muzzle at the younger boy. "put it away, or I'll kill you to!"

"How?" Loud Noise jeered, "I knocked the pan open, you have no powder to fire the gun!"

Sinnatha glanced down at the open rifle pan. Loud Noise took advantage of the distraction and charged, his knife raised to strike. Sinnatha sidestepped the boy's charge and clubbed him across the back with the rifle stock. Loud Noise crashed to the ground hard, losing his grip on his knife.

The white boy picked up the knife and advanced on his prone attacker. Sinnatha roughly flipped the heavy set boy over. He was shocked by what he saw. Loud Noise held his hands over his right eye, blood flowing through his fingers. His body shook in pain and his mouth was twisted in agony. Sinnatha could see the bloody tip of a broken arrow lying on the ground where Loud Noise had landed. The shaft had pierced the boy's eye when he hit the ground. Sinnatha shook growled and put the knife blade to Loud Noise's throat.

"No, Please don't kill me!" Loud Noise pleaded, holding a bloody hand out. "What would you say to Tecumseh?"

That statement saved the boy's life. Sinnatha looked down at the groveling wretch and frowned. As dearly as he wanted to, he could not kill his best friend's brother. Instead, he grabbed the wounded boy by the hair and yanked him to his knees.

"I have killed a man today because of you." Sinnatha hissed. "You have lost an eye and will be reminded of this fight every day for the rest of your life. I hope you have learned your lesson. I will not speak of this to Tecumseh or my father, unless you make up some lie about me attacking you; then I will tell the truth. I think we both know who everyone will believe, don't we?"

Loud Noise shook his head.

"Good," Sinnatha replied, removing the knife from the wounded boy's throat. "I'll let you live, but if you ever come after me again, I'll kill you. Now get out of my sight."

Loud Noise scrambled to his feet and staggered away, clutching his ruined eye. Sinnatha glanced over at the dead Red Hawk and down at the rifle he held in his hands. He spat on the ground before hoisting the rifle and starting in the direction of the village, stopping to pick up his brace of rabbits along the way.

"Incredible!" Dr. Draper cried, his eyes gleaming. "You were responsible for the Prophet losing his eye? How did Tecumseh react?"

The old man shook his head. "I already told you Loud Noise was never any prophet. You're startin' to make me huffy by referin' to him as such." Stephen growled, glaring at the younger man. "I never told Tecumseh, and neither did Loud Noise. I reckon he believed what I told him. He run back and told everyone he had hurt himself out hunting. Since the fat bastard rarely hunted, most of the people believed him. When I came in and informed everyone that I had kilt Red Hawk in a fight, there was some that suspicioned different, includin' Tecumseh. He never said anything. We were best friends, but Loud Noise was his kin. It's hard to turn away from somebody you share blood with. Tecumseh always tried to look after him, no matter how ornery he was!"

Stephen rose from his seat and wandered to the edge of the porch. "I always respected that about Tecumseh. I really can't say I was the same way. Abe and I fought before we were taken, and then we lost what bond we had in those years apart. Did you know that Abe couldn't speak English when we went back to our Pa after the Treaty of Greenville? Poor man was stuck between two different worlds. He always resented the Shawnee for killin' Ma and takin' us away. He found ways to lash out as he grew to be a man. There was always alcohol available from the different traders, and we all know how well Indians use whiskey and such."

"Yes, they certainly seem to enjoy it," Draper cut in.

"Enjoy it?" The old man spat. "I have seen precious few that didn't become drunks after they tried it. It changed many a good Indian brave into a wretch. They'd do things they'd never consider doin' if they weren't corned. It was so bad that most tribes wouldn't hold a warrior accountable for any crimes they committed when they were drunk. Abe knew that. I heard many a tale of Abe getting corned with other braves and killin' them in a fight."

"Did you not kill several warriors yourself over the years? I mean, was Abe so different?" the younger man dared ask, scribbling notes furiously.

Stephen ran his hand through his white hair. "Aye, I kilt some braves, and white men too for a matter of fact," he replied, his face hardening. "I ain't proud of it, but I never kilt unless it was in self defense or in defense of those I loved."

He folded his hands behind his back. "Abe was different; he kilt out of hate. Once, he was working a maple syrup camp with several other Shawnee. He was watchin' the kettles with another young warrior while the rest were out collecting syrup. Abe cut a couple of reeds from a creek and stuck one in the boiling syrup. The boy saw what he was doing and asked him about it. Abe told him that he was drinking warm syrup from the bottom of the kettle. He told the boy that the straw cooled it and that it was very good. He even showed the boy that he had some of the syrup in his mouth. The boy had not seen him take some syrup that had cooled from a different pot. Abe explained to the boy that it was best to draw a right smart amount into the back of his throat through the straw in order to get the best syrup. The Shawnee boy believed him and did as Abe instructed. Can you imagine what happened?"

Draper shuddered and shook his head.

"That boiling syrup hit the back of that boy's throat like liquid fire. He couldn't spit it out quick enough. I can only reckon what his last few moments were like as his throat swelled shut and he suffocated beside the fire. When the others got back Abe told them the cully had drunk the syrup before he could stop him." Stephen shook his head and frowned deeply. "Abe told me that story not long after we come back to Kentucky. He seemed to think it was chirk and was not the least bit remorseful. Hate had turned him into a different person. I didn't have much to do with him after that."

"What happened to him?"

Stephen shrugged. "Abe was like many of the children that were raised by Indians. He didn't fit in white society and was shunned. He kept his hair long and had split his ear lobes like many other Shawnee braves. As I said, he could not speak English well. I fared better, thanks to Tecumseh. All those years of readin' and speakin' English with him kept me fluent. Oh, Abe was able to make a livin' for himself. He was a considerable hunter and tracker. He spent several years workin' as an interpreter for the army on the frontier. Eventually, he married and moved to Arkansas. That was the last I heard of him. I couldn't even tell you if he was still alive."

"Were you punished for killing Red Hawk? What happened next?" Draper questioned eagerly.

Ruddell held up his hands. "Settle down, Doc. Don't have a conniption fit. Give me a moment to remember everything." The old man refilled and lit his pipe and looked across the river.

"No, I wasn't punished, because Red Hawk came after me. The Shawnee saw his killin' as self defense. They didn't need any trial to say I had the right to protect my own life like we would do today. I took the rifle he carried and I could have taken his scalp if I had chosen to. I had earned them both fairly"

Draper shuddered at the mental picture.

Stephen blew a smoke ring and rocked back in his chair. "The war may have ended for the United States and Great Britain, but not much changed for the Shawnee. The United States was still weak and couldn't push the terms of the Treaty of Paris. The British kept their posts among the tribes and continued tradin' with them. The English encouraged the tribes to keep fighting.

They hoped the Shawnee, Miami, and the other tribes of the Ohio Valley could act as a buffer between the United States and Canada. The British had few troops of circumstance in Canada and were always cow-hearted the Americans would try and take Canada away from them."

"The fightin' calmed down for a while. There was a grist of claims made on the lands in Ohio by the different states. The Virginia Military District was formed in 1784, the Seven Ranges and Connecticut Western Reserve in 1786. Those claims 'awarded' lands to Revolutionary war soldiers as payment for their service. Few of them wanted to give up lands they already had back east and travel to the wilderness, so they sold their claims to speculators. Through it all, Chiksika refused to accept the Long Knives' settlin' onto Shawnee lands. This added to the bad blood between him and Black Hoof over leadership of the tribe. So, by 1786 Chiksika had decided to head west and visit the Shawnee in Missouri and the tribes south of the Ohio Valley. It was a journey he would take Tecumseh on."

The old man leaned forward in his chair, his eyes glistening. "Little did we know how much it would end up changin' Tecumseh's life, and mine."

CHAPTER 8

CHILLICOTHE VILLAGE
SUMMER, 1786

TECUMSEH WALKED FROM THE FOREST, a large buck slung across his shoulders. He had grown tall and slim, with well defined muscles and narrow hips. He looked down at the village beside the Little Miami River. This was the third Chillicothe he had lived in during his eighteen summers of life. This town was not as large or as well built as the previous ones, but the Shawnee that lived there were doing their best to live through the challenges they were facing. The young man adjusted the weight of the carcass on his shoulder and moved toward the Shawnee settlement.

Tecumseh smiled as he caught sight of his sister, Tecumpese, grinding corn outside her wigwam. Several children played around the woman who had been as much a mother to him as if he was her own. She looked up and smiled brightly as the hunter lay the deer down beside the fire.

"You bring us too much food, little brother," she scolded good-naturedly. "Soon we will all be fat from eating so well!"

"We can give what we don't use to others who need it," Tecumseh declared, his smile widening. "I enjoy the hunt, and gladly share what I take."

Tecumseh took note of a group of young men wrestling at the edge of the village. In the center of the circle stood Sinnatha. The white boy had grown tall and powerful; his thick neck and shoulders a testament to the incredible strength the young man possessed. Sinnatha had easily defeated all the young men around the circle and now awaited other challengers.

Tecumseh smiled as Sinnatha caught sight of him and waved. The powerful young man motioned for him to join him. Tecumseh chuckled, reading the obvious challenge set out in his friend's gesture and expression. A glint of anticipation appeared in Tecumseh's eye and he moved forward to meet his friend. He was so intent upon the wrestling that Tecumseh almost missed Chiksika sitting beside the wigwam.

"I have been waiting for you," the older warrior stated quietly.

Tecumseh smiled. "It is good to see you, brother. I didn't know you had returned. We could have hunted together."

Chiksika waved his hand toward the west. "We'll have more than enough time to hunt together. I needed to finish preparing for our journey."

"Journey?" Tecumseh repeated, turning to see two heavily loaded horses standing behind the wigwam. He turned back toward his older brother, his eyes gleaming. "Do you mean it? Are we really going?"

Chiksika nodded. "It's the right time."

Tecumseh's smile faded. "What about Tecumpese and our brothers? Who will care for them?"

The older warrior smiled. "You forget that our sister is married to a great warrior and hunter," he stated, referring to Stands Firm, Tecumpese's sturdy husband. "Our brothers are old enough to care for themselves. Now is the time to go."

Tecumseh glanced toward Sinnatha. Chiksika followed his gaze.

"This is a journey for us, brother," the older man stated firmly. "Sinnatha may travel with you some other time. Go, tell him goodbye."

Tecumseh nodded and made his way toward his best friend.

Sinnatha sat across from Tecumseh inside Black Hoof's wigwam, frowning.

"I wish I could go."

Tecumseh nodded and took a puff from the tomahawk pipe Chiksika had given him as a gift a year earlier. He blew out the tobacco smoke and passed the pipe to his friend. "So do I, but I don't know how long we will be gone. I want you to look after my sister and my brothers."

Sinnatha puffed on the pipe and winced at the request. "Tecumseh, you know that I'd do anything for you. I got no problem looking after your sister, but you want me to look after Loud Noise as well?"

Tecumseh smiled. "Thank you, my friend. I am sure we will both have many stories to tell when I return."

Sinnatha gripped his best friend's wrist. "I will miss you, brother. I wish you well on your journey and for a safe return."

Tecumseh gripped the powerful young man's wrist tightly and quickly exited the wigwam.

"How long was Tecumseh gone?" Draper asked, looking up from his notes.

Ruddell sat back in his rocking chair, calculating. "Over a year. He and Chiksika traveled to the Great Lakes to visit with the Ottawa. They hunted buffalo on the plains with the Sioux, and they sat in council with the Creeks and Cherokee. They visited dozens of tribes along the Ohio and Mississippi. Tecumseh made a name for himself and earned the respect of every nation they visited. The alliances he formed would serve him well in the years to come."

"When did you see him again?"

The old man stroked his beard. "It was the fall of 87'. Settlers began to push into Cherokee lands in Tennessee and war broke out again. The Shawnee and Cherokee had fit over Kentucky for years, but sat their differences aside when it came to their common enemy, the Long Knives. Shawnee warriors headed south to help the Cherokee in their struggle. I reckoned Tecumseh and Chiksika would find their way there, so I headed south as well."

Chiksika and Tecumseh rode into a Cherokee village situated in a small valley of the Cumberland River. The brothers had been traveling northeast from the Creek lands of Northern Alabama for over a week. Several squat Cherokee warriors waved at the pair as they made their way toward the center of the village and the chief's longhouse. Tecumseh knew they were not far from the lands white settlers from Kentucky and Virginian were pushing into. The Cumberland River drained fertile lands and was easily accessible to the *Shemanese* who continued to pour through the Cumberland Gap. Every warrior was armed and ready for a fight.

The brothers dismounted as a large bellied Cherokee chief lumbered out to meet them. "*Bezon*," The portly chief stated, using the Shawnee word for hello. "I welcome our Shawnee brothers to the village of Clear Water. I am Big Eagle, village chief."

Chiksika stepped forward and clasped the large man's wrist. "We have come to help you fight the *Shemanese* who are trying to take your land."

Big Eagle smiled. "Yes, we knew you were coming. Some of your warriors are already here."

Tecumseh and Chiksika looked at each other in confusion. "There are Shawnee warriors here?" Tecumseh questioned.

Big Eagle nodded vigorously. "A war party. They are led by a white Shawnee. He is a powerful man with red hair and is a great wrestler."

Tecumseh and Chiksika smiled at each other knowingly. "Where is he?"

Tecumseh shook his head as he and Chiksika quietly slipped into the lodge Sinnatha had been given. A bear skin was pulled up over two prone figures. Tecumseh recognized Big Fish's deep voice, muffled by the cover. A young woman's voice emitted in the form of a giggle as the couple laughed and romped under the pile of skins. Chiksika sneered and winked at Tecumseh, before reaching down and cocking his rifle. The figures stopped moving and the lodge went silent at the sound.

"Do you have a husband?" Tecumseh heard Sinnatha ask from under the bear skin.

Tecumseh reached down and yanked the covering back, revealing a naked Sinnatha and a young Cherokee woman. The girl screamed at the sight of the armed warriors. She grabbed her doeskin dress from the floor and ran naked from the lodge.

"Sinnatha, it's good to see you," Tecumseh stated, struggling to contain his laughter.

The white warrior glared at the brothers as he struggled into his leggings. "I wish I could say the same, Tecumseh! Do you know how long it took me to get her into my bed?"

"Either too long or not long enough," Chiksika observed, causing Tecumseh to howl in laughter.

Sinnatha managed to pull on his leggings and rose to his feet. The big man smiled and hugged Tecumseh and then Chiksika close. "I missed you, my brothers!"

"How did you know that we would come here?" Chiksika asked.

Sinnatha flashed the older man a wry smile. "There's going to be a fight with the *Shemanese* here. I knew you would come. So I put together a band of warriors and came this way."

All three men laughed.

"How do our people fare?" Tecumseh asked.

The big man shrugged. "Black Hoof has built a new village further up the Auglaize River. He did not name it Chillicothe, but called it Black Hoof's town. The people did not like the name and have renamed it Wapakoneta. Black Hoof hopes that it is far enough from the Ohio that we will be out of the reach of the Long Knives and their armies."

"There is no place far enough away to be out of their reach." Chiksika stated, his eyes flashing.

Sinnatha nodded. "I fear you are right, but Black Hoof is doing all he can to protect the people. Tecumpese sends her love," he added with a smile. "If she did not have a wigwam full of children to care for, I am sure she would have come herself. Stands Firm and Blue Jacket also send their greetings as well."

Sinnatha had packed a pipe as he spoke and used an ember from the fire to light it. He puffed the tobacco to life and passed the pipe to Tecumseh. "How was your journey? I heard that you hurt your leg."

Tecumseh shook his head and stuck out his leg for his friend to see. "I did more then hurt it. I broke it. I am lucky to be alive. My horse fell when we were hunting buffalo and rolled on top of me. If I had been thrown clear of the horse, I would have been trampled to death."

"His clumsiness cost us three months of our journey," Chiksika scolded half-heartedly. "I think he learned his lesson not be so reckless when hunting buffalo. We Shawnee are of the forest, not the plains. He had watched the Sioux hunt on horseback too much. I think they are born on a horse. He will be reminded of his foolishness every time he rises in the morning."

"Does it still hurt?" Sinnatha asked, noticing the limb had not healed quite straight.

Tecumseh smiled. "Only on cold nights or if I run a long distance. As my brother said, I learned my lesson and I will be reminded of my recklessness every morning that I wake after I have slept on the hard ground."

"Did you see your mother?" Sinnatha asked, puffing on the pipe once again.

The smile disappeared from Tecumseh's face.

"Our mother is gone," Chiksika stated quietly. "She was not among the Shawnee across the Mississippi. We discovered that she had gone to visit her family among the Creeks. We traveled south to see her after the winter thaw, but white sickness took her just a week before we arrived."

"I am sorry to hear that," Sinnatha sighed. "Too many people have been lost in such a way."

The big man reached over and clasped Tecumseh's wrist tightly. "It has been too long since I have seen my brothers. Now that we are together, we will show the Long Knives how Shawnee fight."

All three men laughed and passed around the pipe, swapping stories of their adventures of the past year.

"You actually fought against your own people?" Dr. Draper gasped.

The old man ran his hands through his thick, white hair and shook his head. "I reckon that it's hard for you to cotton to, Doc. I had become a man livin' among the Shawnee and for the most part, they had treated me considerable. My adopted mother, White Swan, was as good of a woman as I ever knew. She treated me as well as my own ma and never laid a hand on me. I loved Tecumseh as a brother and respected Chiksika and Black Hoof more than most white men I've known in my life. Yes, I fought against other whites. I did so to protect the people I'd come to love."

"Do you regret it?" Draper dared ask.

Ruddell chewed his bottom lip. "I regret that so many good people, both red and white, died over the years. I regret that we never found a way to live together in peace. I regret all that was lost in the growth of this country."

Draper could hear the anger and despair creeping into the old man's voice and decided to move on. "How long did you stay among the Cherokee?"

Ruddell smiled. "Over two years. Those were some of the best times of my life. We traveled and hunted the mountains and fought many a battle against the militia up and down the Cumberland River. We all made names for ourselves as warriors and hunters. Them young Cherokee girls were appreciative of us as well," the old man added with a wink. "Few were the nights that Tecumseh, Chiksika, or I had to worry about lying in a cold wigwam alone."

Stephen chuckled as the younger man shifted uncomfortably on the porch. The smile faded from the old man's face as he gazed toward the river. "It couldn't last; nothin' good does," he whispered. "Did you know that Tecumseh's father had a vision of his death before the battle of Point Pleasant?"

Draper shook his head.

"Well, it seemed to be a gift, or a curse for the men in Tecumseh's family. Hard Striker had foretold that he would fall in battle. Chiksika did the same thing."

Draper snorted. "Surely you don't believe he knew he was going to die, Mr. Ruddell."

The old man leaned forward. "I've seen many a considerable thing in my life, young man," he replied, his eyes narrowing. "I've seen enough to know that God does exist, miracles do happen, and don't doubt when an Indian has a vision. Sure I allow it; I was standin' there when he told Tecumseh."

The fort had been built by a man named Buchanan along a sweeping, horseshoe shaped bend of the Cumberland River. The fortification was deep inside Cherokee lands and could not be allowed to stand. Tecumseh, Sinnatha, Chiksika, and Big Eagle observed the stockade from a grove of hickory trees. Close to a hundred Shawnee and Cherokee warriors crouched behind them, silently waiting for their leaders to signal the attack.

"There could be fifty men on those walls," Sinnatha observed. "They'll have long rifles and you can bet they all know how to use them to."

"The logs they have built the fort out of are hickory; tough and green. They will not burn well," Big Eagle added, rubbing his hands together nervously.

Chiksika smiled. "We will attack the gate. Enough fire arrows and torches will keep it blazing. Once it falls, we will take the fort."

The Shawnee war leader turned to Big Eagle. "I will lead the fire attack against the gate. You will direct warriors to attack other areas of the fort from this position. That should draw some fire away from those attacking the gate."

The large man sighed in relief and nodded eagerly in acceptance of the plan.

Chiksika turned to Tecumseh, Sinnatha, and the Shawnee warriors that had been following his lead for two years. "You will cover the gate attack with your rifles. The *Shemanese* will see the danger of the fire and will try and use their guns on the warriors attacking the gate. You must not allow them to have easy targets. As Sinnatha has said, they will all be very good shots. Go, prepare for the attack."

Chiksika grasped Tecumseh's arm and pulled the young warrior aside as the rest of the Shawnee gathered up their rifles and moved to take positions among the trees. Sinnatha stepped to the side and patiently waited for Tecumseh to join him.

"Stay close to me today, brother," Chiksika whispered. "If I fall, you must lead the attack."

Tecumseh looked at his brother, his eyes wide. "What do you mean? You will not fall!"

Chiksika smiled sadly. "I had a vision of my death last night. I fear that this is my last battle."

Tecumseh began to tremble. "No! You are wrong! We won't attack the fort, or you can stay behind."

Chiksika put his arm around the younger man's shoulders. "You know that I cannot do that. If this is the destiny that Weshemoneto has set forth for me, then so be it!" The older man held Tecumseh at arms length. "You are the hope of the Shawnee, Tecumseh." he stated, his voice strong. "You were born under the Eye of the Panther. You shall lead our people; I have seen it. Promise me that you will never make peace with the Long Knives."

"I swear on my own blood, *ni-je-ni-nuh!*" Tecumseh replied, his voice cracking.

Chiksika smiled. "I can die a happy man. Come, let us join the fight!"

The war leader gathered up his rifle and moved forward. He paused in front of Sinnatha. "Stay beside him and help him through the difficult days ahead, Big Fish. He will need your strength."

Sinnatha scratched his head and frowned, but remained silent as Chiksika moved on. The redheaded warrior fell in beside Tecumseh as he moved slowly by.

"What's wrong!" he demanded.

Tecumseh looked up, tears streaming down his face. "Chiksika had a vision that he would die in battle today."

Sinnatha looked after the war leader. "Maybe he's wrong," he whispered.

Tecumseh nodded. "It is all we can hope. I tried to get him to stay out of the attack, but he refused."

"Help me protect him today, my friend," Tecumseh continued, wiping the tears from his cheek. "I can't bear the thought of losing him."

Sinnatha nodded. "Me either. I will do all I can to help keep him safe."

Tecumseh gripped the big man's wrist in thanks and turned to follow his brother toward the fort, his chest still tight with fear.

Sinnatha steadied his rifle and exhaled before gently squeezing the trigger. The gun bucked against his shoulder and another frontiersman disappeared from the wall. The redheaded warrior had no time to admire his marksmanship; he ducked back down behind the boulder he was using as cover as several riflemen fired at his location. He was showered by rock chips as several bullets struck the top of the boulder. He wiped sweat and soot from his gun smoke-blackened face. He looked over at Tecumseh, hidden behind a stump some twenty feet away, and flashed the warrior a smile.

The battle had raged all the morning and into the afternoon. The frontiersmen had put up a fierce defense. Several warriors had been killed or wounded by the accurate fire of the seasoned defenders. Big Eagle had been hesitant and ineffective in attacking the fort walls. As a result, the assault on the gate had come under heavy fire. Several warriors lay dead within a few feet of the gate, their torches smoldering beside them. A few small fires had been started within the compound and on the gate by fire arrows, but these had all been extinguished quickly. Only the sharp shooting of Sinnatha, Tecumseh, and the Shawnee warriors held the defenders at bay and kept the attackers from being routed.

Suddenly, a Cherokee warrior burst from cover and rushed forward, his torch held high. A shot range out from above the gate, and the warrior dropped his torch and stumbled to the ground. Chiksika rose from behind the stump he was using as cover and fired quickly, knocking another defender from the wall. The war leader dropped his rifle and sprinted toward the gate, stooping to gather up a pair of burning torches from the ground beside the dead warriors that had previously carried them.

"Chiksika! No!" Tecumseh screamed.

Tecumseh and Sinnatha both rose and fired their rifles, scoring hits on two more settlers and providing Chiksika cover as he rushed forward. The Shawnee leader moved in close and tossed the torches at its base. At the same time, he pulled a bottle of whiskey from a pouch at his side and dashed it against the green wood. The alcohol ignited and the gate began to burn.

Chiksika turned and ran back toward Tecumseh, a smile on his face. As he reached his brother, another shot range out from the wall. The war chief's eyes widened and his smile became a grimace of pain as he collapsed into Tecumseh's arms.

"Watch over our family, *ni-je-ni-nuh*," Chiksika gasped. "I go to our father's side."

"No, Chiksika!" Tecumseh wailed. "Don't leave us!"

Tecumseh sobbed as he held his brother's lifeless body. After several moments, he looked up, his eyes filled with tears. The young warrior gently lay Chiksika's body down and grabbed his rifle. Sinnatha rushed to his side and pulled his distraught friend down behind another stump.

"What are you doing?" Sinnatha hissed, holding tight to the struggling warrior.

"Let me go!" Tecumseh demanded. "We must press the attack. The gates are burning and will soon collapse. We must make them pay for Chiksika's death!"

"The Cherokee are pulling back," Sinnatha stated evenly. "They saw Chiksika fall, and Big Eagle does not want to risk anymore of his warriors on this attack. You and I cannot take the fort alone."

Tecumseh struggled against the big man's firm grip once again.

"We have already lost Chiksika." Sinnatha growled. "Don't dishonor him by getting yourself killed as well."

Tecumseh sagged against his friend, overwhelmed with grief and anger.

"Come, I will help you carry him from here," the big man stated softly, patting the grief stricken warrior on the back. "We must not leave him for the *Shemanese* to scalp and mutilate. We will bury him in a place where he will find peace."

Tecumseh nodded. Together, the young men lifted Chiksika's body and staggered toward the woods as black smoke from the burning gates covered their retreat.

The hill provided a scenic view of the setting sun overlooking the Cumberland River and surrounding valley. Tecumseh kneeled in front of a fresh grave as Sinnatha stood behind him. The redheaded warrior stepped forward and placed a hand on his friend's shoulder.

"He is with your father now," he whispered, "and at peace."

Tecumseh shook his head slightly in agreement, but remained silent.

After several minutes, Sinnatha spoke again. "What now, brother? Do we go home or stay here? We will follow you as we followed Chiksika."

Tecumseh stood and turned to face Sinnatha and the assembled Shawnee warriors.

"The war is here," he replied, his face somber. "I will stay and fight the Long Knives; those who wish to go home may do so. I will think no less of anyone who does; you are all brave warriors who I would be honored to lead."

"I will stay with you," Sinnatha replied, his jaw set. "I will be at your side as long as you need me."

Tecumseh managed a smile. "Thank you, *jai-nai-nuh.*"

The two warriors clasped hands as the remaining Shawnee warriors stepped forward to join them as the sun set over the hill and the grave that now adorned it.

CHAPTER 9

QUINCY, ILLINOIS
SUMMER, 1845

"HOW LONG did you and Tecumseh stay with the Cherokee?"
Lyman asked, wiping sweat from his brow with a white
handkerchief. The summer sun was beating down on the porch
and the cool morning air had vanished as the day descended into
afternoon. Draper's stomach rumbled in hunger, but he had no
wish to interrupt the old man's story to request anything to eat or
drink.

Stephen did not seem to notice the younger man's discom-
fort. "Over a year. It took a coon's age for Tecumseh to get over
Chiksika's death. We raided and fought over most of Tennessee
and Southern Kentucky. It didn't take long for Tecumseh to
become well known among the Southern tribes as a warrior and
leader. He built a reputation that would serve him well in the years
to come."

The old man rose and walked to the edge of the porch and
stretched. "I do believe there is some ham and other doings left in
Mrs. Ruddell's kitchen. Are you hungry?"

Draper nodded vigorously.

"Good! You fetch us a bucket of water from the well, and I'll
see what I can scrounge together."

Lyman closed his escritoire and made his way to the well behind
the house. He drew up the bucket and used a dipper attached

to the crank to quench his thirst. He was pleasantly surprised by how sweet and crisp the cool water was. He refilled the bucket and entered the house through the back door. He found Ruddell in the kitchen, slicing thick chunks from a side of ham with a large butcher knife. Draper sat the bucket on the table and commented on the quality of the water.

Ruddell smiled and nodded. "I know. It's one of the reasons why I built diggings here. That well is fed by a limestone spring. The limestone filters the water and improves the taste. There's little chance of anyone gettin' peaked drinkin' from our well. It makes the quality of our tea and coffee better too." The old man reached over and shook the clay jug he had carried with him into the kitchen.

"Not to mention our old orchard," he added with a smile, uncorking the jug and taking a swig of the whiskey.

Stephen tore off two hunks of bread from a loaf on the table and passed one to Draper, along with a heaping plate of ham.

"Thank you, Mr. Ruddell," Lyman said, eagerly accepting the plate.

The old man grunted in response and fell silent as both men set to eating. Finally, both men pushed their empty plates forward.

Stephen belched loudly and rubbed his stomach. "I'm thankful my son married a good cook. I reckon we'd both be skinny if we had to depend on our own cookin'."

Draper smiled and opened his writing box once again. "When did you come back to Ohio?"

The old man ran his tongue inside his lips and sucked the remains of the meal from between his teeth. "It was the winter of 1790, after that coot Harmer tried to attack the Shawnee and Miami along the Wabash."

"Oh, yes," Lyman cried, his eyes lighting up. "Harmer's defeat. What can you tell me about it?"

Stephen shrugged. "Probably no more then you already know; it was one of the few battles that Tecumseh and I weren't at."

"They say that Blue Jacket and Little Turtle were able to defeat Harmer because William Wells advised the Indian leaders how to attack."

The old man's eyes flashed. "Wells? That lump of buffalo shit didn't 'advise' on anything. Oh, he was there, but I'm cock-sure he was hidin' as far from the fightin' as he could be."

"Surely you exaggerate, Mr. Ruddell," Draper argued. "By all accounts, Mr. Wells was devoted to Little Turtle and remained close to him while remaining a champion of the Miami after he returned to white society and became an Indian agent. It is said his death at the hands of Potawatomi warriors during the Fort Dearborn massacre was mourned greatly. It seems to me that you both had a great deal in common"

Ruddell snorted. "More like his death was greatly celebrated. Wells and Little Turtle were both good at looking out for their own designs."

The old man leaned forward, scowling. "We were close to the same age, Wells and I. We were both twelve when we were adopted by Indians, but that's all we had in common,"

Draper was startled when the former frontiersman picked up the butcher knife and rammed it deep into the oak table top and pointed one of his gnarled fingers at the younger man. "Wells married Little Turtle's daughter, Sweet Breeze, to gain power in the tribe. When he became Indian agent, he left her and married a white woman. I came back to help the Indians as a preacher; Wells came back to profit off them! I would appreciate it if you wouldn't allow that he and I had all creation in common again, for your sake," the old man growled.

Lyman swallowed and cleared his throat. "Yes, well... tell me about the battle, please."

Stephen uncorked his jug and took a swig before sitting back in the chair. "Well, there wasn't any trickery involved in Harmer's defeat, or any other fight in which the Indians bested a white army, for a matter of fact. It was a case of poor leadership and a lack of respect for the abilities of your enemy," the old man explained, the anger fading from his eyes. "The land north of the Ohio had become know as the Northwest Territory and an old Revolutionary war general, Arthur St. Clair, was named Secretary of the Territory, as I am sure you already knew. Well, St. Clair decided he needed to make an impression on everyone by sending an army against the tribes in retaliation for all the raids along the Ohio. So, he put that drunkard Joe Harmar in charge of a force of 1,500 men and sent the army north to attack the Indian towns in upper Ohio and along the Wabash."

"Drunkard?" Draper gasped. "What do you mean? General Harmar was the highest ranking officer in Ohio other then

Governor St. Clair and had been an officer under President Washington during the Revolution."

"That don't make him any less of a drunkard, and everyone knew it." Ruddell continued. "Harmar bein' put in charge was the best thing that could have happened for the tribes. They were used to facing Clark, Boone, and more experienced frontier commanders. Harmar had no idea what he was doin'. Still, he had a large force that the Shawnee could not match head to head. So, they fled before him and drew his force deeper into Indian country. They ambushed his scouts and nipped at his heels like wolves. Harmar's main objective was to destroy the Miami capital of Kekionga on the Maumee River."

The old man looked through the kitchen window, his expression growing distant as he remembered the past. "It was there that Blue Jacket and Little Turtle made their stand."

Blue Jacket gazed upon the four hundred man force of mixed militia and army regulars making their way through the swampy river bottom toward Kekionga. The Shawnee leader shook his head and grinned wolfishly.

"This General Harmar is more foolish then I thought," he commented to Stands Firm, who had moved through the undergrowth to stand beside him. "He sends only part of his army against us. He is either a fool or a coward, but either way, it is good for us."

Stands Firm nodded in agreement. The Shawnee leaders and close to three hundred warriors were concealed in the thick undergrowth at the western edge of the Great Black Swamp, patiently waiting to attack the enemy force. Blue Jacket thanked Weshemoneto once again for the good fortune he blessed upon the people in the last several days.

Harmar's army had moved steadily up the Great Miami River from Fort Washington, burning several Shawnee towns. Blue Jacket knew that the Shawnee could not face the Long Knife force alone, so he had formed an alliance with the Miami and their war chief, Little Turtle. Together, the war leaders came up with a plan to face the advancing force.

The Miami leader was not a large man. He was middle aged, with a large head and long nose. Often, warriors had joked that his name fit his appearance. *Mishikinakwa* had risen to a position of power and respect ten year earlier after his defeat of a French force bent on attacking Fort Detroit. The French had been led by Augustine De La Balme, a glory seeking French cavalry colonel determined to make a name for himself. Little Turtle and his warriors had ambushed the French force on the Eel River north of Kekionga and wiped it out. Mishikinakwa had killed De La Balme in hand-to-hand combat and still carried the Frenchman's scalp as a trophy.

Little Turtle and Blue Jacket had met on the Maumee River at the edge of the Great Black Swamp. The little man had greeted the Shawnee war leader warmly.

"How many warriors can you gather?" Little Turtle asked.

"Perhaps four hundred, given enough time. What about the Miami?"

Mishikinakwa rubbed his high forehead slowly. "Five hundred. We will have little support from the Piankashaw, who live close to Vincennes. A few Wea will come, but most will remain at their villages near Fort Quiatenon."

"Can we draw on any other allies?" Blue Jacket questioned. "The Delaware might send some warriors. *Buckongahelas* has always been friendly to the Shawnee. What of the Potawatomi?"

Little Turtle frowned, causing his face to resemble that of a snapping turtle.

"The Potawatomi cannot be trusted," he hissed. "They follow no main chief and care only for what profits them."

Blue Jacket stared at the smaller man intently. "The Miami and the Potawatomi have fought in the past, but is the *Shemanese* threat not enough to set aside old differences?"

"You are right, *ne-kah-noh*," Little Turtle rattled. "I will send word for *Aubenaubee* and *Kewanna* to come to Kekionga. There is a British trading post there and the chance to get some whiskey should be too much for their warriors to pass up," he added.

Blue Jacket ignored the comment. "We will have close to a thousand warriors, so we will still be outnumbered. At least the Long Knives are attacking after the harvest. We will be able to abandon towns and avoid battle until we are ready without starving."

Little Turtle gestured to the swamp. "Your women and children can shelter along the Maumee. There is much game and cover to hide. Bring you warriors to Kekionga, and we will use the swamp and the river bottoms against this General Harmar. By the time he reaches the headwaters of the Maumee, we will be ready for him."

True to his word, Little Turtle had gathered over five hundred warriors to the Miami village by the time Blue Jacket and the Shawnee had arrived. The Delaware chief Buckongahelas had sent a party of fifty warriors in support of the Shawnee and Miami. A force of almost two hundred Potawatomi under a zealous war leader named Turkey Foot had camped north of the village as well. Little Turtle had called all the war leaders together at the village's council house to plan for the upcoming battle.

Blue Jacket noticed that Little Turtle was accompanied by a redheaded, white warrior. The Miami chief introduced the man as *Apekonit*. The Miami Chief explained that the white man had been adopted by the Miami and had lived among them for close to ten years. He had recently married Little Turtle's daughter and had become the chief's son-in-law. Apekonit had fidgeted nervously as the heavily armed warriors had assembled together.

The plan had been simple. The Indians would work to split Harmar's larger force so it could be more easily defeated. Kekionga was initially abandoned as Harmar's army camped south of the town and burned part of the village. Eager for action, a militia colonel named John Hardin had taken a force of two hundred and fifty militia, cavalry, and regulars to scout north of Kekionga along the Eel River. A small party of Shawnee warriors had fired on the force and fled down a narrow trail toward the river. Hardin had ordered his force to follow the escaping warriors and led his men into a trap.

Hardin's troop stumbled into a spongy river bottom that was densely covered in undergrowth. Little Turtle and his warriors attacked the confused troops from three sides. Most of the militia fled in panic, leaving the army regulars to be overwhelmed by Little Turtle's warriors. In all, Colonel Hardin lost close to a hundred men with few Indian casualties.

General Harmar arrived at the scene of the battle the next day and sent another force of three hundred troops under a regular officer named Hartshorn along the retreating Indian's trail. The reckless Hartshorn and his command were ambushed in another river bottom by Turkey Foot and his warriors as well as Stands Firm and a large number of Shawnee. Hartshorn and fifty of his troops fell during the furious attack. The remaining troops retreated in such disarray that they left the bodies of their dead on the battle field.

General Harmar had been shaken by two decisive losses in as many days. He had ordered his force to pull back south of the Miami capital. Little Turtle had Apekonit dress as a militia and sneak into the army's defensive position to gather information. He had returned well after nightfall to report to Blue Jacket and the Miami leader.

"The *Shemanese* are upset with their general," the redheaded man reported, his nose twitching. "They think he is a coward. I saw him argue with the officer named Hardin. Hardin wants to be given a force to return and bury the dead. Harmar does not want to leave the place he has put his troops in."

"We should attack them now," Turkey Foot cried, his eyes glistening. The Potawatomi leader had freshly shaved his head, leaving only his Mohawk untouched. He had also painted his face red from his nose to his forehead, enhancing further his wild appearance. "They will all fall before us!"

Blue Jacket shook his head slowly. "We must not be foolish. To attack them would be to the Long Knives advantage. Our warriors are all brave, but we cannot match their guns. We must be patient."

Turkey Foot looked at the ground, disappointed by the Shawnee leader's rebuke.

Little Turtle rubbed his pointy chin and turned back to Apekonit. "Will Harmer send more men out?"

The redheaded warrior nodded. "I heard him tell Hardin he can go out tomorrow."

"Then we will be able to ambush them again," Blue Jacket began.

"There is more," Apekonit interrupted, rubbing his hands together. "This General Harmar likes whiskey. I saw him drinking during and after his argument with Hardin. By the time I left, he could not get out of his chair."

Little Turtle and Blue Jacket looked at each other and smiled. "This is also good news," the Miami leader rasped.

Colonel Hardin held up his hand and signaled the column to stop when he saw one of his scouts galloping toward him. The man reined his horse up in front of the colonel and saluted.

"Well? What did you see?" Hardin stated impatiently.

"There must be eight hundred warriors in that village!" the scout gasped. "I don't have a mind where they all came from."

Hardin shook his fist triumphantly. "These savages have finally decided to face us in the open! Go, report to General Harmar and tell him we're moving against the village. He'll bring up the rest of the army to support us and we'll crush these red devils once and for all."

The scout saluted again and kicked his horse into a gallop. Hardin then called in his senior officers.

"You'll each lead your regiments against the enemy's flank," he instructed two of his officers. "Major Fontaine will range forward with his cavalry and Major Wyllys and his regulars will remain in support until General Harmar arrives."

"Shouldn't we wait for General Harmar and the rest of the army?" Wyllys dared ask.

"What?" Hardin sneered. "Would you have me allow these savages to get away? We must strike now!"

Wyllys bit his lip and remained silent. The other officers were all militia and did not offer any type of protest toward Colonel Hardin's plan. They had already lost over a hundred men on this campaign and unlike Hardin, Wyllys was a regular soldier and had a healthy respect for the Indians' fighting ability.

Blue Jacket could not believe his eyes as he watched as the Long Knife colonel divided his force into four smaller groups and sent them forward. He grabbed the tall warrior Cold Water by the shoulder. "Go tell Little Turtle to draw the *Shemanese* away from the regular soldiers. We will take care of the horse soldiers." The young warrior bound away toward Kekionga.

The war leader then turned toward Tecumseh's younger brother, Sauwaseekau. "Go and watch the rest of the army, young brother. You are the swiftest of our warriors; you will be our eyes and ears. Watch the *Shemanese* closely."

Sauwaseekau smiled at the war leader's praise and darted through the trees toward Harmar's encamped force. Blue Jacket turned toward Stands Firm. "Is your son ready?"

The Shawnee warrior motioned his fifteen-year-old son forward. Blue Jacket placed his hands on the boy's shoulders. "We will draw the horse soldiers to us. You must be a rabbit and lead these dogs into our trap."

The boy nodded and moved forward fearlessly.

"General Harmar!" the ensign repeated loudly, shaking the sleeping officer roughly. "There's a courier here from Colonel Hardin."

The white haired General snorted and blinked his blood shot eyes in confusion.

"What did you say?" he mumbled drunkenly.

The ensign sighed and tried to hide his look of disdain. He had called for the general from his tent entrance repeatedly before entering to find the commander passed out on his cot, an empty whiskey bottle still in his hand.

"Colonel Hardin has sent a courier with word on the Indians."

Harmer shook his head to clear his senses. "Very good," he mumbled. "Well, what does the good colonel have to say?"

The courier stepped forward, his hat in his hand. "Colonel Hardin is movin' against a group of Indians gathered in the village. He wants you bring up the rest of the army to support his attack."

"Oh? He has almost four hundred men. What is the size of the native force that he faces that would require more troops to support his attack?" the general demanded, irritated with the brash colonel's request.

"We reckon there are over eight hundred warriors in the village alone," the courier replied.

"What?" Harmar whispered, his eyes widening.

"The scouts have reported several hundred warriors assembled in the village. I saw them myself," the courier continued. "The colonel wants to press the attack before the savages have a chance to go to brush."

"The fool!" Harmar bellowed. "There could be twice that many warriors hiding in the forest! Go back and tell Colonel Hardin to pull back. It's too risky to launch an all out attack."

The courier saluted the general and scrambled to his horse's back, galloping from the camp.

"Captain Armstrong!" Harmar cried, calling for one of his senior regular officers.

"Sir?" Armstrong replied, hurrying to the general's side.

Harmar sat down on his chair, wiping sweat from his forehead with a trembling hand. "Form the troops into a defensive square. We must be prepared in case these savages try to overwhelm our position."

"Sir, shouldn't we move to support Colonel Hardin?" the captain dared ask.

"That fool of a militia commander would be the death of us all." Harmar cried, rising from his seat. "He's been ordered to pull back; we'll form a considerable defensive position and protect ourselves from any attack, now!"

Armstrong saluted stiffly and rushed off to carry out his orders, calling out instructions to junior officers as he went. Meanwhile, General Harmer struggled to buckle on his saber, his hands shaking uncontrollably.

The courier never made it back to Hardin's command. Sauwaseekau took note of the army's defensive movements and realized that the Long Knives were not coming out to support the force moving against Kekionga. The young warrior hid himself in a wooded area along the trail and waited patiently for the courier to ride by. Sauwaseekau could shoot a bow almost as well as Tecumseh. His well placed shot punched through the soldier's throat and knocked him from the saddle. The young Shawnee drug the man's body into the woods and quickly scalped him. Sauwaseekau gathered up the horse's reins and leapt into the saddle, a triumphant smile on his face. He steered the horse onto a trail that would take him around the advancing militia. He kicked his horse into a gallop and rode toward Kekionga.

Major Fontaine reined his mount up and called his cavalry force to a halt. He scanned the tree line uneasily, looking for any signs of a hidden Indian force. A grizzled frontiersman in dirty buckskins rode up beside him, his rifle across his saddle.

"What,d 'ya reckon, Major?" the man drawled, spitting tobacco juice onto the ground. "There don't seem to be any savages here. Maybe they all gone to brush when they saw us headin' this way."

"No, Timmins, they're out there. I can feel them watching us," Fontaine replied, reining his horse away from the foul smelling militia man. "Of that I am certain."

Suddenly, a rifle shot echoed across the little valley and Fontaine heard Timmins grunt beside him. The major turned to find the frontiersman clutching a wound in his chest. Blood burst from Timmins's mouth and he tumbled from the saddle, dead before he hit the ground. Major Fountaine looked up to see a teenage Indian standing on the trail ahead of him, smoke still rising from the rifle he held in his hands. The youth let out a whoop, turned around and bent over. The boy then pulled down his leggings and exposed his buttocks to the shocked commander.

"You can all kiss my ass," the boy yelled in perfect English. Laughing heartily, he scooped up his rifle and looped up the trail.

"Get that heathen bastard," Fontaine cried, his face reddening. The entire cavalry force galloped after the fleeing Indian as he disappeared into the forest.

Major Fontaine realized the boy was a decoy too late. The militia officer reined up his horse within fifty yards of entering the forest. He raised his hand to signal for his men to stop. He opened his mouth to yell a warning that they were riding into a trap, but he did not get a chance to utter a word. Fontaine felt the air blast from his lungs and looked down to see an arrow buried deep in his chest. The officer slumped forward on his horse and watched as the forest erupted in a hail of lead and arrows. Nearly half the cavalry went down in the first volley, the rest milled around in confusion and panic as wounded men and horses cried and struggled to rise around them. The major looked on helplessly as hundreds of Shawnee rushed from cover to overwhelm his remaining command. Within minutes, the entire cavalry force had been wiped out. Fountain slipped from his mount's back and fell to the ground, but felt no pain. He knew he was dying, but was surprised by how calm he felt. The sounds from the brief battle had subsided and the dying man closed his eyes for a moment. When he reopened them, an Indian war chief was standing in front of him.

Blue Jacket looked down at the militia officer, his teeth bared. He raised his war club and crushed the dying man's skull. The Shawnee whooped triumphantly, gathering around their war chief. Cold Water and Sauwaseekau appeared, having returned from Kekionga. Blue Jacket raised his hand to quiet the warriors and stepped forward to meet the messengers.

"Little Turtle's warriors have drawn the Long Knives away from the *Shemaganas*," Cold Water reported, using the Shawnee term for soldiers. "He now moves to attack them along with Turkey Foot and his Potawatomies."

"What of the rest of the *Shemanese* army?" Blue Jacket asked, swinging toward Sauwaseekau.

The warrior smiled. "Their general hides in fear. He has made the rest of his army to defend his camp against attack. He will not come out to meet us." Sauwaseekau held up a bloody scalp. "His messenger never made it to the Long Knife colonel."

Blue Jacket offered a prayer to Weshemoneto. "The creator has blessed us on this day!"

The war chief picked up his rifle and turned toward the assembled Shawnee. "We will help Little Turtle and the Miami kill these *Shemaganas* and drive the rest of the Long Knives from the Wabash. Their great white father in Washington will think long before he sends another force against us!"

The warriors cheered loudly upon hearing their war chief's confident statement and eagerly moved forward.

Major Wyllys bit his lip and shook his head. Damn Colonel Hardin! The inexperienced commander had divided up his forces and had eagerly pursued groups of Indians that had fled before them. Now Wyllys and his 1st American Regiment were isolated from the rest of Hardin's command. Wyllys sensed something was wrong with the attack and had formed his sixty regulars and supporting militia into a defensive position. The young officer continued to look over his shoulder for signs of General Harmar and the rest of the army. He would like to have sent a scout to determine how long it would be before the rest of the army arrived, but Major Fountaine and his cavalry force had all charged into a wooded area. Wyllys shook his head again. Damn all militia and their inability to follow orders! The regulars would have to remain in a defensive position until General Harmar and the rest of the army arrived. Major Wyllys prayed it would be soon.

Sounds of battle erupted from the forest that the cavalry had disappeared into. Wyllys clenched his fists as the distant gunfire died down and Fountaine's force did not emerge from the forest. Gunfire and the sounds of battle grew louder in the directions that Majors Hall and McMullen had led their militia in flanking attacks. Wyllys's remaining militia began to edge forward restlessly.

"Hold your positions," the regular army officer ordered.

A bearded frontiersman spat tobacco juice on the ground. "We're missin' the fight," he protested. "If we stand here, we won't get any scalps."

"The only scalp you need to fret about is your own," Wyllys growled, drawing his pistol and pointing it at the frontiersman. "I'll shoot the next man who breaks rank!"

The militia grumbled, but held their positions. The men who survived the battle would later state that it was Major Wyllys's actions that allowed any of them to live through what happened next.

The men of Major Wyllys's command stood wide-eyed as groups of militia fled past them, running for their lives. Hundreds of Indians attacked the regular troops as the militia retreated around them in disarray. To their credit, the militia assigned to Wyllys held their ground alongside the commander who had just threatened their lives. Soon, the combined force of warriors was attacking Wyllys's position from three sides.

The battle lasted for over two bloody hours. Finally, Blue Jacket and Stands Firm led the Shawnee in a fearless charge that broke the 1st regiment's line and the fighting became hand-to-hand. Stands Firm was pierced through the lung by a bayonet, but tomahawked the soldier who stabbed him before he was carried from the field. Sauwaseekau was slashed across the ribs by a sword wielded by the commanding officer. He would surely have been killed if it had not been for Blue Jacket. The War leader threw his tomahawk and buried it in the officer's chest as he raised his saber to finish the young warrior.

With Major Wyllys dead, the remaining regulars and militia retreated from the field. Well over a hundred warriors had perished in the brutal battle and an equal number had been wounded, including Stands Firm and the Potawatomi leader, Turkey Foot.

Little Turtle called for the warriors to fall back and sent scouts to watch General Harmar's remaining force. The little war chief moved up beside Blue Jacket and smiled.

"You fought bravely, *ne-kah-noh.* Your warriors carried the day for us."

Blue Jacket gave a toothy smile. "We carried the day together. The Shawnee could not have won alone, nor the Miami. The Potawatomi and Delaware fought bravely as well. Together, we created our own army that the *Shemanese* could not defeat."

Apekonit moved up beside the war leaders. Blue Jacket could not remember seeing the redheaded man among the other Miami warriors who took part in the battle.

"What now? Do we attack the rest of Harmar's army?" Apekonit asked, nervously looking after the retreating soldiers.

Little Turtle shook his head slowly. "No. This General Harmar has no heart to come against us again. We will let him lick his wounds and crawl back to the Ohio and tell others of what will happen if the *Shemanese* come against us again. Besides, we have many wounded warriors to care for and winter is coming."

Blue Jacket remained silent. He would have liked to have destroyed the rest of the army, knowing that they might well have to face many of the same men again. Yet the Shawnee war chief knew that he could not accomplish this without the support of the large Miami force. The allied tribes had won a great victory under Little Turtle's leadership. He could not risk losing the support of the Miami war chief and his braves by going against his decision. The rest of the *Shemaganas* and their drunken general would survive their disastrous campaign in which a full third of their army had perished.

The late fall day was slipping into dusk and the air had grown cold. Little Turtle turned to look across the battlefield and gave a short laugh. Blue Jacket turned to see what the smaller man found amusing. Close to a hundred and fifty white men lay scattered across the field. Indian warriors were moving among the bodies, collecting weapons, spoils, and scalps. Steam rose from the freshly scalped skulls.

"It looks like a field of harvested pumpkins," Little Turtle rasped, bring a chorus of laughter from the surrounding warriors.

So it was the Harmar's defeat, the first loss by a United States army to a native force, became known to the Indians as the Battle of Pumpkin Fields

CHAPTER 10

WAPAKONETA VILLAGE
WINTER, 1791

TECUMPESE WAS GRINDING CORN outside her wigwam. Snow had fallen the night before and the late morning air was cold, but the Shawnee woman did not complain. She had bundled herself in a bear skin robe and worked steadily with her grinding stone, turning the hard kernels into a meal she could boil and feed to her children and wounded husband. The hard work and her pride in the victory her people had won late in the fall kept the woman warm. Tecumpese was lost in her own thoughts and the task at hand, and therefore did not hear the warrior who had arrived and now stood silently behind her.

"*Bezon, ni-t-kweem-a,*" Tecumseh stated merrily. "What are you making me to eat?"

The woman stopped working, but did not look back. Tecumpese closed her eyes and gave thanks to Weshemoneto.

"I knew you would be home soon," she replied, rising to her feet, "looking to fill your belly from my cook pot!"

Tecumpese turned and rushed to her younger brother and threw her arms around the warrior's neck. Tecumseh held his sister close. His smile faded and he held the woman at arm's length.

"There is something that I must tell you," he whispered softly.

Tecumpese shook her head. "Chiksika is dead," she stated. "I know. I have known for some time. My heart is still heavy, but it was the path he chose."

She examined Tecumseh from head to toe. "Look at you! You have grown into a fine warrior. All the stories must be true!"

Tecumseh raised an eyebrow. "What stories?"

"Why, those of the great Tecumseh," Tecumpese stated proudly. "He who strikes like the panther, all enemies falling before him!"

Tecumseh laughed. "I did not think you would believe such foolishness, *ni-t-kweem-a*!"

The woman patted the warrior on the cheek. "Such foolishness brings our people hope and pride."

A large crowd had gathered, hearing of the celebrated warrior's return. The excited mass began making their way toward the siblings.

"Do you see?" Tecumpese stated, indicating the crowd. "Your return has brought everyone great joy!"

The crowd surrounded Tecumseh as his sister stepped out of the way. Old men, women, and even warriors pushed near to offer their greetings and to touch the young man as children looked on. Tecumseh responded by laughing and welcoming them all warmly.

Sinnatha sat upon his horse and chuckled at the scene. He had purposely left Tecumseh at the edge of the village. The white warrior had known what would happen when Tecumseh arrived, and he wanted no part of it. He turned and slowly walked his horse toward the center of the village and the wigwam of his adopted father, Black Hoof.

Sinnatha reined his mount up short as he rode up behind a young woman scraping a deer hide. The girl had staked the hide out on the ground and was on her knees before it, methodically scraping the last bits of flesh away with a piece of flint. The red-headed warrior smiled as he admired the woman's slender waist and firm backside through her doeskin skirt as she stretched to reach the far corners of the hide.

"Do you like what you see?" The girl asked without turning around.

"What?" Sinnatha replied, his eyes snapping up.

The Indian girl turned around and flashed the warrior a toothy smile. "I asked if you like what you see. Or should I raise my skirt so you can get a better look?"

Sinnatha laughed at her boldness. The girl was pretty, with a pert little nose and fair complexion. Her dark eyes were piercing, and vaguely familiar.

"Do I know you?" he asked.

She smiled and ran a hand through her long, dark hair. "You do not remember me? You ate many meals beside my mother's fire."

Sinnatha raised an eyebrow. "Who are you?

"I am Nika, daughter of Stands Firm," she replied.

Sinnatha's eyes widened. "Stands Firm? Then your mother is…"

"Tecumpese," She finished for him, her eyes sparkling mischievously.

Sinnatha scratched his cheek, the Nika he remembered had been a shy and awkward child when he had went south. He now gave Tecumseh's niece a more appraising look. She had seen seventeen summers and was now a woman. "You have changed much since last I saw you," he observed.

Nika put her hands on her hips. "I would think so, three years is a long time to be away. How did you and my uncle stay warm at night for so long? It is known that the blood of a Cherokee girl does not burn as hot as that of a Shawnee woman!"

Sinnatha laughed once again at the young woman's boldness. "It is good to see you again, daughter of Stands Firm. I would like to stay longer, but my father will have heard that I am home by now and will be angry if I don't go to his wigwam."

Nika smiled once again. "You should not wait three more years before you see me again. Come to my father's wigwam tomorrow and bring something for me to cook. My father was wounded in the battle and has not been able to hunt. He will be much happier about you coming to see me if you bring him something to eat."

The redheaded warrior returned her smile. "Then I will make sure I bring enough for a feast. I will see you tomorrow"

He gave the young woman a final wave and nudged his mount into a trot, a smile still spread across his face.

The old chief was standing beside the lodge, frowning as the people of his village continued to rush to welcome Tecumseh home. He finally noticed Sinnatha riding toward him and a smile returned to his craggy face.

The warrior dismounted beside the lodge and embraced the chief. "It is good to see you, *no'tha.*"

"And you as well, *ni-kwith-ehi,*" Black Hoof replied, patting the younger man on the back. "You have been gone for far too long."

The chief walked to the lodge opening and signaled for the warrior to join him. "Come, smoke with me and tell me of your time away."

Sinnatha hesitated, glancing in Tecumseh's direction.

"You are not his dog!" Black Hoof grumbled, glaring in Tecumseh's direction. "Let the 'Great Warrior' take care of himself!"

The old warrior stormed into the wigwam. Sinnatha rubbed his forehead and sighed. He glanced toward his best friend one more time before following his father into the lodge.

Tecumseh looked at the dilapidated wigwam and shook his head. The flimsy structure had been erected some distance away from the village and looked as if might collapse with the next gust of strong wind. Tecumseh could hear drunken chanting from inside the shelter as he neared. He frowned as he made his way inside.

Loud Noise, fat and drunk, was sitting on a dirty pallet of rotting skins. The fat man held a mostly empty whiskey bottle in one hand as he chanted aimlessly. Realizing someone was present, he swept his greasy hair from in front of his one good eye and squinted at the visitor.

"Tecumseh?" Loud Noise whispered, a light of recognition appearing in his blood shot eye.

"Yes, little brother," Tecumseh replied, his voice cold. "I have returned."

Loud Noise staggered to his feet and stumbled forward, throwing his arms around the warrior. The fat man reeked of sweat, alcohol, and urine. The Shawnee were a tribe that took pride in their appearance and personal hygiene, something the drunkard obviously had forgotten. Tecumseh wrinkled his nose and pushed his brother back beyond arm's length.

"You were not there to welcome me home," he stated grimly.

Loud Noise looked at the ground. "I'm sorry. I was gathering herbs in the forest. I am learning to be a medicine man."

"You were drunk," Tecumseh replied evenly.

"*Mat-tah!* No!" Loud Noise cried, his eye twitching. "Who told you that?"

"Our sister," Tecumseh countered. "She tells me you do nothing but drink. You do not hunt or help the village. You live off the charity of others..."

Loud Noise turned his back on his brother and swept up his bottle of whiskey. He took a long drink and offered the bottle to Tecumseh, sneering. Tecumseh shook his head and turned to leave.

"So what if I drink?" Loud Noise growled, the liquor giving him courage to speak. "It gives me great visions. I will be a great medicine man. What does that bitch Tecumpese know? She has no right to judge me."

Tecumseh turned back toward the fat man, his eyes narrowing.

"What of you, brother?" Loud Noise continued, taking another swig. "You dare look down on me? Did your greatness save Kumsaka? What about Chiksika? What did you do to...?"

People in the village may have heard the would-be medicine man scream. Loud Noise had not had a chance to finish his statement as Tecumseh had leapt across the wigwam and grabbed him. Loud Noise was a large and powerful man, but he was no match for the angry warrior. He screamed as he sailed through the lodge entrance and landed hard on the ground. Tecumseh stalked after his shaken and stunned sibling. He grabbed Loud Noise by the collar and dragged him toward the nearby stream.

The fat man struggled and protested as they reached the bank. A thin sheet of ice covered the small stream. Tecumseh ignored Loud Noise's pleas and drove the drunkard's face through the ice and into the cold water below. The warrior dunked his brother into the frigid water several times before finally tossing the sputtering and gasping wretch to the bank. Tecumseh straddled Loud Noise and grabbed him by the throat.

"If you ever insult the memory of our brothers again, I will kill you!" Tecumseh hissed. "Do you understand?"

"Yes, brother," Loud Noise sputtered, grasping at Tecumseh's legs. "Please don't hurt me!"

Tecumseh looked down at the trembling heap at his feet and sighed, his rage falling away. "A great destiny has been laid upon us, brother" he said calmly. "We were both born under great signs from *Weshemoneto*. Together, we must help our people."

The war leader picked up the empty whiskey bottle that had rolled down to the stream bank during the dousing. "This is not the way to become a great medicine man. This is *Shemanese* poison; you must cast it away!" Tecumseh tossed the bottle into the stream to emphasis his point.

Loud Noise lay upon the ground. "I don't know if I can," he sobbed.

Tecumseh reached down and pulled his wretched brother to his feet.

"I will help you, *ni-je-ni-nuh*," he replied soothingly. "I am home. Together, we will help our people regain what we have lost."

Stands Firm winced as he shifted closer to the fire that burned outside his wigwam. The puncture wound in his chest hurt, but his wife had packed it with moss and it was slowly healing. He had refused to lay in his wigwam to be tended to as if he were a baby. It hurt the warrior to breath, but he knew the crisp, clean air would help him to recover more quickly. The old warrior had managed to pull out his pipe and was packing it with tobacco when Sinnatha strolled up, a pair of turkeys strung over his shoulder.

"*Bezon,* my friend," Stands Firm called out. "What brings you to my fire?"

"Me," Nika answered, stepping from the Wigwam and flashing a smile at the redheaded warrior. "I told him he could come to our fire as long as he brought something for me to cook."

Stands Firm turned back to the young warrior and raised an eyebrow. "Oh? It seems like he has succeeded."

Nika took the turkeys from Sinnatha and gave them an appraising look. "Not bad," she stated. "It would be nice if they were fatter."

"It is the middle of the winter," the white warrior protested.

"Yes, but it would still be nice if they were bigger," she repeated with a smile. "They will still make a fine meal. Sit and smoke with father while I prepare them."

Sinnatha did as he was told and sat near the wounded man as he finished packing his pipe. Stands Firm lit the pipe and took several puffs before passing it to the younger man. Both men watched as the young woman expertly gutted and plucked the birds. She then tied a length of sinew around the neck of each turkey and then strung them from a metal tripod over the fire. Finally, she sat a slab of green bark underneath each bird to catch the drippings in order to baste the meat as the turkey slowly roasted over the fire.

"Well done," Sinnatha observed.

"Yes," Nika replied, wiping her hands on patch of grass before casting her bold eyes in the warrior's direction. "You will find that I do many things well."

The redheaded warrior stammered and stuttered, but could not find a reply. The young woman laughed and turned on her heel and entered the wigwam. Stands Firm shook his head and took another puff of tobacco before looking at the younger man.

"Many warriors have tried to win *ni-da-ne-thuh* heart," Stands Firm observed, blowing a smoke ring. "None have succeeded in keeping her interest for long. You are a strong warrior and good hunter, so you have my blessing to try."

Neahw, my friend," Sinnatha replied.

"Do not thank me," Stands Firm chuckled. "It is difficult to catch a wild cat with only your hands."

"That is what makes it interesting," The white warrior replied with a smile.

CHAPTER 11

KEKIONGA VILLAGE
SPRING, 1791

THE WINTER THAW HAD BROUGHT FRESH NEWS of the activities of the *Shemanese* along the Ohio and the lower Wabash. Harmar's defeat had not been taken well by the Long Knife leaders in the east. President Washington had ordered General St. Clair to raise a new, larger force to crush the native resistance. The old revolutionary war general was assembling a force of two thousand men at Fort Washington, on the banks of the Ohio. Little Turtle had sent runners to all the tribes of the Great Lakes, biding them to join him at Kekionga to discuss what to do about the new *Shemanese* threat. Encouraged by the victory of the previous fall, hundreds of warriors and their chiefs responded eagerly. By May 1791, representatives from the Potawatomi, Ottawa, Delaware, Kickapoo, and Shawnee had joined the Miami war chief for a grand council.

The great Miami council house was packed full of warriors, all eager to hear Little Turtle and the assembled tribal leaders. Blue Jacket and Black Hoof represented the Shawnee, Turkey Foot led the Potawatomi, and the Delaware followed the tall and powerful Buckongahelas. The Kickapoo, Ottawa and various other tribes were represented as well. All had come to hear the Miami leader, Little Turtle. Tecumseh and Sinnatha had both been allowed a place in the council and now sat close to Blue Jacket and Black

Hoof. Tecumseh elbowed Sinnatha and smiled, indicating the redheaded white Indian who sat beside the Miami leader.

"You have the same hair; be thankful you do not have the same name," Tecumseh whispered. "His name means 'The Carrot'."

Sinnatha snorted. "I don't know that 'Big Fish' is much better."

Tecumseh chuckled, but took note of *Apekonit's* nervous expression and shifting eyes. There was something that he did not like about Little Turtle's son-in-law. The crowded lodge grew quiet and the Little Miami war chief slowly rose to speak.

"A year ago, Blue Jacket of the Shawnee came to me when a *Shemanese* army marched north to destroy my home and offered to bring his warriors to our aide," he stated in a surprisingly deep voice.

"The Miami are in his debt," he continued, nodding in respect toward the Shawnee war chief. "So it is that we are equally in debt to Turkey Foot of the Potawatomi and Buckongahelas of the Delaware for sending their warriors to fight by our side. Together, we stood against the *Shemanese* and drove them back. It was one of the greatest victories in the history of all our peoples."

The lodge erupted in cheers at the mention of the previous fall's victory. Little Turtle remained standing, his head held high. After a few moments he held up his hand to silence the crowd.

"Alone, we Miami could not have stood against the Long Knives," he continued as the lodge grew quiet. "None of our nations could have defeated them alone; we have all tried." he added, bringing murmurs of agreement from among the assembled chiefs. "It was the power of our combined strength and courage, and the blessing of *Weshemoneto* that led us to victory that day."

Little Turtle frowned. "The *Shemanese* did not learn from their defeat. They are sending an even larger army against us. There will be more *Shemaganas* in this army, and it is said that their General St. Clair will lead it himself."

Murmurs of anger and alarm rose throughout the lodge. Little Turtle raised his hands again. "I speak for the Miami, but I wish to hear what the other nations have to say. Whatever we do, we must do together."

The little war chief once again sat down as the lodge quieted. Black Hoof, his long hair showing streaks of gray, rose to speak. Sinnatha leaned forward, eager to hear what his adopted father had to say. The Shawnee principal chief's expression was troubled; his wrinkled mouth was set in a deep frown.

"The victory over the white chief was great. My heart sang with joy and pride when I heard the news," he began, his deep voice resounding throughout the lodge. "I have spent my entire life fighting the *Shemanese,*" he added proudly, looking around at the assembled warriors. "I have never heard of such a great victory against the Long Knives by any nation. It was greater than that against the English General Braddock or any of Pontiac's victories years ago."

The chief's frown deepened as he continued. "If the Shawnee or any of our tribes suffered such a loss, we would not go against the enemy who defeated us for many years, if every again. Do you remember the tales our grandfather's told of fleeing before the Iroquois when only they had the gun?" Many older chiefs nodded in agreement. "It was many years, and not until we traded for guns with the French that we were able to stand against them."

Black Hoof shook his head. "Now the *Shemanese* send an even greater army led by a greater chief against us less then a year since we defeated them soundly. This is not good. They are able to take such a defeat so lightly? It tells me they are far stronger then we ever knew. Maybe we should use our victory to our advantage and talk peace with this General St. Clair...."

Tecumseh jumped to his feet. "Peace?" he cried incredulously. "Peace is something the Long Knives will never give us! At least not until we are all dead and they have all our land!"

Black Hoof glared at Tecumseh. "It is not your place to speak. These decisions are best left to older and wiser men then you."

"Being older does not always make a warrior wiser," Tecumseh retorted. "It certainly does not seem to give him more heart to fight for his people."

Black Hoof trembled in anger at the younger man's insult and looked to Little Turtle for support. The Miami leader rose and quietly studied the Shawnee warrior he had heard so much about.

"I respect the opinion of any warrior who has proven himself," he stated carefully. "I know of you, Tecumseh. I knew your father well. You are a great warrior. What chief speaks for you, that you may address this council?"

Blue Jacket rose to stand beside the Shawnee warrior. "Tecumseh is my brother," he stated, his eyes glimmering wolf-like in the dark lodge. "He is a great warrior who only wishes to serve all of our people, not just his own tribe. Hear him, for he is wise beyond his years."

The Shawnee war chief nodded toward Little Turtle and quietly sat down without even glancing in Black Hoof's direction. The Miami chief nodded slightly and indicated for Tecumseh to continue. Black Hoof snorted in disgust and stalked from the lodge. Tecumseh waited for him to leave before he turned to address the assembly.

"Brothers!" Tecumseh began, his strong voice drawing their full attention. "For years, our tribes have all suffered at the hands of the *Shemanese.* Many times the Long Knives have sent their armies to burn our villages and destroy our crops. Many are the memories of my childhood in which I was hungry in the winter because the *Shemanese* destroyed our winter stores."

Tecumseh shook his head and raised his hands. "The Shawnee are a brave people, as is every tribe represented here today. Yet we could never defeat the Long Knives alone. A year ago, Little Turtle and Blue Jacket stood together with Turkey Foot and our Grandfathers, the Delaware." he continued, gesturing toward Buckongahelas. "Look what happened? They defeated the *Shemanese* army! What we might achieve if all Indians joined together to oppose the Long Knives? We must put aside old feuds and differences. The whites are our enemies now. Let the Miami and Shawnee join with the Ottawa, Potawatomi, and Sioux! Together we can turn back any white army!"

The lodge erupted in approving whoops and yelps as Tecumseh finished.

"Have your own stories made you crazy?" Apekonit cried out above the crowd. "The Miami will never join with the Sioux!"

The redheaded warrior turned toward Little Turtle. "Father, we would be foolish to listen to a man with such a weak mind."

"Better to listen to a man with a weak mind than to listen to one with a weak heart!" Tecumseh retorted calmly.

Apekonit's eyes narrowed at the insult and he moved to stand, but Little Turtle stopped him by placing a hand on his wrist. The war chief indicated for Tecumseh to continue.

"All our people are threatened by the *Shemanese*. It is time that we all stood against them together, or we will surely die before them alone," Tecumseh added grimly.

The lodge was silent for several moments after Tecumseh took his seat. Finally, Buckongahelas, chief of the Delaware, rose to speak. The chief had lived seventy winters and his hair was nearly white. Even so, the Delaware was still powerful and erect as he stood before the other leaders. Well respected by all the tribes, Buckongahelas' opinion carried great influence, a fact not lost on the proud leader. He looked around at the lodge his eye's shining.

"We Delaware are known by many names," he began slowly. "Our history is long and many tribes trace their roots to us, thus we are called 'grandfather' by many nations. We call ourselves the '*Lenape*,' which means 'the people'. We were not called the Delaware until the *Shemanese* came many generations ago. Our elders tell how our people once lived along the great eastern sea."

The old man's voice became sad. "Since the white men came, we Lenape have been pushed ever west. In my own time, I have seen our people driven from the headwaters of the Ohio. Now we live on the White River, guests of the Shawnee and Miami."

The war chief's eye's flashed and he shook his head. "The Lenape have signed many peace treaties with the *Shemanese*. Each one has caused us to leave behind our lands in the name of peace. We do not wish to move anymore. So, I will lead all my warriors to fight alongside the Shawnee, Miami, and any tribe that will stand with us against the Long Knives!"

The Delaware leader took his seat as most of the warriors in the lodge shouted their approval once again. Little Turtle rose to his feet and signaled for silence once again.

"I speak for the Miami," the little man began, "and we will fight. The Shawnee and Delaware have made their positions clear. Who else will join us in this fight?"

Slowly and then in mass, the entire lodge stood.

Little Turtle nodded his head in approval. "We will send runners to every nation from the lakes to the Ohio and beyond the Mississippi. When this General St. Clair arrives, we will be ready for him!"

Tecumseh was well hidden in the forest outside the settlement of Fort Washington. He patiently watched the trail leading into the fort for signs of Sinnatha. It had been Tecumseh's idea to send the former white man into the settlement to gather information about St. Clair and his army. The redheaded warrior was not pleased.

"What if they figure out who I am?" Sinnatha argued. "They'll hang me for sure! Why can't one of the Girty brothers go?"

Tecumseh had shaken his head. "The Girty's are known among the *Shemanese,* and you are not. You also still speak English as well as the first day you came to Chillicothe. Nobody will know you; you are the best choice."

Still protesting and grumbling, Sinnatha had changed from his leggings into a pair of breeches and linen shirt. He had loaded a spare pack horse full of furs and entered the town under the guise of a trapper looking to sell his pelts.

Tecumseh had waited two days for Sinnatha to return. He gave thanks to Weshemoneto when he saw the powerful young man making his way back up the trail, his empty pack horse in tow. Sinnatha circled the campsite and covered his trail carefully in case he was followed. Finally, he entered the camp and seated himself beside the small, smokeless fire that Tecumseh had built.

"Well, what did you see?" Tecumseh asked impatiently. "Will St. Clair bring two thousand *Shemaganas* against us?"

Sinnatha shook his head. "That old general ain't got two thousand men in his army, let along soldiers. He has two regiments of regulars, about six hundred men. The rest of his force is made up of militia. He's got fifteen hundred, at best."

Tecumseh's heart raced. This was good news! Together, all the tribes of the western confederacy could raise close to fifteen hundred warriors. At the very least, it would be an even fight.

"How long before this army moves against us?" Tecumseh pressed. "Soon it will be time for the harvest and our people can ill afford for their crops to be destroyed again."

"St. Clair ain't close to movin' yet," Sinnatha snorted. "That whole settlement is one confusin' mess. Not one soldier stopped me or asked what my business was. I saw St. Clair ridin' down the street. He's grown old and fat and is crippled up with gout. He can hardly even walk. Most of the militia are just sittin' around and waitin'. Nobody really seems to know what the hell they're doin'. I reckon it'll be at least a month before they head north."

Tecumseh clapped the big man on the back. "We must take this news to Blue Jacket and Little Turtle," he said with a smile. "You did well, my friend."

Sinnatha winced. "Next time you go. I stink after two days in that place, and I think I got fleas," he complained, itching at his back.

Tecumseh laughed as the big man stripped of his dirty clothes and headed for the nearby stream, desperate to wash evidence of his visit to the white settlement from his body.

Sinnatha's prediction that St. Clair's army would not set forth for a month had proven to be correct. It was October before the force left Fort Washington and slowly made it's way up the Great Miami toward the headwaters of the Wabash and Kekionga. The timing could not have been more beneficial for the Indians. All the fields of corn, beans, and squash had been harvested and carried away before the advancing army could arrive. Anything that could not be used was burned, leaving nothing for St. Clair's hungry force. Blue Jacket had watched the plodding army from a distance and smiled coldly.

"We will be like the wolves who hunt the lone buffalo," he stated to Tecumseh. "We will nip at St. Clair's flanks and weaken him. When he falters, we will go for his throat."

Pressured by Washington to attack before the end of the year, St. Clair had made the grievous error of leading the army out before it had been properly supplied. The General had left orders for supply lines to be established to provision the army as it advanced north. Trains of horses and mules had followed the slow moving force as it crawled farther and farther away from the safety of Fort Washington. Tecumseh had led Sinnatha, Cold Water, Sauwaseekau, and a dozen other young warriors on lightning raids of the vulnerable supply trains. The attacks had been devastating for St. Clair's main force. Morale declined and desertions increased among the militia as everyone was forced to go hungry. Game was scarce and the fields surrounding the empty Indian villages had been picked cleaned or burned in the army's advance. The few hunters that did risk venturing deeper into the forest never came back.

Blue Jacket and Little Turtle sent war parties under Stands Firm and Turkey Foot to attack St. Clair's advance scouts. The attacks frustrated the general. The Indians would not meet his force in head-to-head combat, and they inflicted such heavy casualties on his scouts that St. Clair was forced to advance blindly into the hostile countryside. Still, the old general refused to turn back.

"We will force them into battle when we reach Kekionga," he assured his officers. "There they must stand and fight; they have no other place to go."

So it was that St. Clair's hungry and demoralized force reached the headwaters of the Wabash in November of 1791. Illness and desertion had taken a toll; nearly a third of the force was gone. Less then a thousand men and another two hundred camp followers, wives, children, and prostitutes, set up camp in a meadow overlooking the Wabash on the night of November 3rd. The day had grown cold, and snow began to fall as dusk settled across the land. Not a single officer thought to order the exhausted men to construct any defensive works as they all hunkered around their camp fires. It was a decision they would all regret.

A thousand warriors crept toward the camp as dawn approached on the morning of November 4th. A blanket of light snow covered the ground as many of the sentries had fallen asleep at their posts. They awoke in surprise and pain as silent warriors slit their throats and lowered their bodies to the snowy ground. Satisfied that enough of his warriors were in place, Blue Jacket raised his fist in the air and let out a bloodthirsty war cry. Hundreds of voices took up the call across the meadow as the warriors fell upon the sleeping camp.

The landscape erupted in screams of pain and shouts of confusion and alarm. General St. Clair stumbled from his tent, dressed only in his long nightshirt. The old man stared at the mass confusion, his jaw slack. Finally, he grabbed a junior officer as he ran past.

"Form up!" St. Clair commanded, struggling into his wool coat. "We're under attack! Form up and stand your ground, for God's sake!"

The militia panicked under the furious attack and fled before the Indian forces. St. Clair's regulars managed to form a battle line under the direction of their officers and fired a volley at Blue

Jacket's warriors, stalling the attack. Unfortunately, the camp had been surrounded and Little Turtle and Apekonit led a flanking assault that killed most of the officers and shattered their line.

Colonel John Drake formed his battalion and ordered his men to fix bayonets. He then led his command in a desperate attack on Little Turtle's force. The warriors gave way and retreated into the woods before the advancing soldiers. Tecumseh and his warriors were waiting. They joined Little Turtle's force as they encircled the advancing battalion and destroyed it.

General St. Clair had finally mounted a horse and surveyed the increasingly desperate situation. He turned his mount toward his artillery, praying the gunners were wheeling the cannons into position to drive the Indians back. The general's hopes were dashed when he saw the artillery being overran by Delaware warriors led by Buckongahelas. Most of the gun crews were down, killed by native marksmen. The rest were racing toward the camp, desperately seeking a safe position. The horse that St. Clair sat upon whinnied in pain and collapsed to the ground, sending the general sprawling in the mud. St. Clair rose to his feet and limped toward another mount. He had to rally his forces or face total destruction.

The mud-splattered commander rode through the camp, shouting out commands among the chaos. Many of the militia cowered in fear under wagons as women and children picked up guns to join the fight.

"Cowards!" St. Clair bellowed. "Stand and fight, I say. Stand and fight if you want to live!"

As hard as he tried, St. Clair could not rally his troops into an effective fighting force. A few groups of soldiers and militia rallied around their officers and counter attacked, only to be cut down by the combined attack of the fierce warriors. Another horse was shot out from under St. Clair as he rode among the combatants. Finally, the old general called his remaining officers together.

"The battle is lost, and we must break through and flee for our lives," he cried hoarsely.

"What of our wounded?" a young captain dared ask.

St. Clair shook his head. "We must leave them behind or we'll all die."

The remaining soldiers and militia formed up and charged forward desperately.

Little Turtle's warriors retreated before them, not realizing that the force was escaping, not attacking. When they were free of the battleground, the remaining troops broke and ran for their lives. A few warriors pursued the fleeing survivors for a short time, but most returned to the meadow to celebrate their victory.

By dusk, over eight hundred bodies lay strewn across the cold ground. The snow had all been turned into red slush as the warriors made their way through the camp, dispatching the wounded and taking scalps. Only twenty warriors had been killed in the fight. No one could remember such a one sided victory ever taking place in the entire history of their nation. The warriors of a dozen tribes surrounded Blue Jacket and Little Turtle as they stood on the bloody field, their arms raised in victory.

Lyman sighed. "St. Clair's Massacre," he stated. "I can't believe you were there. It was certainly one of the darkest days in our country's history."

Ruddell looked at the historian, his eyebrows raised. "What makes you say it was a massacre? I allow it was a fair fight."

Lyman rolled his eyes. "Heavens, Mr. Ruddell. Surely you jest! The Indians killed over six hundred soldiers and wounded just about all the rest. They killed every camp follower as well. That's the death of over two hundred innocent women and children. If that's not a massacre, I don't know what is."

The old man pulled at his whiskered chin. "I recall many a campaign in which white armies wiped out defenseless villages, killin' a boodle of Indian women and children, that were proclaimed considerable victories," he replied quietly. "Fact is the only difference is whether you look at the fix from the daylights of a white man or that of an Indian. In the end, innocent people die in war, on both sides. To the Indians, the defeat of St. Clair was the greatest victory they had ever had."

The writer shook his head. "Still, it's hard to believe that a white man led the Indians to such a victory."

Ruddell raised an eyebrow. "Who do you mean? Wells?"

"I mean Blue Jacket," Draper explained. I've seen many reports that he was actually a Dutch settler named Marmaduke Van Swearingen. He was captured by the Shawnee before the Revolution began and eventually became the war chief that you knew."

The old man snorted. "Blue Jacket was no more white man then you are an Indian."

"What about the accounts of people who knew him?" the writer argued.

"It's all blab!" Ruddell growled. "I knew Blue Jacket for thirty years; I reckon I'd known if he had been adopted into the tribe. The man was born a Shawnee. Now, he married a white woman who had been adopted into the tribe as a child and they had several half breed children, but Blue Jacket himself was a full blooded Shawnee. Them stories are just a bunch of gum made up because folks can't accept losin' to Indians."

Draper decided to move on. "It was a costly defeat for the United States. A good portion of our standing army was wiped out and General St. Clair was forced to resign by President Washington."

Ruddell chuckled. "They say George had himself quite a temper. I sure wouldn't have wanted to be there when he found out what happened!"

President George Washington looked up from his breakfast as his personal secretary entered the room. The sixty-year-old former general vainly adjusted the false teeth he had never grown accustomed to wearing. A formal man, the President was slightly annoyed that the younger man had entered without knocking.

"Good morning, Tobias," he said, wiping his mouth. Washington noticed the younger man's grim stare. "What's wrong?"

Tobias Lear stepped forward and handed the President a slip of paper. "News from the northwest, Mr. President," he replied hesitantly.

Washington reached into his frock coat pocket and took out a pair of glasses and put them on. The president's irritation increased; he detested the glasses as a sign of weakness. He had become a national hero and his ego and vanity caused him to struggle accepting the effects aging was having on his body. Breaking the wax seal, the president scanned the contents of the letter. As he read, Washington's face reddened.

"This has to be a mistake," the president whispered. "The whole army destroyed! How could this happen?"

"It seems that the savages surprised General St. Clair," The secretary began. "The general had neglected to set up breastworks."

The younger man went silent as the President threw the letter down and knocked his breakfast tray from the table before jumping to his feet. Washington slammed his fist into the table with surprising force for a man of sixty.

"Dash!" he raged. "I warned that fat fool! I told him to watch for surprises. I told him how the Indians would fight! To allow the army to be massacred! That no account black guard! Now the whole northwest lies open to the savages!"

The President slammed his hand on the table again in frustration. He removed his glasses and rubbed his temples. Washington moved to the window and placed his arms behind his back. He took a deep breath and contemplated the situation.

"We'll offer them a peace treaty," he stated softly. "After this debacle, there's no reason they will sign it. They'll have a mind they can defeat any force we might send against them. By God, why shouldn't they?"

Washington turned and faced Lear, his jaw set. "We will offer them the treaty. Hopefully, it will stall any designs they have to attack Kentucky. They'll hold councils to decide what to do. That will give us time to raise a new army."

The President walked over to Tobias. At six feet two, Washington towered over the smaller man.

"Find me a general, Tobias," he implored, squeezing the secretary's shoulder. "Find me a man whose brains are in his head instead of his arse! Find me a leader who will be as ruthless as these savages, yet understands and respects his enemies."

Lear swallowed hard and looked up at the man he practically worshiped. "I'll do my best, Mr. President!"

Washington nodded. "See that you do, my boy. Our country is still young and growing. We cannot let a few red devils beat us! How would it look to the British? Or the French? We must handle this quickly, or risk fighting another war. That is something that we cannot afford to do."

Tobias bowed sharply to the President and turned on his heel, exiting the room quickly as one of the house slaves slipped into the room to clean up the remains of Washington's breakfast.

"Begging your pardon, Mr. President" The slave whispered, his eyes looking at the floor. "But do you want me to bring you more fixin's?"

"No, Percy," Washington replied, turning back toward the window. "I've lost my appetite."

CHAPTER 12

QUINCY, ILLINOIS
SUMMER, 1845

"THE OHIO FRONTIER seemed to be defenseless after the losses suffered by Harmar and St. Clair," the blond writer observed, squinting against the afternoon sun. "I would have thought Blue Jacket and Little Turtle would have followed their victories up with an offensive to drive the settlers south of the Ohio River."

The old man snorted. "It shows how little you know about frontier war!" he growled. "Defenseless? Far from it! Those Kentucky and Ohio militiamen were bluff fighters. Any war party sent against Vincennes, Clarksville, or Fort Washington would have suffered powerful losses. Every warrior kilt meant one less hunter for the tribe. Life is much more precious to Indians then it is to white people. Oh, there were plenty of raids back and forth across the Ohio for the next couple of years, to be sure! All and all, most of the fighting wasn't much more then skirmishes."

"All right," Draper conceded. "Were there any 'skirmishes' during this time that you thought were more memorable than others?"

Ruddell scratched his chin for a moment and smiled. "Well, there was that fight Tecumseh and I had with Simon Kenton and his boys down on the East Fork."

"You fought against Simon Kenton?" Lyman gasped.

The former warrior chuckled. "Sure did. Hell, I shot him!"

"You shot him?" the writer repeated, his eyes widening.

The old man smiled. "I didn't kill him. We talked about it years later. I reckon it's a likely story."

Tecumseh, Sinnatha, and a group of ten warriors had been on an extended hunting trip near the mouth of the Little Miami River for over a week. The spring air had warmed and the hardwood trees were beginning to bud and bloom in the lengthening daylight. Game had been plentiful as deer and even a few buffalo had emerged to graze upon the fresh shoots of green grass along the river banks. The hunt had been so successful that Tecumseh had sent the warrior Cold Water back up the Little Miami to return with several women and children to help butcher and smoke the venison. The Shawnee had established a butchering camp on the East Fork of the Little Miami and happily set about curing the meat. The Indians had set up a pair of large canvas tents that had been spoils of the defeat of St. Clair to help ward off some of the chill that still remained in the air during the early spring nights.

The hunters were unaware of a raid a mixed party of Wyandot, Potawatomi, and a few Shawnee had carried out across the river into Kentucky, killing several settlers and stealing a large number of horses. The raiders had triumphantly returned to the Ohio side of the mighty river and headed north, leaving a significant trail not far from the hunting camp. Back in Kentucky, a group of rangers led by the powerful Simon Kenton had set out in pursuit of the raiders.

One of the hunting party's horses had not been hobbled properly and had wandered away from the camp. Tecumseh was preparing to go in search of the animal when an old warrior named Hocaka had insisted on going in his place. Tecumseh had been pleased with the older warrior's enthusiasm and had even let him take his own horse to track the wayward animal. Such was the man's esteem for the young war chief that Hocaka had ridden from the camp on Tecumseh's horse with his chest stuck out in pride.

Darkness had fallen upon the camp without Hocaka returning. Tecumseh had been worried for the older man, but several warriors reminded their leader that it was not the first time the old warrior had lost his way away from camp. Still, Tecumseh had felt uneasy and remained alert for Hocaka's return. The hunters had celebrated and danced into the night before finally retiring to the tents for sleep. Sinnatha had turned to Tecumseh, who remained sitting beside the fire.

"Are you coming?" the redheaded warrior asked.

Tecumseh shook his head. "I cannot sleep in those tents; they still smell too much like the *Shemaganas* that they once belonged to. Nothing smells much worse then a white man."

"Do not be offended," he added, smiling slightly.

"None taken," Sinnatha replied with a chuckle. "I'm quite happy you would rather sleep under the cold stars. The women are all in the tents and are much softer than the ground."

"Be thankful that Stands Firm did not join this hunt," Tecumseh observed. "He may not share your views when it comes to his daughter."

"I believe you are right," Sinnatha replied, his smile broadening. "I will make sure I say a prayer to the Great Spirit before I close my eyes."

Tecumseh shook his head, but did not reply. He had seen the looks that had passed between his niece and best friend over the last few months. He did not disapprove of the relationship. Sinnatha was a good hunter and brave warrior. His skin might be white, but his heart was true. He would make a fine husband for Nika.

Tecumseh waved his friend into the tent and lay down beside the fire, his war club within his reach and his rifle not far away.

Hocaka would not return. The old warrior had been ambushed and killed by the Kentucky rangers a couple of miles away from the camp. The Kentuckians had scalped the Indian and hidden his body in the thick brush along the river bank. Kenton had easily picked up the lone Indian's trail and backtracked the warrior to the camp on the East Fork. The big frontiersman had brought his party of twenty four rangers up within a hundred yards of the tents after the fall of darkness. He turned to the Kentuckians and laid out his plans.

"We'll give'em time to go to sleep," he whispered. "Then we'll move in close on em' and get a volley off into their tents 'fore they know we're here. They should have a conniption fit and run. We'll be able to track down most of the survivors and finish them off with knife and tomahawk."

Nobody questioned the legendary frontiersman's logic. At thirty-seven, he had spent more then twenty years on the frontier. He fame was second to that of only Daniel Boone.

Kenton had left Virginia and fled to the Kentucky frontier when he was only sixteen. The big youth had fought an older man over a girl and had hit his opponent so hard that he was certain he killed him. Fearing punishment by the local authorities, the lad had grabbed his rifle and a few provisions and disappeared into the wilderness. He had gone by the name of Simon Butler and had established a reputation as a hunter and Indian fighter. The man's feats of strength were legendary. He had once saved Daniel Boone from certain death outside of Boonesborough. Kenton had been hunting with the famous scout when they were attacked by a Shawnee war party. The big man had scooped up the wounded frontiersman at a dead run in one arm while holding on to his rifle with the other. He had out paced a score of the Shawnee's best runners with Boone draped over his shoulder and had brought the wounded man back to the fort safely.

To the Shawnee, Kenton was the second most hated frontiersman, behind only Boone as well. He had killed many warriors in fights over the years and every Shawnee warrior dreamed of taking the feared and respected fighter's scalp for themselves. He was called *Psaiwiwuhkernekah Petweowa*, The Great White Wolf. The Shawnee had even captured him a decade earlier and made their powerful enemy run the gauntlet over a dozen times before Simon Girty had asked for his life to be spared and took the man to Detroit.

Since that time, the frontiersman had returned to using his given name and had fought in every major campaign launched against the Shawnee as a scout in the past decade. If caught again, there would be no pardon for the Great White Wolf.

The rangers split into three groups and moved silently to surround the camp. The frontiersmen worked their way to within twenty yards of the large tents before a camp dog caught their scent in the air and began to growl.

Tecumseh's eyes snapped open at the sound of the dog and he rolled to his feet beside a large poplar tree.

"NOW!" Kenton bellowed.

The night erupted in gun fire as the Kentuckians unloaded their rifles into the tents and began to reload. Tecumseh leapt forward with his war club and crushed the skull of the nearest rifleman.

"Sinnatha!" he shouted. "Where are you?"

The big warrior rolled naked from the tent, his rifle in his hand. The darkness was filled with the frightened and confused cries of the women in the tents and the shouts of the warriors and Kentuckians as Tecumseh kicked the fire out.

"I'm here!" Sinnatha dared call, rising to his feet.

"Attack them on your left," Tecumseh called from the darkness. "My warriors will finish those to the right!"

Tecumseh had called out in English for all the rangers to hear. The redheaded warrior knew that his leader was hoping to confuse and frighten the Kentuckians into believing there were more Indians in the camp then they had thought. Hopefully, it would give the Shawnee a few moments to organize a defense.

Sinnatha stepped forward and was knocked from his feet by a powerful figure even bigger then he was. The white warrior lost his grip on his gun as he rolled across the ground. Simon Kenton charged him as he came to his feet, his tomahawk raised to strike. Sinnatha caught the big man in a hip toss and flipped him to the hard ground. Kenton landed with a grunt and rolled to his feet, agile as a panther. The Shawnee warrior had left his tomahawk in the tent and now circled the Kentuckian with only his bare hands as weapons. Kenton leapt forward and took a mighty swing at his adversary. Sinnatha swayed to his left and avoided a blow that would surely have decapitated him. He followed the frontiersman's attack with a powerful left hook to the big man's jaw. Kenton grunted again and stumbled to the ground.

The white warrior leapt back and noticed his rifle lying nearby. He grabbed the gun as the big man regained his senses and charged. Kenton's eyes went wide as Sinnatha shoved the muzzle of the rifle into his chest and pulled the trigger.

The warrior heard a small pop as only a fraction of the powder within the rifle ignited. The summer night air had dampened the charge and caused the gun to misfire. Still, the weapon had discharged with enough force to knock the Kentuckian back, clutching his bruised chest and gasping for air.

Sinnatha tried to seize the advantage and leapt forward, his rifle stock held like a war club. He took a savage swing at the staggering man, but missed. A second ranger appeared in his path, and the white warrior reversed his swing, connecting with the man's head with a sickening thud.

Kenton had seen enough. He scooped up his tomahawk and rifle and sprinted from the camp.

"Scatter!" he bellowed, still gasping in pain.

Unnerved by the darkness and the Indians unexpected defense, the rangers had retreated away from the camp at the sound of their wounded leader's command. Within a minute, the East Fork fight was over.

Tecumseh studied the trail, scowling. Cold Water and the now clothed Sinnatha stood by as their leader examined the tracks. Several Shawnee had been wounded when the Kentuckians had fired their volley into the tents. Tecumseh and his remaining warriors had waited until dawn to check the trail of the retreating *Shemanese*. It seemed that most of the rangers had scattered into the forest as their leader had instructed. The various trails all headed south along the Little Miami toward Kentucky. The Shawnee had moved quickly to pursue their enemies, but found more then half of their own horses missing. Tecumseh had been able to determine that the mounts had been taken by a lone man, riding Tecumseh's own horse. Sending a pair of warriors to scout after the main force of Kentuckians that had headed south, Tecumseh had kept Cold Water, Sinnatha, and two additional warriors to track the horse thief that had headed west.

Tecumseh picked up a piece of horse dung and smashed it between his fingers. "Still fresh," he observed, wiping his hand on the long grass beside the trail. "We are not far behind."

The warriors had silently followed their leader as he moved steadily along the trail. Within a mile, they started to smell smoke from a campfire. Tecumseh signaled for the Shawnee to stop. He edged along the trail and peered through the brush toward small meadow. There he saw a single Kentuckian roasting a rabbit on a spit over a small fire. The ranger was a small, wiry man with dark, curly hair. Behind him, the Shawnee's missing horses grazed in the meadow. The man was dirty and preoccupied with cooking his breakfast. Still, his Kentucky long rifle was at his side.

Tecumseh turned to his warriors and signaled that there was only one man. Without hesitation, the Shawnee leader picked up his rife and charged down the trail as his warriors looked on in surprise. Tecumseh let out a whoop that startled the little man. The ranger grabbed his rifle and bolted from the camp as Tecumseh and his men pursued him. The Kentuckian's short legs could not outdistance the Indians' long strides. Desperate, the little red-headed man turned and raised his rifle. Tecumseh continued to charge as Cold Water and the other Indians dove for cover. Sinnatha watched as the ranger took sight on his friend. Seeing a round stone on the trail, Sinnatha scooped it up and continued forward. The rock was close to the size of his fist and heavy. The big warrior stopped in the middle of the trail and flung the stone at the little man as he prepared to fire, praying to throw off his aim.

Sinnatha's throw was true, almost. The heavy stone whizzed by Tecumseh's head and struck the ranger in the groin. The Kentuckian grimaced in pain and involuntarily fired his rifle, missing the advancing Tecumseh. The little man fell gasping to his knees, holding his injured genitals. Tecumseh ran to his side and knocked his rifle and tomahawk away. The Shawnee leader then shoved the smaller man to his belly and bound his hands with a leather thong he pulled from a pouch at his side. He looked up at Sinnatha and smiled.

"You are a cruel man, Big Fish," he laughed. "You should have hit him in his other head; he would be in less pain."

"I didn't have time to aim." Sinnatha replied, irritated by his friend's recklessness. "You could have been killed."

"No," Tecumseh replied. "He panicked. He could not hold his rifle still enough to have hit me. Still, it pleases me that you are here to protect my life!" he added with a smile.

The Shawnee turned his attention to the little man still gasping at his feet. He reached down and pulled his head back by his curly hair. "Who are you?" Tecumseh demanded in English.

"Alexander McIntyre," the little man replied in a thick Irish accent, still wincing from the pain in his groin.

"Where is Hocaka?" the Shawnee leader continued, glaring at the Irishman.

"Who?" the little man replied, staring blankly.

Tecumseh pointed at his black gelding which still grazed in the meadow. "The warrior you stole this horse from! Where is he?"

The white man shrugged nervously. "Mr. Kenton had us kill him and follow his trail to your camp."

Sinnatha stepped forward. "Kenton? Simon Kenton?" he asked.

McIntyre looked the big man over. "Aye!" he replied. "Mr. Kenton led us up from Maysville after these red devils raided the settlement. They kilt some good people and stole over fifty hosses, includin' a couple of my own! I circled around after the fight to get some of them back."

"You should be ashamed of yourself," the little man added accusingly, "a white man fighting against his own kind!"

"You attacked a peaceful hunting camp and wounded several women," Sinnatha growled. "Our party had nothing to do with the raid on your settlement. Kenton should have realized that when he saw the size of our camp."

"The White Wolf led your attack?" Tecumseh interrupted, hearing the legendary frontiersman's name.

"Aye!" the little Irishman replied proudly. "I followed him into the camp. We would've killed all of you if he hadn't called the attack off after he was wounded."

Tecumseh looked at Big Fish, his eyes sparkling. "The man you shot was Kenton? Brother, if you would have been more careful to not get your guns wet last night, you could have claimed his scalp!" He laughed, referring to the reason why the redheaded warrior had come out of the tent naked.

Sinnatha glared at Tecumseh. "What? And have you and every other Shawnee warrior be jealous of me for the rest of my life because I killed *Psaiwiwuhkernekah Petweowa?* No! I enjoyed gettin' my gun wet a Hell of a lot more then fighting that big bastard."

Most of the horses had startled and run from the meadow when the Irishman had fired his gun. Tecumseh had ordered a pair of warriors to guard the prisoner while he, Sinnatha, and Cold Water rounded up the missing animals. McIntyre had looked on nervously as the trio left the camp. The little man sat beside the fire, his hands tied behind his back.

"You reckon I might have a drink?" he asked, nodding toward a water skin lying not far away.

The warriors ignored him.

"It's whiskey," he added, getting the Indians' attention immediately.

The Irishman smiled and winked. "Untie me, lads! I'd be happy to share a bit of my nectar with ya!"

Several of the horses had strayed far, and it took some time for Tecumseh and the others to round them up. Still, the trio where in a good mood when they worked their way back up the trail toward McIntyre's little camp. They had outfought a larger force of Kentuckians led by the legendary frontiersman and had won. The prisoner that they had taken could be adopted into the tribe or ransomed back to his family in Kentucky. Overall, the Shawnee had come out of the surprise raid victorious.

Tecumseh pulled back on the reins and stopped his horse in the middle of the trail as they rode into sight of the camp. Sinnatha was busy guiding the horses along and looked up in confusion to see why the warrior had stopped so abruptly. He was shocked by the sight before him.

Alexander McIntyre's mutilated and decapitated body lay in the middle of the trail. The Shawnee warriors that had been left to guard him were gleefully kicking his severed head back and forth across the meadow. The warriors whooped and staggered around, the white man's empty water skin lying nearby.

"What have you done?" Tecumseh cried, aghast.

One of the warriors looked up and smiled drunkenly. "We have made a new game!" he slurred. "It is like *baaga'adowe*! We score by kicking the *Shemanese* head past each other. You must try it!"

The drunken warrior's smile disappeared when he saw the furious expression on Tecumseh's face.

"You worthless coward!" Tecumseh raged. "How dare you kill my prisoner?"

"He tried to escape," the other warrior stammered. "He gave us his whiskey and tried to run."

"How could he do that with his hands still tied?" Sinnatha observed, riding up beside the mutilated body.

Tecumseh's eyes narrowed. "You are cowards and liars! I should kill you both."

"The *Shemanese* killed Hocaka and wounded other Shawnee in the camp," the first warrior dared argue. "We killed him to out of revenge for our people."

"He was my prisoner!" Tecumseh hissed. "It was not for you to decide what should happen to him."

The Shawnee war leader shook his head and indicated the body on the trail. "Bury it," he ordered, turning his horse around.

"Come on," he growled at Sinnatha and Cold Water. "We will not stay here any longer."

The drunken warriors looked on in alarm. "What about us?" the second cried, staggering forward. "We need horses."

Tecumseh cocked his rifle and pointed it at the stunned man.

"You cowards will never ride with me again," he replied coldly. "Bury the body and find your own way home. If you ever speak to me again, I will kill you."

Tecumseh rested the stock of his rifle on his hip and rode up the trail, scowling. Cold Water followed silently after his leader.

Sinnatha turned back to the stunned warriors, his expression hard. "Do what he said," he instructed, indicating the body. "Then take any family you have and go to the Shawnee who have moved to the other side of the Mississippi. There you will be safe. If you stay in Ohio, Tecumseh will kill you. He is not a forgiving man, whether you be white or Indian."

Neither warrior argued the big man's point as he turned and nudged his string of horses up the trail after the departing war leader.

CHAPTER 13

QUINCY, ILLINOIS
SUMMER, 1845

LYMAN CLOSED THE LID OF HIS WRITING BOX and stretched his back. He already had pages of notes that would take weeks to review and write in more detail. The afternoon sun had faded in the western sky and dusk began to settle over the Mississippi River. Wisps of fog were beginning to form over the land as the summer air cooled. John Ruddell and his family had returned home from church, ending Draper's interview session with the old man. Stephen had gone out to take care of the team of horses.

"I'll do it, Pa," John had protested. "Why don't you keep talkin' with Dr. Draper?"

The old man looked at his son sharply. "What the Sam Hill do you reckon I been doin' all day? I'll take care of the hosses. I haven't done all creation useful today and it don't sit well with me. Besides, I'm better with hosses then you are. You sit with the dude and talk if you're so concerned about him being entertained."

John threw up his hands, surrendering to his father's scolding. Shaking his head, he walked from the barn as the old man began unhitching and rubbing down the horses. Lyman was waiting outside the barn.

John flashed him a smile. "Well, you're alive. I take it that the day wasn't plum bad?"

Lyman ran his hand through his hair and shook his head. "Your father is certainly the most interesting figure I have ever interviewed. He was there for almost every important event that took place in the early history of the Ohio Valley. I could write an entire book on his amazing life, and he has only told me part of it."

John nodded. "I thought you would be able to get through to him. I know he can be rambunctious, but stick with him, Dr. Draper. His story only gets better, but it's hard on him to tell the end. It may take all your skill to get it out of him."

"Oh, I will certainly do my best. I cannot thank you enough for bringing me here," Draper said.

Both men fell silent as Stephen stalked out of the barn. "What are you two doing here gossipin' like old women? Don't your noses work? Mrs. Ruddell just about has dinner ready."

The old man sniffed loudly and smacked his lips as the aroma of roasting turkey drifted down from the house.

"Come on," he ordered, hurrying past the younger men. "I don't like to eat my turkey cold."

John chuckled. "Nothing can put my father back into a chirk mood more then Sarah's cooking. You might get more of that story out of him yet tonight."

"Well, I must say that I agree with him on at least one point. Your wife is an excellent cook, and I am looking forward to some of that turkey myself," Draper replied, his mouth watering.

The smaller man stumbled forward as John clapped him on the back.

"We'd better hurry up then," he laughed, "or Pa and the boy won't leave any for the rest of us!"

Both men quickened their pace as Sarah Ruddell's supper bell rang out from the back porch.

It had been an excellent meal, as good as Lyman had eaten in years. Sarah had prepared roasted potatoes, biscuits, and green beans fried in bacon fat to go along with the turkey. The little family had laughed and talked, and the little boy had shared how he brought a grasshopper into church and put it down the back of a young girl's dress. The young lady had bound around the pews, screaming and shaking her skirts to get the insect out.

Sarah looked at her son, shaking her head in disapproval.

"That was not a nice thing to do, Stephen," she said sternly.

"Sure it was," the old man cackled. "I reckon it improved the preacher's sermon."

With supper completed, Lyman wandered back to the front porch and packed a pipe of tobacco. As he smoked, Draper looked out into the evening sky.

"It's a nice night," a voice from behind Draper stated, startling him. Lyman turned to see the old man moving out of the shadows.

"I didn't hear you come out of the house, Mr. Ruddell," Lyman replied.

Ruddell signaled for Draper to hand him his tobacco pouch. The old man packed and lit his own pipe. He puffed away for several moments as he looked out into the night.

"The summer of 94' was like this one," he stated. "Hot and dry. Tecumseh and I both enjoyed the nights; it seemed like the only time it cooled down."

Stephen moved to his rocking chair and sat down. "I know you didn't hear me; I didn't want you to," he stated matter-of-factly. "Livin' with the Indians, I learned how to move like an Indian. I spent many a night in the summer of 94' movin' so I wouldn't be heard. I reckon I spent that entire summer watchin' Wayne's army."

"General Anthony Wayne?" Draper gasped, fumbling to open his writing box. He managed to pull out a sheet of paper and a sharpened pencil.

Stephen nodded. "The very same. Washington found his general in Wayne. I know that many people took to callin' him 'mad', but he was smart as a steel trap. Wayne was the most considerable enemy the Indians ever faced."

The old man shook his head. "Wayne did all creation right. He put together a large army and he whipped them into a powerful force. He drilled those men for months, ignorin' all the calls from the east for a fast victory. The man spent over a year plannin' his campaign. When he finally marched north from Fort Washington, he was leadin' an army of four thousand fighting men. That wasn't all, either. He didn't make the same mistakes that Harmer and St. Clair made. He moved slow, buildin' forts along the way and keepin' his supply lines short. His camps were always well-defended and he showed no sign of weakness. It didn't take long for the Indians to give him a new name. They called him the 'general who never sleeps.' They could not surprise him, be it day or night."

Stephen stared off into the night. "I remember it like it was yesterday."

Tecumseh and Sinnatha lay hidden at the edge of a forested ridge as dusk settled over the Ohio Valley. Tecumseh was holding a spy glass to his eye, studying the army encampment that lay before them. He passed the glass to Sinnatha with a frown.

"This *Shemanese* is different. He never lets down his guard."

Sinnatha scanned the camp, observing the strong defensive perimeter that surrounded the camp. "He moves like a turtle; he does not come out of his shell for long. Maybe he fears us."

Tecumseh shook his head in disagreement as he took the spy glass back. "No, this one does not fear us. He understands us and the way we must fight. That makes him a dangerous enemy."

Tecumseh adjusted the lens on the glass and scanned the camp again, intently seeking a sign of weakness.

General Anthony Wayne sat back in his camp chair outside of his tent and observed the army with a small nod of satisfaction. His "Legion of the United States" had met his expectations as the army moved north. A full year of training had made the Legion a disciplined fighting force, and it was all because of Wayne. At fifty, the general was not a young man. He had served with distinction in the Revolutionary War and had experience dealing with The Creek and Cherokee Indians in Georgia. Wayne had left the army for over a decade, but he could not deny the call of President Washington and had returned to lead these troops against the savages that had decimated two previous American forces.

Wayne's long, pointed, nose often reminded those around him of the beak of a bird. Many soldiers had taken to calling the general more then a few names when no officer was around. Yet it was the nickname that had stuck with him through most of his military career that was remembered the most. He was "Mad" Anthony Wayne.

The general chuckled at the thought before wincing as he rose from his seat. The gout in his feet was acting up again, and camp life was beginning to take a toll on the Wayne's body. Ignoring the pain, he slowly made his way to the nearest campfire to warm his hands.

The army commander settled himself down beside the fire and used a burning twig to light his pipe. As he smoked, his aide returned from the evening watch and poured two cups of coffee from a pot hanging beside the fire. The young man offered a cup to the aging general.

"Thank you, Harrison," Wayne said, accepting the cup. "How goes the watch?"

"Quiet, Sir" the young man replied, frowning slightly.

Wayne blew a smoke ring from his pipe and looked at the young man intently. "You say that as if it is a bad thing. Speak up, boy. What's on your mind?"

"We've been on the move for almost two months, Sir," William Henry Harrison sighed. "When will these cowards stand and face us?"

Wayne puffed on his pipe for a moment and studied the younger man. Only twenty one years old, Wayne had promoted the young Virginian up through the ranks because of his attention to detail and discipline. Harrison was not an imposing figure; he was of average height, with dark hair and eyes. His most distinguishing characteristic was a large nose that seemed too big for his face. Still, he had a quick mind and followed orders to the letter.

Wayne took the pipe out of his mouth and cleared his throat. "I like you, Harrison. You might make a considerable soldier someday, if your designs for fame and glory don't get you killed. I have a mind to give you some advice."

The general held his hands out toward the fire and stared into the flames. "Don't ever call these natives cowards. They're more bluff fighting men than any two of our own put together. Respect them for the noble adversary that they are. That was the mistake that those fools Harmer and St. Clair made. Look what happened to them. Are you a fool, Harrison?"

The younger man stiffened sharply and frowned. "No, Sir!"

General Wayne turned away from the fire to face Harrison. "I know what they are saying about me, boy. Some say that I'm frightened to face these savages. Well, they're right," he admitted, his eyes narrowing. "That's why I'll defeat them. If we rush out and attack, we'll be doing exactly what they want. The Shawnee and their allies would slaughter us, just like they did St. Clair. To beat them, we must make them fight the way we desire."

Wayne looked out into the darkness beyond the campfire. "They are out there right now, watching us. I'm certain some of them would give their own scalp to have a chance at me right now."

Harrison smiled. "There's little chance of that happening, Sir. They would have to fight our own men to have the first shot at you."

The old officer chuckled and put his pipe to his lips. "Dash! I'll allow it's a fix I don't want to consider when we finally do see battle."

Tecumseh caught his breath as his spy glass came to rest on the young officer who stood beside a fire at the edge of the camp. The warrior's throat tightened as the young man turned his gaze in their direction. It seemed as if he knew they were watching him, Tecumseh put the glass down.

"What's wrong?" Sinnatha asked, noticing Tecumseh's alarm.

Tecumseh frowned. "I don't know. I think this general has great medicine. The *Shemaganas* who watch over him are very powerful. I fear that we will not find a way to surprise him."

Tecumseh began working his way back into the forest. "Come, we must take this news to Blue Jacket," he whispered.

With a final glance at the camp, Sinnatha followed Tecumseh into the darkness.

"General Wayne seemed to be very canny," Lyman observed, continuing to scribble down notes as the old man rocked on the porch.

Ruddell snorted. "Well, Doc, I reckon that's all creation we agree upon. The son of a bitch was a genius. He knew exactly what he needed to do to beat the Indians. Still, we would have had a chance if it weren't for Little Turtle and Wells, may they both rot in Hell!"

"I don't understand," Draper interjected.

"Damn!" the old man spat. "If you'd quit askin' questions before I'm finished talkin' I'd explain!"

Draper bit his lip and nodded, waiting.

"You need to have a mind that the confederacy that Blue Jacket and Little Turtle had put together was made up of a dozen tribes, many of which were still old enemies," Ruddell explained. "They set aside their differences for a time to fight a common enemy, the

Long Knives. It had been two years since the victory over St. Clair, a coon's age for warriors used to fighting. Some old feuds surfaced among the Potawatomi and Ojibwas and many of their warriors went home before Wayne's army moved north. That wasn't good, but it got worse."

Ruddell leaned back in his chair and looked up at the stars. "Little Turtle got himself a bad feeling about Wayne and announced that he believed that he couldn't be beaten. So, after two victories over American armies the Miami war leader went home and said he wouldn't fight again. A grist of the Miami went with him."

"I reckon I could respect that, wantin' to live in peace," the old man stated, his voice hardening. "Except for the fact that Wells did not go back to Kekionga with the Miami. He joined up with army and became a scout and advisor to Wayne. He betrayed his own people. Oh, how I wanted to meet him on the battlefield."

"No offense, Mr. Ruddell," Draper dared argue, "but William Wells was born white and taken from his family by force. Is he really a traitor if he is returning to his own people?"

Ruddell's eyes flashed, but he remained calm. "All creation Wells did in his life was for his own benefit. He maintained no loyalty to anyone but himself, which is a matter we already discussed."

The younger man held up his hands in submission. "Well, what happened after Little Turtle left?" he asked, changing the topic.

The old man scratched his beard and continued to glare at Draper for several moments before finally sitting back in his chair. "Well, we still had over fifteen hundred warriors to face Wayne, and Blue Jacket was leading us. He knew we wouldn't be able to ambush Wayne or face his army in a head-to-head battle, so he looked for a place that would allow the Indians to stand against Wayne's stronger force.

"You're talking about Fallen Timbers?" Draper gasped.

The old man nodded. "The very same."

Blue Jacket and Tecumseh stood on a low ridge overlooking an expanse of down trees. Fallen Timbers, as the Indians called the area, had been created by a tornado ripping through the forest some years before. Several acres of large trees had been flattened by the storm, scattering the trunks across the ground. Fort

Miami, one of the British posts that still remained south of the Great Lakes, could be seen in the distance.

"So this is where we will fight," Tecumseh stated, observing the battlefield.

Blue Jacket nodded, his expression solemn. "Yes, it's the best ground. The *Shemanese* will not be able to use their cavalry. It is the only chance we have to make the fight more even with Little Turtle and so many other warriors gone," he added sourly.

Tecumseh looked toward the fort. "Will the British help us?"

Blue Jacket shrugged. "They say they will. If we beat the Long Knives back, I am sure they will come out of their fort to help chase them. If we don't, then who knows what they will do?"

Tecumseh shook his head. "This is not our way. This General Wayne makes us fight as the white men do."

"We will not surprise them this time, brother," Blue Jacket sighed. "We cannot retreat before them anymore or they will destroy our winter villages and food stores. We will make our stand here."

Tecumseh turned toward the war chief. "I will stand with you, brother!"

Blue Jacket managed a smile. "I know, Tecumseh. You will lead your warriors well tomorrow."

As they turned to leave, Tecumseh looked toward the vast web of dead trees, wondering if it would prove a strong defensive position or a burial ground in the battle to come.

Blue Jacket's warriors had purged their bodies and prepared for battle when Wayne's army had encamped on the banks of the Maumee, less then two miles from Fallen Timbers. They had prayed to Weshemoneto and fasted the entire day before applying their war paint and taking up their positions among the ruined trees as dawn broke across the Ohio sky. They silently held their positions and waited for the *Shemaganas* to move forward.

General Wayne was shaving his face with the help of small mirror as the camp came to life around him. He carefully ran the razor under his chin and dipped the blade in a pan of water to rinse it. He noticed the edge of the blade was beginning to dull and he deftly sharpened it on his leather strop as William Henry Harrison rode up to his tent and dismounted. The junior officer saluted the general sharply. Wayne acknowledged the younger man with a nod and went back to shaving. When he was finished, he turned toward the waiting Harrison.

"What news from the scouts?" Wayne asked, wiping his face with a white towel.

"The savages have massed behind a patch of fallen trees about two miles away." Harrison reported excitedly. "Do you wish for me to call assembly, General?"

Wayne picked up his mirror and examined his shaven face, running his hand down his throat to check for stubble. "No."

"Sir?" Harrison asked, his excitement vanishing.

Wayne moved to his writing table and sat down. He dipped his pen in an ink well and began scribbling down some notes. Finally, he looked up at the young officer.

"Blue Jacket has his warriors ready to fight. They have fasted and sung their death songs," the general explained. "To attack then right now would be suicidal! We will wait. Let their empty bellies growl and weaken them! Spread the word; any man not on duty has a day of rest."

Harrison saluted General Wayne once again. "Yes, Sir!"

The younger man turned to leave, but hesitated. "General, you're either a military genius or a fool."

Wayne smiled broadly at the honest statement and chuckled. "Many have said that about me. You may be the first to say it to my face, outside of President Washington, that is!"

The General winked at Harrison. "I suppose we'll find out which it is in the days ahead."

Harrison shook his head and turned on his heel to leave the tent. He had orders to issue.

The morning fog had burned away from the land around the battlefield as the warriors waited impatiently. The summer sun beat down on the open field as the day slipped into early afternoon. Tecumseh's gaze never wavered from the Maumee and the direction of Wayne's camp. A feeling of uneasiness had taken root in the pit of his stomach. He stood up as he caught sight of his brother, Sauwaseekau, running through the woods. The younger warrior had been placed as a scout and was to report back any information to Blue Jacket and Tecumseh. Tecumseh broke into an easy trot and reached Blue Jacket as Sauwaseekau arrived, winded from the long run.

"Well?" Blue Jacket barked impatiently as the scout caught his breath.

"They do not come!" Sauwaseekau gasped. "I watched the camp all morning. Most of the *Shemaganas* lay sleeping or play games."

Stands Firm had moved up beside Blue Jacket and Tecumseh to hear the report. The grizzled warrior frowned and turned toward Blue Jacket. "What do we do?"

Blue Jacket scowled and shook his head. "We wait. There is nothing else we can do."

Tecumseh pulled Sauwaseekau aside. "Go back and watch the *Shemaganas* carefully, brother. Let me know the moment anything changes. This general is like a fox; we must not take our eyes off him. You are our eyes; don't let us down!"

Sauwaseekau nodded solemnly. "I'll watch them like an eagle," he stated, turning and running swiftly along the river valley toward the camp.

Tecumseh watched him go, confident in the younger man's abilities. He waited for Sauwaseekau to disappear into the forest and turned to take his place among the downed trees. He frowned when he caught sight of Loud Noise lumbering across the field toward him.

"You should be with the rest of our warriors, brother," Tecumseh stated as the large man arrived. "What's wrong?"

Loud Noise looked up at Tecumseh, shifting nervously and rubbing his hands together. He had painted a black stripe across his eyes. Tecumseh thought his brother now reminded him of a fat raccoon seeking some way to escape as he stood before him. The war leader could see the fear in the man's one good eye.

"I came to see what I could do for you, brother," Loud Noise mumbled. "Maybe I could go back to the village and get more herbs to take care of the wounded?" he added hopefully.

Tecumseh shook his head. "Our people need you here; I need you here! All our men must fight if we are to win this battle. Now, go back to your place among the timbers. When the fighting starts, I will be beside you."

Loud Noise hung his head at his brother's reprimand and shuffled off without another word. Sinnatha moved up to stand beside Tecumseh. The powerful man had his red hair tied back in a pony tail and was wearing a white linen shirt to help protect his pale skin from the summer sun.

"You should have let him go," Sinnatha observed. "He is frightened and will be no use to us in battle. I would wager that he might run when the fighting starts."

"No, he will fight, as will we all." Tecumseh replied evenly. "This battle might very well determine the future of our people. Even Loud Noise will play his part."

Sinnatha smiled. "I'll say. I think half a dozen warriors have passed out from all the wind he has made behind his log. Many of them would have you send him to the village for a while just so they can breathe clean air."

Tecumseh snorted.

Sinnatha could not stop. "Better yet, you should put him at the head of the valley. When Wayne's army arrives, he can shit himself and drive the whole force back to the Ohio."

Tecumseh chuckled softly and shook his head. "I don't know which of you is worse. You both try my patience. Go back to your place before I mistake you for a *Shemanese* and have our warriors kill you."

Sinnatha snickered, noticing the slight smile that now creased his friend's stress filled face.

"Very well," he conceded, "but don't expect me to stand next to that wind bag brother of yours. That place is reserved for you and any other warrior foolish enough to come within ten feet of him!"

Sinnatha turned and made his way through the trees, smiling as he heard the quiet laughter continue as he left.

Sauwaseekau and a young Delaware warrior continued to watch the movements of the *Shemaganas* that remained camped outside the Maumee River valley. The Shawnee scout sighed and frowned at the quiet camp. He had diligently watched Wayne's army through the night, looking for signs of movement. As night turned toward dawn, the young warrior had become nervous with anticipation. The sun had risen steadily in the eastern sky and the camp continued to remain silent. An hour of daylight had passed and Sauwaseekau knew that both Tecumseh and Blue Jacket would be expecting a report. Finally, he turned toward the Delaware scout.

"Go tell Tecumseh that the Long Knives still won't leave their camp," he sighed. "I will stay behind and watch what they do."

The Delaware nodded and looped off to take the news to the Indian leaders.

Tecumseh had gathered with Blue Jacket and the other war leaders after one of the scouts had appeared and made his way through the tangle of fallen trees. Tecumseh recognized the young Delaware that he had assigned to assist Sauwaseekau. The warrior came to a halt in front of the war leaders, his expression troubled.

"The Long Knives do not move." he gasped. "They remain in their camp as they did yesterday!.."

Tecumseh cursed and kicked the dirt. Turkey Foot, the Potawatomi leader who had led his forces in both previous victories over the Long Knives stepped forward, a scowling.

"Our warriors must eat," he stated. "They grow weak and will soon be unable to fight. Let this coward Wayne sit in his camp, we will starve to death before he comes out to face us."

Several other war chiefs murmured their agreement. Tecumseh frowned and shook his head. "It would not be wise to let any of our warriors leave; the Long Knives could attack at any time."

All eyes turned toward Blue Jacket. He rubbed his eyes and growled in frustration. "Release every third warrior to get food; we cannot fight for long if we have no strength."

The war leaders dispersed to relay the orders to their warriors.

Blue Jacket turned back to the Delaware scout. "Get something to eat and rest. You can return to Sauwaseekau later in the day."

The young Delaware nodded gratefully and made his way down the valley toward the villages. Tecumseh remained behind, Sinnatha at his side.

"Something is not right," he said to Blue Jacket, glancing in the direction of Wayne's camp. "This general is no fool, nor is he a coward. He doesn't move against us for a reason. Splitting up our warriors may be what he wants to happen by waiting so long to attack."

Blue Jacket squeezed the younger warrior's shoulder. "I understand your concern, brother, but we don't have a choice. Turkey Foot is right; we cannot fight if we are weak."

General Wayne stepped out of his tent at noon. The bright summer sun had driven all coolness from the Maumee valley. Wayne adjusted his knee high leather boots and placed his trifold cap upon his head. William Henry Harrison rushed to the General's side as he finished adjusting his battle uniform.

"Is everything ready?" Wayne inquired, unbuttoning his coat against the stifling heat.

"The men are prepared to assemble on your command, general." Harrison replied evenly.

Wayne nodded in calm satisfaction. "Then the command is given."

Sauwaseekau was startled awake by the sound of a drum. The Shawnee scout had grown tired in the summer heat and had fallen asleep while observing the camp. The warrior's eyes widened as he watched the soldiers quickly form ranks and begin to march toward the Maumee Valley with speed and discipline. The scout rubbed his eyes, convinced he was dreaming the impending attack. His mouth went dry and his heart raced in fear of what he was seeing. He had to warn Tecumseh and Blue Jacket before it was too late. The scout jumped to his feet and rushed through the forest, willing all speed from his athletic frame to warn the Indian forces of Wayne's surprise move.

Sinnatha and Tecumseh rose from their places behind a large poplar log as the sounds of drums beating became clear. Sunlight glinted off rifle barrels in the distance and the sound of four thousand sets of boots marching in beat to the drums could be heard across the valley. Sauwaseekau burst from the forest and rushed toward the Indian's position.

"They're coming!" he shouted, his eyes wide. "The entire army is coming!"

Sinnatha cursed and grabbed his rifle, checking the flint and making sure it was primed. Tecumseh looked around at the Indian force. Many of the warriors sent to find food were still gone. Less then a thousand remained to face the full attack of Wayne's army. The Indians were outnumbered close to four to one! Sauwaseekau ran to his brother's side.

"I'm sorry," the young warrior sobbed. "I fell asleep and did not see the army preparing to move. It's my fault that we have been surprised."

"No, the fault is mine," Tecumseh replied calmly. "I knew that the *Shemanese* were doing something to fool us, and I did not see what was happening. I also didn't send someone to take your place after you had watched the camp all night."

Tecumseh placed his hand on his brother's shoulder. "None of that matters now. We must fight as we have never fought before. Take your place among the trees. We will need the strength of all our warriors to win this battle."

Sauwaseekau wiped the tears from his eyes and nodded in understanding. He gathered up his rifle and ran off to find Loud Noise.

Blue Jacket was moving among the trees, his teeth bared. "The Long Knives are finally here," he snarled, his deep voice booming across the battlefield. "Prepare yourselves!"

Tecumseh moved to his place in the center of the valley. Here is where the fighting would be the heaviest and where Blue Jacket had placed Tecumseh and the Shawnee warriors to bear the brunt of the attack. Sinnatha stood silently next to Tecumseh, his rifle ready. Nearby, Loud Noise hunched behind a log, shaking in fear. Sauwaseekau had regained his composure and taken a place to the left of Tecumseh with Cold Water and Stands Firm. Tecumseh took a deep breath and exhaled slowly. Their position was still strong and manned by experienced fighters. Wayne's army would pay a high cost in attempting to push the Shawnee back.

Wayne's force continued to move forward deliberately. The disciplined ranks marched steadily closer to the mass of fallen trees. Tecumseh was not certain how many of the *Shemaganas* had moved within striking distance, but he could tell that the entire army was not engaged. When the soldiers and advanced within fifty yards, Blue Jacket signaled to attack.

The mass of warriors rose up from behind the downed trees and fired. A score of soldiers collapsed to the ground and the advance halted. The Long Knives returned fire as the Indians took cover behind the trees. A second volley from Blue Jacket's warriors caused the line to falter, and then finally break as the soldiers retreated from the deadly fire.

Turkey Foot, the zealous Potawatomi leader, had been placed in charge of a group of mixed warriors to the right of Tecumseh's position. The war chief gave a triumphant whoop and eagerly led his warriors after the retreating *Shemaganas*. Warriors all along the defensive line eagerly leapt forward to join the Potawatomi's attack. Tecumseh grabbed Stands Firm as he made to move out into the open.

"No! Stop!" Tecumseh commanded, yelling after the attacking warriors in vain. "It's a trick!"

Few heard his warning and continued chasing the retreating soldiers.

Turkey Foot pulled up at the sound of hoof beats, realizing his mistake too late. Wayne's Calvary, led by Harrison, thundered in from the left flank and decimated the warriors who had so eagerly raced into the open. The Indians tried to run to the safety of the fallen trees, but most were cut down. Tecumseh saw Turkey Foot fall. The Potawatomi leader had bravely stood his ground and was killed by a sword thrust from the aide Tecumseh had observed through his spyglass a few nights before. Tecumseh took aim at the officer, but the man rode out of range before he could get off a shot.

General Wayne smiled slightly as he watched the battle from the crest of a small hill. "Beautiful! Now use the cannons." he commanded.

An ensign used a flag to relay the order to Captain Porter's artillery company that had taken position on a low ridge well behind Wayne's force. The general had experienced the results of effective artillery fire during the revolution and intended to use what he had learned on this campaign. Wayne had not only drilled his infantry relentlessly, but his artillery force as well. The results were devastating for the Indians.

The cannons thundered and accurately dropped shells full of grapeshot among the Indians defensive position, decimating scores of warriors and causing those that were not hit to scramble for cover. The uprooted trees proved to be as much danger as cover for the warriors as the exploding shells ripped through the wood and showered the Indians with flying splinters that caused as much damages as the cannon balls.

Wayne smiled as the artillery pounded the Indian forces into disarray. He turned toward an aide.

"Send in the rest of the troops," he ordered. "Now is the time to break them."

The soldier saluted and ran to issue the General's orders as Wayne turned back toward the battle, his arms crossed behind his back.

Ignoring the deadly barrage, Tecumseh watched as two thousand soldiers rushed forward, their bayonets gleaming in the afternoon sun. The precise artillery fire ceased when the advancing force was within one hundred and fifty yards of the Indian's position. The war leader gritted his teeth.

"*Oui-shi-cat-to-oui*, be strong!" he bellowed. "Hold your positions!"

"Mad" Anthony Wayne had drilled his infantry relentlessly to prepare them for this moment. The disciplined troops swarmed over the logs and threw their superior numbers against the struggling warriors. This was not the militia of Harmar or St. Clair. These were soldiers who had been hardened for battle and fought as such. Yet, these Indians had defeated every army that had been sent against them and they were fighting desperately to protect their land and homes.

The battle quickly reduced to close quarter, hand-to-hand combat. Shawnee, Delaware, and Miami warriors were clubbed by rifle stocks and pinned to fallen trees by thrusting bayonets. Soldiers fell to blows from tomahawks and war clubs. Gun fire erupted across the battlefield and mingled with the grunts and screams of the men locked in deadly combat.

Tecumseh crushed the skull of a red-bearded soldier with his war club and blocked the bayonet thrust of another with his tomahawk. A tall officer appeared behind him as he grappled with his bayonet-welding adversary. The officer raised his sword to strike, but crumbled to the ground as Sinnatha shot him through the heart. Tecumseh clubbed the soldier and nodded toward his friend in thanks.

A blond soldier had Loud Noise on the ground, his rifle pressed to the fat Indian's throat. Loud Noise's considerable strength was the only thing keeping him from being strangled by the rifle stock. The soldier gritted his teeth and growled, pressing down on the Indian with all his strength. Loud Noise could smell the stench of the soldier's breath and felt the rifle tighten against his throat, choking the life from him.

Suddenly, Sauwaseekau appeared above the struggling pair and drove his tomahawk into the soldier's skull. Loud Noise was splattered with blood and brain as the dead man slumped forward. He pushed the lifeless body aside and gasped for air. Sauwaseekau yanked his twin to his feet. He was bleeding from several wounds, but Sauwaseekau showed no fear. He thrust a tomahawk into Loud Noise's hand.

"Fight, Brother!" he cried, turning to engage another advancing soldier.

Loud Noise rubbed his throat and looked across the battlefield. The situation was hopeless. Wayne's army was steadily pushing the defenders back. Dead and dying warriors lay strewn in the wake of the awful *Shemaganas*. Loud Noise looked to Tecumseh as he desperately tried to rally his warriors. Cold Water, Stands Firm, and the hated Sinnatha all fought beside him. Sauwaseekau had dispatched another soldier and was moving to Tecumseh's side as well. Loud Noise gripped the tomahawk tightly and shook his head. He did not want to die. Glancing to his left, he saw an open path to the forest. Looking one final time toward his brothers, Loud Noise slipped over a log and fled the battlefield as Wayne's infantry pressed the relentless attack.

Tecumseh and his core of Shawnee warriors stubbornly held their ground as the mass of soldiers drove the other defenders back. Soon, the Shawnee were engaged on three sides. An infantry captain took careful aim at Tecumseh with a flintlock pistol as the warrior blocked a soldier's bayonet thrust and crushed the man's skull with his war club. Sauwaseekau knocked a young soldier from his feet and saw the officer cock the hammer of his pistol. Without hesitation, the brave warrior stepped in front of his brother as the officer fired. The lead ball burrowed into Sauwaseekau's forehead, killing him instantly.

Tecumseh saw his younger brother fall and cried out in anguish. With a growl of rage, the war chief rushed the officer before the man could react. Tecumseh struck the soldier a savage blow to the neck with his tomahawk, nearly decapitating him. As the man fell, Tecumseh dropped to his knees at his brother's side.

Sinnatha saw Tecumseh cradle Sauwaseekau in his arms. The powerful warrior rushed to his leader's aid, knocking several soldiers aside as he charged. Sinnatha arrived in time to block the bayonet thrust of another soldier that had appeared behind the kneeling warrior. The surprised man looked up as Sinnatha swung his rifle like a club. There was a sickening crack as the soldier's neck broke under the force of the blow. Sinnatha shook the grieving war chief roughly.

"Come on, Tecumseh!" he shouted. "We must retreat!"

The warrior pulled away. "NO!"

"The battle is lost here!" Sinnatha pleaded. "Maybe we can regroup at the fort. If you stay here, they will kill you. Your brother would have died for nothing."

Tecumseh looked up, tears running down his cheeks. "Help me carry him. I will not leave him to be scalped by the Long Knives."

Sinnatha nodded and helped his friend lift the dead warrior. Together, they staggered from the field as Wayne's infantry drove the last of the defenders from their defensive positions among the trees.

British Major Thomas Campbell looked down at the warriors massing below the closed gates of Ft. Miami. Campbell had been ordered to provision the natives and to observe the battle, but nothing more. His superiors in Canada had issued a clear directive that the British soldiers of Ft. Miami were in no way to take part in the battle or provide protection for any of the combatants. Not only could Campbell not help the Indians, but he had to deny shelter for Captain Alexander McKillop and his company of Canadian volunteers who had fought beside the Indians as well. When the battle had begun, Campbell had ordered the gates closed and barred.

The massed warriors had begun the pound on the gate, pleading for the British to help them. Campbell watched silently as Blue Jacket limped to the front of the crowd. The Shawnee leader looked up at the British Commander, his angry face covered in blood.

"Open the gates, Campbell," he howled in English. "Your king promised us protection."

"I cannot," Campbell replied, unable to look the war chief in the face. "My orders are to only observe."

"We call still win with your help." Blue Jacket pleaded. "Use your cannons on the Long Knives! Help us!"

"I cannot," Campbell repeated forcefully. "His majesty will not allow it. You should flee before the Americans capture you."

Blue Jacket pounded his fist against the heavy gate.

He gritted his teeth and glared at the British officer. "No white man can be trusted. We will remember your treachery! Pray that I never find you outside your walls!"

The defeated Shawnee chief signaled for the gathering warriors to fall back into the forest.

General Wayne chuckled as he observed the scene through his telescope from his position on the hill overlooking the battlefield. William Henry Harrison had dismounted from his horse and joined the victorious commander.

"The British won't open their gates," Wayne exclaimed. "I knew they didn't have the balls to risk another war."

The general put down the telescope and turned toward Harrison. "Well, my boy. It seems that we have won a great victory."

Harrison nodded in agreement. "You will be a hero, Sir!"

Wayne laughed. "So it seems, as will you."

You have a chance to go far, Harrison," Wayne added, shaking the younger man's hand. "Remember what you have learned from this campaign."

Harrison saluted his commander sharply. "I will, General. Perhaps I will someday have the honor of being called 'Mad' as well."

Wayne chuckled heartily. "Come, let's go tell those English bastards that they need to get their arses off American soil."

General "Mad" Anthony Wayne mounted his horse and rode toward Ft. Miami as his soldiers cheered his name. William Henry Harrison sat erect in the saddle, basking in the moment, as he rode beside the victorious commander.

Tecumseh stood silently looking down at Sauwaseekau's fresh grave. Sinnatha, Loud Noise, Blue Jacket, and a score of Shawnee warriors stood behind him.

"What will happen now?" Tecumseh asked Blue Jacket, not taking his eyes from the grave.

"They will make us sign another treaty," Blue Jacket replied softly. "We will lose most of our lands."

Tecumseh looked up, his face dark. "I will not sign."

Blue Jacket sighed. "We don't have any choice; we are beaten."

Tecumseh turned to face his war leader, his eyes hard. "We are beaten, but not defeated. I will never make peace with the Long Knives; too much of my family's blood has been shed."

Blue Jacket shook his head. "I am tired of fighting, brother. I have seen too many of our young men die. I grow weary of our women and children starving in the winter because our crops have been destroyed and our homes burned. It is time for peace. I will sign the treaty."

Tecumseh frowned. "So be it," he whispered.

Tecumseh turned and walked away from Blue Jacket, closely followed by Loud Noise and Stands Firm. Sinnatha made to follow his friend, but Blue Jacket stopped him.

"Reason with him, Big Fish," the older man pleaded. "There is nothing more that we can do. We must try and protect what we have left."

"At what cost?" Sinnatha countered. "Will you now dress as a white man and give up our way of life? I once lived in such a way and will never do so again. Do you believe that Tecumseh could live as the *Shemanese*? You might as well ask the sun to stop rising. As long as his heart still beats, Tecumseh will continue to fight."

Blue Jacket looked at the ground, defeated. "Someday, I will mourn his death greatly. I hope it is later, rather then sooner. Watch over him, for all our sakes."

Sinnatha gripped the former war chief's wrist and nodded, before turning to follow the man he now recognized as the leader of the Shawnee people.

CHAPTER 14

FORT GREENVILLE, OHIO
AUGUST, 1795

SINNATHA CAUTIOUSLY MOVED DOWN the trail toward the new fort General Wayne had constructed after his victory at Fallen Timbers. The stockade was bigger than any ever before built on the frontier, its log walls encompassing over fifty acres of land. Soldiers of Wayne's "Legion of the United States" were everywhere. Sinnatha felt his stomach tighten as he stood outside of the main gate. He could feel the eyes of a dozen men he still considered his enemies watching him as he walked through the gate. Inside the fort, warriors and chiefs of tribes throughout the Great Lakes had gathered to make peace with the *Shemagana* chief who had so soundly defeated their combined forces a year earlier. Sinnatha shook his head as he thought back on the events of the past year.

Wayne had not ended his campaign with his decisive victory at Fallen Timbers. The canny leader had burned villages and destroyed crops, weakening the tribes further with the onset of winter. Wayne forced all the British soldiers and traders to leave the lands south of the Great Lakes. He burned the British forts and trading posts so they could no longer supply the tribes and stir up trouble. The general had then ordered the construction of the massive fort in the spring of 1795. With the structure complete, he called for all tribes to send representatives to meet with him so a "lasting" peace could be agreed upon between the tribes of the lakes and the United States.

Tecumseh refused to attend the peace negotiations. Instead, he sent Sinnatha to observe the talks and report back what was decided. The white warrior had agreed to go reluctantly.

"You should not do this," Nika had argued a final time as he handed her the reins of his chestnut mare. She had insisted on riding with Sinnatha to the negotiations despite her misgivings. "Blue Jacket will be able to tell my uncle what happens," she reminded him once again when he had dismounted just out of sight of the fort. "You are to be *ni-da-ne-thuh*, my husband. Your place is with me."

"You already sound like *ni-wa*, my wife," he replied with a smile. "I thought you are suppose to do what I say."

Nika snorted and tossed her long hair in response.

"Tecumseh trusts me to tell him everything the *Shemanese* say and do at this treaty," he reminded her, patting his bride-to-be on the thigh as she sat her horse at the edge of the trail. "I use to be one of them. I speak their language and know the ways of the *Shemanese*, Blue Jacket does not. Tecumseh knows this. You must trust me as well."

"It is the *Shemanese* that I do not trust," she retorted, tears streaming down her face.

Sinnatha pulled Nika close and kissed her deeply. "I will return in a few days," he assured her before heading down the trail on foot.

Now he stood at the edge of the crowd of Indians, silently watching the proceedings and hoping they would end quickly so he could collect Nika and report back to his chief.

A platform had been built in the center of the fort specifically for the signing of the new treaty. General Wayne, his legs swollen with gout, sat on a sturdy wooden chair in the center of the platform. A clerk sat at a small table to his right, drawing up the treaty papers as William Wells stood nearby. The former Miami warrior was very much a white man again, dressing as such and using his Christian name once again. He had worked as a scout for Wayne's army and had become a confidant of the General during the past year, working closely with the commander to arrange for the different tribes to be represented at Greenville. Sinnatha felt the bile rise in his throat as he stared at the hated traitor. Oh, what he would give to have the chance to face the man alone!

Wayne looked over the assembled Indian leaders and nodded toward Wells. The redheaded man stepped forward, his face emotionless. He unrolled the terms of the treaty and cleared his throat. "All chiefs who sign this treaty promise to never take up the hatchet against the United States again. All lands between the Ohio and the Auglaize River now belong to the United States, and all tribes will leave these lands within the next year."

Wells looked up as a murmur of dismay rose from the crowd. He noticed Sinnatha standing to the side of the group, his arms folded across his chest. The former Miami warrior smiled slightly as he continued to read the terms of the agreement.

"Finally, all white captives will be turned over to the United States immediately. Failure to do so will bring swift punishment on any tribe who withholds said captives from returning to their rightful families."

Wells rolled the document up and stepped back as General "Mad" Anthony Wayne rose from his chair. The commander stepped forward, his arms folded behind his back. He gazed upon the assembled Indian leaders, his face stoic.

"You are all warriors, as am I," he stated matter-of-factly. "I will hold you to your word. If you break this treaty, I will break you," he added forcefully, looking directly at Little Turtle and Blue Jacket.

"This is a good treaty, one that will last many lifetimes. It is time for peace between our peoples. Enough blood has been shed," he added, a hint of remorse in his voice.

Wayne signaled to the sentries and the appointed chiefs were escorted forward. Little Turtle glanced at William Wells and then became the first to mark the treaty. Sinnatha felt his stomach tighten as Black Hoof stepped forward and signed the treaty without hesitation. Several chiefs of the Delaware, Potawatomi, Ottawa, and other tribes stepped forward and made their mark. Finally, Blue Jacket made his way to the platform. The old war leader hesitated for several moments, his lined face tormented by the decision he was forced to make. Finally, the former war chief picked up the quill and signed his name to the treaty.

Sinnatha shook his head and moved to leave the fort. He walked through the gate and made his way to where he had left his mount. A pair of soldiers blocked his path just outside the gate. William Wells stepped out from the shadows, a triumphant smile on his face.

"Howdy, Sinnatha," he sneered. "Where are you going?"

"I'm leaving," the powerful man replied, looking down his nose at the soldiers in front of him. "The stench of this place sickens me."

"Didn't you hear the terms of the treaty?" Wells chuckled. "You're white, and you're staying here!"

Sinnatha glared at the former Indian. "I'm my own man," he declared. "I'll go where I please."

He turned back toward his horse, but another pair of soldiers moved to block his path.

Wells stepped forward. "Come now, Stephen. That is your real name, ain't it?" he mocked. "The life of an Indian is finished. Come back to your own kind. What? Do you have a squaw? Bring her along to take care of your home when you get a white wife. That's what I'm doing. Two is always better than one, if you know what I mean."

The soldiers laughed at the crude joke. Sinnatha turned and took advantage of the distraction to hammer Wells to the ground. He jumped on the hated man and punched him repeatedly. The surprised soldiers leapt forward and drug the furious man off the former Indian. Wells shook his head to recover his senses. He pushed a soldier away and rose to his feet, wiping blood from his face and spitting out one of his teeth. Enraged, he pulled a knife from his belt and advanced on Sinnatha, a murderous look in his eye.

"STOP!" a deep voice boomed.

A large officer with thick, auburn hair stalked through the gates. The big man inserted himself between Sinnatha and the enraged scout. "What is the meaning of this, Wells?" he demanded, scowling at the smaller man.

"Nothing I can't handle, Lieutenant Clark," Wells responded, his face twitching. "This white Indian was trying to go to brush and he blasted me when I tried to stop him. I was just about to fix his flint."

William Clark turned an appraising eye on the warrior. He took note of the man's powerful frame and red hair, similar to that of his own. Wells was telling the truth; the warrior restrained before him was a white man. The sentries had stripped their prisoner of his weapons and had pinned his arms behind his back. Even so subdued, the big man glared at Wells, his chin thrust forward defiantly.

"Go ahead, you hen-hearted black guard!" Sinnatha growled in English, "Five against one is the only way I reckon a cully like you could ever best me."

Wells' eyes widened at the string of insults. The former Miami warrior raised his knife and stepped forward with a snarl.

"Stand down, Mr. Wells," Clark ordered, blocking the smaller man's path once again.

"I'll not hear his gum," the scout protested, still holding his knife ready to strike.

"Then you are dismissed," the big officer retorted, placing his hand on the hilt of his sword. "I will take charge of this prisoner; it is evident you have a personal grudge against the man. As you said, he is white and being such must remain unharmed. I'm cock-sure his safety is in doubt if he is left in your care."

Wells hesitated. He wanted nothing more then to thrust his blade into the white Shawnee's heart, but he had also witnessed the formidable Virginian's prowess in battle at Fallen Timbers. The big man was strong and fearless and the former Miami warrior had no wish to fight him. He decided to change tactics.

Wells sheathed his knife and folded his arms across his chest. "General Wayne will hear of this."

"I will tell him myself," Clark retorted, still fingering the hilt of his sword. "After all, it was General Wayne who signed my commission into the legion at the request of my brother, George Rogers Clark."

William smiled when the scout's eyes widened at the mention of his famous brother. "The General thought it was the least he could do for a hero of the revolution," Clark added pointedly, finally releasing the hilt of his sword. "By all means, file any protest that you wish. I will certainly hear what the General has to say when he and I take tea in the afternoon."

Clark leaned in close so only Wells could hear him. "I've grown sour of your company," he whispered. "General Wayne does not cotton to fools. I suspicion that he might find your usefulness in decline should I report this incident to him."

Wells swallowed hard, knowing he would gain no favor from the general against the young officer. He turned on his heel and stalked away, casting Sinnatha a final murderous glare as he went.

Clark turned back to the soldiers restraining the redheaded warrior. "Release him," the big officer ordered.

"He's a hostile, Sir!" one of the men argued.

"Dash!" Clark snorted. "I reckon he's no more hostile then I. Now do as you are told before I have your court martialed."

The sentries released their hold on Sinnatha and stepped back. The warrior rubbed his wrists and eyed the young officer carefully. "Thank you," he stated evenly.

"Welcome," the big man replied, hooking his thumbs into his belt. "What is your name?"

"Sinnatha."

Clark smiled. "I meant your Christian name."

Sinnatha hesitated. He was thankful the officer had come to his aide and sent Wells away, but the warrior knew that he was still a prisoner and this man was his enemy. "I was known as Stephen," he finally offered, "but it has been many years since I have been known by that name."

The big officer nodded. "Do you remember your last name?"

"Ruddell."

William Clark offered the former white man his hand. "Stephen Ruddell, I am pleased to meet you."

Sinnatha frowned but shook the officer's extended hand. He hoped his cooperation might assure his release to return to Tecumseh.

"I hope you understand I cannot release you," Clark stated apologetically, dashing Sinnatha's hopes. "The terms of the treaty are clear; all white captives shall be returned to their families."

"I am not a captive," the warrior argued. "I wish to remain with the Shawnee."

Clark shook his head. "That is not possible. General Wayne will not allow it. I understand your attachment to your adopted people, but what of the family that birthed and raised you? Your return will surely bring your mother joy."

"My mother is dead," Sinnatha replied, wincing at the painful memory. "I have not seen my father or sisters in fifteen years. I don't know if they are even alive."

The officer nodded sympathetically. He had heard similar stories from other former captives that had been returned during his time on the frontier. Still, the terms of the treaty must be adhered to.

"That may be, but there may be other kin who wish to see your return," Clark stated, raising his hand to cut off the warrior's reply. "Allow me to offer you some advice, Ruddell," he continued, seeing the man's face flush with anger. "Cooperation is your only course of reasonable action. Return to your family and you will have met the terms of the treaty. You can then make your own choice to remain with your kin or leave."

"And if I choose not to cooperate?" Sinnatha countered.

"Then I will be forced to place you in chains and put you in the stockade until arrangements can be made for your return," Clark replied, his eyes hardening.

Sinnatha hung his head and sighed in defeat. He did not doubt the big officer's words. "I'll go back," he replied softly, continuing to stare at the ground.

"Very good," Clark replied, motioning toward the sentries. "Escort Mr. Ruddell to the barracks. I will speak with General Wayne about the arrangements for your return myself."

Sinnatha looked up as he reentered the fort, catching sight of Black Hoof and several warriors as they exited the gate. He was hopeful for a moment that the former war chief might intercede on his behalf. Those hopes faded when he looked at Black Hoof's face. The Shawnee leader frowned and shook his head sadly. The once proud warrior raised his hand in farewell and continued out the gate without stopping.

Sinnatha's shoulders sagged. He covered his eyes with his hand to hide his tears.

The old man sat back in his rocking chair, his eyes closed against the pain of the memory.

"You did not want to go home?" Draper whispered, the shock evident in his voice.

The rocking chair stopped. It was past midnight and the darkness of night covered the expression on the old frontiersman's face. He rose from his chair and stalked toward the house.

"It's time to go to bed," he announced, his voice strained.

Lyman did not reply but remained where he was sitting. He hoped that he had not offended the old man to the point he might refuse to speak to him in more detail. Worse yet, Draper did not doubt that the former preacher might still resort to violence if he had been personally offended. It was with this thought fresh in his mind that he entered the house.

Ruddell had retired to his room and Lyman breathed a sigh of relief. He made his way to the guest room and undressed quickly. He was exhausted from the strain of the day. He was asleep not long after he put his head on the pillow.

Lyman's heart skipped a beat when he awoke to find the former frontiersman sitting at the foot of his bed. It was obvious that the sun had been up for some time, as had Ruddell.

"Get dressed," the old man ordered gruffly. "Everyone else is gone. John needed Sarah's help at the store today and they took the boy with them. She left you some doings on the stove, if you're hungry."

Stephen rose without waiting for a response and exited the room. Draper dressed quickly and moved to the kitchen. The old man had placed a warm plate of food on the table and was pouring two cups of strong coffee. He sat one on the table for Lyman and took a sip from the other.

"That's good," he said, smacking his lips. "I'd allow hot coffee in the mornin' is the one comfort that I longed for during the time I was with the Shawnee."

Draper yawned and took his place at the table, his stomach growling. "Thank you for letting me sleep, Mr. Ruddell."

Stephen waved off the comment and sat quietly sipping his coffee as Draper ate the late breakfast of fried eggs and bacon. Finally, the old man refilled his coffee cup and moved toward the front door.

"When you're done, join me on the porch and we'll talk about my joyful reunion with my kin," the old man stated sarcastically.

Draper swallowed hard and nodded.

Lyman found the old man sitting in his rocking chair, nursing his cup of coffee. He had finished his breakfast and had gone back to his room to collect his escritoire before returning to the porch. Ruddell was staring in the direction of the river and took no notice of the younger man's arrival. After several moments, he turned his gaze toward the writer.

"No, I reckon I didn't want to go home," he admitted quietly. "I don't recall many whites that were raised among the Indians who truly did, though you could not get many of them to acknowledge the corn today. I had lived with the Shawnee for fifteen years, more then half of my life. I had forgotten what it was like to live as a white man. I was lucky, I reckon. Thanks to Tecumseh wanting to learn English, I had kept my ability to speak the language. Abe was a plum different story."

The old man shook his head. "Abe had never cotton to livin' with the Shawnee, but he had spent a coon's age away and no longer hankered to live as a white man either. He only spoke broken English, and he had split his ears to wear feathers and ringlets like many Indians do. He was plum streaked when the Shawnee brought him in. All-fired, I don't reckon he recognized me as his own brother. General Wayne made contact with our pa and he come up from Kentucky to get us."

Ruddell ran his hand through his white hair and rocked back in the chair. "I still recall the look on Pa's face when he saw us for the first time in fifteen years."

Stephen looked up as the door opened and William Clark entered the barracks.

"He's here," Clark stated. "Your father is meeting with General Wayne as we speak. I am to take you to him."

"What is he saying?" Abe questioned in Shawnee.

Stephen looked at his younger brother. It had been two months since the Treaty of Greenville had returned the sons of Isaac Ruddell to white society. Missionaries had given both men new clothes to wear. Stephen had accepted the linen shirt, but would not give up his buckskin leggings. Abe had refused everything and remained dressed in the same deerskins that he was wearing when he had been brought in. His split earlobes dangled about his shoulders as he stared suspiciously at the big Virginian.

"We are to go with him," Stephen replied in Shawnee. "Our father waits for us."

Abe snorted in response but followed his brother's lead when he rose from his seat and followed the officer out of the barracks.

General Wayne's quarters were dimly lit by a single window and it took a few moments for Stephen's eyes to adjust to the darkness after Clark had led him through the door. He was able to finally make out the General's portly frame seated behind a maple desk. Wayne nodded toward the corner of the room.

"Here they are, Mr. Ruddell," he stated softly. "I hope you will see the boys you left behind in the faces of the men who now stand before you."

Stephen turned as a figure rose from a chair in the darkened corner and stepped out of the shadows. He did not know the old man frowning before him. His hair was completely white and sixty years of hard living had left him stooped and frail. It was not until he looked into the old man's eyes that Stephen recognized his father.

"Is this our father?" Abe called out in Shawnee from the place he had taken beside the door.

The old man's frown deepened upon hearing his son speak. Both men looked like Indians, not the sons that had been taken from him fifteen years earlier. It was more then he could stand. Isaac sat back down heavily and put his face in his hands. "My children are Indians!" he sobbed.

Stephen stepped forward and place his hand gently on the old man's shoulder "Hold your heart, father," he softly stated in English. "Hold your heart."

Isaac glanced up when he heard the big man call out in English, but his tears continued to flow. He had held his heart for fifteen years, dreaming of the day he would be reunited with his boys. This was far from what he had envisioned.

Stephen sat across the campfire from his father as the old man puffed on a long stemmed clay pipe. General Wayne had assigned a detachment of men under a Colonel named Trabue to escort the Ruddells back to Fort Washington. From there they would return to Kentucky where Isaac had established a sawmill and gristmill just south of their old settlement on the Licking River. William Clark had taken Stephen's hand the morning the party had mounted up to leave.

"Good luck to you, Ruddell," he had said. "You might find it difficult to return to the life you had before the Shawnee took you. Should that be the case, remember that there is always a need for interpreters on the frontier. Your years among the Indians have made you a valuable man."

Stephen did not sense that his father shared William Clark's sentiments. The old man could not look at either of his sons without frowning.

"He should let us go," Abraham stated in Shawnee as they sat beside the fire. "We do not belong with him and he hates us for becoming Shawnee."

"Speak English!" the old man commanded. "I can't understand what you are saying."

"He does not remember how," Stephen replied quietly.

Isaac shook his head and took another puff from his pipe. "I reckon I should not be surprised. How is it that you at least remember how to speak like a white man?"

"Tecumseh wanted to learn," the younger man began.

"So you taught him," The old man finished, glaring at his eldest son. "Don't tell me anymore. I had hoped for better from you. I would not think you would have been so helpful to the savages who killed your mother."

Stephen had listened to enough. "I remember who killed my mother," he growled. "I was the one who killed him, not you. You surrendered the fort to the British and Ma ended up getting killed because of it. You told me to stay put and wait for you to come back when they marched you off to Canada. I did just what you said, but you never came back," he added, pointing a finger at his father accusingly. "The war ended and you still did not return. What was I suppose to do? I thought you were dead, so I did what I could to survive."

The old man stared at the ground, crestfallen by his son's harsh words. "There was nothing I could do," he whispered.

Stephen took a deep breath to cool his anger; already regretting what he had said to the old man. "What happened to you father?" he asked softly.

Isaac stared into the fire and continued to absently puff on the clay pipe. "Byrd marched us on to Detroit after we left you boys. I was able to gain audience with the Commandant there and I filed a complaint against Captain Byrd for his treatment of prisoners of war. He cottoned to my grit and allowed me to settle on some land outside of Detroit and grow corn to help feed the other prisoners. I worked that rocky soil for two years, doin' all creation to help out all those from Kentucky that I could. I was even able to help a few escape. Finally the war ended and they allowed me to take your sisters and go back south."

The old man's frown returned. "I would have come for you then, except I was charged with treason and had to stand trial in Fredrick County."

"What?' Stephen interrupted, his jaw dropping.

"Some of the other prisoners suspicioned I had been given special treatment and allowed it was because I was working for the British. I was accused of being a traitor and had to stand trial," he spat. "I had fought with Clark and was a Captain in the militia, but I had to answer questions about my loyalty. My wife and baby were dead and I had lost my boys, yet my loyalty was still questioned."

Isaac stirred the fire with a stick, sending a cloud of sparks streaming into the October night. "I was acquitted, but several people had to speak on my behalf before that could happen. I didn't have much left after that. So I took your sisters and went back to Kentucky. I couldn't care for the girls by myself so I remarried. I was able to start the mills, but it took some time before they were profitable enough for me to ransom you back. The fighting between the United States and Shawnee had gotten worse and I couldn't find a trader who was willing to take my ransom in to get you back. It wasn't until after Fallen Timbers that I was able to find any trace of you. I was already headed north when General Wayne's letter found me. "

A commotion at the edge of the camp drew the attention of both men.

Nika walked into the camp leading Stephen's chestnut mare.

"Stop," Colonel Trabue ordered, stepping into the woman's path. "What do you want here, squaw?"

Stephen stepped forward. "She's with me, Colonel."

Trabue hesitated. His orders were to escort the Ruddells back to Ft. Washington, not deal with indians. He nodded to the former warrior and walked back to the fire he shared with his men.

Nika dropped the horse's reins and fell into the big man's arms. "You have been gone longer then a few days," she reminded him.

Stephen chuckled at her directness. He took her hand and led the young woman back to the fire. "Pa, this is Nika," he stated proudly.

Isaac looked down his nose at the Indian woman and let out another puff of smoke. "Who is she?"

"She is to be my wife," he replied with a smile.

"Send her back," The old man stated bluntly. "She will not be welcomed in Kentucky."

Stephen's smile disappeared. "She is to be my wife," he repeated.

The old man shook his head. "Folks will already be hostile to you boys for all the time you spent with the Shawnee. How well do you reckon they will treat her? Her place is with her people, not yours."

Stephen stuck his chin out defiantly. "Her place is with me," he declared. "I will not send her away."

"So be it," Isaac sighed. "I reckon you'll figure out the truth of the matter soon enough."

Stephen responded by pulling Nika closer to his side, determined to hold on to the last thing that remained of his old life.

CHAPTER 15

Paris, Kentucky
June, 1796

Stephen stepped out of the church and jammed his felt hat on his head. He had ridden into Paris to speak with Reverend Thomas about marrying he and Nika, but the conversation had not gone as the big man had hoped.

"I can't do it," the thin minister had replied firmly when he heard the request. "The woman is a heathen. She has not been baptized in the eyes of the lord and refuses to come to church."

"She is not allowed to sit in a pew next to me," Ruddell countered. "She would be forced to remain in the back of the church and is shunned by the rest of your congregation. Who would hanker to be treated in such a way?"

"That may be," Thomas said, adjusting his wire-rimmed spectacles nervously, 'but there are other matters to consider."

"Such as?" Stephen pressed, his cheeks beginning to flush in anger.

"You spent fifteen years among the savages and have yet to redeem your own soul," the minister blurted. "You must be baptized again to wash away the sins you committed while you lived among the heathen."

Stephen was speechless. He had done his best to adjust back into white society over the past several months. The big man had worked and sweated at his father's mills and attended church diligently. Retaining the ability to read had allowed him to study the bible again as well, a skill he now called upon.

"I reckon I did spend a coon's age with the Shawnee," he began, fixing the minister with an intense stare. "I recollect that Moses and his people spent forty years in the desert before the lord led them to the Promised Land."

"You speak of the Book of Exodus," Thomas replied, adjusting his spectacles once again. "What of it?"

"Well, the good lord led me home in fifteen years. I reckon that's twenty-five years better than Moses and his folks. Maybe my sins ain't as bad as you suspicion."

The minister's face turned bright red. "Good day, Mr. Ruddell," he whispered, his bottom lip quivering. "I suggest you find a different church to attend, you and your squaw are beyond any salvation I could provide."

Stephen had mounted his horse and ridden north out of Paris toward his father's gristmill. The June sun was hot, but the big man remained cool in his buckskin leggings. The fact that he had refused to give up his Indian garments was just another detail of his life that Stephen and the elder Ruddell continued to disagree upon.

Issac looked up from his ledger as his eldest son entered the mill. The old man took note of Stephen frown and set his quill down on the old table that served as his desk. "Well?"

"He refused, as you said he would," the big man admitted, dropping into a chair opposite his father. "He didn't cotton to what I had to say on the matter. I suspicion you will have to talk to him before Reverend Thomas allows any of us back in his church."

The old man shook his head and sighed in exasperation. "I had plum forgotten how stubborn you could be. You never listened when you was a brat, I reckon I shouldn't be expectin' you to listen as a grown man."

"Your squaw is leaving." Isaac continued, picking his quill back up.

"What?" Stephen cried, his jaw falling open.

"I saw her and your no account brother talkin' with some other Injun out on the trail. She come in and started packing her things," Isaac explained, gesturing toward the storeroom that had served as Nika's bedroom since their arrival back in Kentucky.

Stephen leapt to his feet and bound out of the room.

"I told you she did not belong here!" his father called after him.

Stephen found Nika on the loading dock. She had rolled her belongings in a blanket and was strapping the roll to the back of her bay gelding. Abe sat on the edge of the dock, sipping whiskey from a clay jug as he watched Nika prepare to leave.

"Where are you going?" he demanded.

Nika looked up at the big man, brushing her dark hair out of her troubled expression. "My brother is waiting on the trail. He is going to visit some of our family among the Creek. I have decided to go with him."

It took several moments for her statement to sink in before Stephen could reply. "When will you return?"

"My brother has brought other news," She continued, ignoring his question. White Swan wishes to leave Ohio and travel to the Shawnee who live on the other side of the great river. Black Hoof will not leave his village. Your mother asks for you to take her there."

"When will you return?" the big man repeated.

Nika sighed and looked Stephen in the eyes. "There is no place for me in your world, *ni-da-ne-thuh*. I will not return."

Stephen took the young woman's hand. "Don't go," he pleaded softly. "I just need more time to get folks to accept you."

Nika caressed the redheaded man's cheek gently. "The *Shemanese* will never accept me, their hatred runs too deep. I do not belong here, we must both accept this."

Abe chuckled drunkenly as he watched the exchange. *Ni-je-ni-nuh* does not understand," he slurred in Shawnee. "He still believes he can change people's hearts."

"Don't you have some maple syrup to boil?" Stephen snapped.

Abe's smile disappeared. He hurled his empty whiskey jug against the mill wall and staggered to his feet. Stephen stepped forward, waiting for the smaller man to attack. Drunk as he was, Abe hesitated. Not for love of his brother, that bond had long since been broken. Stephen's prowess as a fighter was well known and the younger man had no true desire to face him. Abe glared at his older brother before stumbling away from the dock.

Nika pulled the angry man back to her side. She wrapped her arms around his powerful neck and gave him a long kiss before leaping to her horse's back.

"*Ni-wa*," Stephen began, reaching out for her.

"No!" she stated forcefully. "We will never be married. I cannot live in two worlds, Sinnatha. I will remain with the Creeks and you will remain here. We will not see each other again," she added, tears streaming down her cheeks.

Stephen watched helplessly as Nika kicked her horse into a gallop and disappeared down the trail.

It was another month before Stephen finally decided to leave. He strapped his pack and rifle to the back of his chestnut mare and went looking for his father. He found the old man at the ruins of the old fort, smoking his pipe on the cabin steps.

"Your leaving," Isaac stated matter-of-factly.

"White Swan needs me," Stephen explained. "She wants to move beyond the Mississippi, but has nobody to take her. She treated me as a son while I lived with the Shawnee, I reckon I need to take care of her."

"Your mother died right over there," the old man whispered, pointing toward the gate. "You would leave your own people behind to run back to the very savages that murdered her?"

"I don't belong here anymore, pa," the big man stated gently. "We both know it."

"Because of the Shawnee," Isaac argued. They kilt your Ma and turned you and your brother into one of them. It is bad enough that they kilt my wife, but I reckon it burns my soul to see my boy go back to livin' as savages!"

"It's not your fault, Pa," Stephen replied, placing his hand on his father's shoulder. "It was the war that killed Ma and took us away from you."

The old man grimaced and slapped the big man's hand away. "Go," he cried hoarsely, "I want no more to do with you. All that I have will go to your sisters and half-brother when I die. I can't abide with you choosin' to be with murderin' heathens. Who's mother do you reckon you'll kill? Who's child will you steal away and turn into a savage?"

Stephen bit his tongue and swung onto the mare's back. He looked down at his father for the last time. "I've killed more then my share of men in my day, both red and white," he admitted, his expression hardening. "I reckon I've seen enough death for a dozen lifetimes. I'll spend the rest of this one doin' my best to prevent bloodshed, be it white man or Indian. I wish you well, pa. I don't reckon we'll meet again."

The big man did not wait for a response. He pulled the horse around and galloped north without looking back.

"So what did you do after you left Kentucky?" Draper asked.

The former frontiersman smiled. " I helped White Swan settle with some of the other Shawnee in Missouri. I hunted for the tribe and cared for White Swan. She was old when we left and only lasted two years. Still, she spent her last days in peace and comfort. It was during that time in Missouri that I decided that I could best serve the Shawnee people by helping them work for peace. I realized that the Indians wouldn't be able to whip the United States in battle, not in the end. So, I joined the Baptist church and became a missionary preacher with designs to go among the Shawnee and help them find a peaceful way to live with the Long Knives."

Draper scribbled notes down furiously. "What happened to Tecumseh during this time?"

Ruddell scratched his chin, his expression troubled. "The years after Fallen Timbers and the Treaty of Greenville were hard for Tecumseh. It always haunted me that I wasn't with him during those bad times. He was huffed at Black Hoof for making peace and broke from the Shawnees at Wapakoneta. He moved beyond the treaty lands and started a village on the White Water River in Indiana. Many Shawnee went with him, including Loud Noise and Tecumpese. Tecumseh married and had a son, but his wife died in childbirth. He gave the boy to Tecumpese to rear and rode back to Ohio alone."

Stephen shook his head. "It may have been the saddest days of Tecumseh's life, the time that he felt the most defeated."

Tecumseh rode his black mare along a trail beside the Little Miami River. "I am now on white man lands," he thought bitterly.

The trail opened into a wide field that Tecumseh recognized as the site of the former Shawnee capital of Chillicothe, his childhood home. The warrior dismounted at the edge of the field and moved forward slowly. It had been almost twenty years since Chillicothe had occupied the site, but Tecumseh remembered it well. He made his way to where Black Fish's wigwam had stood. Noticing something in the dirt, he bent to inspect it. He smiled slightly as he wiped dust away from the bowl of an old tobacco pipe. He was certain it was the remains of one of Black Fish's pipes that he had always been so fond of quietly smoking outside the wigwam entrance.

The warrior heard a whisper of movement behind him. He rose to his feet and allowed his hand to trail close to the handle of his knife. Suddenly, Tecumseh whirled and pulled the blade from the sheath at his side, ready for a fight. A lone white man was standing beside a hickory tree some twenty feet from the warrior. The bearded man held his hands out in a gesture of peace.

"Easy, friend," the man stated calmly, a slight smile appearing on his bearded face. "I mean you no harm. I just had a mind to see what you were doing in my hayfield."

The man's friendly manner helped the warrior to relax and Tecumseh sheathed his knife.

"This was my home..." he replied hesitantly, "many years ago."

"Ah," the white man replied, his smile broadening. "I knew there had been a village here. You are a Shawnee?"

Tecumseh nodded. "Yes, my name is Tecumseh."

"Tecumseh?" the man repeated, stepping forward. "Well, I say any man should be welcome in his old home. I'm James Galloway, and I'm pleased to meet you."

Galloway stuck his hand out toward the warrior and smiled. Tecumseh looked at the outstretched hand. He hesitated briefly, then shook Galloway's hand and returned the smile.

"My wife has supper almost ready; would you join us?" the white man offered sincerely.

"Yes," Tecumseh replied, surprising himself. "Are you sure that eating with an Indian would not frighten your family?"

Galloway laughed heartily. "Wait until you meet my family. I'd allow more concern about you being streaked to eat with us."

The two men made their way toward the distant cabin as dusk settled over the open field.

James Galloway had built a sturdy, two story cabin of old growth hickory for his large family. The house was full of children of various ages, from teenagers down to a giggling infant. Tecumseh smiled as the settler wrestled with one of his small sons. Mrs. Galloway, a blond woman in her mid thirties, brought a large platter of meat from the kitchen and sat it on the wooden plank table.

"Please, Tecumseh," she stated warmly. "Help yourself. James shot a deer this morning, so there's plenty to eat."

Tecumseh smiled. "*Neahw*, thank you."

"No, thank you for coming." she countered. "We have few visitors here. It's good to have someone else to talk to."

The woman turned back toward the kitchen. "Rebecca! Bring the bread."

Rebecca Galloway entered the room carrying a loaf of brown bread. Tecumseh was drawn to the child. She was a pretty girl of about twelve years of age with long, blond hair and striking blue eyes. She sat the loaf on the table.

"It's fresh from the oven," she stated in a soft, cheerful voice.

The girl glanced at Tecumseh and looked at the floor.

"Now don't be rude, Rebecca," Galloway coaxed. "Say hello to our guest. This is Mr. Tecumseh, and he's a considerable Indian chief who use to live here!"

Tecumseh stood as the girl blushed and curtsied politely.

"Hello, Mr. Tecumseh," she said, smiling at him shyly.

"Please, just call me Tecumseh."

The meal had ended and Galloway's sons went out to check the stock while Mrs. Galloway put the younger children to bed. James made his way to the sitting room with Tecumseh. He winced and let out a low moan and rubbed the side of his neck as he settled into his favorite chair.

"The weather is changin'," Galloway exclaimed. "I can feel it comin' on."

"Old wound?" Tecumseh asked, taking notice of the scar that the man was rubbing.

"Aye!" Galloway replied. "Courtesy of one Simon Girty. He gave it to me back in 82'. The black guard near done me in."

"I know Simon Girty," Tecumseh replied innocently. "He has always been a friend to the Shawnee."

The settler packed his pipe with tobacco and used an ember from the fireplace to light it. He smiled and passed his tobacco pouch to Tecumseh. "It seems we have differin' opinions of the man. I'm just thankful he can't shoot straighter."

Galloway slapped his leg and laughed at his own joke. Tecumseh managed a smile and packed his own pipe. The warrior took several puffs and looked around the cabin. His gaze settled on a bookcase on the far side of the room. He rose from his place beside the fire and moved to examine the shelves.

"You have many books." Tecumseh stated in amazement.

"Yes! My wife was a school teacher," Galloway replied proudly. "When we moved here she made me tote every one of them books with us! She said our children weren't going into the wilderness without the necessities to provide them a proper education."

Rebecca had moved into the room and watched their guest with obvious interest as he ran his hands over the rows of books. "Do you read, Tecumseh?" she asked, moving to stand beside her father.

"A little," he admitted. "I had a friend who taught me to speak English and to read. I wish that I knew more."

"I could teach you," the girl replied excitedly, turning toward her father. "Would it be alright, Papa?"

Galloway puffed his pipe for a moment, silently contemplating the situation. "Well, I reckon so, if Tecumseh wants to learn. He may have more important designs then spendin' his time here."

"I will stay, at least for a while," the warrior replied thoughtfully. "It is good to see my homeland."

Galloway rose from his chair and smiled, holding his hand out toward his guest. "Our friends are always welcome, Tecumseh. I hope you will come to our home whenever you like."

Tecumseh returned the smile and took the settler's outstretched hand. "Then I will come often. You are a good man, Galloway, and you are my friend."

"Ah!" Draper interrupted. "I have heard about Tecumseh's relationship with the Galloway family in Ohio. There was always speculation that Tecumseh fell in love with the daughter, Rebecca.

Some say he wanted to marry her, but she wanted him to give up the life of an Indian. He refused, and they went their separate ways. I always assumed the stories were nothing more then romantic fiction."

The old man scowled. "You seem to have quite an opinion about a fix that you got no first hand knowledge of."

Draper began to reply, but the former frontiersman cut him off. "The Galloways were some of the first settlers to budge up the Little Miami and settle in the old Shawnee lands. That land was sacred to Tecumseh, and all Shawnee. It was likely for different warriors to return to the area, especially the old men. A boodle came back to die where they had been born. Tecumseh spent a coon's age with the Galloways. He learned about history and speech from Rebecca and her father kept him up to date on all the changes goin' on in the United States and Ohio. It was from Galloway that Tecumseh first heard about William Henry Harrison, and how powerful a body he was becomin' on the frontier."

Tecumseh and James Galloway sat before the cabin fire, smoking their pipes. The war chief had spent a great deal of time with the Galloway family in the past year, staying for weeks at a time. The settler smiled through his thick beard.

"You've learned right smart durin' your visits with us, Tecumseh," he observed, blowing a smoke ring. "We are all pleased when you visit, especially Rebecca."

Tecumseh returned the smile. "It is always good to see you, my friend. I enjoy spending time with your family. It does my spirit good to be in this place."

The warrior lowered his pipe and looked at Galloway, his expression serious. "I have questions for you, *ne-kah-noh*," he state solemnly. "They are questions that only a white man can answer for me. Will you tell me the truth?"

Galloway puffed on his pipe for a minute before nodding respectfully. "I've never lied to you, Tecumseh. I don't hanker to start now."

Tecumseh nodded in satisfaction. "There are many rumors of this man, Harrison. Will you tell me about him?"

Galloway leaned forward in his chair, always eager to talk. "Well, you know that he was at Fallen Timbers. He became a hero of some circumstance and used that fame to become a considerable man in the territory. He got himself appointed Secretary of the Northwest. They say he wants to separate the Northwest Territory into two parts, Ohio and Indiana Territory. Ohio could soon be a state."

Tecumseh frowned. "I remember when there were no states. Now they are like rabbits; more come every day. Will it never end?"

The settler blinked and looked at the floor. "It is a terrible thing, my friend, but it will not end," Galloway admitted. "In the east, there is no land. Here, there seems to be plenty...."

He could not finish his statement as Tecumseh leapt to his feet, his eyes flashing. "My land! My people's land!"

Seeing the settler's startled expression, Tecumseh calmed himself and sat back down. "Forgive me, *ne-kah-noh*," he stated quietly.

Galloway shook his head. "You have a right to be huffed, Tecumseh. When I was younger, I didn't see that. As I grow older, I become wiser, or at least less stubborn. You don't need to apologize."

The bearded settler repacked tobacco into his clay pipe and lit it again. He puffed silently for several moments before turning toward Tecumseh. "If they do form a new territory, there'll be a new governor. You reckon who that might be?"

Tecumseh's brow wrinkled. "Harrison? That would be as bad as having Wells as the Indian agent."

Galloway nodded. "Maybe worse, my friend. He's got highfalutin designs, could be President some day. Watch out for him, Tecumseh."

The warrior frowned and emptied out his pipe. Finally, he held his hand out toward Galloway. "I must leave tomorrow, *ne-kah-noh*. It may be some time before I return."

Galloway took Tecumseh's hand. "My door is always open."

Tecumseh mounted his horse in front of the cabin. The entire family had assembled to see him off, with the exception of Rebecca. He smiled at the Galloway family. "I will return when I can."

Without waiting for a reply, the war chief nudged his mount into a trot. Out of the corner of his eye, Tecumseh noticed a figure on the ridge overlooking the trail. He reined the horse to a halt and waved at the blond-haired girl. Rebecca managed a smile and waved in return.

With one last glance at his former home, Tecumseh kicked his horse into a gallop toward the western horizon.

CHAPTER 16

WAPAKONETA VILLAGE
SPRING, 1800

A LONE RIDER reined his horse up at the crest of a hill over-looking the Shawnee village. He shook his head as he took in the view. The cluster of homes before him looked much like many of the small, white communities he had passed through on his journey, only more ramshackle and destitute. Stephen Ruddell sighed. The black shirt and white collar of a minister that he wore over his buckskin leggings seemed out of place on the big man. Adjusting his collar, he nudged his horse and descended the trail into the village.

It had been five years since he had left the Shawnee. Ruddell was not coming back as *Sinnatha*, the warrior who had fought at Fallen Timbers. He was once again a white man. Stephen rode into the village as a Baptist minister, sent to save the heathen. He looked around as his horse cantered down the muddy street. Several Shawnee men sat or lay on rough cabin porches, clutching whiskey bottles and staring listlessly. All the village occupants were dressed in the wool and linen clothing of frontier settlers. Pigs and chickens wandered about the filthy streets. Few of the villagers even glanced at the white man as he rode among them.

Stephen caught a glimpse of a familiar figure working in a small garden at the edge of the village. Dismounting, the large man walked toward the garden. A stooped Shawnee man worked at breaking the muddy soil with a hoe. Intent on the task at hand, he did not hear the minister's approach.

"*Bezon, no'tha,*" Ruddell stated warmly.

Black Hoof stopped hoeing. A slight smile cross his wrinkled features as the old chief pushed his gray hair out of his face and turned to face the younger man.

"*Bezon, ni-kwith-ehi,*" he replied, his voice still strong. "My heart rejoices that you have returned."

"I never thought I would see the day you would work in the fields."

Black Hoof looked down at the hoe and frowned. "Much has changed. We are no longer warriors; we live as the great white father says we must. Look around! We beg for everything we have from the *Shemanese.*"

"Even you, *ni-kwith-ehi,*" he added, a hint of disappointment in his voice. "Have you not returned to us as a white man once again?"

Stephen stepped forward and took the hoe from the old man's hands. "I am a servant of God. I care not the color of a man's skin. I am here to help the people, *no'tha.*"

Tears fell from the old chief's eyes. "I'm happy you have come back."

Black Hoof stepped forward and hugged the younger man close as many of the villagers began to gather around the pair, ready to welcome one of their own home.

Lyman put down his pen and rubbed his eyes. The old man had stopped the interview to do some morning chores. He now stood in the barnyard, scattering corn for the chickens. Draper closed his writing box and walked down the porch steps to join him. Ruddell looked up as the writer stopped at the edge of the flock.

"Did you keep chickens when you were a brat?" Stephen asked, tossing out another handful of corn.

Draper nodded. "It was one of the first chores I remember having as a child. I had to feed the chickens and gather the eggs for my mother."

Ruddell cast out another handful of kernels. "It really is a simple task. We whites teach our children how to do it when they are young, and that chore is passed down from family member to family member. It becomes second nature."

The old man dumped out the last of the corn for the hungry chickens and looked at Draper. "How would you know how to take care of chickens if you or anyone around you had never seen a chicken before in your life?"

Lyman thought about the question for a moment before shrugging. "I don't know; I never considered the possibility."

Ruddell shook his head. "Neither had I, until I was the one trying to teach the Shawnee how to care for chickens and hogs. It was plum fat-headed for Shawnee men and they struggled with the different aspects of farming mightily."

"But the Shawnee had raised corn, pumpkins, and beans," Draper argued. "You have said so yourself. I fail to see how the farming would be that different."

Shawnee *women* raised corn and beans," the old man replied pointedly. "Shawnee *men* hunted and fought. Warriors used to torment male prisoner's who hankered to work in the fields with the women. A man who wanted to stay and work with the women was not considered a man. You can't change a way of life by handing a warrior a hoe and tellin' him to grow potatoes! Those men felt they were being forced to give up being men and they were ashamed. So, very few were successful farmers and many turned to alcohol to ease the shame they felt. I spent the next five years ministering to them, teaching them to farm, and helping the Shawnee to build a better life."

Ruddell leaned against the barn and looked out over the barnyard. He pulled a plug of tobacco from his pocket and bit off a hunk.

"I never saw Tecumseh during that time," he stated, spitting tobacco juice at one of the hens that had wandered too close, sending her flapping away. "There were always stories about him. He spent most of his time among the other tribes of the Northwest, warning them of the ambitions of Harrison and the United States."

The former preacher shook his head. "Little did we know that an unexpected source would change our lives and bring us together again after ten long years."

Loud Noise sulked before the wigwam fire, nursing a bottle of whiskey. The decade following Fallen Timbers had not been good for the would-be medicine man. He had followed Tecumseh to Indiana Territory and had spent a great deal of time living off his brother's charity. The other people of the village tolerated him because of his relationship to the Shawnee leader, a fact the fat man never failed to take advantage of. Unfortunately, Tecumseh was often gone and his brother was left to his own devices. Loud Noise had learned enough from Change of Feathers to gather herbs and care for basic ailments, but he could do little to care for those who were very sick.

He had married the plump daughter of a warrior who had died at Fallen Timbers and together they had produced several screaming and hungry children. Loud Noise was a poor hunter and the family often depended on Tecumseh and Stands Firm to provide them enough to eat. His wife never said anything as the fat man lay around drinking, but the complete disappointment was evident in her eyes anytime she looked at her pathetic husband.

Loud Noise wiped the greasy hair out of his face and rubbed his empty eye socket. It was all Tecumseh's fault, he reminded himself bitterly. If only he had spent more time teaching me to hunt and to be a warrior rather then wasting his time with that white traitor, Sinnatha! Then, Loud Noise would never have fled Fallen Timbers in disgrace and he would have the skills to care for his own family! The fat man snorted and raised the bottle to his lips. Suddenly, a great pain gripped his heart and the one eyed man gasped and dropped the bottle. He gripped his chest tightly as the precious whiskey spilled into the fire, causing the blaze to sizzle and grow. Finally, his eyes rolled back in his head and the medicine man collapsed beside the blaze.

Tecumseh rode toward his village on the White Water River, a small group of warriors trailing him. He had spent over a month visiting with the Sauk and Fox Indians south of the Great Lakes. It had been a good trip and Tecumseh had secured the promise of several chiefs that they would not consider any offers to sell land to the *Shemanese*.

As he rode into the village, Tecumseh could see something was amiss. He reined his horse to a halt as Tecumpese hurried forward, her expression concerned.

"What's wrong?" Tecumseh asked as his sister moved beside his horse.

"Come quickly!" she replied urgently. "Something has happened to our brother!"

Tecumseh frowned. "What has the fool done now?"

Tecumpese looked up, tears in her eyes. "He's dying."

Tecumseh kicked his horse into a gallop and raced through the village. He leapt to the ground in front of Loud Noise's wigwam and rushed inside. It took a moment for his eyes to adjust to the darkness of the lodge as he listened to the sound of his brother's wife weep. Loud Noise lay upon a pallet beside the fire, unmoving. Tecumseh turned toward the crying woman.

"How long has he been like this?"

"Three days," she sobbed. "He collapsed beside the fire and has not risen since."

Take the children and go outside," Tecumseh demanded. "Give me some time with him."

She nodded and left the wigwam, her children in tow. Tecumseh stared at his brother for several moments, his eyes moist with tears. Finally, he moved forward to kneel beside the motionless body and placed his hand on Loud Noise's forehead.

"Watch over my brother, *Weshemoneto*," he prayed. "Give him the peace he could never find in life..."

Tecumseh stopped praying as a low moan issued from the prone man's throat. Loud Noise's eyes fluttered before finally opening. With a start, the large man sat up.

"Brother!" Tecumseh gasped, grabbing Loud Noise by the shoulders to support him. "We thought you were dead!"

Loud Noise looked around in confusion ,his eye wide. "I was dead," he cried, "but *Weshemoneto* sent me back! He said there was much work for me to do for the people!"

Tecumseh shook his head and began to rise, but Loud Noise caught his wrist.

"Tecumseh, I have not been a good man," he stated, tears rolling down his face. "I have given you little reason to trust me, but I speak the truth! I have much to tell the people. Will you have them come in the morning to hear what I have to say?"

Tecumseh looked down at the fat man's hopeful face, shocked by his words. Finally, he shook his head in agreement.

"Thank you, Tecumseh!" Loud Noise sobbed, as his wife and children rushed back into the wigwam. "You will be happy to hear what *Weshemoneto* has taught me."

Tecumseh looked back at his younger brother, but said nothing as Loud Noise embraced his wife and children. The warrior stepped from the wigwam and looked up at the sky. Could the Great Spirit have chosen one such as his brother as a vessel of hope for the people?

The entire village had gathered outside Loud Noise's wigwam. The sun had risen in the eastern sky and the villagers waited impatiently. It was only out of respect to Tecumseh that they had gathered to hear the medicine man. Many of the gathered Indians began to murmur and shift restlessly. Tecumseh stepped out of the wigwam and the crowd quieted. The village leader silently looked the crowd over and moved aside. Loud Noise stepped from the wigwam entrance. Many of the Indians gasped at the change in the drunkard's appearance. Loud Noise had washed and combed his hair, pulling it back over his ears so that his empty eye socket was exposed. He had cleaned his body and changed out of his soiled clothing. He now stood before them in a deerskin robe. He looked around the crowd, his head held high. Finally, he spread his hands and addressed the assembly.

"Listen to me, my people!" he cried, his voice booming across the village.

Nobody had heard the medicine man address a crowd before. His voice was deep and strong, and held all their attention. "I died and *Weshemoneto* showed me many things before he sent me back to you. He showed me a happy hunting ground where all those who have gone on before us live in peace. I saw my father, brothers, and mother there. It was such a wonderful place that I began to weep in joy."

An excited murmur went up from the crowd, but Loud Noise raised his hands to quiet the noise. "My heart was full and I asked to Great Spirit if I was to remain there with all those that I loved," he cried, gathering the crowd's full attention once again. "The creator told me that I was not worthy and he showed me the place of the *Matchemenetoo*, the bad spirit. There I watched in fear as people that I had known, people of weak heart and spirit, drink molten lead from a great ladle of the *Matchemenetoo*! I dared ask the Creator if this was to be my fate. The fear in my heart was great, but his answer was clear."

Loud Noise hesitated and looked around at the crowd before closing his good eye and raising his head to the sky.

"*Weshemoneto* showed me that evil place to warn me of what awaits all of his red children if we do not change our ways," the one-eyed man declared.

An astonished murmur and moans of dismay rose from the crowd at the revelation. Loud Noise raised his hands again, quieting the voices instantly.

"I have been the greatest sinner of us all," he stated, tears rolling down his face. "I drank the white man's whiskey. I stole, I lied, and I was a coward. All those things were of the man, Loud Noise. I tell you now that I am no longer that man. From this day forth, I will never drink whiskey again, for that is something from the white men. We must give up the things that we have taken from the *Shemanese* and return to the old ways if we are to save ourselves," he declared, raising his voice toward the sky. "From now on I will teach our people the words of the Great Spirit. I will be the Open Door. My name is now *Tenskwatawa*. I am the prophet and I will show you the way!"

The crowd rose to their feet and cheered for the Prophet as Tecumseh looked on in amazement and pride. Tenskwatawa raised his hands and smiled as the crowd gathered around him. Tecumpese moved up beside Tecumseh, shaking her head.

"Can you believe it? Has our brother truly been saved to help lead our people forward?"

Tecumseh looked on as the crowd continued to surround the man who had previously been a source of shame and embarrassment for Tecumseh and the rest of his family.

"I have often prayed to *Weshemoneto* to send us a sign of hope. Maybe we have been blessed with that sign today," he answered quietly.

"He will not be able to unite our people by himself," Tecumpese continued. "He is still only one man."

Tecumseh nodded. "I will be there to guide and help him. Together, we may accomplish great things."

The woman put her arm around her brother's waist. "So you will," she stated with a smile. "This is a great day for our family and people."

The old man rocked back in his chair and sighed. "So it was that a former drunkard and laggard brought hope to the Indians. With Tecumseh by his side, he went among the different tribes to preach his gospel. He called for a return to the old ways with the promise that *Weshemoneto* would help the Indians drive the *Shemanese* from their homelands. They listened to him in every village they visited and his following grew considerable."

Draper chuckled and shook his head. "I can't fathom why so many believed his teachings. It was madness."

Ruddell stopped rocking his chair. "Religion is a powerful thing," he stated quietly. "A man's beliefs can help him weather the worst of times. Belief in something gives you hope for the future. Without hope, a body has no future. As much as I hated him, I have to allow that Loud Noise gave the Indians hope, at least for a little while."

The former minister reached down and lifted his jug up from beside the chair and uncorked it. He took a long swig and sighed. He leaned back and closed his eyes as the morning sun filtered onto the porch.

"So, Tecumseh helped the Prophet?" Draper asked, drawing the old man's attention once again.

Ruddell nodded. "He sure did. Loud Noise was a good preacher, but he was as organized as chickens taking a shit. Tecumseh met with the different chiefs and set up alliances and visits to the Prophet's village. Without Tecumseh, I suspicion the religious movement among the Indians around the Great Lakes wouldn't have been so considerable."

The old man chuckled. "Not everyone who lived north of the Ohio was pleased with the Indians new found religious spirit."

Governor William Henry Harrison and his wife Anna were eating their breakfast in the garden of their Grousland estate when the messenger arrived. Harrison had arranged for the bricks that were used to build the home to be ferried up the Wabash from Louisville to Vincennes. Now the thirty-three-year old former military aide owned the largest brick home in the Indiana Territory. The land purchases he had arranged with the various tribes around Vincennes and the southern part of the territory were quickly making him wealthy and powerful. Harrison nodded in satisfaction as the messenger removed his hat and waited patiently outside the garden entrance. He wiped his mouth with his napkin and signaled for the man to enter the garden. The messenger hurried to the governor's side, a wax-sealed envelope in his hand.

"Pardon me, Governor," the messenger stated nervously, holding the envelope forward. "Mr. Wells sends his regards. He wanted this message delivered to your hand only."

Harrison took the note for the man's outstretched hand and nodded. "Thank you. You must be tired and hungry. You have my leave to refresh yourself. Go to the kitchen and tell the slaves there that I desire them to give you something to eat. Return to me this afternoon. I will have correspondence for you to deliver back to Mr. Wells."

The messenger saluted the governor and wandered out of the garden. Harrison broke the seal on the letter and began reading the contents of the message. His expression became grim as he finished the note.

Anna Symmes Harrison looked at her husband as he rose from his place at the table.

"What is wrong, Henry?" she asked in concern.

"More news on that bloody prophet," Harrison replied. "It seems that Mr. Wells is quite alarmed with his activities."

"You'll have to excuse me, my dear," he added, patting his wife's hand and kissing her cheek. "I have some work that I must attend to in my office."

The governor stalked from the garden as his wife looked on.

Harrison's office was a spacious second story room in his own home. He sat down at his oak desk and stared out of the large window at the distant Wabash River. He drummed his fingers on the desk top and contemplated what he should do. After several minutes, he took out a clean sheet of paper from the desk drawer and dipped a quill into an inkpot. He rubbed his forehead with his left hand for a moment longer, deciding how he should word his letter.

Harrison was not a religious man, but he certainly understood how powerful religion could be. Wells had indicated that the Prophet was convincing Indians not to buy or drink any liquor from the American traders in Ft. Wayne. Not just the Shawnee, but the Indians of many different tribes as well. This was cause to worry as it was a sign of the tribes moving toward unity once again. This threat had to be ended. Harrison put the tip of the quill to the paper and began to write.

My Red Children,

It is with great sorrow that I learned that many tribes have ceased trading with the great white father's agents in the Great Lakes. This worries the leaders of the United States greatly as we have all enjoyed a decade of peace and trust between our people since the Battle of Fallen Timbers. What reason is there for our people to not continue to trade in peace? I have been told there is a so called prophet who is telling the leaders of many nations bad things. He encourages you to not deal with traders of the United States and to give up using the items that have been provided to your people out of friendship for many years past.

I admire and respect your faith in the Great Spirit, but I remain doubtful that this Shawnee medicine man is a true prophet sent to guide the Indian people. If this man has truly been sent by the creator, should he not prove himself before you follow his words? This man should provide some sign that he is Weshemoneto's chosen one. Have him make the sun stand still, turn day into night, or perform some other miracle to validate his claim as a savior of the Indian peoples.

If he cannot produce a sign, then I say he does not speak for the Great Spirit and should not be listened to. Please consider the choices you have made carefully. Do not let the ramblings of one man end a profitable relationship that has endured for all of our people.

Respectfully,

W.H. Harrison

The Governor signed the letter and sealed it with wax. Harrison then rang a small hand bell, signaling his secretary to enter the room.

"James, find that courier and have him carry this message back to Mr. Wells," Harrison instructed, handing the young man the note. "I want it read in every Indian village between Vincennes and Ft. Wayne."

James nodded and walked briskly from the room as the governor sat back in his chair and looked out of the window once again. A confident smile spread across his face as he watched James pass the note to the courier outside the kitchen entrance. Harrison was certain that the problems caused by the Shawnee prophet would soon be over.

Tecumseh was sitting beside the fire of the Galloway home. Rebecca was sitting close to him as he studied the book that he held in his lap. James Galloway sat in his favorite chair, smiling as he smoked his pipe. It had been several months since his last visit and the Galloways had been pleased when Tecumseh had arrived the previous morning. Rebecca, grown into a beautiful teenager, had presented Tecumseh with a new book titled *"A History of the United States."* The war chief had spent the next two days eagerly examining the contents.

"'We hold these truths to be self evident'," he read aloud. "'That all men are created equal, that they are endowed by their creator with certain unalienable rights, that among these are life, liberty, and the pursuit of happiness'?"

"Very good, Tecumseh!" Rebecca cried proudly. "You read that perfectly!"

"You say this is the Declaration of Independence?" he questioned. "This paper let you break from the king in England?"

James Galloway took the pipe from his mouth and nodded. "Yes, Tecumseh. That paper started it all. Now we have our own country, and are ruled by no king."

Tecumseh smiled. "It is a country that was once all ours. We Indians should write our own Declaration of Independence. Do you think your government will give us our land back?"

Galloway looked down at the ground, his face reddening. "I'm sorry, my friend. Sometimes I forget your pain."

"You are a good man, Galloway," Tecumseh replied sincerely. "More whites should be like you."

The warrior rose from his seat and moved to the hearth, staring at the fire that was burning brightly. Rebecca moved up beside him.

"We heard about Governor Harrison's letter. What will you do?"

Tecumseh shrugged. "Harrison fears my brother's teachings. The tribes have pride again and are uniting behind the words of the Creator. It will make it harder for him to steal our land. He challenges the Prophet to produce some type of miracle to prove he has been blessed by *Weshemoneto*. Even many of our own people still doubt and want a sign they can believe. What will we do? That is not for me to say."

Rebecca looked to her father, silently imploring him to allow her to share the information they had discussed. James hesitated a moment before shaking his head in consent. Rebecca moved across the room to the bookcase and retrieved a slender book. She walked back to Tecumseh, the book extended before her.

"This is our Almanac," she explained, thumbing through the pages. "It tells many things to farmers about how hard the winter is going to be and when crops should be planted. It also talks about certain scientific events such as an eclipse."

Tecumseh looked at the girl, puzzled. "What is this eclipse?"

"When the moon passes in front of the sun or likewise," she explained. "The day would turn to night for a short period of time. There is supposed to be one soon."

Tecumseh's eyes light up. "When?"

"The almanac estimates that it will occur on June 16."

Tecumseh had learned the basic of the Christian calendar and compared it in his mind to the seasons of the Shawnee year.

"That is a little more then a month away," he cried excitedly. He looked between the father and daughter. "Why are you telling me this?"

"We want to help, Tecumseh," Galloway replied solemnly. "We think you can use this knowledge to help your people."

"Yes!" Tecumseh cried. "This could be the sign our people have asked for. Thank you, my friends!"

"Will you be leaving tomorrow?" Rebecca asked, her smile disappearing.

Tecumseh nodded. "Yes, I must bring what you have told me to my brother. We have much to do."

"We shall miss you."

Tecumseh hugged the girl. "I will miss you too," he replied warmly. "I will return as soon as I can. I will not stay long from my friends."

Rebecca smiled brightly and wrapped the Indian leader in another hug. James Galloway looked on, his expression worried. He saw too clearly the feelings his daughter was developing for the Shawnee warrior. Falling in love with an Indian warrior was something folks on the frontier tended to look down on. Galloway respected Tecumseh greatly and was fond of the Indian, but the thought of his daughter becoming the chief's wife worried him. He would have to watch the situation carefully and make sure it did not get out of hand.

CHAPTER 17

WHITEWATER VILLAGE
JUNE, 1806

WORD HAD SPREAD across the Ohio Valley that the Prophet would meet Governor Harrison's challenge. He promised all the tribes that he would produce a sign that he was *Weshemoneto's* chosen one. He welcomed all who wished to come see him prove his claims. The Whitewater village quickly crowded with believers and skeptics. Stephen Ruddell was sent by Black Hoof to observe the spectacle.

The frontier preacher rode down the trail toward the crowded village. A few other white men were mixed in the crowd, but the large man received many curious stares as he dismounted his horse and slowly made his way toward the center of the village. Nobody moved to stop him, but Ruddell could sense that all the eyes fixed upon him were not friendly. It did not matter to him; he was here to see Tecumseh as much as anything else. It had been ten years since he had last seen his best friend. His heart beat rapidly as he scanned the crowd, hoping to locate the Shawnee leader.

"Has *ni-je-ni-nuh* returned to me?" a familiar voiced called from behind the redheaded man.

Stephen turned to find Tecumseh and several warriors standing behind him. He smiled widely and chuckled. "Didn't I promise I would?"

Tecumseh stepped forward and embraced the big man. "Ten years is a long time, my friend. Are you well?"

"Yes, brother," Ruddell replied, clasping Tecumseh's shoulders. He looked around at the crowded village. "It seems the years have been good to you as well."

Tecumseh smiled slightly. "Have you come to see the power of the Prophet?"

Stephen did his best to hide his disdain at the mention of Loud Noise's new name. "Partly, but mostly to see you. We have much to talk about."

Tecumseh motioned toward a small wigwam located off the main trail. "There is time before the Prophet speaks. Come, we will smoke."

The two old friends entered the wigwam, and Tecumseh signaled for the group of warriors to wait outside. Alone, the two men settled onto the ground and packed tobacco into their pipes. Lighting them from a small fire, they both smoked for several moments in silence. Tecumseh studied his friend carefully.

"I see you now wear the black shirt," the warrior observed. "When did you become a priest?"

"I am a minister, brother," Stephen explained. "I began following the Lord not long after I was sent back to my father. I believe in God, just like a priest. The difference is that I may take a wife."

Tecumseh smiled. "That is good! I remember your appetite for young women. I don't think you would do well without them."

Ruddell blushed and cleared his throat. "I hear you have a son?" he asked, changing the subject.

"Yes, he lives with my sister. His mother died birthing him," Tecumseh replied sadly. "Why have you come, *ni-je-ni-nuh?* Did Black Hoof send you?"

Stephen nodded. "He feared he wouldn't be welcome."

"He's right!" Tecumseh stated, his eyes hardening. "He has many of our people living as the white man's *ni-ki!* Dogs! in Wapakoneta!"

The frontier preacher sighed. "He only wants what is best for the people, Tecumseh. Your brother has many settlers worried that there will be another war. Black Hoof only wants peace."

The Shawnee chief spat in the fire. "Peace? The *Shemanese* will never give us peace as long as we have one speck of land left. In his heart, Black Hoof knows this. He fought against them. Now he is a tired old man who ready for his grave."

The beat of a drum interrupted the conversation. Tecumseh rose to his feet. "It's time. It has been good to see you, my friend. I had hoped that you would stay with us," he added quietly.

Stephen felt his chest tighten as he looked into his friend's hazel eyes. "You know I cannot," he replied sadly.

Tecumseh sighed. "Then stay and watch as the Prophet gives our people hope. Then go back to Black Hoof. Tell him I hope that he is happy being a *Shemanese ni-ki*, living off the scraps that are tossed to him."

Tecumseh turned and stalked from the wigwam, leaving Ruddell to contemplate his friend's words.

The crowd outside had grown considerably by the time Stephen exited the lodge. People were gathered around a large platform that had been constructed in the middle of the village. The crowd shifted impatiently as the frontiersman made his way to the back of the gathering, hoping for a clear view. The murmurs ceased as the Prophet made his way to the platform, Tecumseh at his side. Ruddell stepped up on a hickory stump for a better view and gave the prophet an appraising stare. The fat man was dressed in deer skin robes tied with a white sash, and his face was painted black. He wore silver hoops in his ears and nose and his dark hair was wrapped in a red silk turban. He waved at the crowd as they cheered his entrance. Stephen ignored the rest of the Indians and focused on the would-be prophet. He could see sweat running down the man's brow and his eye darted nervously. Ruddell shook his head. How could so many put their faith in a man such as this?

"Are you sure that it is time?" the Prophet whispered to his brother, looking around nervously.

Tecumseh grasped the large man's elbow to steady him. "Yes, brother," he replied soothingly. "*Weshemoneto* is with us. Begin your ritual."

Tenskwatawa nodded and stepped onto the platform. Tecumseh moved away; he wanted all the focus of this moment to be on the holy man. The Prophet looked around for a moment before clearing his throat and pulling a pouch and rattle from his side. He was so nervous that he dropped the rattle to the platform floor. He quickly stooped to pick it up, cursing his nerves.

Finally, he took a deep breath and raised his hands into the air and addressed the crowd, his voice booming across the village.

"Oh *Weshemoneto!*" he cried. "I call upon you to give us a sign that we are your chosen ones. Please show the people that you have sent me to teach them of your greatness!"

The Medicine man emptied the pouch into his hand and sprinkled *nilu famu,* sacred tobacco, about the platform. He then began to chant and shake his rattle. His voice started low, but grew in strength as he continued to chant. Soon his face became drenched with sweat as the chanting continued. Finally, after almost two hours, the Prophet collapsed to the platform.

Tecumseh swallowed hard and took one step toward the prone figure. Suddenly, the daylight began to fade, even though it was midday. The crowd began to murmur in awe and excitement. Many of the spectators gasped and pointed toward the sky. The moon was moving in front of the sun! Tecumseh leapt to the platform and grabbed his brother.

"Get up!" he ordered. "It has started. Tell the people it is *Weshemoneto's* sign!"

Tenskwatawa staggered to his feet as the daylight faded into night. "Behold *Weshemoneto's* greatness!" the medicine man cried excitedly, gesturing toward the sky.

"Does anyone here still doubt me?" he challenged. "If you believe, kneel and give thanks to the creator for sending you his prophet to spread his words!"

The stunned crowd fell to their knees before the triumphant medicine man and began to cry and chant. After several minutes, the eclipse began to pass and daylight returned to reveal Stephen Ruddell, grimly standing alone at the edge of the crowd. The frontiersman shook his head and moved to where he had tethered his horse and mounted to leave. He had seen enough of the Prophet's "miracle." He had much to report to Black Hoof, none of which would make the old chief happy. He looked back at the crowd as he turned his horse up the trail out of the village. Tecumseh alone was watching him leave. Stephen raised his hand to wave goodbye. Tecumseh responded with a slight nod, before focusing his attention back on his brother as he continued to address the crowd.

"The Indians saw the eclipse as the sign they had been waiting for" the old man stated, casting rocks into the wide river. Lyman sat on a driftwood log that had washed up on the riverbank, diligently writing down notes as Ruddell paced the Mississippi River bank. "The Prophet's message spread through the Great Lakes like a prairie fire. Tecumseh knew that Harrison and the government wouldn't stand for it. We both knew that the days ahead was very dark, much darker then any eclipse had ever been."

"The eclipse could be explained through science," Draper argued. "Why didn't Governor Harrison address this with the Indians? You said that Tecumseh got the information about the eclipse from an almanac, so why didn't the governor just provide almanacs as proof to the tribes that the Prophet did not produce a miracle?"

Ruddell snorted. "You don't reckon he didn't try to do exactly that? None of the tribes that had allied themselves with Tecumseh would believe anything Harrison or any white man might tell them. They wanted to believe that Loud Noise was a prophet and they figured he had proven himself through the eclipse. No white man was going to come in and denounce the word of their Great Spirit through blab about science."

Lyman dropped the point. "What happened next?"

Stephen skipped a flat stone across the water, watching it hit several times before sinking below the surface. "Indians flocked to the village on the Whitewater River to meet with the Prophet and listen to his teachings. I returned to Wapakoneta and told Black Hoof about the Prophet's 'miracle' and my meetin' with Tecumseh."

"What was his reaction?" Draper interjected.

"How do you think he reacted?" the old man grumbled. "Black Hoof had been a leader among the Shawnee for over fifty years. He had always been sour on Tecumseh's popularity and he plum hated Loud Noise. He saw their actions as a challenge to his leadership of the tribe. He wanted to put a war party together and attack Tecumseh's village, but I convinced him it wasn't a likely idea."

The old frontiersman chuckled at the memory. "Black Hoof was old by that time, but he still had some fire left in him. Tecumseh's village continued to grow as boodles of Indians visited from as far away as the other side of the Mississippi. Soon, it began to worry many of the settlers that had moved in along the Ohio border and the Governor of Ohio. Then something happened that caused Black Hoof and Tecumseh to square off against each other."

John Boyer had been working to clear a field on his homestead near the Mad River when a shot range out in May of 1807. His wife had looked out of their log cabin window in time to see a pair of Indian warriors standing over Boyer's motionless body. One of the Indians reached down and deftly removed the white man's scalp with a skinning knife. Mrs. Boyer stepped back from the window and quietly ushered her three children out the back door. The family escaped into the woods and headed in the direction of the nearest settlement. The exhausted woman and her children arrived in the village of Urbana the following morning. Her tale of what happened set off a panic. Soon, a group of heavily armed men had mounted horses and returned to the cabin. There they found Boyer's scalped and mutilated body lying face down in the field. The Indians had left a set of black-dyed feathers and a small deer hoof rattle on the man's body. This was no random raid; Boyer's death had been a calculated murder.

Speculation and accusations of who had killed the settler began to fly. A story circulated that the Shawnee prophet had sent some of his new disciples to carry out the attack, the first of more to come. Tecumseh had been away from the village hunting when word of this accusation had come in. Tenskwatawa had quickly denied the accusation and shifted the blame toward Black Hoof and the Shawnee at Wapakoneta. The Prophet claimed that the old Shawnee leader had arranged the murder in order to implicate the true followers of Weshemoneto who lived with him at the White Water Village.

Black Hoof had angrily denied the Prophet's claim. He had Stephen Ruddell write a letter to Benjamin Whiteman, the Ohio Militia officer that Governor Kirker had placed in charge of the investigation of Boyer's death. The Shawnee leader had asked to meet with Whiteman and any other Ohio leaders who were concerned so he could reaffirm the peaceful intentions of the Wapakoneta Shawnee and clear any misunderstanding of the incident. With a great deal of coaxing from Ruddell, Black Hoof had suggested that Tecumseh and Tenskwatawa be invited to this meeting as well.

Whiteman had responded enthusiastically, eager to determine the cause of the settler's murder. He invited both rival leaders to the settlement of Springfield to discuss the matter.

Stephen Ruddell sat on his horse beside Black Hoof, his expression concerned. The silver haired Shawnee chief had insisted on bringing over sixty of his most loyal and heavily armed warriors with him to the council. Hearing of this, Tecumseh had shown up at the small Ohio settlement with a similar number of warriors. Luckily, Blue Jacket had arrived at the council as well. The former war chief looked older then his actual age of fifty-four and had developed a nagging cough. Still, the once powerful leader was respected by both Shawnee factions. It was Blue Jacket who suggested that each group stack their weapons beside cabins at opposite ends of the village and make their way to the maple grove in which Worthington had arranged for the council to be held. Both leaders had grudgingly agreed. Now Ruddell sat beside his adopted father, eyeing the White Water Indians warily.

"It would be best if you enter the grove," Stephen whispered into the old warrior's ear. "The *Shemanese* are well armed and nothing will happen in their presence. I'll greet Tecumseh."

Black Hoof nodded in agreement. "Tell him to choose his words wisely," he warned. "We will not tolerate being called murders or cowards!"

Ruddell exhaled deeply as the Wapakoneta Shawnee followed their chief into the grove and arranged themselves around him. The frontier minister dismounted his horse and walked across the clearing to greet his old friend. He stopped when he noticed a pair of white men moving out to join him. The first was obviously Benjamin Whiteman, dressed in his militia uniform. The second man was dressed in buckskins and seemed familiar to Stephen. He was a big man with shoulder length hair that was graying at the temples. The large hooked nose protruding from his careworn face gave him the appearance of a buzzard as he stalked confidently across the field. He held out a big hand as he approached.

"Howdy, Reverend Ruddell," he stated in a rich, deep voice. "I'm Simon Kenton."

Ruddell took the big man's hand with a smile. The grip was still stronger than that of most men half his age. Kenton had recently built a mill near the settlement of Urbana and had been appointed by Governor Kirker to the commission looking into Boyer's death. At fifty-two, the famous Indian fighter was still formidable.

"I'm pleased to meet you, Mr. Kenton," Stephen replied warmly as Tecumseh stepped forward.

"Call me Si," the older man replied, turning toward the Shawnee warrior.

Tecumseh smiled at Stephen, his eyes shining with amusement. "That's better then the last time you met," he observed.

Kenton's brow wrinkled in confusion. "What? I don't ever recall meetin' the good reverend before."

Stephen felt his cheeks redden in embarrassment as he realized the direction the conversation was going. He gave the Shawnee warrior a pleading look, but it was too late.

"Sinnatha shot you the last time we were all together." Tecumseh chuckled. "Many years ago, when you attacked our camp on the East Fork."

The big frontiersman turned toward the red-faced minister. "That was you?" he asked.

"I reckon so, Si," Stephen replied apologetically. "I was a different body back then, before I was called to serve the good Lord!"

Kenton threw his head back and laughed deeply. He then reached inside his linen shirt and pulled out a flattened lead bullet that he had attached to a leather thong and wore as a necklace. He held up the keepsake proudly for all to see.

"It was the closest I ever come to death, and that's a powerful fact," he boasted. "I was cock-sure I was done for when you turned your rifle on me. I reckon the good lord was watchin' over me that day. This bullet hit a buckle on my shootin' pouch and cut through my clothes. I found it in my shirt the next day. If your powder had been dry, I wouldn't be standin' here showin' you my bullet," he explained. "Still, it hit me considerable, enough to break one of my ribs. It still pains me when the weather turns cold."

Ruddell shook his head in amazement as he examined the flattened ball. "I apologize for any hardship I might have caused you," he reiterated.

The older man slapped him on the shoulder. "No hard fee-lins'," he chuckled. "I did have my boys shoot up your tents while you were all sleepin'. I reckon it wasn't a chirk visit."

Kenton turned toward Tecumseh and raised an eyebrow. "Well, *Psai-wi ne-noth-tu,*" he stated, using the Shawnee term for "Great Warrior". "I never suspicioned we'd be meetin' as friends! We sure have had a grist of fights. I always reckoned one of us would end up kilt!"

Tecumseh smiled mischievously. "Who says we still won't?"

Kenton slapped his thigh and laughed heartily.

Benjamin Whiteman stepped forward in his freshly tailored militia uniform. He cleared his throat to get Kenton's attention.

"Oh!" the frontiersman grunted, taking a step back. "Tecumseh, this is Ben Whiteman. He was one of the men who was with me in that fight on the East Fork!"

Tecumseh looked the Militia officer over critically. "Are you an important man?" he asked abruptly.

Whiteman stiffened, taken back by the warrior's brash manner. "I am the main representative of the United States government at this council," he replied sharply.

"I'm a bigger man than you," Tecumseh continued, smiling.

"How's that?" Whiteman retorted with a frown.

The Shawnee leader stepped forward and fingered the officer's fine coat. "I whipped you when we were younger," he laughed. "I reckon you were wearing the same uniform when you run out of my camp on the East Fork."

Kenton and several of the other assembled militia laughed at the warrior's joke.

Whiteman finally smiled and shook his head in relief. He nodded toward the Maple Grove. "I'd allow that it's time to start the council"

Most of the militia and Tecumseh's warriors had already entered the grove. Black Hoof and his followers remained on the opposite side of the council grounds as the Shawnee from the White Water village. Blue Jacket and a few men from his village sat apart from the other, silently watching. Stephen had entered the grove and moved to Black Hoof's side when the old chief had growled and pulled on the big man's arm.

"He brings his tomahawk into the council," the Wapakoneta leader hissed. "We all promised to bring no weapons."

Ruddell patted the old man's arm as an angry murmur went up among the Indians standing behind Black Hoof. "I'll see to it," he whispered, moving to the grove entrance.

Stephen managed to catch Simon Kenton's attention and motioned toward Tecumseh. The Shawnee leader held his silver trimmed pipe tomahawk in the crook of his left elbow as he walked toward the grove. Kenton nodded and stepped forward.

"*Ne-kah-noh!* My friend! Why do you bring your tomahawk?" the frontiersman called, causing Tecumseh to halt.

The warrior turned. "*La-yah-mah?* This?" he replied innocently. "Black Hoof is here. I may need to use one end or the other before we are finished."

Stephen shook his head in exasperation at his friend's statement, half made in jest, but half in threat as well. He could feel his adopted father's angry scowl on his back as he stepped in front of Tecumseh.

"What are you doing?" he demanded. "If you bring that tomahawk in, this council will be over before it even begins."

Benjamin Whiteman stepped forward, concerned. "He's right, chief. No weapons allowed for any warriors, including you."

"What am I to do if I want to smoke?" Tecumseh protested, his expression darkening in anger.

Nathaniel Pinckard, a bony little schoolmaster with wire glasses stepped forward.

"Here, chief!" he called affably, offering Tecumseh his long stemmed clay pipe. "If you need to smoke, you can use this."

Tecumseh looked at the little man incredulously and took the pipe. The Shawnee leader examined the dirty instrument in dismay. He sniffed the clay bowl and crinkled his nose in disgust. Tecumseh carelessly tossed the pipe over his shoulder and into the brush. The mounting tension of the situation melted away as the assembled militia and Indians laughed as the little schoolteacher scrambled to find his pipe.

Tecumseh turned toward Whiteman and held out his tomahawk pipe. "I would be glad if Blue Jacket would hold this for me until we are finished. His stance is neutral," he conceded, nodding toward his old friend.

Whiteman nodded in relief and had the pipe handed over to the respected Shawnee elder. Ruddell knew that Black Hoof was still not pleased by Tecumseh's actions, but the compromise would have to do if this matter was going to be resolved. The frontiersman moved back to his adopted father's side.

Whiteman stepped forward to address the council, his expression stern. "Governor Kirker sends his regards to the leaders of the Shawnee people and bids them welcome. The governor has appointed Simon Kenton and I to lead the commission to investigate the death of Mr. John Boyer, who was shot down in his own field as his wife and children looked on."

The militia officer looked around at the assembled warrior solemnly. "All signs suggest this is a case of cold blooded murder, committed by Indians of the lakes."

A murmur of anger and protest began among the warriors, but Whiteman held up his hands to silence them. "I'm not here to accuse any man of this crime without proof," he stated. "If you value peace, I am cock-sure you should share as much information as you have concerning this matter."

Black Hoof stepped forward, his head held high. He held up a friendship medal that he had received from President Jefferson to remind everyone that he had signed the Treaty of Greenville and had remained peaceful ever since. "All the men who live in my village were at home when the settler was killed!" he stated in his deep voice. "You say that this man was murdered by Indians who left feathers on his body? This tells me that it was a revenge killing," the Wapakoneta leader argued.

"There are so many different tribes from all over the lakes roaming through the country that it is hard for us to know who they all are," he added, clearly insinuating that the guilt lay with the Indians who were visiting the Prophet in the Whitewater village.

Tecumseh rose to his feet to speak. All eyes were on the Shawnee warrior as he smiled warmly and spread his hands wide.

"The people who live and visit with the Prophet at our village could not have killed this man," he stated eloquently. "This would go against the teachings of Tenskwatawa and the vision *Weshemoneto* has set forth for all our people. We wish to remain at peace with the white men who now live in Ohio, as the Great Spirit has directed us. If we knew who had killed this man, we would certainly give this information to Governor Kirker's commission."

He then looked directly at Black Hoof. "I would allow that any of our chiefs or warriors here would do the same. You may wish to ask each one of them, or just to ask Chief Black Hoof again, though I believe you would be wasting your time."

The old man's eyes widened in anger at the younger man's statement, thinking he was being called a liar. His jaw set firmly and he opened his mouth to respond, but Tecumseh cut him off.

"I say this because I don't believe Black Hoof knows who killed this white man," Tecumseh stated confidently.

"Black Hoof has remained loyal to the Treaty of Greenville since the day he signed it. He will never take up the tomahawk against the United States again, no matter the circumstance," he added pointedly. Tecumseh turned toward Simon Kenton and Benjamin Whiteman. We cannot answer your questions, so now I would ask for you to answer one of mine."

Kenton nodded, studying the Shawnee leader carefully. "Very well, *ne-noth'tu.*"

"Do you still have the items that were left on the settler's body?" Tecumseh asked.

Kenton nodded slightly.

Tecumseh smiled. "Good! May we see them?"

Ben Whiteman and Kenton spoke in hushed tones for a moment before the militia officer signaled for the items to be brought forward and laid upon a table that had been set in the grove. Both Black Hoof and Tecumseh stepped forward to examine the deer rattle and the brace of eagle feathers. Wordlessly the Shawnee leaders inspected the items before placing them back on the table.

"These were not made by a Shawnee," Tecumseh stated confidently. Black Hoof shook his head in agreement

Kenton grunted and scowled. "What is there to prove what you say is the truth?"

Tecumseh held up the rattle and pointed to the hoof. "This is the hoof of a deer from the Illinois country. Do you see how it is longer? This is for running on the plain. Woodland deer have a shorter hoof," Tecumseh explained.

Black Hoof stepped forward, holding up the eagle feathers. "Eagle feathers are important to a Shawnee warrior," the old man added. "Not even a warrior living at peace would leave one on an enemy's body. Eagles are more plentiful along the Mississippi and the tribes that live there do not hold them in such importance as the Shawnee."

"What exactly are you saying?" Whiteman replied in confusion. "That some wandering Indians from a tribe along the Mississippi killed John Boyer?"

Tecumseh smiled. "See, your commission has found the answer yourself. You can tell Governor Kirker and the settlers in Ohio to rest easy. All the Shawnee that live near them remain their friends and only wish to live in peace."

Whiteman looked to Simon Kenton. The big frontiersman scratched his chin and shrugged, at a loss for words. This was not how they had expected this council to progress. Neither rival Shawnee leader had implicated the other and both even seemed to be grudgingly working together. It was not the result Whiteman or Kenton either one were expecting. Kenton stepped forward, scowling. "We looked for facts to have been brought to light at this council," he stated, an edge in his deep voice. "Instead we are left in the dark. You say the Indians that murdered this man were not Shawnee? So be it. You profess that you are still friends with the seventeen fires. As friends, we would expect you to do everything in your power to find and help bring these murders to justice."

His scowl deepened as he looked specifically at Tecumseh and Black Hoof. "If you choose to not help us, then do not expect to be welcomed back to another council as friends."

It seemed fitting that thunder and lighting began to dance across the sky as the frontiersman made his threat clear to the assembled Shawnee. Rain began to fall as a summer storm rolled in, ending the council on an ominous note.

CHAPTER 18

QUINCY, ILLINOIS
SUMMER, 1845

"WHAT HAPPENED NEXT?" Lyman asked.

The old man shrugged. "Tecumseh had the gift of the gab. He talked those commissioners right into allowing that neither group of Shawnee was at fault. They sure didn't like it though; they needed all creation to blame. Hell, Boyer's own family didn't have a mind the Shawnee had kilt him. Still, it was put on the tribe to come up with some information. So, that's what Black Hoof did. He was familiar with a Potawatomi chief named Big Son who told Black Hoof that Boyer had been killed by some Potawatomi warriors looking to avenge the death of some kin who had been done in four years earlier. Big Son also told Black Hoof that the feathers and deer rattle belonged to the dead warrior. He said that the warriors involved feared the wrath of the *Shemanese* and had went to brush in the Wisconsin Territory soon after the killin'."

Ruddell smiled. "Black Hoof took this information to Whiteman who declared the flint fixed. Tecumseh had been busy shinin' the eyes of the settlers around Springfield. He and his boys had took part in several games with the settlement's young men. Tecumseh won most of them, beating Indian warriors and white men that were half his age."

Stephen's smile faded. "He spent considerable time with Blue Jacket and some of the other peaceful Shawnee, trying to strengthen the bond between the two groups. He didn't avoid me, but neither of us was very chirk to the other. I had sided with Black Hoof and that hurt Tecumseh. A considerable rift was forming between us. Still, he had convinced most of the whites and Indians that had met with him that his designs were peaceful by the time he returned to his village."

Ruddell shook his head. "The man was smart as a steel trap. He could talk a squirrel out of his winter supply of nuts!"

Draper shuffled back through his notes. "You said that the village was growing before Tecumseh had gone to Springfield. I suspicion that many of the settlers were still uneasy with that many Indians so close to the Ohio border."

The old man nodded. "You bet they were. Not only that, but feeding everyone who lived there as well as all those that came to visit had become a powerful fix. Game in the area was becoming scarce and the hunters were ranging farther to find a grist for everyone to eat. Simple fact was that Tecumseh's village was outgrowing its resources. Two major events occurred that caused Tecumseh to budge from the Whitewater."

Main Poc, war chief and medicine man of the Illinois Potawatomi, rode slowly down the trail into the Whitewater village. The Potawatomi sat proud and erect as the villagers gathered to see the well known war leader. He was very large, well over six feet tall and heavily muscled. His body was covered with scars from his many battles and he carried himself with an arrogant manner. His name meant "Withered Hand," as he had been born without fingers or thumb on his left hand. Main Poc made no effort to hide the deformity he had overcome to become a war chief of his people. He led his large group of warriors into the village and dismounted in front of the council house where Tecumseh was patiently waiting for him.

The Potawatomi looked the Shawnee warrior over deliberately. "You are Tecumseh," he stated matter-of-factly.

Tecumseh nodded and stepped forward. "I am honored that the great Main Poc has come to visit the Prophet. You are a welcome guest; what is ours is yours as well."

Main Poc nodded and smiled slightly. "The trail has been long and hard. I desire some whiskey to celebrate our arrival."

Tecumseh frowned. "Whiskey is for the white man, great chief. There is none in this village, and we do not allow any to be brought in. I will not allow the drinking of the white man's poison by anyone who stays with us."

The Potawatomi scowled. "No whiskey?"

"No" Tecumseh repeated firmly.

Main Poc smiled. "Very well, Tecumseh. I wish to stay with you and listen to the Prophet. I have heard much about you and hope to learn more of you as well. My warriors and I are guests in your village and will respect your words."

Tecumseh returned the smile and grasped the big man's wrist. "Come, *ne-kah-noh*. The Prophet is eager to meet you as well."

Main Poc and his warriors spent nearly the entire summer of 1809 visiting with Tecumseh and the Prophet. He took a great liking to both brothers and visited with each of them daily. As August came to a close, the big warrior prepared to return to the Illinois country. He had eaten with the brothers a final time and they sat smoking around the fire when the Potawatomi leader made the Shawnee an offer.

"My people have much land," he stated, making a sweeping gesture with his deformed hand. "There is a place near where the Wabash turns south that none of my people live. The ground is fertile, the river is full of fish, and the game is plentiful. It would be a good place for your village to grow. You would also be far from the *Shemanese*! My people would be honored if the Prophet would move his village to our land beside the Wabash."

Tecumseh and the Tenskwatawa looked at each other, their eyes widening. Main Poc was a powerful man in both stature and personality. He often dominated conversations and was quick to tell of his exploits and his vast knowledge. He had gone to war extensively with the Osage and enjoyed drinking whiskey, both practices he had no intention of stopping. Yet for all his brashness, the big Potawatomi leader had become an ally to both brothers and had made a most generous offer.

"We don't know what to say," Tecumseh replied.

Main Poc smiled broadly. "Say yes, you can move before the end of autumn. The sooner you are away from the *Shemanese*, the better. You will also be closer to your loyal followers who live around the Great Lakes."

Tenskwatawa took Main Poc's good hand. "*Weshemoneto* has answered our prayers once again by sending you to us, *ne-kah-noh*. We accept. We will build a new, larger village on the Wabash. It will be a place all our people can gather to hear *Weshemoneto's* teachings."

"That village would become Prophetstown," Draper interrupted, looking up from his notes. "I always wondered how the village came to be located beside the Wabash."

Ruddell nodded. "Now you know. Tecumseh laid out the village himself just south of where the Tippecanoe River joins the Wabash. They built a council house that would hold five hundred people and a considerable lodge they named 'The House of the Stranger' for all the Indians that would come to hear Loud Noise speak. The largest diggings belonged to the Prophet, of course. By that time he believed his own gum and had a mind that he was an important man."

"No offense, Mr Ruddell," Lyman dared say, "but it seems to me that he was, at least to the Indians."

The old man bit his lip and shook his head. "I reckon that's true, even though he didn't earn it! The fat headed cully cottoned to the attention he received. He dictated to the Indians how they should live in order to please the Great Spirit, but he had a hanker for more power. Tecumseh was the one who met with the other tribes and made alliances. Loud Noise was just the blab they came to see."

Ruddell was becoming agitated again, and the writer knew it was time to change the subject. "You said there was a second event that influenced the move to Tippecanoe?"

Stephen nodded. "The treaty of Ft. Wayne."

Governor William Henry Harrison adjusted his frock coat and carefully combed his hair forward using a mirror that had been placed in the parlor of William Well's home. He looked up as the Indian agent entered the room.

"Is everything ready?" the governor asked.

Wells nodded. "All the chiefs will sign, Governor," he replied, rubbing his hands nervously. "At least enough that will matter.

There's a boodle of Indians out there. Not all of them are pleased about this treaty. Are you cock-sure you want to do this?"

Harrison glanced at the Indian agent. "Of course," he replied sharply. "We're offering these savages fair compensation for their lands. Why wouldn't I want to purchase an additional three million acres for our country?"

Wells chewed on his lip, hesitant to speak. "Well, beggin' your pardon, Governor. The Indians out there are Potawatomi, Miami, and Delaware. None of them have any claim to the land you're fixin' to buy. Weas, Kickapoos, and Shawnee are the one who live on it, and they ain't been invited to this council."

The Governor sighed. "The Wea are a sub tribe of the Miami and therefore are represented. The Potawatomi certainly have documented claim to the land as well."

"Yes, Sir," Wells nodded, "but the Western Potawatomi claim that land. Winamac and his people represent the eastern tribe."

"Dash, man!" Harrison barked. "What difference does it make? Are you not clear on where you stand on this issue? Do I need to consider appointing a new Indian agent to help represent what is best for the United States on this matter?"

Wells reddened at the rebuke. "No Sir," he stammered. "I stand with you. As you said, it's a likely deal!"

The governor smirked. "I should say so! I think President Madison will be very pleased to know we are purchasing land for two cents an acre. That's better then the Louisiana Purchase."

William Henry Harrison stood before the assembled chiefs, confidently scanning the crowd. A small wooden table had been set up outside William Wells' house and two companies of soldiers stood at attention behind the governor. A double guard had been placed on the fort walls to watch the proceedings as hundreds of Indians had crowded into the fort. Harrison had only invited and admitted representatives of tribes "friendly" to the United States. Several Shawnee and Kickapoo tribesman had been turned away at the fort gate. The territorial leader stepped forward to address the crowd.

"You all know of the land that the United States desires to buy from your tribes," he stated, his voice strong. "I say to you, do all the tribes who claim to this land stand in this council?"

Winamac, chief of a Potawatomi village on the Tippecanoe River stepped forward, smiling. "All are here, Father."

Harrison smiled. The Potawatomi had greeted him eagerly and had followed him around since the beginning of the council, desperate to please the territorial leader. Winamac and his people had fallen on hard times with the price of furs dropping and the dwindling game around their villages. The Potawatomi leader was willing to do anything to be awarded some of the goods and annuities that the Governor was offering for the land between the White and Wabash Rivers, land that Winamac and Harrison both knew his people had no claim to.

Not all the assembled chiefs were as eager to appease the Governor's desires. Miyathwe, Chief of the Mississinewa band of Miami, stepped forward. The middle aged chief crossed his arms in front of his chest defiantly.

"The Wea and the Kickapoo are not here!" he cried, frowning. "How can there be a treaty when those who live on the land that is being sold have no say?"

Winamac cleared his throat. "The Miami are the *ko'tha* of the Wea. They are led by Little Turtle and the other Miami chiefs."

Miyathwe turned away from the Potawatomi leader, his eyes hardening. "I will not listen to what this man has to say," he hissed. "His people have no claim to this land and should not be at this council!"

Murmurs of anger and agreement rose from the crowd after Miyathwe's harsh words. Harrison could see the discontent building in the crowd and knew he had to act fast. He turned to Little Turtle, the most respected and influential Miami leader on the frontier for the past thirty years.

"What say you, Chief?" the governor demanded. "Do the Miami represent the Wea concerning this matter?"

Little Turtle hesitated. The old chief turned his wrinkled face toward Wells, his former son-in-law. The Indian agent gave the old man a slight nod. The Miami leader's shoulders sagged slightly and he sighed.

"The Miami speak for the Wea at this council," he replied quietly. "They will accept the decisions that are made here today or their blood will flow in the Wabash."

The angry murmurs coming from the crowd ceased after the former war chief's statement. Harrison nodded in satisfaction and turned to the clerk seated at the small table.

"Make note of all the chiefs who sign the treaty and the tribe they represent," he instructed. "They will be paid in goods and their annuity will be arranged before they leave."

"Yes, Sir," the clerk replied, dipping his pen into the inkwell that sat on the table.

Winamac was the first chief to step forward. He quickly made his mark on the treaty and stepped aside, rubbing his hands in anticipation of the much needed goods his people would receive. Slowly, Miami and Delaware leaders lined up behind the Potawatomi, ready to sign away over three million acres of land to the Unites States, most of which none of them lived or hunted on.

Harrison smiled. Surely President Madison would approve of the deal. Expanding the interests of the United States at a cheap price was beneficial to both the country and Harrison's personal interests, just the way the governor liked it.

"Mr. Harrison sure seemed to have an ability to arrange good terms on his land deals in a peaceful manner." Draper observed. "The tribes seemed content with the five thousand dollars in goods they were paid and the annuity. I am certain the government was pleased with the arranged payment for the tract of land."

Ruddell snorted and glared at the younger man. "He bought the land from tribes that had no claim to it for less then three cents an acre! It wasn't a treaty, it was theft!"

The former frontiersman pointed a gnarled finger at Draper. "Did you know about Harrison's treaty of 05'? It expressly stated that the Potawatomi had no land claims on the Wabash, a point the good governor forgot all about when he arranged the 09' treaty!"

Ruddell shook his head sadly. "Past treaties and land claims meant nothing to the man. All that mattered was that he got what he wanted. Even then it was never enough. He promised the tribes that the government would not seek anymore land cessions after the 09' treaty, a promise he forgot in eighteen months!"

He spat on the ground and pulled at his whiskers. "All-fired, it wasn't just Harrison. The United States has never stopped breakin' the treaties it signed with the Indians, even today. Still, I'm huffed to know just how no account the man was!"

The old man chuckled. "Tecumseh and his brother sent a message to Governor Harrison from their village on the Wabash. They wanted to make cock-sure he understood how they felt about his land deal. The message they sent was clear."

William Henry Harrison was dressed in his finest uniform as he welcomed his guests in the foyer of his Grousland estate. He had arranged for a ball to be held in celebration of the Treaty of Ft. Wayne and the successful purchase of the large tract of land that would soon open for settlement east of Vincennes. A large number of the most important people in the Indiana territory were now gathering to greet and congratulate the Governor and his wife Anna on the successful acquisition. The sound of violin music and laughter drifted into the foyer from the estate's great room as one of Harrison's sentries made his way quickly to the governor's side and saluted.

"Beggin' your pardon, Governor!" The man whispered into Harrison's ear. "There's an Indian outside who has a message for you from the Prophet."

"Well?" The governor replied, irritation creeping into his voice. "What is it?"

The soldier's face reddened. "He won't tell me, sir."

Harrison sighed in frustration. "Well, I suppose I had better see him. I would not want an emissary of the Prophet to be kept waiting!"

William smiled at Anna and kissed her forehead. "Excuse me, my dear. There is a territorial matter I must attend to. Please continue to welcome our guests, I'll be back soon."

Anna returned her husband's smile. "Oh course, my dear. Don't be gone long; it's you everyone is here to see. We would not want to be rude!"

Harrison chuckled and followed the soldier through the house and exited out the back door. A Shawnee brave sat stone-faced upon his horse ten feet from the estate entrance. Harrison glanced at the pair of guards to make sure they were prepared in case the Indian should attack. Satisfied, he boldly moved within a few feet of the motionless warrior.

"Well?" he stated, looking up at the warrior's stern face.

Without a word, the messenger handed the governor a folded note. He then swung his horse around and nudged the steed into a gentle trot. Harrison handed the slip of paper to the officer of the watch as the Indian rode away.

"What does it say?" Harrison asked, looking after the departing warrior.

The young officer scanned the note and cleared his throat nervously. "*Your people should not come any closer to me; I smell them too strongly already!*"

Harrison's eyes narrowed and he held his hand out, motioning for the man to give him the message. The officer handed it over and the governor scanned the contents himself. He looked after the departing warrior once again, his jaw tightening. He slowly crumbled the note and dropped it to the ground. Without another word, he turned on his heel and reentered the house to greet the rest of his guests. Only now he would do so without a cheerful smile.

CHAPTER 19

QUINCY, ILLINOIS
SUMMER, 1845

"THE SIGNING of that damn treaty became a rally cry for every tribe that stood against whites settlin' on their lands," the old man explained as he gently curried the mane of one of John Ruddell's mares.

The younger Ruddell had returned from Quincy with his family late in the afternoon. Stephen had wordlessly unhitched the team and set about grooming them. Draper had sat aside his writing box for a time in the afternoon and fished with the old man on the banks of a stream that emptied into the Mississippi. They had been successful in landing several catfish that Sarah Ruddell was now busy stuffing and preparing for dinner. Draper had wandered into the barn as dusk settled over the farm and the old man was finishing up with the horses.

"Those sons of bitches, Wells and Harrison, damn near done up any peace we had made with their fat headed designs! Tecumseh was more then a bit huffed. He was stirrin' up every tribe around the lakes for a fight. By then he had considerable influence and all creation listened to what he had to say. So, nobody stopped him when he decided to come speak with the peaceful Shawnee at Wapakoneta. By then, Black Hoof was sour on the power and fame Tecumseh had achieved and refused to attend any meeting.

Instead, he sent me to speak in his place," Ruddell continued, hanging bridles on the wall.

"You spoke against Tecumseh?" the reported asked, his writing box open in front of him.

The old man shook his head. "I was forty years old at the time and allowed I could still control what was happening around me. It clouded my judgment. I was fat headed enough to agree to read a letter Governor Harrison had sent for Black Hoof. I wish I had never done it, but the only thing I was frettin' about was to find a way to keep the peace."

John Ruddell entered the barn, frowning. "Pa? Why is my son running into the house and telling my wife about the 'sons of bitches' that his Grandpa knows? I've told you to mind your chops around him. Sarah's madder then a wet hen! She's threatening to make you eat on the porch and to send the boy to bed without his supper."

Stephen chuckled. "Tell her I'll accept the punishment, but don't send my grandson to bed without his supper for listening to an ornery old man!"

John sighed and shook his head. "Just come eat; you know she won't stay huffed at you."

The younger man stalked from the barn as his father and the writer followed behind.

"I'd allow this, Tecumseh was a powerful speaker! The son of a bitch turned a boodle of peaceful Indians back to the war path!" the older Ruddell added.

"Pa!" John cried.

Stephen laughed once again. "It ain't a sin to acknowledge the corn!"

A barn on the outskirts of Wapakoneta was the only structure that could accommodate the large crowd that had come to hear the famous Shawnee warrior. Wapakoneta did not have a council house and none of the village cabins were large enough for the occasion. Most of the Shawnee that now crowded the barn were dressed in linen shirts and wool trousers, the attire of peaceful Indians. Scattered among them were more then a few warriors dressed in deerskins, silk turbans, and calico blouses. Tecumseh stood proudly before the assembled Shawnee, dressed in doeskin leggings and a fringed leather shirt with a red sash. A pair of eagle feathers were tied in his long hair along with a set of silver armbands clasped around his biceps. He had completed his impressive attire with a silver gorget hung from his neck. The Indian leader stepped to the center of the barn and looked around at the crowd, his eyes shining with emotion.

"Brothers! It is time that the Shawnee people were one again!" he cried, his voice resounding through the crowd. "Look around you. Is this the life that our ancestors fought and died to protect? No! You now live a life that the *Shemanese* have forced upon you. You live as their *wi-si*, begging for the scraps from their table! It is time for you to join us, *ni-je-ni-nuh*. The Shawnee must live in the way *Weshemoneto* had set forth for us in the beginning. Our old chiefs have forgotten this. Come, join our people at Prophetstown!"

"It's time for peace!"

The crowd turned at the proclamation. Stephen Ruddell stepped into the barn and shouldered his way to the center of the crowd. The big man now wore the black shirt and white collar of a Baptist minister. He carrier a letter in his large hand as he stepped before Tecumseh and nodded toward his friend.

"Tecumseh is my brother and I love him, but anger burns in his heart. Black Hoof has led our people well. We have made a good life and are at peace with the *Shemanese*. We cannot return to the past. We must live the best life that we can. Black Hoof knows this and he wants our people to live, not die for a lost dream of days of old!"

Ruddell raised his hand, showing the assembled Indians the letter he held.

"I have a message from Governor Harrison. He praises our people for their efforts to keep peace. He is proud of the Shawnee at Wapakoneta for the way they have adapted to the new life we must all live!"

Tecumseh stalked toward Stephen, his expression cold. The warrior snatched the letter out of the minister's hand. He then opened the note and scanned the message. His eyes hardened as he finished reading the governor's words, and he looked up at his former best friend.

"The praise of a thief!" he spat. "Oh, you have much to be proud of, my people! Where is your payment for this land that was sold? It is in the hands of Little Turtle and other *wi-si*. None of the chiefs who signed this treaty had claim to the lands that were taken!"

Tecumseh crumbled the letter in his hand and threw it into a small fire that had been built in the center of the barn.

"If Harrison was here, I would do the same to him." he stated darkly. "I am leaving. I will be returning to Prophetstown and anyone who is still a true Shawnee may come with me. The rest of you may stay and continue to live off scraps. I will mourn you all, as you will now be dead to me and all those true Shawnee who still live."

"Tecumseh..." Ruddell began, reaching out toward the warrior.

Tecumseh smacked the big man's hand away. "You were once Shawnee. You were my brother, *Sinnatha*. Now you are just another white man that I cannot trust."

Tecumseh turned his back on the frontiersman and stalked from the barn. Several of the men in the crowd, both those dressed in skins and linen, joined him. Stephen watched as they left; sadness gripped his heart and he could find no words to say.

Rebecca Galloway was preoccupied milking one of the family's cows and did not hear the barn door open or close. She patted the Jersey's flank and rose from her stool, a full pail of milk in her hand. She turned and abruptly came face to face with Tecumseh. Startled, she dropped her pail and the milk spilled on the barn floor.

"Hello, Galloway girl," he stated, quickly picking up the pail before all of its contents spilled out.

"Oh, Tecumseh," she gasped. "You scared me! I did not hear you come in."

Tecumseh smiled. "I am Indian. When I do not wish to be heard, I am not."

Rebecca laughed. "Everyone will be chirk to see you! Let's go tell Pa!"

Tecumseh caught the young woman by the wrist as she moved to leave. Puzzled, she looked back at him.

"I have come to say goodbye," he stated sadly.

"Goodbye?" she replied in confusion. "You just got here!"

"No, I will not see you again," Tecumseh explained.

The girls eyes widened in bewilderment. "Why?" she cried. "Have I done to make you sour on me? Please, tell me what's wrong!"

Tecumseh patted the girls hand as she began to sob.

"War is coming between our people," he explained. "I must make my people ready for what lies ahead. Soon, it will not be safe for me to come here."

"Pa said that you'll always be welcome here," she sobbed, wiping tears from her blue eyes. "I don't want you to leave! I thought..."

Tecumseh raised his hand before she could finish the statement.

"We are different. You do not belong with my people any more then I belong with yours. I will always care for you and your family. Remember, you will always be safe here, no matter what happens."

The warrior kissed the frontier girl on the forehead and quickly exited the barn without looking back. Rebecca Galloway dropped the pail of milk once again and covered her face with her hands and continued to sob as the barn door closed behind the vanishing warrior.

Governor Harrison was sitting at his desk in the office of his Grousland home. He was carefully examining several treaties and other territorial documents. He looked up when his secretary entered the room.

"He's here, Governor."

Harrison nodded. "Good, send him in."

The governor stood and smiled as Stephen Ruddell entered the room. The frontiersman towered over the territorial leader. Harrison extended his hand and his smile turned to a grimace when the big man seized his hand in a vise like grip.

"It's good to finally meet you, Reverend Ruddell," Harrison stated, flexing his hand to return the flow of blood to his fingers. "I have heard much about you. You are a considerable man on the frontier."

Stephen shrugged. "I'm pleased to meet you, Governor Harrison. I'm cock-sure you're of more circumstance then me."

Harrison's smile returned and he pointed to a set of chairs beside the fireplace. "Please, have a seat. Would you care for a drink?"

"No self-respectin' preacher could refuse!" Ruddell replied.

Harrison chuckled and poured two glasses of bourbon. He handed one to the frontiersman. Stephen smiled and drained the glass.

"Thank you, Governor. It was a chapped ride here."

Surprised, Harrison drained his own glass, before falling into a fit of coughs as the strong liquor washed down his throat. Finally, the governor reached over and poured both men a second drink. Stephen took his glass and swirled the caramel colored contents around before looking the smaller man in the eye.

"Governor, I reckon you didn't ask me here to drink all your Kentucky whiskey. What can I do for you?"

Harrison took a sip from his glass before returning the frontiersman's stare. "Ruddell, I need your help," he admitted. "I have been told that you know the leaders of these Indians on the Wabash. Is that true?"

Stephen took a sip of his bourbon before nodding. " I grew up with them after I was captured by the Shawnee."

Harrison nodded. "That's what I had heard. What can you tell me about this Prophet and his brother?"

Ruddell scratched his chin and sat down his drink. "Many Indians have come to believe in the Prophet's words, but he doesn't command the Shawnee. His older brother, Tecumseh, leads them."

Harrison took another sip of bourbon. "Yes, I've heard right smart discussion about him. Do you know him well?"

The frontiersman nodded. "We grew up almost as brothers. We fought and rode together, until I was sent back to my father after Fallen Timbers. I'd allow that he's the most powerful leader I've ever known." Stephen took another swallow of his whiskey and smiled. "Including you, Governor Harrison."

The governor managed a slight smile and rose from his seat and walked to the office window. He folded his arms behind his back and gazed out over the Wabash.

"These Indians have caused me considerable trouble since the Treaty of Fort Wayne." Harrison stated. "Every surveyor I've sent into these new lands have had all their equipment broken and they have been sent back home with threats against their lives should they ever return. Every emissary that I've sent up the Wabash has been refused entrance into their village and has been sent back accused of being spies."

Ruddell swirled the bourbon around in the delicate crystal glass. "Were they spies?" he questioned, before draining his glass and refilling it from the decanter.

Harrison turned back to the preacher, amused.

"I like you, Ruddell," the governor chuckled. "You're an honest man. I suspicion that you're as much Indian as you are white. That means you really don't cotton to me, but that doesn't matter. It should suffice that the outcome of this situation effects many people, including your congregation at Wapakoneta."

Stephen frowned, not liking the veiled threat of the smaller man. "What do you want from me, Governor?"

Harrison drained the last of his bourbon and set the glass down on his desk. "I want you to take a message to Tecumseh and the Prophet. I wish to meet with them to try and resolve our differences in a sensible manner. Tensions between the British and our own government are becoming arduous, so maintaining peace on the frontier is vital. Nobody wants another Indian war."

The frontiersman stared at Harrison intently. "Why me?"

"He knows and trusts you," the governor stated. "I need a body who I'm certain will talk to Tecumseh personally. Our situation grows more precarious every day. We must talk before there is any bloodshed. Keeping peace is best for everyone involved, red and white men alike. What do you say?"

Ruddell looked at the floor a moment before draining his third glass of whiskey. He fixed his gaze on Harrison and nodded. "Alright, Governor. I'll take your message to Tecumseh. I can't promise that he'll talk to me anymore then he did your envoys. Your right, I don't cotton to you much. Still, I'm a man of God and I'll do whatever I can to keep the peace. People I care for on both sides would end up kilt in another war, and not doin' all creation about it wouldn't sit well with me."

"Good, I had a notion I could count of you," Harrison replied with a smile. The governor moved behind his desk and withdrew a sealed letter from one of the drawers. He held it out for the minister.

Ruddell moved across the room and took the letter from Harrison's outstretched hand. The governor sat down behind the large desk.

"Perhaps we can put an end to these disagreements," he stated smugly. "I hope that Tecumseh is a reasonable man. Our government does not want to fight another war at this time, but it does not mean we won't defend ourselves if threatened or provoked. I hope these savages understand that."

Stephen put on his hat. "I'm sure he's as reasonable as you are, Governor Harrison. I'll make sure he gets your message," he stated smoothly. "With your permission, I'll take my leave. It's a long ride to Prophetstown."

Harrison waved the frontiersman out without turning. Harrison's aide, Richard Spencer, entered the room as the big man left. The governor had moved back to his desk and was looking over land claims as the younger man moved up beside him.

"Pardon me, governor," Spencer said hesitantly. "Are you sure this man can be trusted? Everyone says he's more Shawnee then white man. He went back to live with them after he was returned to his family. Don't you suspicion he'll reveal more to the Shawnee then you desire?"

Harrison smiled. "That's exactly why I'm sending him. The Shawnee will trust him, even if we don't. The simple fact is that I need to meet with this Tecumseh in a safe place in order to determine how much of a threat he and his confederacy are. War with Britain is coming again. We cannot allow these savages to become allies of the British in Canada. We'll do all we can, within reason, to placate Tecumseh until we've dealt with the British. When the time is right, we'll handle both he and his brother."

The governor looked out of the window at the Wabash once again. "The land along the upper Wabash is some of the most fertile in the world. We cannot leave it in the hands of savages when our own settlers could feed the nation from the bounty they could raise upon those lands. In time, we will control the Wabash and no Indian prophet or frontier preacher will stand in our way."

Harrison watched as Stephen Ruddell galloped northward out of Vincennes, the invitation for Tecumseh tucked away in his saddlebag.

Stephen walked his tired horse up the well beaten path toward Prophetstown. It was July and the summer heat was stifling as the frontiersman used a handkerchief to wipe the sweat from his brow and neck. His white linen shirt was soaked with sweat and stained with the dirt and grime accumulated from over a week of steady travel. Ruddell was impressed by the structure of the village that had not been in existence for a full year. He shook his head at the size of the council house and the medicine lodge that dominated the landscape. The settlement was larger then any Indian village Stephen had seen during his youth in Ohio. He estimated that there were no less then two thousand Indians in Prophetstown. Governor Harrison had reason to worry; the brothers' influence and power over the different tribes around the Great Lakes was expanding rapidly.

Stephen stopped in the middle of the trail as a group of warriors on horseback rode out to meet him. He made no move toward his rifle, which remained holstered across his horse's back. The frontiersman recognized the warrior Cold Water leading the group as they surrounded him, their weapons ready. Ruddell held his right hand up toward the warrior, his palm extended in a sign of peace.

"What do you want?" Cold Water demanded, recognizing his former Lacrosse team mate. "*Shemanese* are not welcome in Prophetstown"

"I'm here to see Tecumseh," the frontiersman replied, showing no fear toward the well armed warriors. "I come bearing a message from the *Shemanese* Chief Harrison to Tecumseh and his brother."

Cold Water extended his hand toward the frontiersman. "Give it to me," he ordered. "I will take the message to them."

"No," Ruddell stated. "I'll hand the message to them myself and await their reply."

Cold Water's eyes hardened, but he made no move toward the big man. He had been instructed to stop any messengers sent by the governor in Vincennes and deny their entry into Prophetstown. The warrior had not been instructed to kill any white man, at least not yet. He remembered the redheaded man well and was wary of fighting him. He also did not think Tecumseh would want his once close friend killed over a message. He leaned close to the warrior next to him and whispered in the man's ear. The man nodded and swung his horse around and galloped toward the village. Cold Water turned his gaze back to Ruddell.

"We will wait for word from Tecumseh and the Prophet. If they want you to enter Prophetstown, then I will bring you before them myself. If they want you to leave, then so it will be."

A slight smile appeared on the warrior's face and his voice became slightly malicious. "If they want your scalp to be brought to them, then I will gladly remove it from your head as well."

Stephen returned the cold stare. "Your boys might return with my scalp, *ne-kah-noh,* but you would not. You would be lying cold on the ground beside me. No matter what else happens, I promise you that!"

Cold Water smirked at the comment, but felt a tinge of fear as he looked into the former warrior's icy blue eyes. They spoke no more as they waited for word from the leaders of the village. Finally, the warrior Cold Water had sent into the village returned.

"He is to be brought to the medicine lodge. The Prophet is waiting to see him," the man explained, eyeing the frontiersman curiously.

Cold Water shook his head. "Today may not be your day to die," he stated in disappointment.

Stephen snorted and uncocked the flintlock pistol hidden in his belt. He held the weapon up and tossed it to the surprised Shawnee. "Nor is it yours, at least not by my hand."

The frontiersman also handed over his rifle and hunting knife to his would-be escorts as well. "I'll be havin' all those back after I see Tecumseh," he added pointedly.

Ruddell blinked to adjust to the darkness inside the medicine lodge as he entered. He was able to make out a platform in the middle of the room with a wooden throne set upon it. Stephen felt his throat tighten as his gaze settled on Loud Noise, sitting upon the throne and glaring at the frontiersman angrily.

"What do you want, Ruddell? Why have you come to our home uninvited?" the Prophet demanded.

"I bring a message from the governor at Vincennes," he replied politely. "Where's Tecumseh?"

Tenskwatawa leapt to his feet and shook his fist at the messenger.

"Your concern should be with me!" he raged. "You carry a message from Harrison? This says to me that you are a spy! I warned all the others what would happen the next time a *Shemanese* spy was sent to my village! Look to the ground at your feet; there is your grave!"

Stephen's eyes narrowed at the threat, and his jaw tightened in anger toward his old adversary.

"I see that some things never change," he retorted coldly. "Your chops are as big as they ever was when you were a brat and you're still full of buffalo shit!"

Tenskwatawa's eyes widened at the insult, and he yanked a knife from a sheath at his side and advanced a step toward the frontiersman.

"STOP."

Tecumseh's voice caused everyone to halt and turn toward the chief as he entered the lodge. The warrior was dressed only in a doe skin loin cloth in an attempt to remain comfortable in the stifling July heat. He crossed his arms in front of his muscular chest and regarded the scene, scowling.

The Prophet looked to his brother for support. "Harrison has sent us another spy; I think we should kill this one to teach the others a lesson!"

Tecumseh flashed his brother an impatient stare, causing the medicine man to bow his head and sit back on the dais. The Shawnee leader then turned toward his former friend.

"Why have you come here?" he demanded

Stephen pulled the letter from his side pouch. "The governor sent me with a message. He thought you might listen to me since we are old friends," he explained. "I told him I didn't reckon you would want to see or hear me."

Tecumseh managed a slight smile at the big man's honesty. "This may be the first time I have known your governor to be right. Come, we will talk."

Both men glanced at the scowling Prophet as they exited the lodge.

Ruddell sat across from Tecumseh inside his wigwam as the warrior broke the seal on the letter and opened it. He scanned the message for several moments. Finally, he looked up at the preacher.

"Do you know what this says?"

Stephen nodded slightly. Tecumseh shook his head in amazement and began to read the note aloud.

"What reason have you to complain of the United States? Have they taken anything from you? Have they ever violated the treaties made with the red men?"

Tecumseh looked at Ruddell, aghast. "They have taken everything. Every treaty we signed has been violated."

The Shawnee leader tossed the letter down in disgust. "He wished to meet with me? It is men like Harrison who are destroying our way of life. He takes without asking, and then expects us to kneel to him as if he were a king. Why should I meet with such a man?" he demanded.

Stephen sighed. "Tecumseh, you are the only one who can speak for your people. Harrison is giving you a chance to have your say; you must take it."

Tecumseh looked skeptical. "What if it is a trap? Maybe he wants me to come to Vincennes so he can kill me. He asks that I only bring three warriors with me!"

Ruddell shrugged and smiled. "Bring three chiefs with you. Those chiefs will have to bring their own warriors to protect them. The chiefs will protect you and the others will protect their chiefs."

Tecumseh smiled. "You were always cunning, Sinnatha. If I come to Vincennes, will you be there?"

Stephen grasped his friend's wrist tightly. "Yes, *jai-nai-nah.* I'll be there to help keep the peace between all our people."

Tecumseh nodded and looked into the small fire for several moments. "Tell Harrison that I will come in a month's time to talk of our differences. Maybe he is a man who can be reasoned with. I don't think so, but I must try for our people. I will need you there to help speak to this man."

The frontiersman nodded and filled a pipe with tobacco. He took several puffs before passing it to his friend with a smile.

"I look forward to you meetin' the governor. I suspicion the conversation will be lively. I don't intend to miss it."

CHAPTER 20

VINCENNES, INDIANA TERRITORY
AUGUST, 1810

STEPHEN RUDDELL WATCHED as almost a hundred canoes floated down the Wabash toward Vincennes. Tecumseh had been true to his word and had arrived from Prophetstown a month from the day he had promised. His warriors had made camp north of the town and were now finishing the short trip to Harrison's estate for Tecumseh to meet with the territorial leader. Harrison and the peaceful Potawatomi chief, Winamac, now stood beside the frontiersman, watching the canoes land on the bank of the river. Harrison was dressed in his finest clothes to greet the Shawnee chief. He wore a high collared frock coat adorned with heavy brass buttons and a pair of white breeches. He had finished off the outfit with his best black leather riding boots and an ornamental sword hanging from a red silk sash at his side.

"I told him to bring three warriors! The devil has brought a war party!" Harrison whispered, his voice strained. The governor pulled a white handkerchief from his coat pocket to wipe the sweat from his brow.

Ruddell looked at the smaller man. The day was already growing warm and the heavy frock coat was impractical. The sweat that the garment would produce would not be worth any impression of finery the governor was trying to portray. If anything, Tecumseh and his warriors would think the *Shemanese* leader a fool for his dress in the summer heat. The frontiersman shrugged, quite cool in his buckskin leggings and blue linen shirt. It was not his job to tell the man how to dress; he was here as an interpreter.

"They haven't brought their guns," he reminded Harrison. "So many warriors have come because they fear for their chief's life and are here to help protect him."

"Or maybe kill me," The governor retorted. "The guard will remain ready. My, he is a striking fellow."

Stephen transferred his gaze to Tecumseh as he led his warriors up from the river bank. The Shawnee wore a pair of fringed doeskin leggings and moccasins. A white wampum belt was strung from his left shoulder and his pipe tomahawk hung at his side. He had placed a bear claw necklace around his neck that hung over his muscular chest. A brace of eagle feathers were strung in his shoulder length dark hair. "The governor is right for once," Stephen thought with a smile. Tecumseh was an impressive figure to behold.

Harrison smiled and stepped forward with his hand extended as Tecumseh drew near. The Shawnee leader examined the governor from head to toe and hesitated a moment before gripping the man's extended hand solemnly.

"It is good to meet the great Tecumseh," Harrison declared. "I have heard much about you."

"We have seen each other before," Tecumseh replied.

Harrison's brow furrowed. "Fallen Timbers?"

Tecumseh nodded, remaining silent.

"Then it is good to speak with a former enemy as an honored friend," the governor replied. "Come, we will go inside. We have much to discuss."

"No," Tecumseh stated, crossing his arms in front of his chest

"What?" Harrison replied, more then a little confused.

Tecumseh spread his hands wide. "I want to be in the sun. We can talk outside where there is fresh air to breathe and wind to cool us from the summer heat. There will be neither inside your house of stone. I have no wish to smell the stench of your soldiers crowded around me. Also, everyone will be able to hear what we say to each other outside where only a few would know what is said behind your walls. Has not everyone come to hear us?" he added with a smile.

Before Harrison could respond, Tecumseh signaled for his warriors to sit down on the grass around a large oak tree. The governor frowned, but shrugged indifferently. He turned to a nearby officer.

"Bring a table and chairs," he ordered.

The officer saluted and rushed off as the governor turned back to the sitting Shawnee.

"Tecumseh, this is Chief Winamac," he said, presenting the Potawatomi leader.

"I know who he was," the Shawnee warrior replied without looking up.

"Was?" Harrison questioned.

"I don't speak to dead men," Tecumseh replied harshly, glaring at the chief who had signed the Treaty of Fort Wayne. "One who sells land that is not his could not have a soul."

Winamac frowned and took a step closer to the governor. Stephen sighed and shook his head. So much for a smooth beginning to this visit!

The old man was splitting kindling wood for the kitchen stove when Draper exited the back door of the Ruddell home. The former minister had stopped his story late in the evening with Tecumseh's arrival in Vincennes. Lyman could hardly go to sleep, excited to hear more details of the famous meeting. When he did finally sleep, he once again woke late. Sarah Ruddell was in the kitchen and smiled kindly at the writer. She fixed him a heaping plate of hotcakes and bacon as well as several cups of steaming coffee.

"Where is Mr. Ruddell?" he asked politely as she cleared the table.

"Well, he was grumbling about doing something useful this morning," she replied, rolling her eyes. "I suspicion you'll find him out at the woodpile."

Ruddell did not even look up as the door closed behind the younger man. He was methodically splitting rounds of hickory into thin strips.

"Hickory makes the best kindling," he commented, splitting another round. "It's easy to light and it burns longer."

Lyman nodded and picked up a spare axe. The old man raised a questioning eyebrow as the writer set up a round and split it deftly.

"My father was a cooper; I split more then my share of wood when I was a boy," Draper explained.

The former frontiersman chuckled and the pair toiled together at the woodpile for the better part of the morning. Finally, the old man wiped his brow and sat down on a large chunk of hickory.

"We burned a lot of hickory in Vincennes," he stated, "It was plentiful in the forests around the Wabash. I reckon Tecumseh and his boys burned through ten chord of wood during their visit, and that was in the summer."

"I have read many accounts of Tecumseh's visit and the debate he had with Harrison," Draper interjected. "Every witness stated that both the Governor and Tecumseh debated passionately for hours."

The old man snorted at Draper's remark. "Passionate isn't the word I would use. Oh, they was the most powerful pair of speakers that I ever heard. Both were smart as a steel trap in defendin' their positions. Tecumseh argued that one tribe could not sell the land, that it belonged to all the Indians. He allowed that all the tribes had to agree to sell their land, which ain't what happened at Fort Wayne."

Ruddell wiped his sweat drenched brow once again and shook his head. "I can still recollect what he said, and it's been over thirty years. He could speak good English, but refused. He made me translate all creation he said in Shawnee to English."

The old man smiled. "I still remember the look on Harrison's face when I translated Tecumseh's words!"

Tecumseh rose before the crowd of warriors, settlers, and soldiers that had formed in the oak grove where the governor had arranged the table and chairs for their meeting. Harrison sat behind the small table, his hands folded in front of him, patiently waiting to hear what the Indian leader had to say. Tecumseh stood proudly, gazing intently upon the assembled crowd. Stephen stepped to his side and whispered in his ear.

"Why do you need me to translate?" he demanded quietly. "You speak English well enough."

Tecumseh smiled. "It would please the Long Knife to hear me speak his language," he replied in Shawnee. "I trust you to translate everything exactly as I have said it."

Stephen shook his head in frustration. "So be it."

Tecumseh looked around at the crowd once again before settling his gaze upon Harrison. The Governor maintained a slight smile as the Shawnee leader stepped forward and raised his hands.

"Houses are built for you to hold councils in. The Indians hold theirs in the open air," Tecumseh cried, gesturing toward the sky. "I am a Shawnee. My forefathers were warriors. Their son is a warrior. From them I take my only existence. From my tribe I take nothing. I have made myself what I am. If only I could make the red people as great as the conceptions of my own mind! When I think of the Great Spirit that rules over us all, I would not then come to Governor Harrison to ask him to tear up the treaty," he continued, staring directly at the seated man. "I would say to him instead, 'Brother, you have the liberty to return to your own country'."

Tecumseh waited a moment for Ruddell to finish translating his words to English. When he saw Harrison's smile disappear, he continued.

"You wish to prevent the Indians from doing as we see fit, to unite and let them consider their lands as a common property of the whole. You take the tribes aside and advise them not to come into this measure. You want, by your distinctions of Indian tribes, in allotting to each a particular, to make them war with each other. You have never seen an Indian endeavor to make the white people do this. You are continually driving the red people, when at last you will drive them into the great lake, where they can neither stand nor work," he cried, gesturing in the direction of Lake Michigan.

Tecumseh could see that his words were having the desired effect on the governor. Harrison now leaned forward on his table, his hands clenched and a scowl upon his face. The Shawnee leader held back a smile as he moved on with his speech.

"Since my residence at Tippecanoe, we have endeavored to level all distinctions, to destroy village chiefs, by whom all mischief is done. It is they who sell the land to the Americans! Brother, this land that was sold, and the goods that were given for it, was only done by a few. In the future we are prepared to punish those who propose to sell land to the Americans," he declared, glaring at Winamac, who had seated himself beside the Governor. Understanding the clear threat, the Potawatomi stared at the ground, unwilling to meet the Shawnee leader's gaze.

"If you continue to purchase these lands, it will make war among the different tribes, and, at last I do not know what will be the consequences among the white people," Tecumseh warned. "Brother, I wish you would take pity on the red people and do as I have requested. If you will not give up the land and do cross the boundary of our present settlement, it will be vary hard and produce great trouble between us."

The Shawnee leader banged his fist on Harrison's table. "How can we have confidence in the white people? We have good and just reasons to believe we have ample grounds to accuse the white men of injustice, especially when such great acts of injustice have been committed by them upon our race, of which they seem to have no respect or regard."

Tecumseh looked at Harrison again, adding one more statement as Stephen grimly translated the speech. "Everything I have told you is the truth. The Great Spirit has inspired my words today."

"What happened next?" Draper gasped, amazed at the old man's memory.

Stephen had pulled out a small knife and was whittling at a piece of hickory. He snorted and spit on the ground. "Well, the governor was about out of his head. I don't know what made Harrison redder, that damned frock coat or how huffed he was from Tecumseh's speech. He kept his head though, I'll give him that. Harrison wasn't the powerful body that Tecumseh was, but he was a considerable speaker and had a strong voice. The son of a bitch was no less cock-sure about his position on the fix. He spoke of how the Miami and Potawatomi had used the land around the Wabash long before the Shawnee had moved north. He said that all the tribes were different, and spoke different languages. So, he had a mind that it was right for a tribe to sell the land that they claimed."

"How did Tecumseh react?" Lyman asked, his writing box open before him once again.

"How do you reckon?" the old man growled. "He was out of his head! Unfortunately, Tecumseh let his spirit get the best of him."

Tecumseh leapt to his feet and pointed at Harrison. "You are a liar!" he cried in English, shocking the territorial leader. "Everything you say is a lie! I was foolish to come here and try and reason with you! This is better left to the red dog that laps at your feet!"

Hearing the insult directed at him and fearing Tecumseh might attack, Winamac pulled a flintlock pistol from his shirt and pointed it at the Shawnee leader. The warriors who were serving as Tecumseh's bodyguards leapt to their feet and pulled their weapons to protect their chief. Harrison pushed away from the table and withdrew his flimsy sword, his teeth bared. Tecumseh had pulled his tomahawk from his belt as soon as Winamac had brought forth his pistol. The Shawnee leader now seemed ready to strike as his warriors surrounded him. The company of soldiers that stood behind the governor raised their muskets and prepared to fire.

Stephen sprang forward to stand between Tecumseh and the governor, his hands extended toward both men.

"STOP!" he demanded, his voice booming across the grove.

Tecumseh and Harrison eyed each other warily. Ruddell edged closer to his old friend.

"Look around you, brother," he hissed. "You are surrounded by soldiers with loaded guns. If you attack, you will die along will all of your warriors. Put the tomahawk down; now is not the time to let anger guide you!"

Tecumseh glanced at the big man, his enraged features calming. Finally, he relaxed and lowered his tomahawk, exhaling deeply. The warriors protecting him followed suit. Harrison lowered his sword and signaled for the soldiers to stand down.

"I did not invite you here to be insulted!" The governor cried indignantly, jamming the ornamental sword back into its scabbard. "You come to my home and dare draw your weapons and threaten me and my guests? This council is ended."

Harrison stalked away from the table with Winamac close on his heals. Stephen and Tecumseh watched him go in silence. Ruddell could see his hopes of a lasting peace between the government and Tecumseh floating away like driftwood down the Wabash.

Stephen slipped quietly into the governor's office as the enraged man paced the floor. Harrison had removed his coat and was busy wiping his face with a towel when he noticed the frontiersman silently standing in the back of the room.

"All fire, Ruddell," he huffed. "You're as sneaky as one of those damn savages. How did you get in my office?"

"I reckon that didn't go well," the big man observed.

The governor's eyes widened and he snorted in response. Harrison moved across the room and slammed his ornamental sword on his desk before pouring himself a tumbler of whiskey and collapsing in his chair.

"I knew I couldn't reason with these Shawnee fanatics." he cried. "The nerve of the man, to pull his tomahawk on me during a peaceful council."

"After Winamac had drawn a pistol on him," Stephen observed.

"Damnation, man!" the smaller man bellowed, slamming his glass on the table. "He called me a liar in front of all creation. He insulted my honor."

Ruddell sighed and moved to the table and poured himself a glass of the governor's fine whiskey.

"Oh, do help yourself," Harrison stated sarcastically. "You're as impudent as that devil Tecumseh."

Stephen took a sip of the bourbon and exhaled. He smiled slightly. "You didn't allow that he was a powerful speaker, did you governor?"

Harrison opened his mouth to respond, but hesitated. He rose from his chair and poured himself another glass of whiskey. "No, I surely didn't," he admitted grudgingly. "It took me by surprise."

The frontiersman held out his empty glass, his smile growing. "I do recall warning you."

Harrison chuckled and refilled the big man's glass. Finally calm, he sat down at his desk and looked into his own glass.

"This council has become a disaster of epic scale," he observed. "President Madison has instructed me to make every endeavor to preserve the peace with these red devils until the current dispute with the British can be settled. Our efforts today just made that task more difficult."

Ruddell took another swallow of whiskey and looked the governor over. "Do you want my advice on how to handle Tecumseh?"

Harrison raised his eyebrow. "By all means."

"Take away the boodle," the big man instructed. "Meet with him alone. Tecumseh is as smart as a steel trap, contrary to what you might believe. He also cottons to an audience. His mere presence can send them into a conniption fit, and he works to whitewash his image when there's a crowd. Meet with him; you will see that he is a different body."

"How?" the governor asked.

Stephen finished his bourbon and smiled. "Leave that to me. I reckon I can arrange something."

Night had settled upon the river and the encampment Tecumseh had returned to just north of Vincennes. Tecumseh was sitting on a small hickory log, staring into the fire. He looked up as Stephen Ruddell appeared out of the darkness.

"You can still move like an Indian," the Shawnee leader stated, not surprised to see his old friend.

Ruddell nodded. "When I need to. Which seems like it could be more often in the days ahead."

Tecumseh shook his head sadly. "I was a fool to come here, Sinnatha. The white men will never listen."

"Why not try and talk to him alone?" Ruddell suggested as he warmed his hands at the fire. "Just the two of you?"

"How?" Tecumseh replied.

Stephen jerked his head in the direction from which he had come. "He's here! Come on in, Governor!"

William Henry Harrison cautiously entered the firelight, unsure of the course of action the frontier minister had talked him into. He had removed his frock coat and was now dressed in a white linen shirt and breeches. Harrison removed his hat and pointed to a place on the log beside Tecumseh.

"May I sit?" he asked politely.

Momentarily speechless, Tecumseh finally nodded and moved over to give the white man more room. Both leaders sat staring at the fire for several moments before the governor cleared his throat.

"You and I are not so different, Tecumseh. We both want our people to have better lives. Together, we could work together to benefit all of our people."

Tecumseh sighed and scooted closer to Harrison, causing the governor to move closer to the edge of the log.

"We are two different people who wish for two different things. Your people want to change the land; ours wish to live with it," the Shawnee leader explained, inching closer still to the territorial leader.

Harrison moved once again, uncomfortable with the warrior's intrusion into his personal space. "There is plenty of land for all," he argued. "I allow that some of your claims may be valid, but that is not for me to decide."

Tecumseh edged closer, forcing Harrison right to the end of the log.

"Who decides then?"

"The President in Washington," the governor replied impatiently, irritated by the Indian leader's closeness. "Tecumseh, if you continue to crowd me, I'll fall off the log."

Tecumseh smiled and laughed. "Now you know how we Indians feel every time you make a new treaty."

The Shawnee leader stood and walked away chuckling. Harrison shook his head in amazement and watched him go, not quite sure what to say.

The summer sun was beginning to dissipate the ribbons of fog that hung over the Wabash as the Indians packed their belongings into their canoes and prepared to paddle back up the river to Prophetstown. Tecumseh was smoking his tomahawk pipe beside a hickory fire when Governor Harrison and Stephen Ruddell rode into the camp and dismounted.

Ruddell sat down beside his old friend as Harrison took a seat across from them on the very same log that he and Tecumseh had shared the previous night. Tecumseh smiled at the memory and almost laughed after the governor eyed him suspiciously when the Shawnee leader leaned forward to light the pipe he just refilled.

"Don't worry," he chuckled, passing the pipe to Ruddell. "The log is yours; we do not even need to sign a treaty for you to keep it. Think of it as a gift."

Stephen snorted and choked on smoke at the Indian leader's joke. Harrison glared at the minister before turning back to Tecumseh. "I'm sorry to see you go, Tecumseh. Your visit has been interesting, to say the least."

Ruddell had passed the tomahawk pipe back to the Shawnee warrior who offered it to the governor. Harrison took the pipe, not wanting to insult the Indian leader, and drew a couple of tentative puffs.

"I don't want war between our people," Tecumseh stated, his smile fading. "But I will not allow further encroachment onto our land. You say that the great chief in Washington will determine this matter. I hope that the Great Spirit will put sense enough into his head to induce him to have you give up the land. It is true; he is so far off and he will not be injured by the war. He may sit still in his town, and drink his wine, while you and I will have to fight it out."

Harrison passed the pipe back to the Shawnee warrior. "It is not a war that you could win," he stated confidently.

Tecumseh emptied the pipe and stood to leave.

"You may be right, but there is much at stake. I know that trouble between the seventeen fires and the British fathers across the sea grows," he replied, meeting the governor's stare. "Soon, they will fight another war. Your president would not want to fight two wars. It would not be good to have Governor Harrison become the cause of a war with the Indians, especially when there are so many British traders and soldiers in Canada that would support my people in a fight"

Harrison had risen from the log, scowling.

"What are you saying? Are you threatening to enlist British support against the United State of America?" he demanded

Tecumseh did not flinch.

"Do not send anyone into our lands. I cannot guarantee their safety," he replied evenly.

The warrior turned to the redheaded minister. "That includes you, *ne-kah-noh*," he stated sadly. "You will not be able to find a peaceful union between our people. We will fight to keep what is ours."

Tecumseh stepped forward and clasped Stephen's wrist tightly. "Be safe, *Jai-nai-nah*. I hope I see you in better days."

Ruddell swallowed hard. "As do I, brother."

The Shawnee leader nodded to Harrison wordlessly and slipped into the last canoe as it was being pushed into the river. The two white men silently watched for several minutes as the Indians paddled up the Wabash.

"What does it mean?" Harrison asked suddenly.

"What?"

"*Jai-nai-nah.*"

"Blood brother," Stephen replied, watching Tecumseh's canoe disappear around the bend in the river.

Harrison nodded and walked from the river bank. He mounted his horse and pulled the reins around to take one last look at the departing leader.

"It's appropriate," he stated darkly. "Blood may very well be spilled the next time you or any other white man sees him."

The frontier minister remained silent, knowing in his heart that the governor could very well be right.

CHAPTER 21

QUINCY, ILLINOIS
SUMMER, 1845

"I CAN'T IMAGINE THE SCENE!" Draper gasped. "The debate between Tecumseh and President Harrison is well documented, but this is the first account I have ever heard of their private meetings. Tell me, what happened after Tecumseh went back to Prophetstown?"

The pair was sitting underneath a large maple tree beside a stream that emptied into the Mississippi. The afternoon sun was bright, but the maple provided ample shade for the old man to cast a line into one of his favorite fishing holes. He had secured his pole to the ground with a rock and lay back in the shade, his eyes closed as a summer wind stirred the leaves on the tree.

"It would suffice to say he didn't sit on his bumfiddle in Prophetstown long." Ruddell yawned without opening his eyes. "It was certain that war was comin'. So, Tecumseh spent most of his time buildin' his alliances. He visited tribes from New York to Wisconsin, drummin' up opposition against Harrison and the United States. He made several trips to Canada to speak with the British. All the while, Harrison had spies reporting on the happenings along the Wabash. The blood was up between Vincennes and Prophetstown. Harrison had powerful designs. He wanted to force a fight by buying more land and sending settlers into the treaty lands. The leaders in Washington wouldn't allow him to do it with all the trouble brewin' with England. There wasn't any fightin' for a coon's age, but that changed the next summer."

"How so?" the writer pressed.

The old man cracked open one of his eyes, annoyed by the younger man's excitement and the fact that his afternoon nap was being interrupted.

"Tecumseh had many supporters among the different tribes, but he knew he didn't have enough to whip Harrison in a war. So, he had designs to go south to visit the Creeks, Choctaws, and Cherokees to drum up more support. Tecumseh knew that he could be gone for a coon's age, but he reckoned gainin' the southern nations as allies was worth being away so long."

Ruddell sat up as his fishing line moved. He gave the pole a tug and pulled in a large catfish. He tossed the fish into a basket and rebaited his hook before dropping the line back into the water. He glanced at Draper, his expression somber. "The most powerful risks Tecumseh took were leaving his brother in command and visiting Harrison on his way south. Both would prove considerable mistakes."

Tecumseh and Tenskwatawa stood beside his horse outside the House of the Stranger. Nearby, a score of mounted warriors waited patiently for their leader. Tecumseh looked at his younger brother, his eyes hard. Tenskwatawa had taken to painting his face and body various shades of black and red, as well as wearing robes adorned with furs, claws, and various feathers in the last several months. Gone was the simple and modest attire in which he had so sincerely presented himself to the people after his vision from Weshemoneto. His old swagger and boastful tendencies had returned as his status had grown. Tecumseh had chastised him privately on several occasions. Tenskwatawa's behavior would improve after his brother's tongue lashings, but never for long. Tecumseh had to keep constant watch over the brash Prophet and often had to smooth the ruffled feathers of chiefs and Indian leaders who Tenskwatawa had offended or upset in some way. It was a tedious and tiring job.

Tecumseh was hesitant to leave Prophetstown in his brother's care, but he knew that the trip to visit the southern tribes could not be put off any longer. His visits with British officials in Canada had confirmed that tensions between England and the United States had risen to the brink of war. This trip could be the Shawnee leader's last chance to strengthen the Indian confederacy before the conflict began. Leaving the Prophet in charge of the village was a risk that Tecumseh knew he had to take.

"I could be gone for almost a year, *ni-je-ni-nuh*," Tecumseh stated, clasping his younger brother by the wrist. "There is much to do in the south."

Tenskwatawa frowned "I wish that I was going," he replied enviously. "Few of the southern tribesmen have heard the messages that *Weshemoneto* has bestowed upon me to share with the people."

Tecumseh shook his head; they had previously discussed this issue on several occasions. "You are needed here as the voice of *Weshemoneto*. Our home here on the Tippecanoe is too important for both of us to leave. There are more people from many nations coming every day to hear your teachings. If we both go, the bonds we have worked so hard to build could fail. We cannot allow that to happen."

Tecumseh put his arms around the Prophet's wide shoulders. "Many warriors are staying with you, brother," he continued, indicating the assembled leaders. "Listen to their words and lead wisely."

Shabani, a Potawatomi chief who had become one of Tecumseh's closest friends and advisers, nodded in agreement.

"Do not trust Harrison." Tecumseh warned, loud enough for the other village leaders to hear. "I fear he might attempt something while I am away. If he does, don't fight him! Protect the people and flee. What we have accomplished here is too important to attempt any foolishness. Do you understand?"

The Prophet smiled and nodded. "You can trust me, brother. We will await your successful return."

Tecumseh swung up onto his horse's back as Shabani moved up beside his chief.

"Guide him wisely, my friend," he whispered to the Potawatomi. "I put my trust in you!"

Shabani nodded. "I will do my best," he stated, glancing at Tenskwatawa.

Tecumseh looked around at the assembled villagers, Indians from a dozen different tribes, his heart swelling with pride. "Wish me well," he cried, "and *Weshemoneto's* blessing of a safe journey!"

The Prophet smiled and waved along with the other cheering villagers as Tecumseh and his warriors galloped out of the village. When Tecumseh had disappeared from sight, Tenskwatawa turned away, his smile replaced by a scowl.

"I am the Great Spirit's chosen one, not you," Tenskwatawa hissed, glaring in the direction of his departing brother. "I will lead my people as the Great Spirit directs me."

The Prophet stalked across the village toward his medicine lodge. Alarmed, Shabani moved to follow. Tenskwatawa motioned to his personal guards as he entered the lodge. The warriors obediently blocked the Potawatomi's path and would not let him enter the lodge. Shabani shook his head in frustration and moved away. He wished Tecumseh had taken his pompous brother with him. The next year could be the longest of his life.

William Henry Harrison watched Tecumseh and his warriors float down the Wabash, heading south. He had just spent two days at council with the Shawnee leader, with results similar to the talks they had held a year earlier. Tecumseh had skillfully debated the governor on every topic and issue. In the end, neither side had gained a significant advantage. Harrison had been more prepared to deal with the cunning chief then he had been last year, right down to the comfortable fringed buckskin hunting shirt he wore. This council had ended more cordially, with Tecumseh making a surprise announcement.

"I hope that no attempts will be made to settle the land near our village on the Wabash," Tecumseh stated somberly. "I shall be traveling south to visit our Indians brothers, the Cherokee and Creek. There will be a great number of Wyandots coming to settle on the Tippecanoe this fall, and they will need to use those lands as a hunting ground. I would not want them to cause bad feelings by killing some settler's cattle or hogs. It is my wish that despite our differences, everything remain in the present situation until my return. I will stop and meet with Governor Harrison upon my return from the south. It is my hope that we may eventually travel to meet your President and settle all our differences."

The Shawnee leader turned toward Governor Harrison. "I go south to spread our message of unity and peace. Will you maintain the peace between our people while I am away?"

Harrison returned the warrior's stare. "I look forward to your return that we might build a peaceful alliance that will last many generations," he stated smoothly. "If our people are not provoked, then peace will remain."

Tecumseh had been satisfied with the response and the council had ended.

Harrison had watched until the last canoe had disappeared down the Wabash. He had placed his hands behind his back and slowly made his way back to his Grousland home, contemplating his next action. The governor had climbed the stairs to his office and stood staring out of the window for several minutes. Finally, he had taken a sheet of paper and dipped a pen into an ink pot that sat upon his desk. He addressed the letter to William Eustis, President James Madison's Secretary of War.

Dear Mr. Secretary,

Concerning the matter of the Indians who have taken up residency along the Wabash north of Vincennes. They remain active in recruiting other tribes to their cause to resist the settlement of land that has been rightfully purchased in this fair territory. They mask their ambition behind a message of religion, but it is clear they desire the removal of all white settlers from the region. Their main leader is the Shawnee war chief, Tecumseh. The scope of his influence is both alarming and impressive. His influence stretches across the Great Lakes, and he is currently undertaking a mission to the southern tribes to enlist their support in his cause. The obedience and respect which the followers of Tecumseh pay to him is astonishing, and more then any other circumstance bespeaks him one of those uncommon geniuses who spring up occasionally to produce revolutions and overturn the established order of things. If it were not for the vicinity of the United States, he would, perhaps, be the founder of an empire that would rival in glory that of Mexico or Peru. No difficulties deter him. His activity and industry supply the want of letters. For four years he has been in constant motion. You see him today on the Wabash and in a short time you hear of him on the shores of Lake Erie or Michigan, or on the banks of the Mississippi, and wherever he goes he makes an impression favorable to his purpose.

Sir, the situation here grows more tenuous. I believe that it is time to move against the savages that inhabit land that I feel is one of the fairest portions of the globe. Why should this land, fairly purchased, remain in a state of nature? I intended, with your support, to move against the village on the Tippecanoe before the onset of winter to end this threat against our own people and land. With Tecumseh gone, it is the most opportune time to end the confederacy he and his brother have built to oppose our nation.

I shall begin making the necessary arrangements to support a fall campaign. It is my hope that Tecumseh will return to find that part of the fabric, which he considered complete will be demolished, and even its foundation rooted up. I anxiously await your response.

Your humble servant,

W.H. Harrison

Harrison signed his name with a flourish and sealed the letter with wax. He knew that Eustis was concerned with preparing for the impending war with Great Britain. As such, the governor hoped the Secretary of War would be more willing to support his plan to attack Prophetstown and reduce the Indian confederacy, eliminating a possible ally for the British along the Western frontier.

Harrison smiled. Tecumseh's departure for the south could not have come at a more opportune time.

Vincennes was bustling with activity when Stephen Ruddell arrived from Wapakoneta in the middle of September. The governor had sent word that he needed to see the Baptist missionary. Militia and regular soldiers were camped in large numbers north of the town. Stephen was escorted to Harrison's office by an armed guard. The scene inside the office reminded the big man of a chicken coop. Several aides were rushing around the room, filling out orders and provision requests for an army. Governor Harrison stood in front of a floor length mirror as a tailor fitted him for a new uniform. He looked up as the frontiersman entered the room and smiled.

"Ah! Ruddell, do come in. I have some wonderful news!"

Stephen moved across the room and sat down on one of the cushioned chairs in front of the governor's desk. He slowly looked around the bustling room.

"Looks like you're fixin' for a war, governor," he observed.

Harrison chuckled. "I plan for the possibility of one. I intend to march on Prophetstown and put an end to all of this nonsense!"

The frontiersman frowned. "What about Tecumseh? Didn't you promise him that there would be no trouble while he was gone?"

The governor looked at the big man incredulously. "Well of course I did! Would he have left if I said otherwise? Now is the time to strike, while their leader is gone. I need a good man to act as a scout and guide. You've been to the village before. What do you say?"

"No," Ruddell replied sharply.

Harrison's smile disappeared. He signaled for the tailor and all the aides to leave the room. When they were alone, the smaller man leaned forward on his desk.

"I know that you still harbor loyalty for Tecumseh, Ruddell," the governor stated evenly. "It angers you that I would consider attacking his home while he is away. None of that matters!"

Harrison banged his fist on the desk to emphasis his point and glared at the redheaded man. "I've never met another man like this Indian. He almost killed me, by God. He's a natural leader, and therefore dangerous. If he goes unchecked, he could build a force strong enough to wreak havoc on every white man in this territory! That I cannot allow."

Stephen rose from his seat, his eyes cold. "You gave your word, Governor. You figure attackin' Prophetstown is the way to deal with Tecumseh? You're wrong. If you do this, you'll only bring this country closer to war, not prevent it. I'll not be a part of this fat-headed campaign," the frontiersman stated adamantly.

"Fine, Ruddell," Harrison sneered. "Go back to your mission in Ohio. I'd allow that you look at the color of your skin and not that of your heart! You can't sit the fence any longer. It's time for our people to take what is ours!"

The big man reached over and deftly poured himself a glass of Harrison's Kentucky bourbon as the governor looked on in disbelief. Ruddell held the glass up, as if to toast the territorial leader. "Your wrong, Governor. You may destroy the village, but you will not whip their spirit as long as Tecumseh lives."

Ruddell threw back his head and swallowed the liquor in one large gulp. He wiped his mouth with his sleeve and slammed the empty glass down on the table as the governor stood speechless.

With a final nod, the frontier minister turned on his heel and stalked from the office.

Stephen sat upon his horse on the trail outside Vincennes. The path he should take was not clear. Harrison's army could be on the march in a week's time. Ruddell looked south along the trail toward the Wabash. He knew that even now Tecumseh was in the deep south, trying to strengthen his alliances with the Creek. To the north was Prophetstown and Tenskwatawa, a man who hated him with all his heart and would surely attempt to have him killed if the frontiersman rode into the village. To the east was home, working with the peaceful Indians at Wapakoneta to bring in the fall harvest. The decision was not easy.

Finally, Ruddell cursed and swung his horse toward the southern trail. If he traveled hard and had luck, he could reach the Shawnee war chief in time to warn him of Harrison's plans. Perhaps Tecumseh would have time to return to his village to face the threat. If not, then the fate of all their work would lay upon the shoulders of the Prophet.

Stephen shuddered at the thought.

Tecumseh exhaled deeply as he and his warriors completed their war dance for the assembled crowd. The humid southern air was heavy upon their bare skin. Sweat drenched the war chief's powerful chest. The Shawnee had stripped to their breech cloths to perform the dance for the Creeks. Tecumseh and the other warriors had painted their faces black and placed eagle feathers on their heads. Every warrior wore numerous silver bracelets, gorgets, as well as ear and nose rings as part of their attire. The impressive looking northern tribesman had danced with enthusiasm for over an hour as the crowd looked on in amazement.

Tecumseh desperately wanted to make a favorable impression upon the powerful Creek nation. He had been politely welcomed among the Chicksaw and Choctaw, but had been unable to enlist either nation into an alliance with the northern tribes. Many southern Shawnee lived near the Creeks, including more then a few Tecumseh was related to. He hoped the good relations between the tribes would afford him a more favorable response when he arrived at Tuckabatchee, the principle Creek village. Fortunately, Tecumseh already had allies waiting to meet him in the form of

Big Warrior, one of the nation's most important chiefs, and his son, Tuskenau.

Tuskenau had traveled north with a band of Creeks to hear the Prophet a year earlier. Tecumseh had developed a keen admiration for the Creek warrior during his stay on the Wabash. Tuskenau had shared that the Creek were also concerned with the continual encroachment of the Americans onto their land, much the same as it was with the northern tribes. The Creek warrior had impressed upon the Shawnee leader that he would be welcome in council among the Creek Nation. When Tecumseh and his warriors did arrive in Tuckabatchee, Tuskenau was on hand to welcome them on behalf of his father.

Big Warrior's name suited him well. Immense in both height and girth, he towered over all his people. He was speaker for all the Upper Creeks and as such was the most influential leader of the tribe's national council. Most importantly, he maintained sympathy for tribes that stood in opposition to the United States. The large man now watched as the Shawnee finished their war dance, his round face set in an approving smile. Tecumseh had learned enough of Creek society to know that he would have to win over the civil chief of the Upper Creeks, Tame King, as well. The chief was an old man, wrinkled with age and with white hair that hung past his shoulders. More importantly, he was a fierce rival of Big Warrior for leadership of the tribe. Tame King rarely agreed with the large chief and harbored a great resentment of the younger man's popularity and power. The old man saw Big Warrior's smile and scowled deeply as the Shawnee finished the war dance.

Big Warrior rose to his feet and lumbered forward. He grasped Tecumseh's wrists and chuckled heartily.

"Very good, my friend," he stated in a voice that rolled like thunder. "You have stirred the blood of our young men. Everyone is eager to hearTecumseh's words." Smiling, the chief returned to his seat as Tecumseh turned his attention to the crowd.

Hundreds of Creek warriors had gathered to listen to the Shawnee leader. They waited patiently as the other Shawnee warriors moved from the clearing, leaving the war chief standing alone. Tecumseh solemnly looked around the crowd. He inhaled deeply and raised his head proudly.

"Honored Creek warriors! Hear me!" he cried, his strong voice echoing across the village. "You know who I am and why I have come. I am Shawnee, you are Creek. In the time of our grandfathers we were enemies, some may even still see us as such. No matter our differences, we are all the red children of Weshemoneto. It is time that we stand together against the greatest enemy that our nations have ever faced. We must stand against the Long Knives, those who would steal all of our land and put an end to our way of life!"

Tame King rose from his seat and stepped forward, his wizen face somber. "The Long Knives have taken your land, not ours," the old chief pointed out. "The Shawnee trade with the British, enemy of the Americans. Your tribe fought with the French against the British before the Americans made their own country. Your people have always fought against the *Shemanese*, no matter what the reason."

Tame King shook his head. "We Creeks have long traded with the Long Knives and we have stayed at peace. Because of these bonds, our tribe has remained powerful. That is the reason why the Shawnee no longer war with us."

Many of the assembled warriors murmured and shook their heads in agreement. The prospect of losing the trade connections they had with American traders was not pleasant. Unlike the Shawnee, they could not replace the lost trade with British goods. Besides the Americans, only the weakening Spanish settlements in Florida could offer any significant trade. The arrogant Spanish traders had long been unfriendly to the Creek and the goods they offered were of inferior quality to that of the Americans.

Tecumseh shook his head sadly. Slowly he turned and pointed at the distant mountains. "Look to the lands east of the mountains, my brothers!" he cried. "Once, it all belonged to the red man; now none of it does!"

The Shawnee leader turned back to Tame King. "You say the *Shemanese* have not taken your land? It will not be so long before they come to kill all your deer and cut down the forest. They are spreading as quickly across our lands as the diseases that they have brought to our people. Soon, they will no longer trade, but will come to 'buy' your land."

Tecumseh's voice became thick with emotion. "Sell a country! Why not sell the air, the great sea, as well as the earth? Didn't the Great Spirit make them all for the use of his children?" he declared, scanning the faces in the crowd. "The way, the only way to stop this evil is for the red man to unite in claiming a common and equal right in the land, as it was first, and should be now, for it was never divided. No tribe has the right to sell land, even to each other, much less to strangers."

The Creek warriors were enthralled by the Shawnee leader's passionate address. Several rose to their feet whooping in agreement. Tecumseh knew this was the time to act. He pulled a white wampum belt from a pouch at his side and moved to stand before Tame King.

"Together, we can stand against the Long Knives. Together, we will be strong," he stated, holding the belt out toward the old chief. "I ask Tame King, chief of the Creek Nation, will your people join your brothers from the lands of the Great Lakes?"

Tame King stepped forward, his expression solemn. Tecumseh had played the crowd well and had placed the old chief in a precarious position. The gesture of offering the wampum belt to Tame King instead of Big Warrior had caught the old man by surprise. It was a great honor that bestowed a large measure of respect upon the civil chief. Little did he know that Big Warrior and Tecumseh had prearranged the ceremonial passing of the wampum belt in order to win over Big Warrior's rival.

Tame King was no fool. He looked around at the assembled crowd. He knew that refusing the wampum belt would put him out of favor with his people. That he could not afford to do, not with the popular Big Warrior standing by to readily accept the offering. The old chief reached out and took the white belt from the Shawnee warrior. The crowd remained silent as Tame King slowly brought the wampum belt to his chest as a sign of acceptance.

The crowd exploded in joyous shouts and whoops. Creek warriors rushed forward to embrace the Shawnee. Others fired their rifles in the air and began imitating the war dance their allies had just demonstrated. Tecumseh smiled broadly as Big Warrior, Tuskenau, and the rest of his Shawnee warriors came forward.

"Very good," Big Warrior whispered. "We have much to talk of, but your words will move more Creeks to oppose the Long Knives. Soon, many Creek warriors will join you on the Wabash."

Tecumseh smiled up at the big man. "We will welcome them as brothers."

The Shawnee were returning north along the Mississippi in good spirits. The support of the Creeks would hopefully bring many more of the southern tribes into Tecumseh's confederacy. The war chief intended to cross the Mississippi to council with the Osage and the Shawnee who had settled west of the river during his childhood. It was time for the tribe to reunite in a common bond once again. Tecumseh smiled at the happy thought.

His smiled disappeared when he saw a lone rider appear on the trail. He signaled for his warriors to halt. They all took up their rifles and watched carefully as the rider advanced slowly down the trail. The white man reined up his tired horse when he was still several yards out of rifle range and held his hand up in a sign of peace. Tecumseh nudged his horse forward; something was familiar about the frontiersman sitting patiently on the trail. Finally, he recognized him. He signaled for his warriors to wait as he trotted forward to meet with Stephen Ruddell.

Tecumseh pulled up several yards from the big frontiersman. Ruddell looked tired. His clothes were covered in grime and sweat from hard travel. Usually clean shaven, a thick beard was forming on the preacher's face.

"What are you doing here, my friend?" Tecumseh asked, studying the big man carefully.

"Looking for you," Ruddell rasped. "Harrison is marching on Prophetstown as we speak. I suspicion that I have come too late for you to be able to stop the fight that I'm cock-sure is about to happen!"

Tecumseh felt his stomach tighten, Sinnatha had never lied to him. If any other white man had appeared to give him this dreaded news, he would have suspected a trick. The Shawnee leader's greatest fear was coming true. The long anticipated clash with Harrison would take place, and Tecumseh would not be there. The fate of years of work and preparation now lay in the hands of his often misguided brother.

Tecumseh shuddered at the thought.

He rode forward and put his hand on the exhausted man's shoulder. "Thank you, my friend," he whispered sincerely. "I owe you a debt for coming all this way to speak of Harrison's treachery.

I have no more time to talk. My warriors and I must get back to the Wabash before it is too late. Neither you nor your horse would be able to make it far without rest. We cannot wait for you."

Ruddell nodded and nudged his tired mount off the side of the trail. "Good luck," he replied as Tecumseh signaled his warriors forward. "I will pray for your safe and speedy return."

Tecumseh did not reply as he kicked his horse into a gallop up the northern trail.

CHAPTER 22

PROPHETSTOWN
NOVEMBER, 1811

V ILLAGERS MOVED OUT OF THE WAY as a Kickapoo
scout galloped into Prophetstown. The warrior rode up to
Tenskwatawa's medicine lodge and leapt from his mount's back
before he had reined the horse to a complete stop. He rushed into
the lodge, his expression grim. Inside, the Prophet was sitting on
the dais, surrounded by several village leaders and visiting chiefs.
The Kickapoo stepped before the one eyed medicine man and
bowed his head respectfully.

"The *Shemanese* have crossed the river," the scout reported.
"They will be here before nightfall!"

The Prophet muttered a curse under his breath. His spies had
kept close watch over Harrison's force since it had marched out of
Vincennes two months earlier. The scouts had reported back that
the Long Knife army numbered over a thousand men, twice the
number of warriors available to defend the village. Harrison had
camped where the Wabash made its southwestern turn and began
constructing a fort on a high bank overlooking the river. This was
near the boundary of the disputed treaty lands and the Prophet
had become hopeful that the governor would construct and gar-
rison the fortification and then return to his base at Vincennes.

Luck had not been with Tenskwatawa. Harrison had marched
his force out of the newly constructed Fort Harrison, named in

the governor's honor, a week earlier. The territorial leader had shrewdly sent a delegation of peaceful Miami and Delaware ahead of him to lay out his latest terms of peace. The Prophet had wrongly assumed that Harrison would await his response to the terms before he continued his advance. Just two days earlier, Tenskwatawa had sent Little Eyes, a Miami chief, down the east side of the Wabash with his reply. Unfortunately, the Miami had missed Harrison's army as it crossed to the west side of the Wabash and had quickly advanced to within a mile of the village. The American force had camped on a narrow plateau overlooking a small stream that would become known as Burnett's Creek. Now the governor cautiously awaited the Indians next move.

Shabani stepped forward, frowning deeply. "We must leave the village! We may still be able to hide some of our winter stores and disappear into the forest."

White Loon, a middle aged Wea chief, stepped forward. His lips parted in a sneer and he shook his head vigorously in opposition of the Potawatomi's statement.

"We must not run from these white dogs!" he declared. "They will destroy everything we have built."

The Wea leader turned toward Tenskwatawa. "Great Prophet, you must use your magic to help us stand against them."

"Tecumseh does not want us to fight," Shabani declared, interrupting White Loon's fanatical request. "He told us so before he journeyed south."

"Enough!" the Prophet cried, cutting both warriors off. "My brother is far from here. I lead our people and will deal with Harrison."

"But..." Shabani began.

The medicine man turned toward the Potawatomi leader, his face set in an angry scowl. "Do you dare question me? I am the Open Door, the Great Spirit's chosen one!"

Shabani bowed his head in submission. Tenskwatawa sneered triumphantly and turned back to the scout.

"Go to Harrison and tell him that I will meet with him tomorrow," he instructed the Kickapoo warrior.

"Now, leave me," he commanded, gesturing to everyone within the lodge. "I must commune with *Weshemoneto,* that he may give us guidance in this matter."

The Indian leaders silently exited the lodge. Several were convinced of the Prophet's confident statements and were eager for the battle to come. A few left with concerned etched on their face as the smiling medicine man began to chant and dance about the lodge.

General Harrison eyed the Indian messenger that stood before him suspiciously. His army was busy setting up a defensive perimeter along the small plateau the governor had chosen as a campsite. The contour of the ground had forced the army to form into the shape of a rough trapezoid that covered an area of land equal to about ten acres. Harrison now sat at his small camp desk outside his tent. The messenger's somber gaze rested solely on the governor, but the two warriors that accompanied him were watching the soldier's preparations intently.

"The Prophet will meet with me in the morning? Well, how gracious of him!" the governor stated sarcastically.

"The Open Door wishes for peace between our people," the messenger replied, his face betraying no emotion. "He does not want to see blood spilled."

Harrison snorted. "Go back and tell him I will be expecting him an hour after sunrise."

The governor watched the warriors as they silently filed from the camp. He waited until they were on the prairie that lay between the plateau and Prophetstown before he turned to his aide, a forty-year-old colonel named Abraham Owen.

"Double the guard tonight, Colonel," Harrison commanded. "I don't trust any of these red devils. There's all creation afoot and I don't intend for us to be surprised."

Owen saluted the army commander sharply. "Yes, Sir!" he replied, quickly moving off to carry out the order as Harrison watched the messengers disappear into the forest.

Shabani, White Loon, and the other village chiefs had gathered at the House of the Stranger and were once again arguing the best course of action to take against the strong enemy force that was now camped just over a mile away.

"We should attack them tonight," White Loon stated, his face flush with excitement. "We can surprise them while they sleep."

"No!" Shabani cried. "Harrison's army outnumbers our warriors two to one. He fought at Fallen Timbers and will expect an attack."

Shanbani shook his head. "Tecumseh did not want this." he reiterated. "We must wait until he says the time is right."

"Tecumseh is not here," White Loon reminded the Potawatomi leader. "How do you know that he would not attack the *Shemanese*?" the Wea demanded. "The Prophet's village must be defended!"

The chiefs fell silent as Tenskwatawa entered the House of the Stranger. The Prophet had dressed in his finest doeskin robes, fringed with quills and animal claws. A large black bear skull sat upon his head, and he had painted his entire face red, with the exception of his missing eye socket which he had painted black. The medicine man folded his hands across his chest and stared at the chiefs solemnly.

White Loon stepped forward. "What have you seen, father?" he asked eagerly. "Does the Great Spirit favor us?"

The Prophet smiled. "He does."

The chiefs began to chatter excitedly. Tenskwatawa raised his hand to silence the group. "*Weshemoneto* came to me in a vision and told me many things. He said we can win this battle, but Harrison must die. We must strike him down in the night while he sleeps. With their leader dead, the rest of the army will flee before us!"

"He will be well protected," Shabani dared state.

The Prophet scowled at the Potawatomi. "Do you think that I cannot protect you?" he demanded.

Shabani shook his head. "No, *no'tha*. I only fear that it will be difficult for any warriors to go after Harrison. They would surely find death waiting."

Tenskwatawa shook his head and held up his hand to cut the chief off. "No! Our warriors will be safe. The *Shemanese* bullets will not harm you! *Weshemoneto* has shown me this in my vision. I will go to the cliffs above the battlefield. There I will work my magic and protect all who will go against Harrison. We will kill the governor and destroy his army. It will be the greatest victory in the history of all our people!"

Several of the chiefs and assembled warriors whooped with delight and surrounded the boastful leader.

Shabani shook his head and sighed in frustration. "This is not the way," he whispered sadly.

White Loon and his warriors crouched silently in the creek bed outside the camp. The Wea leader had eagerly volunteered to lead the initial assault on the camp to assassinate Harrison. A short climb up the steep creek bank would bring them close to the outer edge of the camp and their objective. White Loon and a handful of warriors would slip into the perimeter while a Kickapoo chief named Mengowa would lead his warriors in an assault on the opposite side of the camp to distract the army while White Loon's force killed Harrison.

"Remember," White Loon whispered into the darkness. "Harrison rides a gray horse. If we don't get him in his tent, we will kill him in the saddle!"

Harrison tossed about on his cot, unable to sleep. Finally, he rose from the camp bed and moved across the tent to his desk. The general lit a candle and poured a glass of bourbon. He ran his hand through his hair and sat down on a chair beside the small desk. He rubbed his forehead and took a swallow of the whiskey.

Suddenly, shots range out and the dark night erupted in cries of alarm, anger, and pain. The governor rushed to the tent flap and looked out into the darkness. Several bonfires still burned brightly inside the camp perimeter, illuminating the area. Harrison was able to make out the image of Indian warriors rushing into the camp, attacking soldiers as they rose from their bedrolls.

"Damn!" he cursed. "We're under attack!"

Harrison grabbed his sword and a pistol and rushed outside the tent. "To arms! To arms!" he bellowed, buckling on his sword and thrusting the pistol into his belt. "Owen! Where's my horse?"

Abe Owen swung onto the back of the governor's gray mare and galloped toward the sound of the commander's voice. The aide reined the horse up near one of the bonfires, struggling to recognize the governor in the confused mass of soldiers rushing around the camp. The light from the fire distinguished the horse and rider from the mass of soldiers as he spotted Harrison and kicked the steed forward. Several warriors raised their guns and fired. Both Owen and the mount collapsed in front of Harrison, struck by several bullets.

White Loon buried his tomahawk in a militia officer's skull. He saw the grey horse topple and he leapt forward eagerly, sweeping up the officer's saber as he ran. The chief was certain his warriors had killed Harrison and he intended to take the white man's head back to the Prophet. He jumped over the dying horse and found himself face to face with the hated man. White Loon let out a war whoop and charged. Harrison calmly pulled his flintlock pistol from his belt and shot the warrior as he closed within feet of him.

The Wea chief grunted and looked down at the hole that had suddenly appeared in his chest. White Loon sank to his knees and looked up at Harrison, his eyes wide in disbelief.

"It cannot be!" he gasped, blood appearing on his lips. "The Prophet said he would protect ..."

The officer watched as the warrior collapsed in front of him. He glanced at Owen's corpse and shook his head. He quickly reloaded his pistol and calmly appraised the situation. His soldiers were regrouping and organizing behind the line. Doubling the sentries for the night had allowed the soldiers to quickly counterattack the Prophet's warriors. The governor could see that his force was slowly beginning to regain control of the lines and push the savages back. He grabbed a young officer as he rushed by.

"Get me another horse!" he commanded. "We'll put an end to these savages tonight!"

The young man saluted nervously and rushed off to find the governor a mount. Harrison turned his attention back to the battle. The heaviest fighting seemed to be concentrated on the rear line where Captain Barton's regulars were struggling to hold their position against the ferocious attack. The commander calmly mounted a horse that was brought before him and rode forward. Several new recruits rushed frantically away from the fighting, but the governor blocked their path.

"Turn about, lads!" he cried sternly. "You're leaving your friends to die! Follow me; we'll drive these red devils back."

Ashamed, the recruits calmed themselves and fell in behind the general as he rode toward the sound of musket fire and the screams of the wounded and dying.

Tenskwatawa sat beside a small fire on a high bluff overlooking the prairie and the battlefield below. A large rock shielded the fire from the elements and the Prophet sat with his back to the stone, beating a deer hide drum and shaking a rattle as he chanted loudly. Sweat beaded the one-eyed Indian's forehead. He could hear the sounds of the battle and he exhaled nervously. A pair of his bodyguards stood silently watching over the Shawnee leader. The warriors raised their weapons as the sound of a galloping horse interrupted the medicine man's chants. They lowered their guns when a Kickapoo messenger appeared on the trail. He leapt from the horse's back and ran to the Prophet's side.

"Father," the Kickapoo gasped. "Your medicine does not work! Our warriors fall to the *Shemanese* bullets. White Loon is dead. Shabani sent me to tell you this so you may instruct us on what to do."

Tenskwatawa swallowed hard and glanced into the darkness toward the raging battle. He looked back at the messenger. "I will pray harder." he stated, wiping the sweat from his brow. "Tell Shabani and the others to keep fighting. We must have faith in the Great Spirit in order to gain victory!"

The Kickapoo leapt back onto the horse and galloped down the trail. Tenskwatawa resumed his chanting and drumming at a louder and more frantic pace.

Dawn had broken over the eastern sky before the Battle of Tippecanoe had finally ended. The desperate warriors had circled the plateau in the darkness and thrown themselves against the army's lines, probing for a weak point. The regulars and militia had stubbornly held their ground and driven back every furious assault. Finally, the Indians had launched one final desperate attack against the army's front as darkness faded from the sky. The line did not break. The governor had launched a strong counter attack from both flanks and driven the remaining warriors from the plateau and onto the prairie. Lead and powder supplies had been exhausted and the number of dead and wounded warriors had finally forced Shabani to call an end to the assault. The remaining warriors retreated to Prophetstown, bringing with them all the dead and wounded they could carry

William Henry Harrison observed the scene around him grimly. His face was smudged with soot and mud. He had lost his frock coat in the battle and his fine linen shirt was torn. Dead and wounded soldiers and Indians lay scattered across the plateau. Several of the tents had been given over to the treatment of the wounded. Even now the groans and cries of the men inside carried across the prairie. A few militia were moving among the dead warriors, collecting scalps and other grizzly trophies of war. Harrison ran his hand through his hair and shuddered at the sight before him. The battle had lasted two and a half hours, but it had seemed like days.

Over two hundred men, nearly a quarter of his entire force, had been wounded or killed in that short period of time. In addition, five of Harrison's company commanders had perished in the fight, including his aide, Abraham Owen and Joseph Daviess, the brash and gallant leader of the Kentucky volunteers. Harrison did not know if the Indians were regrouping for another attack, but he could clearly see that his own force was crippled and needed time to regroup. He ordered the construction of breastworks and assigned a detail to care for the wounded and bury the dead. He then returned to his tent to complete a report of the battle while it was fresh in his mind. He hoped he would have the opportunity to deliver it to Secretary of War Eustis.

Another attack did not come that day or the next. Finally, Harrison sent out scouts to observe the Indian's movements the following afternoon. Within an hour, a buckskin clad frontiersman rode back into the camp and dismounted in front of the General's tent. Harrison stepped outside, concerned by the scout's early return.

"Well?" the governor stated impatiently as the frontiersman stepped forward.

"They're gone, General," the scout replied. "That village is empty. Every one of the red bastards has gone to brush!"

Harrison closed his eyes and sighed in relief. His remaining officers had gathered quickly upon the scout's return. Their commander looked at them, his expression grave.

"We've won," he stated softly, "but the cost has been high. Tecumseh was not here, but he will return. Many good men died here, and many more could surely join them before this fight is over."

Colonel John Boyd, commander of the 4th regular army regiment that made up almost half of Harrison's remaining force stepped forward. Boyd's regulars had held the line during the heaviest fighting while many of the militia had faltered. The colonel had little faith left in any of the soldiers or militia left outside of his own regiment and had adamantly voiced his concerns to the governor.

"What are your orders, Sir?" he asked, his voice strained.

Harrison remained silent for a moment, contemplating the situation. "The militia will remain in the camp to care for the wounded and prepare for our withdrawal to Vincennes in the morning."

The governor turned toward Boyd. "Take your regulars and advance on the village, make sure the savages are gone. If our scouts are right, the village is ours. I want it burned to the ground. Leave not a single structure standing. Let's see them rebuild from the ashes of failure."

Tecumseh kneeled in the ashes of what had been the House of the Stranger. Shabani and Stephen Ruddell stood behind him, their expressions solemn. The Shawnee chief picked up a handful of ash, letting it sift through his fingers and back to the ground. He shook his head and sighed in despair. Shabani cleared his throat.

"I failed you, my chief," he whispered sadly. "I tried to do as you said, but the Prophet and the others would not listen."

Tecumseh shook his head again. "It is not your fault, *ne-kah-noh*. Does my brother still live?"

"Yes," the Potawatomi replied, his eyes hardening. "Most of the warriors want to kill him, but I stopped them. They called the Prophet a liar, and most of them returned to their villages."

Tecumseh rose from the ground, frowning. "Take me to him."

Tecumseh, Shabani, and Ruddell rode into a small Indian camp on Wildcat Creek. Tecumseh leapt from his horse and stalked toward one of the wigwams. Tecumpese stepped in front of him.

"Out of the way, *ni-t-kweem-a*." he stated darkly.

Tecumpese held her ground. "I am as angry at him as you are. Whatever you do, remember that he is our brother."

Tecumseh snorted in disgust. "How could I ever forget?"

The war chief brushed past the older woman and entered the wigwam.

Tenskwatawa sat dejected upon the ground, tied by a set of leather thongs to a post in the center of the structure. He slowly rose to his feet when he saw Tecumseh enter the room. His eyes widened in dread as his brother drew a knife from his belt and advanced forward.

"I am *Weshemoneto's* chosen one!" cried pitifully. "Do not..."

The fat man was unable to finish the sentence as Tecumseh struck him in the face and knocked him to the ground. He sliced the thongs from the post and rolled the frightened man to his back and placed the razor sharp blade against his throat.

"You are nothing." Tecumseh hissed, his eyes wide with rage. "Everything that we have built is gone! Gone because you were weak and greedy, as you have been your entire life."

The Prophet gasped sharply as Tecumseh pressed down on the blade.

"STOP!" Stephen cried, stepping from the shadows. "Tecumseh, you cannot kill your own brother!"

The war chief looked up at his friend. "He deserves it, as he has so often proven. You speak for him, Big Fish? You tell me not to kill the man who would have killed you?"

Ruddell placed a strong hand on his friend's shoulder. "Oh, I'm as sour of Loud Noise as he's of me," the big man stated softly. "I just don't want to see you become like him. Please, let him live."

Tecumseh let out a long breath and sheathed his knife. He turned back to the prone medicine man. "If you weren't of my own blood, I would still cut your throat. If you ever disobey me again, I will kill you."

Tecumseh yanked the quivering man to his feet. "We will do our best to rebuild. We must show the *Shemanese* and our people that we are still strong. To that, you will dedicate the rest of your wretched life. Do you understand?"

Tenskwatawa nodded his head vigorously. Tecumseh turned and stalked from the wigwam. Both Tenskwatawa and Stephen following a distance behind. A large crowd of warriors, many still bearing fresh wounds from the Battle of Tippecanoe, had gathered as the war chief exited the wigwam.

The Shawnee leader looked around at the assembled Indians, his expression stern. "A terrible thing has been done, my people. The *Shemanese* have broken their word and have made war on us once again. They think that they have beaten us, but we are still strong! We will gather together once again, but not in peace. I say that the *Shemanese* have broken the peace and it is time to take up the hatchet against them once again!"

Tecumseh pulled his tomahawk from his belt and thrust it into the air. Many of the warriors cheered and raised their own weapons in response. An old Piankashaw chief stepped forward, frowning.

"How will we fight them?" the old man demanded. "We don't have enough guns and all our powder is gone!"

Tecumseh pointed north.

"Soon there will be war between the English and the *Shemanese*," he stated confidently. "We will stand with our English fathers. They will give us everything we need if we will fight with them. We will join them in driving the Long Knives from our land! I will go to Detroit. Our people will have revenge for everything the white men have done to us."

Tecumseh leapt onto his horse as the crowd roared their approval. He thrust his tomahawk into the air, and shouted a battle cry. He spun the horse around to face the Prophet.

"You will not come with me," he stated coldly. "You will remain with our sister and help to rebuild whatever you can in our village. You will continue to deliver the Great Spirit's teachings to any who will listen. You are not worth anything else!"

The fat man cringed at his brother's harsh words, but nodded in silent submission. He retreated into the wigwam in order to avoid Tecumseh's icy glare. Cold Water and Stands Firm had mounted their own steeds and moved up beside their chief. He signaled the warriors ahead of him as he reined his mount up in front of Stephen Ruddell.

"Fine speech!" the big man stated. "You already gained a boodle of your allies back."

"What about you?" Tecumseh replied, fixing his gaze upon the redheaded man. "Will you ride with me, Sinnatha?"

Stephen swallowed hard. "I will not," he replied evenly. "I will return to Wapakoneta to live in peace. I will have no part in this war!"

Tecumseh nodded, expecting the response. "I am grateful for all that you have done. We will leave you and the Wapakoneta Shawnee at peace. I doubt that Harrison will do the same."

Stephen could not disagree. "I wish you well, *Jai-nai-nah*," he stated. "May the Good Lord and the Great Spirit both keep you safe!"

Tecumseh smiled slightly as he kicked his horse into a gallop along the northern trail. The frontiersman watched as England's newest ally disappeared after his warriors. A feeling of sadness welled up within the big man. He knew that the days of bloody warfare would quickly return for all the peoples of the Great Lakes, and there wasn't anything he could do about it.

CHAPTER 23

QUINCY, ILLINOIS
SUMMER, 1845

THE OLD MAN SAT BACK in his rocking chair and closed his eyes. Dusk had settled over the summer landscape and stars were beginning to appear in the evening sky. Lyman put his pencil down and flexed his fingers. The pair had spent the afternoon cleaning fish and doing chores around the farm. Draper had noticed that the former frontiersman grew winded as the day went on and he had closed up his writing box to help with several of the chores. Ruddell had protested, but did not refuse the younger man's assistance. By the end of the afternoon, the older man was exhausted and retired to his room to rest before the evening meal. Lyman was concerned and sought out John Ruddell to discuss his father's health.

"It's his heart," John admitted with a rueful smile. "I made him go to a doctor about a year ago. He told Pa his heart was weakening and that he needed to slow down.

I reckon you have a mind how well that went over." the younger Ruddell added dryly. "I have tried to hire hands to work around the farm, but Pa drives them to brush. Most days, he can still out-work any man half his age, but there are times when he's tired and can't catch his breath. Sadly, those days are comin' on more often."

"Surely he allows that he must slow down." Draper stated, alarmed at the revelation. "He's an old man."

John Ruddell chuckled. "Do you want to tell him that?"

"No," the writer admitted.

John shook his head sadly. "Grit has gotten my father through some considerable times, as I suspicion you well know. His strength fails him now and he can't allow it. Time is man's greatest enemy. I used to think there wasn't anything Pa was afraid of. I was wrong; he's cow-hearted of becoming feeble and useless."

"Growing old is a part of life," Draper argued. "It happens to us all."

"Sure it does," John conceded. "I can't do all creation that I did when I was twenty, but that doesn't mean I don't still try every now and then. How well do you handle growing older, Dr. Draper? Do you just accept it?"

Lyman hesitated. "I see your point," he admitted. "But your father's going to drive himself into an early grave."

John laughed. "He's seventy-seven years old and has lived a life on the frontier. He fought in Lord knows how many battles and had boodle of folks try and kill him. I reckon if he was headed to an early grave, the good Lord would have already taken him!"

Lyman seemed about to reply, but the big man cut him off. "I appreciate your concern, Dr. Draper, but my father's not going to change who he is. I accept that and cherish every day that I have with him," he stated, his expression serious. "I can see him beginning to fade, which is why I contacted you. I want his story written before it is too late. I'm pleased that he has made such an impression on you, that you would express so much concern for his health."

Lyman shook his head. "He's a considerable man, maybe the most extraordinary that I've ever interviewed."

John smiled and clapped the smaller man on the shoulder. "On that, we both agree."

Lyman stared intently at the former frontiersman. The old man had risen for supper and had eaten his meal in silence. Afterwards, he had retired to the front porch to smoke his pipe and look at the stars. Lyman had not joined him until he saw Ruddell settle into the rocking chair. Now the writer sat in silence, struggling to find the words for all the questions he wanted to ask.

"I ain't cold as a wagon tire just yet," the old man growled, "even though there are days I wish I was." He cracked his eyes opened and peered intently at the blond haired writer. "I'm more than well enough to answer any questions you have for me. So, don't sit there like a cully. What do you want to know?"

"Tell me about the war," Lyman replied, hesitantly opening the writing box. "What role did you play? Did you see Tecumseh before he...?"

"Before he was killed," Ruddell finished for him, his expression pained.

"Yes," Draper replied uncomfortably. "I understand if you have no wish to talk about it."

The old man held up his hand, silencing the writer. He sighed and rocked back in the chair, looking up into the night sky.

"Tecumseh was right. England and the United States did go to war again. Tecumseh and his warriors allied themselves with the British in Canada. The War of 1812 was no different on the frontier than the Revolution had been. Most of the battles and skirmishes were fought between the militia and Indians. Many a settler and Indian alike died in the fighting. The tribes massacred wounded prisoners at the River Rasin and Ft. Dearborn. I can't say I was grum when the Potawatomie kilt that bastard William Wells at Ft. Dearborn, though I was sad for all those who died with him."

Ruddell shook his head. "Did you know we outnumber the British and Canadian forces five to one? That war would have ended quickly if it wasn't for Tecumseh. The British leaders in Canada cotton to him and put Tecumseh in command of both Indian and redcoats troops. I don't reckon there's ever been another red man respected as much. He fought with Isaac Brock before he was kilt at Queenston Heights. He might have been able to invade and take the whole Ohio Valley if he hadn't been stuck with that fat-headed coot, Henry Proctor."

"I suspicion you were displeased when Mr. Harrison was named commander of the Army of the Northwest," Draper suggested.

Stephen snorted. "That would be whitewashin' my stance. Oh, he was the best choice after that timid old woman, General Hull, surrendered at Detroit. Tecumseh almost had him at Ft. Meigs, but Proctor's artillery failed to force a surrender and they had to give up the siege."

Ruddell smiled. "Did you know that Tecumseh challenged Harrison to come out and fight him to determine the outcome of the battle?"

Draper nodded. "They say that Harrison was tempted by the challenge, but his officers dissuaded him."

"Bullshit," the old man growled. "Harrison wanted no part of fighting Tecumseh.."

"What about the Ft. Miami Massacre?" Draper asked, changing the subject.

Stephen frowned. "That was a shameful event. Tecumseh and his warriors defeated a boodle of Kentuckians that had been sent to reinforce the fort. He sent the prisoners to the ruins of the old fort to be held. There were over fifty British regulars there to guard them and they should have been safe. A no account Ojibwa named Split Nose gathered a group of warriors into a gauntlet and forced the prisoners to run it. They didn't use sticks; they used tomahawk, knives, and rifles on those poor devils. I think they kilt over thirty of 'em before Tecumseh showed up."

"He was well remembered by the survivors for saving their lives," Lyman interjected.

The old man nodded sadly. "Those fifty British guards were too cow-hearted to stop Split Nose and his warriors, but Tecumseh did it by himself. He rode in and called them all cowards and told them they were a disgrace to all Indian nations. Split Nose argued with him and tried to kill another prisoner. Tecumseh gave him a bellyful and promised to kill any warrior who laid another hand on the Kentuckians. The massacre stopped."

"When did you next see Tecumseh?" Lyman questioned. "Were you able to stay out of the fighting?"

"No," Ruddell whispered, hanging his head. "I tried to keep the Shawnee at Wapakoneta out of the fighting, but it wasn't to be."

Tears formed in the old man's eyes as he looked again toward the night sky.

Late summer storms had turned the dirt streets of Wapakoneta into a quagmire as Stephen Ruddell navigated his way through the mud, his face grim. The big minister stopped in front of an old cabin at the edge of the village, hesitating before moving to the door. Black Hoof had sent word that he needed to see his adopted son. Ruddell knew that the old chief had met with local militia leaders and an officer sent by General Harrison. He dreaded what news the old man might have to share.

The big man stepped into the cabin. Black Hoof, old and withered, sat beside the hearth.

"How is your wound, father?" Stephen asked, moving up beside the old man.

Black Hoof winced and rubbed his bandaged face. "You warned me not to visit that *Shemanese* camp to offer my help," he rasped. "I was lucky, the man who shot me was so scared he could not shoot straight. I have learned that it does not matter what clothes we wear or how we live, whether we are peaceful or hostile, the only thing some white men see is the color of our skin."

"You sent for me, *no'tha?*" Ruddell stated quietly.

Wordlessly, the old man held a letter out to his adopted son. Black Hoof now dressed in the linen and wool of a white farmer, but he could not read and was dependent on the big man to translate for him. Stephen knew by the chief's sad expression that Harrison's officer had already informed Black Hoof of the letter's contents. Ruddell took the note and scanned its contents. His eyes widened as he finished the note.

"Harrison must be out of his head," he hissed. "He demands that we provide scouts for his army in fighting our own people. We cannot do this!"

"We must," Black Hoof replied sadly. "We have no choice."

Stephen crumbled the note in anger. "I will speak with Congressman Worthington. He will see the folly of this order and will come to our aide."

The old chief shook his head and laid a withered hand on the younger man's wrist. "The *Shemanese* are at war with England. Their Congress has told Harrison to do what he must to gain victory. Worthington will do nothing. If we don't do as Harrison asks, we will be branded as enemies and the Long Knives will take everything we have left!" Black Hoof looked down, defeated. "We will send what men we can."

The former Shawnee war leader looked up at his adopted son, tears in his eyes. "You must lead them."

The frontiersman's eyes widened, "Me?" he gasped. "I cannot..."

"There's no one else!" Black Hoof cried in despair.

"Only you can protect our people, on both sides of the battle lines. I am too old to lead," he whispered in shame. "You must go in my place!"

The old chief put his head in his hands. "I only wanted peace for our people," he sobbed. "Now I wish that I could stand beside Tecumseh. At least then I would die a warrior."

Stephen heart ached to see the proud warrior broken before him. He moved forward and wrapped his arms around the old man's bony shoulders.

"Alright, *no'tha*," he whispered into his ear. "I will go in your place, though I doubt I will be able to protect our people. I'm not sure there is anyone who could anymore, not even Tecumseh."

Tecumseh and his closest followers were sitting beside a fire, smoking their pipes. The Thames River flowed gently southward west of their position and the bulk of Tecumseh's remaining force of five hundred warriors had been placed in front of a small swamp north of the village of Moraviantown. Five hundred British troops had been placed to the right of the Indian's position. Tomorrow, the combined British and Indian force would face off against General Harrison and an army that outnumbered their force three to one. Shabani, Stands Firm, and Cold Water had all joined their chief on the eve of the battle. Tecumseh still wore the red officer's coat that General Brock had presented to him before he had died in battle over a year earlier. The Shawnee chief was enjoying the peaceful company of his friends and the last of his tobacco when a young warrior rushed up and whispered into the war leader's ear. Tecumseh raised an eyebrow and nodded, sending the youngster back into the darkness.

"We have captured a *Shemanese* scout," he explained in amusement. "One who speaks Shawnee."

The Indians watched as a powerful hooded figure was led into the firelight. Tecumseh rose to his feet and examined the big man. He reached up and yanked the hood off of the man's head. Stephen Ruddell stood before him.

"Hello, *jai-nai-nah*," Tecumseh stated calmly. "It has been long since we have seen each other."

Ruddell nodded. "Too long, *ni-je-ni-nuh.*"

The Shawnee chief pulled out his knife and cut the leather thongs that bound the big man's hands. He motioned for the white man to sit beside him at the fire. After the frontiersman had seated himself, Tecumseh took a long puff from his pipe and passed it to his former brother.

"Do you lead the Shawnee who have been scouting for Harrison?" the Shawnee leader asked suddenly.

Ruddell coughed, his expression grim. "Black Hoof sent me in his place. He reckoned I would be able to keep the people out of the fighting."

Tecumseh nodded sadly. "We both have failed. Harrison is likely to win this battle and our own people will fight each other in the morning"

The war chief took another long puff from his pipe. "Why have you come, Sinnatha?"

"General Harrison knows that most of the British troops have abandoned you, Tecumseh," the frontiersman replied softly. "Tomorrow you will be outnumbered and outgunned. The general has sent me to ask for your surrender."

Tecumseh smiled. "You knew what I would say before you left Harrison's camp!"

"You have won many great victories in this war, my brother. We both know that you will not win tomorrow. Let's end this fighting now, before the Shawnee suffer more." Ruddell pleaded.

Tecumseh waved for all the other warriors at the fire to leave. Stands Firm, grown old and gray, hesitated.

"Go *ni-je-ni-nuh.* Spend tonight with you wife and children," Tecumseh commanded. "Tomorrow will be a long day. I am safe with our brother, Sinnatha."

Stands Firm nodded in submission. He cast one final distrusting glance at the big frontiersman and left the fire. Tecumseh smoked his pipe and stared into the fire for several minutes. Finally, he turned toward Ruddell.

"For us, it was never about winning a battle against an enemy," he stated sadly. "We have fought to remain who we are. Those who die in battle tomorrow will do so as Shawnee warriors."

"You'll always be Shawnee," Stephen argued, tears forming in his eyes. "You don't have to die to prove it."

Tecumseh chuckled. "You are of two worlds, Sinnatha. I am of only one. Both of them cannot remain. You will go on, I will not."

"What are you saying?" Stephen whispered.

Tecumseh stared into the fire. "Did you know that my father foretold his death?" he stated calmly. "Do you remember that Chiksika told me he would die before we went into battle so many years ago?"

Stephen's chest tightened in fear. "Tecumseh!"

The Shawnee leader held up his hand, cutting his friend off. "Hear me, *jai-nai-nah*," he said, gazing at the big man. "There are things that I need you to do for me."

Tecumseh pointed at a young warrior sitting beside one of the nearby fires. The young man smiled and waved at his chief. Tecumseh smiled at the boy.

"That is my *ni-kwith-ehi*," he explained. "I have not been a good father to him. I have spent so much time away that we hardly know each other. I have had little time to train him as a warrior. Still, he is determined to fight beside me tomorrow. Should he be proud or frightened?"

"Both." Stephen replied with a smile.

"Are you a father, Sinnatha?" the war leader asked.

"Stephen nodded, " I have a boy who is a couple of years old. I miss him dearly and hope to return to him and his mother soon."

"Is he white?" Tecumseh questioned, staring at the frontiersman intently

"Yes," Ruddell answered evenly. "My wife is the daughter of a missionary."

"Good!" Tecumseh replied. "Life is hard for half-breed children in your world, more so in the years to come. Your son will have and easier life then mine will," he added sadly, looking toward the boy.

The Shawnee warrior turned to face the frontiersman. "I ask that you look after him tomorrow."

Stephen began to protest, but Tecumseh cut him off again.

"I have seen it, *Jai-nai-nah*. Tomorrow is my last fight, and the last battle of our people.

"You will be there when I fall," he stated confidently. "I ask that you keep my son safe. Will you do this for me?"

Sinnatha nodded as he choked back tears, unable to speak. Tecumseh smiled and put his hand on the redheaded man's broad shoulder. "Much time has passed for us, brother. We are no longer young men. I grow tired of war," he admitted with a sigh. "Tomorrow there shall be peace. You must go now, we will speak again soon."

Sinnatha struggled to find something to say, but could not. Finally, he turned and disappeared into the darkness, leaving the Shawnee chief alone beside the fire.

CHAPTER 24

MORAVIANTOWN, CANADA
OCTOBER, 1813

INDIAN WARRIORS AND BRITISH SOLDIERS milled around in confusion along the road that led to the village. Many watched nervously as the Army of the Northwest began forming a line to the south of their wooded position. The British had been on half rations for several days, and a retreat up the Thames had been ordered before the troop's breakfast had been cooked. No orders had been issued since and the road lay open to Harrison's force. Several warriors and British officers looked toward the general who had placed them in this position.

General Henry Proctor, fifty years of age and portly, bit his lip and cast about helplessly. His thick jowls quivered like those of a bulldog as he shook his head and sighed in despair. He removed his shako and wiped his sweat drenched brow with a white handkerchief. Colonel Augustus Warburton, commander of the 41st Regiment, stepped forward, his expression grave. The general had ordered all of their remaining cannon sent forward and placed in Moraviantown. One single field piece now sat in the road.

"What are your orders, Sir?" Warburton asked, saluting the general.

Proctor looked up, his eyes wide. "Orders?"

The Colonel bit his lip, struggling to maintain his composure in front of the incompetent leader.

"Where do you want the troops? The cannon?" he pressed.

"Where is Tecumseh?" Proctor demanded. "He should have been here by now.

None of these blasted savages will fight without him. We'll have to forfeit this position and retreat to the village."

Warburton pointed behind the general. Proctor turned to see Tecumseh riding down the road on a black gelding. The Shawnee leader had removed his officer's coat and was adorned in simple buckskins tied with a red silk sash. He had placed a single eagle feather in his hair, and his face was painted half red and black, split right down the center of his brow. The war leader rode forward with his head held high in confidence and pride. Shabani, Stands Firm, and Cold Water all rode solemnly behind their chief. Tecumseh reined his horse up in front of the British general.

"Thank goodness you're here." Proctor sighed in relief. "Everything is a bloody mess. I was just about to call a retreat."

"There is no place to go, General," the Indian leader replied calmly. "We must stop Harrison's army here or he will lead them on to Canada"

Tecumseh pointed toward and area of downed trees to the left of the road. "General, you will have good cover if you put your men there. My warriors will hold the black ash grove on your right. The land along the river is swampy and the *Shemaganas* will have a hard time advancing and using their calvary well. If we are strong, we can hold this place."

"What about the cannon?" the fat man stated, gesturing toward the field piece.

Tecumseh shook his head. "There's no time for that, General. See to your men, and be strong. If we hold together, we can win!"

General Proctor nodded weakly and wandered away, shouting out orders to his junior officers. Warriors gathered around Tecumseh as he leapt from his horse's back to stand on a large maple stump. The Shawnee chief looked the force over silently. Many of these warriors had followed him to Canada two years earlier, but there were also many young men who would be taking part in their first battle, including his son, Paukeesa.

"Today, we fight for all of those who have come before us, and all those who will follow us. We battle for our way of life," he cried, his voice full of emotion. "We will be strong. We pray for the blessings of *Weshemoneto* that we will prevail!"

The warriors raised their voices in a chorus of cheers and war cries as Tecumseh shook his rifle defiantly at Harrison's gathering troops.

General Harrison was intently observing the assembled warriors through his spy glass. His second in command, Colonel Richard Mentor Johnson of the mounted Kentucky volunteers, stood anxiously behind him. Nearby, Stephen Ruddell leaned on his rifle beside Simon Kenton. Kenton, nearly sixty, had been appointed chief scout by Harrison. The title was not honorary. The grizzled frontiersman was still twice as valuable as a hunter, fighter, and scout as any other man attached to the Army of the Northwest. He observed the Indians' preparations with a keen eye.

"They seem optimistic," Johnson stated, moving up beside the general.

Harrison smiled. "Tecumseh inspires them. I cannot count the times he had challenged me to single combat to determine the outcome of a battle. Such foolishness!"

"If it's so foolish, why don't you accept his offer?" Stephen called, loud enough for everyone to hear.

The general put his spy glass down and slowly turned toward the preacher, frowning is disdain.

"Because I'm no fool!" he replied. "I will defeat him with the might of my army against his. He has little chance against those odds."

Harrison pointed toward the battlefield. "That is why we will always win. The Indian is a great individual fighter, but they cannot maintain the discipline and order it takes to operate as an army to win a war."

He peered through his spy glass once again, scanning the enemy position. "I respect Tecumseh," Harrison added, "but his time has come to end."

Satisfied, the general tuned toward Colonel Johnson. "Form your Calvary up. You will strike at Tecumseh's position on the right flank while the infantry assaults the British position on the left."

Harrison looked toward Ruddell. "The Indian scouts will join the Kentucky volunteers to help provide covering fire during their assault."

"You're out of your head!" Stephen cried angrily. "You can't expect them to fight their own people. We won't do it!"

Colonel Johnson stepped forward. "You'll do as you are commanded or you will be court martialed as a traitor and shot." he stated hotly.

Stephen felt the hair on the back of his neck stand up as his chest tightened in anger. He moved his hand toward his pistol, but Simon Kenton stepped forward and gently took him by the elbow, stopping the motion.

"Beggin' the general's pardon," the legendary scout drawled, "but I reckon we might want to consider this design a bit!"

Harrison raised his eyebrow. "How so, Mr. Kenton? You have taken part in many campaigns over the years. I value your opinion."

"Well, my diggings are in Ohio, but I'm more Kentuckian then most of these brats that are ridin' with Mr. Johnson," the old scout stated with a smile. "We Kentuckians hold a considerable grudge against the Shawnee and damned near any Indian that might be over in that Black Ash. Some of Johnson's boys were at the River Raisin and are itchin' for some revenge. Ruddell's right, to a certain extent. If you send our own Indians in there, our boys will end up gettin' confused and shoot our own red skins."

Many of the assembled officers chuckled at the scout's reasoning.

"It would make more sense to send our Indians with the infantry to attack the British on the left flank," Kenton continued. "I suspicion there's not much fight left in them redcoats, but Tecumseh and his boys will make a tough time of it. Our Ohio scouts can support Colonel Johnson and his Kentuckians. Then we're cock-sure any Indian we shoot at ain't friendly."

The big man grinned. "That's what I'd do, General, but the decision is yours. I don't reckon I want to face a court martial if you don't agree."

Harrison snorted. "I have more chance of being court martialed than someone as considerable as you, Mr. Kenton."

The general scratched his chin, contemplating. "Very well," he conceded. "The Indian scouts will join the infantry, but I want you to lead them, Mr. Kenton. I trust your judgment. Ruddell can ride with you."

Stephen relaxed upon hearing the concession and Simon removed his hand from his elbow.

"Good enough," the old scout replied.

Harrison glanced at Stephen once again, frowning. "I hope you are able to recall which side you fight for today, Ruddell. For your own sake."

Stephen turned and stalked away from the command post. "How could I forget." he whispered bitterly.

Tecumseh rode down the British line, greeting and encouraging many of the officers he had fought alongside the past two years. He reined his horse up in front on Colonel Warburton and extended his hand.

"Good luck, Colonel," he stated. "I know you will fight well."

Warburton took the extended hand and nodded.

"Thank you, Chief," he replied with a smile. "I'd hoped to be placed alongside you and your warriors."

Tecumseh leaned in, his expression serious. "I fear General Proctor will not hold for long. It will be up to you to rally your men."

Warburton nodded in agreement. "I'll do my best; my lads are more than a bit worn, but I allow we still have some fight left in us."

Tecumseh smiled. "As do my warriors."

With a final wave, the war chief galloped toward the right flank and the swamp where his warriors waited. He dismounted beside a large maple and took his position beside Stands Firm and Paukeesa. They watched silently as the American infantry began to slowly march up the road toward the British lines. Tecumseh shook his head when he recognized Indian scouts moving forward among the American lines.

"There are so many of them," Paukeesa whispered nervously.

Tecumseh placed his hand on the boy's head. "Be strong, my son," he replied calmly. "You are a Shawnee warrior."

An explosion erupted among the trees behind the Indians' position as the American artillery opened fire. Calvary units began forming for an assault on the right flank. Tecumseh could make out General Harrison sitting upon his white horse in the distance, observing the battle with his spy glass.

Stands Firm recognized the hated man as well.

"Harrison!" the grizzled warrior cried. "Oh, that he would join the attack!"

"No, brother," Tecumseh replied sadly. "He is cautious. He will watch and wait where we cannot get to him, as he has always done."

The beat of a drum signaled the American infantry's advance to quicken.

Tecumseh cocked his rifle and rested the barrel on a fallen ash tree. The stoic warriors around him followed suite.

"*Oui-shi-cat-to-oui*, be strong!" the Shawnee chief shouted.

Fire erupted along the British line as the American infantry came into range. Tecumseh's warriors opened fire on the advancing infantry, slowing the assault. The cavalry force charged forward, splitting as it reached the infantry lines. Colonel Johnson led a smaller force toward the swamp, his sword held high. The remaining cavalry swept past the infantry and into the British lines.

Johnson's force crashed into the forest and met a hail of fire from the Indians. Artillery fire and rifle smoke quickly reduced visibility within the trees and the battle diminished into intense hand to hand combat. Kentucky militia were pulled from their horses and tomahawked while warriors were hacked with swords. Kenton's Ohio scouts and a second line of calvary joined Johnson's force as Tecumseh's warriors stubbornly held their ground.

The left flank was in trouble. The exhausted redcoats had managed one organized volley before the Americans had split their lines. Many of the more seasoned British soldiers were holding their positions, slowing the American advance. Still, the sight of the advancing Kentuckians, thick bearded and wild eyed, was too much for General Proctor.

"There are too many of them," the general cried, his voice panicked. He turned toward his aide, his eyes wide with fear. "Order the retreat!"

Without waiting for a reply, he spun his horse about and galloped from the battlefield.

Colonel Warburton cursed and shook his head in dismay as he watched the General disappear north along the road to Moraviantown. The left flank began to collapse as the drummers signaled the retreat. Warburton's section of the line had held their position and was now cut off from the rest of the 41st regiment as it pulled back along the road.

"Easy now, lads," he shouted. "We've no clear path of retreat and I'll be damned if we run from the field like common rabble."

"What do we do, Colonel?" a young lieutenant asked nervously.

Warburton pulled out a white handkerchief and placed it on the end of his sword. "We surrender," he replied sadly.

"Strike our colors," he commanded, waving the makeshift white flag at the advancing troops. "Our days of fighting in this war are over."

A mighty cheer went up among the American forces. William Henry Harrison, watching the battle through his spy glass, smiled as he saw the British flag lowered. The drummer's continued to beat the call for retreat in the distance.

Tecumseh and his warriors could hear those drums as well. The cavalry's advance into the swamp had stalled, for now. The Shawnee leader knew the rest of the army would soon close on his line.

"Hold your ground!" he shouted as he tomahawked a scout who had charged him through the smoke. "Do not run!"

The smoke cleared and Tecumseh caught a glimpse of the American officer who had led the assault, slashing left and right with his sword as he galloped through the trees. Tecumseh lifted his rifle and took careful aim at the charging officer. Colonel Johnson saw the warrior a moment before he fired and tried to rein his horse to the left.

Tecumseh's bullet missed the officer but buried into his mount's skull. Johnson cried out in rage as the beast collapsed to the ground and rolled on top of him, pinning the Kentuckian to the forest floor.

Seizing the initiative, Tecumseh pulled out his tomahawk and sprinted forward to finish off the American leader. Johnson, his leg broken, struggled to free himself from the dead horse. He heard the Indian's advance and managed to pull his pistol from his belt as the Shawnee warrior leapt over the horse, his tomahawk poised to strike. The officer pointed at the Indian's chest and pulled the trigger.

Tecumseh's eyes widened as the pistol flashed. The Shawnee leader grunted as he felt the lead ball smash into his chest and knock him back. The war leader lowered his tomahawk and looked down at the gaping hole below his left nipple. He took a ragged breath and collapsed to the ground.

Paukeesa and Stands Firm had both seen the great warrior fall. The pair rushed through the trees, desperately trying to reach the mortally wounded chief.

"*No'tha*! No!" the boy wailed inconsolably.

Paukeesa knocked the struggling officer unconscious with the stock of his musket and rushed to his father's side. Stands Firm moved to help lift the war leader. The old warrior gasped in pain and the boy looked up to see a bayonet punch through his uncle's chest. Stands Firm collapsed to his knees beside his chief as a bearded soldier ripped the bayonet from the dying warrior's back. The American flashed a yellow toothed grin as he raised his rifle to strike the boy.

The soldier looked up as Stephen Ruddell galloped through the smoke. The frontiersman clubbed the bearded man across the head with his rifle barrel and leapt from the horse's back. He grabbed Tecumseh in his powerful arms and lifted him into the saddle. The infantry was less the fifty yards from their position as Ruddell turned back to the startled Indian boy and grabbed him by the shoulders.

"If you want to live, do as I say," he hissed. "Get yourself on another hoss, now!"

Paukeesa nodded and rushed through the trees toward a rider-less horse. Stephen swung up behind Tecumseh and pulled him close. He kicked the horse into a gallop as the infantry reached the edge of the woods. Paukeesa swung his mount in beside him and the pair galloped deeper into the swamp.

Word of Tecumseh's fall spread quickly. Demoralized, his warriors ceased fighting and disappeared into the forest before the astonished eyes of the American troops they had battled so hard moments before.

William Henry Harrison smiled as the battle ended and cheers began to erupt from among the troops. The victory had been decisive. He patted his horse on the neck. He hoped to find Tecumseh's body on the battlefield. Sending the great warrior's scalp back to President Madison as a trophy of war would surely secure his status as a hero back east.

Harrison chuckled as he nudged his horse forward. Heroes get elected President!

"William Henry Harrison, President of the United States" the General whispered, as he rode victoriously onto the battlefield.

Stephen slowed the horses to a trot as they crested the bank of a small stream. They had ridden deep into the forest, and the sound of the battle had faded in the distance. The cool October evenings had begun to turn the leaves of the maple and black ash trees that grew beside the stream red and yellow. Afternoon sunlight broke through the canopy of leaves to bath the stream bank in warmth. Tecumseh raised his head and looked around "Stop," he rasped, blood upon his lips.

Stephen reined his horse to a halt and leapt from the saddle. Together, he and Paukeesa lifted the Shawnee leader from the saddle and carried him to the crest of a small rise beside the stream.

"Get some water," Ruddell ordered, as he worked frantically to stop the flow of blood from Tecumseh's chest.

Paukeesa rushed to the stream bank without question. The boy used his hands as a cup to bring the clear, cold water back to his father's side. Stephen raised the wounded man to drink from the boy's hand. Tecumseh's throat worked as he swallowed the water. He coughed violently, bringing fresh blood to his lips. Ruddell gently laid him back on the ground and began working on the terrible wound once again. Tecumseh looked up at his friend and laid a bloody hand on his wrist.

"I'm dying," he whispered calmly.

"I saw this place in my vision," he continued, weakly looking around at the stream bank.

"You're not going to die," Stephen protested, tears in his eyes.

Tecumseh smiled weakly and patted the big man's hand. "I am glad you are with me. Now listen, there are things I must say and there is not much time."

Ruddell wiped the tears from his eyes and nodded.

Tecumseh motioned for Paukeesa to come closer. The boy dutifully moved forward, his face sad.

"You fought well today, *ni-kwith-ehi*" the dying man whispered, squeezing the boy's hand. "I am proud of the man that you have

315

become. You will no longer live as I have. You will have peace and a new way of life. Know that I will always be with you."

The boy sobbed and shook his head, gripping his father's hand to his chest.

Tecumseh turned his face toward Stephen. "You and I have come a long way together, *Jai-nai-nah*," his gasped, his voice weakening.

"Now it is time for us to part. I am tired and wish to rest. I ask that you watch over my son and our people for me. You are of two worlds, *Sinnatha*," he whispered, grasping the big man's hand tightly. "Help what is left of my world to continue in yours. Will you do this for me?"

"I will," Sinnatha replied, his voice cracking. "I will be there for our people until the day I die."

Tecumseh managed a weak smile and took one final gasp of air. The great warrior collapsed against the stream bank, his hand falling to the ground.

Sinnatha embraced his blood brother's lifeless body close and sobbed.

EPILOGUE

QUINCY, ILLINOIS
SUMMER, 1845

LYMAN DRAPER SAT ACROSS THE PORCH from the old frontiersman, speechless. The Sunday afternoon sun shone brightly in the summer sky. Draper had spent an entire week with the old man and his family to get to this point. John Ruddell and his family had once again left for church early, leaving the writer and his subject sitting on the front porch. Ruddell had sipped a cup of coffee as he hesitantly relayed the final chapter of his time with Tecumseh, a tale that he admitted he had never told anyone else. The former frontiersman had finished, his eyes red rimmed with tears. He suddenly looked frailer as he leaned against the front porch rail and stared at the distant Mississippi.

Lyman finally cleared his throat, struggling to find the right words. "I had no idea," he finally whispered.

"Well of course you didn't," the old man growled. "I was the one who was there! Most of the others from that time are gone."

Ruddell snorted. "Soon I will be to. Then, all creation will forget about what we lost. Maybe it's for the best."

The sound of John Ruddell's wagon returning from church interrupted Draper's response. The old man smiled and stepped off the porch as his grandson leapt from the wagon and raced across the yard.

"I have so many questions," Draper said, opening his writing box once again. "What happened to Paukeesa? Did General Harrison find out what you did?"

Ruddell waved off the younger man. "No more questions today. I've told you enough."

"What happened to Tecumseh's body?" the writer pressed.

The old man scowled. "Are you deaf? Or just that fat-headed?"

Little Stephen rushed onto the porch and jumped into his grandfather's arms before Draper could respond.

"Grandpa!" the boy cried in excitement. "There are some Indians down by the river! Can we go see them?"

The old man laughed heartily. "Of course! Maybe Grandpa can trade them for an eagle feather."

The little boy clapped his hands in delight as his grandfather carried him off toward the river.

John Ruddell climbed the porch to stand beside the bewildered writer. "Well, how did it go?"

Lyman shook his head in amazement. "Your father is unlike anyone else I've ever met. There's so much that I still want to ask him."

John chuckled, "Give him time, Dr. Draper. You're welcome to stay with us as long as you need to."

Lyman nodded in response, watching as the old man and little boy made their way toward the river. Finally, he shook his head once again and followed John and Sarah Ruddell into the house.

Three Shawnee Indians stood beside their canoe on the banks of the Mississippi. The two younger men were dressed in linen shirts and trousers, and their hair was shorn above their ears. Between them stood their father, a middle aged man with shoulder length hair. He still wore a buckskin fringed shirt and had tied an eagle feather in his dark hair as his warrior ancestors had done before him. He looked up and smiled as the old man made his way down the riverbank.

Stephen put his grandson down and strolled forward to embrace the former warrior.

"*Bezon*, Paukeesa," he stated warmly. "It's good to see you again!"

THE END

CPSIA information can be obtained at www.ICGtesting.com
Printed in the USA
LVOW12s1746250713

344651LV00024B/1027/P